Reluctant

Angels

By

Dodie Hamilton

Dedication:
For my Friends King and Julie Dexter
And for the 1ˢᵗ Battalion US Ranger POW who escaped in
a dung cart while being paraded through Rome in 1944.

Acknowledgments
to John and Josie Lewin, co-founders of Spirit Knights Paranormal Investigation, to Pat and Lee Jay in Spain, and to Simon Woodward and all good friends around the world, thank you for your support.

Part One
Sparrows

Prologue
Bug's Wings

This is how it started. One day in early Spring Pa took the belt from behind the door to administer discipline. When he was done his arm wrung out and sweat in his eyes he gave Gabe a choice, he could work with them that was already killed or he could do the killing. There weren't no choice. Gabe could never work in a slaughterhouse. Cattle so scared, great eyes pleading for mercy, it would've killed him. So he did the other thing, went to work for Simeon Salmanovitz at the Valley Funeral Parlour.

Mr Smith took him back of the shop. 'This is the preparation room where I do most of my work.'

Gabe peered round the door. A couple of metal tubs and a pulley contraption screwed to the rafters, he daren't think what kind of preparing went on in there. That first day he hovered. 'Come on in,' says Simeon. 'No need to be afeard, nothing happening here but folks getting ready for their last journey.'

Coffins propped along the wall, shadows everywhere and a strong smell of lye eight year-old Gabe thought it an awful place. That smell! There were times in later life when he'd get a drift of that and straight way was back in Virginia watching Simeon Salmanovitz embalming a corpse. Skinny old guy, dry as leather, he'd be standing over a drain, an apron about his waist and his feet encased in outsize rubber boots. 'Come close, young Gabe Templar,' he'd be saying, 'and I'll show you how it's done.'

Gabe didn't want to know. Pa said he was to be making coffins. He said nothing about washing dead bodies. He'd hovered at the door. 'I can't stay, Mr Smith,' he says, 'truly I can't.'

Simeon nodded. 'I'll allow it don't seem fair, the sun shining and me and you and Miss Virginia Ransome here in the gloom. I can see why you'd sooner be some place else as I can see how given the choice Miss Virginia would feel the same. Poor lady dying of dropsy she has no say in the matter, her only hope a Christian burial and to look decent when knocking on the Pearly Gates.'

But for a fly buzzing it was quiet. Still Gabe hovered. Then Simeon had sighed. 'But never mind Miss Virginia's hopes. Cut along home and tell your Pa you weren't able to stay. I guess he'll understand.'

There it was again a choice that was no choice. Gabe stayed. He would like to think it was care of Miss Virginia kept him but there were other considerations, the bank foreclosed on the Mill and Pa out of work and them having to leave Alabama. Of course, there was the two dollars promised end of the week and also the need not be a yellow-belly alone with a dead body. All of those unhappy considerations kept him at the Parlour that day but mostly it was about not having to see Ma's face when returning home empty-handed caused Pa to seek out the belt.

Gabe stayed that day and on til his seventeenth birthday. As for the belt the two dollars earned working from school until late into the night made no difference, discipline was maintained, bloodied wheals crisscrossing his back that by morning would be gone. Yes, there at night yet come five of the morning he'd wake without a blemish. It's why nobody knew overmuch of Pa's fondness *for discipline, nobody yelling, 'stop that Hodge Templar! You're hurting that boy.'*

Ma said the cuts on Gabe's back looked like bug's wings. The overnight healing she put down to good blood her side of the family, 'Sister Belle always quick to heal.' Gabe saw it different. He saw a miracle, a painful miracle while it was happening yet a miracle nonetheless.

After a beating he'd lie on his belly trying not to weep at the pain. Knowing the miracle-maker was close by he'd stare into the darkness. 'It's okay, little gal,' he'd whisper. 'Don't you fret! I know who makes me well and it ain't Aunt Belle.'

On such a night, his back a fiery furnace and his pillow wet, he would twist and turn every muscle aching and yet his heart filled with love. Most nights he'd try staying awake hoping to catch sight of her but dog-tired he'd sleep to rise in the morning healed. 'Cept for dreams he rarely saw his little gal but now and then when real unhappy, kids at school calling him a dummy and Pa extra busy with the belt, she would visit, shining and perfect, his Other Self, a reminder that she was more than a dream.

So it went year-after-year until there was another world war and a dream was made flesh.

One

Niggardly Blessings
Fredericksburg, Virginia.
Spring 1934.

May tied the bow tighter. 'Bend down will you! I ain't standin' on no stepladder. And quit squirmin'!'

'Hey!' Gabriel twitched away. 'You're catchin' the hair back of my neck!'

'That's 'cos I'm trying to get it right. It's the Ferguson kiddie you're plantin' today so you need to look smart.'

'Hiram looks smart and he ain't wearin' a ribbon.'

'Hiram ain't got the hair to wear it. A woolly patch is all he's got. You couldn't tie cotton through that never mind velvet.'

'Other kids have their hair short. Why do I have to have it long?'

'Because Simeon Smith pays the bills!' She tugged the tuft. 'Anyway, it's good hair. You take after your Great-Grandpa. Folks from the old country all got this thick yeller hair.'

'I look like a girl.'

'You could never look like a girl! And less of the lip, Gabriel Howarth Templar! It don't become you.'

'Neither does wearin' a ribbon.'

'Maybe not but it gets another dollar. Now go do your best for Mizz Ferguson. Seven dead babbies, poor woman, you'd think she'd give up tryin'.'

Gabe was gone, so tall he had to bend getting through the door. That's the trouble, coming up seventeen and built strong you'd think him able to handle anything but that ain't the case. He may have the body of a man but with the heart and soul of a loving child he's prey to everything cruel.

Sighing, May swept up ribbon ends. Hodge won't want to see them. They remind him that he hasn't worked in years and that the boy he mocks as stupid is the one putting food on the plate. Always picking fault! 'All them dead bodies! It ain't natural,' he'll say. 'If'n he'd gone to a slaughterhouse like I said he could've brought meat home instead of some filthy disease.'

'He won't catch no disease,' she answers. 'He's a strong and healthy.'

'Yeah and a fool in that coat with his hair gussied up.'

'He wears the coat,' says May, ''cos he's the Parlour mute and paid to mourn the dead. Mr Smith reckons all the fancy city morticians has a mute.'

'And whut would that man know of fancy? Hold up in a room above the shop and never seen unless collectin' bodies, the old miser! And he ain't no Smith. He's Simeon Salmanovitz, a Jew come over on a boat.'

'Miser or not he does a fair trade.'

'Yeah, at the hickory end of the market! You never see uptown bereaved knockin' on his door.'

'That's as maybe. He's good to Gabe, treats him kindly.'

'Phuh!' Hodge laughs. 'Sure he does! A skinny feller he needs the muscle. Couldn't be liftin' corpses on his own.'

'He ain't short of help. Hiram Abrahams and his wife have been with him years. Anyway, he likes Gabe. He says he brings in good business.'

'Then he oughter pay more!'

May won't argue. She knows if she opens her mouth too wide she's like to get a fist in it. Hodge can't stand to be challenged. A bitter man, he sees the move from Selma a failure which it is though according to him not his failure. He says we lost the yard because of interference from the government and not because he's a drunk who can't manage hisself never mind a business. Always blaming some other feller! 'Folk here are blind,' he says of Fredericksburg where he can't get work, none foolish enough to offer. 'They don't see whut's under their noses a government hell bent on destroyin' honest men. I mean, who is this man Hoover? Whut do we know of him? Is he sound?'

Hodge believes the world is against him. 'I don't get any luck. I must've been born under a dark star.' Father a drunk and his father before him it's likely William Hodgeson Templar was born under something dark. For sure he had May fogged with his good looks and promises to whip the yard into shape. 'Don't you worry Miss Marta May. I can run this place with one hand tied behind my back.'

To be fair Pappy dying sudden and things left in a mess the yard was already in trouble. May tried keeping it going but hadn't the skill. It needed a strong man with a firm hand. A weak mind and love of forty-rod whisky Hodge was entirely the wrong man. A year was all it took the bank waiting on any excuse. Sensing foreclosure and wages owing men at the yard took their own way out, tools and machinery disappearing overnight. With nothing left and nowhere to go the Templars had no choice but to come to Virginia and Great-Granma's.

May was four months gone when they moved in. The house was rundown then. First night, the whisky bottle empty and the house not to his liking, Hodge lost his temper his fist slamming into her stomach.

'Don't!' she lay curled up on the floor. 'You'll do the child harm.'

'So whut!' he says. 'One less mouth to feed.'

Life was hard. He couldn't hold a job. He'd turn up for a week or so but a busy mouth and drunk or plain idle he was soon sent packing.

He maintained the baby was the cause of his woes, Gabe being some other feller's doing. 'Whose is it?' he'd yell, face blazing. 'Whut was you doin' in Alabama when I was bustin' a gut tryin' to save that blamed yard?'

It was the preacher Aimee Semple McPherson and a slip of the tongue on May's part that put that idea into his head. The summer they moved there was a revival meeting at the church, billboards all over town saying she was coming, the famous Sister McPherson who talks with Presidents and movie stars. Hodge said they should go. It was a once in a lifetime.

They went and wished they hadn't. A field back of the church set up as a stage the meeting had already begun. Folk singing and clapping their hands! You'd think the Lord God Himself was coming.

The preacher lady had a bullhorn and was calling on folks to confess their sins and be healed in the Blood of the Lamb. A lot of people went to the front and Hodge one of them. Face awash with tears he set off a-running, shoving folk aside as though it was a race and a bottle of Jim Beam the prize.

Sun beating down and ankles swollen May wasn't for budging. She sat on an upturned barrel fanning her cheeks. Looking back the day takes on the feeling of a dream. Done up in a white dress and a long blue cloak the preacher lady asked May's name. Flustered, everyone looking, she gave her maiden name instead of her married. 'I am Marta-May Applethwaite.'

'So Marta May Applethwaite.' Aimee Semple McPherson laid her hand on May's belly. 'How shall you name this boy?'

Folks gasped on hearing her declare the baby a boy. It shook May. Hoping for a daughter to share her life she'd been thinking on girl's names.

The woman asked again. 'How shall you name this boy?'

'I guess if it is a boy I'll name him after my Grand-pappy.'

'And what was Grand-pappy's name?'

'Gabriel.'

The preacher lady smiled. 'Yes,' she says as if she'd known what was coming, 'It's a good name and I doubt the original will object.' With that she was swallowed up in the crowd and the incident forgotten by all except Hodge.

A dirty suspicion got into his head adding his wife and child to those that had done him wrong. Always questioning: 'Why Applethwaite? Why show me up in front of a crowd? Were you ashamed of bein' wed to me or were you sayin' somethin' different?'

Didn't matter what she said, he'd made up his mind. Night-after-night she took a pummelling, if not with his fists then with that other part of his body that means so much to him. It's a wonder she survived never mind her son.

In those days Hodge fetched logs off the river to sell to the saw-mill. He was drinking real heavy. One night the dts got him, May waking to him fending off the air with a knife. He said the Angel of Death had paid him a call.

Eyes popping, he was terrified. 'A female angel,' he said, 'with eyes of fire and wings of pure gold.' He reckoned she threatened him. 'Hung over me with fist clenched she did. 'Kill this child,' she says, 'and you kill one of God's own.''

May asked what she meant by God's own. Hodge said didn't know only that the baby was not to die by human hand. He was to thrive and be of use to God.

For a while that vision gave respite, him circling May like her bulging belly was a Copperhead snake. The child born he wouldn't come near. Three years he loitered on the edge of life fist primed but never striking.

The silent watching lasted until Gabe's third birthday when Hodge threw him across the room. When May tried intervening he punched her. 'This house will come to order!' he yelled. 'I ain't standin' back no longer. I'm master here not a three-year-old kid. See this?' He held up a belt. 'This is how it's gonna be. Step out of line and you get whut's comin' both of you.'

May said, 'aren't you scared of the angel and the killing of God's Own.'

He grins. 'I don't aim to kill him. I aim to chastise. The angel said nothin' about chastisin'. She knows I'm allowed to do that.' He fetches a bible. 'It says so in the Holy Book. Proverbs thirteen, *'he that hateth the rod hateth his child.'* There in black and white God's holy word! Ain't no Angel going against that.'

For sure no angel did! The poorest excuse Hodge beat the boy 'til he bled.

'It's my right,' he says. 'He's some other feller's leavings, maybe not a man, maybe a devil, in which case the devil has to be shook out.'

Foolish talk! There was no other. It is true May had a yearning for Buckminster Rourke, the copper king that lives here on the Green. In the old days Pappy having trade with him. Bucky would come to Selma and he and May would talk. For a time she thought a promise might come of them talking but a silver mine made a rich man of Bucky and Ruby Cropper, her that lives back of Wolfe Street with a price for every man come swinging her hips.

She got a kid by Bucky but he wouldn't marry her. Nothing coming of it she took to religion, going to church every day with a hat on her head and cast-iron drawers. Awful woman! May thinks it was her put the chastising idea into Hodge's head. Certain he wouldn't think of it. He can't hardly sign his name never mind read a bible. Whatever it's a lie and he knows it but still torments them with gabble of angels and devils.

Thinking of angels you couldn't get better than Gabe. Every mother thinks her child special. The same can be said of most fathers. Bucky Rourke doted on his boy; the smartest clothes and latest model Chevrolet, even a plane, his son has it all. Hodge Templar hasn't a good word for Gabe. Thick-headed dummy he calls him. If he is slow it's not his fault. Working at the Parlour he missed schooling and May always wanting him with her must recognise her part. Hodge, Simeon Smith, wounded animals in the pen, one way or another everyone needed Gabe. Seventeen years on and he pays the price.

Pity he ain't got brothers and sisters. May wanted more but Hodge's fist kept Gabe alone. He don't have friends at least none you'd call human. Animals are his friends. Some magic in him is felt by everything that creeps or flies. They come screeching and holding up a paw or. Gabe says if he can find the pain he can usually make it go away.

There's always some critter he's nursing back to life. Nights you hear him talking to a dog or wounded bird he's smuggled in. Now and then he'll talk with another kind of critter, a will-of-the-wisp shimmering thing brought back from the old house in the wood.

Gabe loves that house. It is his church. Missing round the yard you know where to find him. Winter, summer, rain or snow nothing keeps him away. Puzzled, May asks, why do you go there? He says it's a good place to think. She says what do you think about? He says everything. A century old ruin with the roof fallen in May thinks the Eyrie is dangerous. He smiles that golden smile. 'Ain't nothin' dangerous there unless you're callin' quicksilver dangerous.'

Quicksilver is Gabe. He's learned to move real quiet but when entertaining other worlds he forgets to be quiet.

You hear him laughing through the wall. Hodge hears it but a coward keeps his head down afraid to ask what causes his son to laugh. Anyway, there's always another day and another belt.

'I got to do it,' he says, 'gotta beat the strangeness out of him.

A cruel man. Kids can be just as cruel especially if their parents show the way. Ruby Cropper's boy Bobby has a following. Kids trail behind him hee-hawing at his jokes and copying the way he combs his hair. Handsome but cruel, he and his pack make sport of the timid and the small. Only a few weeks ago he hoisted Miss Emilee's terrier up into a tree and left it dangling.

Gabe shinned up and brought it down. May couldn't get over it. 'What's wrong with that boy? Why would he want to hurt a pretty little dog?'

Miss Emilee tightened her lips. 'Some folks can't abide beauty. They want to stomp such things into the dust. It's why they make your boy's life so hard.'

Emilee March is right. Not a day goes by without someone ripping into Gabe. A solitary boy, a lover of the wild animals are no problem. It's human beings he must avoid them that would hoist him up another tree.

Time is getting on. Gabe will have swept the pens and be on his way to the Parlour and the funeral. Becky Ferguson died of pneumonia. A cute little poppet with limbs like gossamer she was on loan to the earth. Her funeral will draw a crowd. It'll be hard on her folks and if Bobby Rourke and his pack of hounds turn up to mock it'll be hard on Gabe. Bless him, he can walk as soft as he likes but six foot three with golden hair and slate grey eyes there's no avoiding the world. Heads turn when he walks by. Miss Emilee says he's beautiful. He is and not only his looks. It's who he is kind and forgiving.

The times he's forgiven his father! Not that Hodge begs forgiveness, though of late when liquored up there is a moment when torment gives way to shame and he hangs his head the belt loose in hand and blood on his vest.

Boots nailed to the floor he stands trembling. It's Gabe who sets him free. He nods. 'It's okay, Pa,' he says. Then Hodge staggers to bed to sleep it off.

He drinks for the whole of Virginia, night after night shouting of devils and golden-haired angels. May thinks now what she thought then there weren't no angel. It was the dts talking. Even so, that visitation brought three years grace and so with that in mind she's every day down on her knees.

Privately, she thinks the angel niggardly. Seventeen years and not once got between the belt and flesh! What's the use of that? So she heals him afterward? So what? Gabriel's back clear the following day Hodge thinks he is being tested and beats the harder.

Knees creaking, May crouches down. Niggardly or not she's all they have and must not be offended. 'Dear Angel, if you are here please keep an eye on my boy. It's his birthday next week. I'm hoping at seventeen he'll get a decent job and his troubles ended.'

She rises and crosses her breast. 'Hoping this finds you well and in good health. Thank you and Amen, Marta-May Templar nee Applethwaite.'

Two
Soldiering

Gabe and Hiram are outside the Ferguson house. They should be heading to the church but there's a hold up.

Here comes Mr Simeon.

'Whut's wrong, sir?' asks Hiram.

'Mizz Ferguson doesn't want to let her child go.'

'Oh Jubilee! Poor lady!'

She says Becky's not dead, she's sleeping. I've talked with her but she's deaf to all even her husband.' He glanced to Gabe. 'Maybe you could talk to her.'

'Me?'

'You're carrying the coffin. Maybe if you go in she'll see sense.'

'Why would she let me take her daughter and not you?'

'Because she knows you are trustful and will take care of her child. *And*, though I advised against it, you did make Becky's coffin.'

Gabe opened his mouth to argue but Simeon made a clicking sound back of his throat which meant end of conversation. 'What shall I say?'

'You'll think of something.'

'Better take this.' Gabe passed the coffin, the old man staggering under the weight. Seasoned oak it is heavy. Mr

Ferguson came last week asking the price of caskets. Gabe was sawing wood. Annie-Lou, Hiram's wife, was sweeping woodchips off the floor. Mr Simeon and Hiram were at the County Morgue collecting the banker, Mr John J Little. 'Rich as Croesus,' says Simeon, 'his wife won't spend another dollar nor will she have him in the family vault. Tuck me in when my time comes, she says, but him you drop in a gofer hole. In this life he slept in every bed but ours. Damned if he'll share mine in the next.'

Mr Ferguson was another wanting a beggar's funeral. Every casket outside of his price he went home empty-handed. 'I ain't begrudgin',' he says. 'If I could I'd bury my Becky in gold. I jest don't have that kind of money.'

Simeon told how Jeb Ferguson worked in the paper mill until '29 when he lost his right hand to the blades. Now with a hook fitted to the stump he hauls carcases in a meat-yard. That evening Gabe stole a door from the Eyrie and made a coffin Ma lining it with velvet left over from the coat. Mr Simeon wasn't happy. He said working for nothing was unprofessional and as with most good deeds has a habit of bouncing back.

Simeon Smith is good to Ma. Gabe didn't want to go against him but with the roof open to the sky he thought the Eyrie wouldn't miss a door.

Angeline Ferguson stood by the window rocking her dead child in her arms. Gabe tapped on the door. 'Afternoon, Mizz Ferguson.'

She looked up. 'Good afternoon, Gabriel Templar.' She smiled. 'I see you're wearin' your hair tied back. I like it. It's becomin' in an old-world chivalry style.'

'Mr Simeon wants it this way.'

'I imagine you come in for some mockery.'

'Yes'm.'

'Let 'em mock. Long hair or not you're the handsomest lad I ever did see.' She turned back to the window, rocking, rocking. 'It's been a long summer. Those purple cornflowers are so bright. Are they late bloomin' this year?'

'I heard my Ma say so.'

'I haven't got to the yard much of late. Everythin' runnin' to seed and the summer passin' and nothin' done.'

'I could give time if it'd help.'

'Jeb could surely use the help and it'd be a change for you tendin' the livin' rather than the dead. I like your coat.' She came toward him and trembling stroked his sleeve. 'Is the velvet from Mr Simeon's shop?'

'It is.'

'And your Ma made it?'

'Yes'm.'

'I like black velvet. I think it becomin' on anyone man or woman. I always wanted a velvet ball-gown. You know, with a string of pearls like the one Jo March wears in Miss Alcott's book.'

Gabe didn't know. He'd never read a book in his life 'specially not one that tells of girls with boy's names who wear velvet gowns.

Mizz Ferguson was lost in memory. 'I love the girls in *Little Women*. Meg and Jo and Amy and Beth are all so different. We called our first one Beth. She died as did the one in the book.' Mouth sadly sweet, she sighed. 'If she'd grown my Becky would've looked pretty in a ball-gown don't you think?'

'Yes'm, she would.'

It was heavy in the room, daises wilting in a jar and Mizz Ferguson with them. Gabe stepped forward. 'Shall I take her? It's gettin' late and you need to rest.'

A sleepwalker she turned so very slowly to lay the cold bundle in his arms. 'I suppose so,' she said. 'It is getting late and as you say we need to rest.'

~

Whatever settled in that box it wasn't Becky Ferguson. China face and limp cotton body it was more a Kewpie doll won at a carny than a child, no life, not so much as a glimmer from a candle. Gabe screwed the lid down and then tied a sash about the box with a sprig of rosemary on top. Mr Simeon grows rosemary back of the yard. 'A good smelling herb it covers other smells.'

Gabe remembers his first corpse, Mizz Virginia Ransome, eighty-five and bald under a knitted wig. Annie-Lou took the wig off during embalming and put it back for the final viewing. Gabe can see that old lady now. Years of arthritis her spine was twisted like a mouse in a trap. Simeon had to do some bending.

That first day he was scared. Conies, skunks, a deer with her throat ripped out, Gabe has seen all manner of dead things but never a bald lady. Bald ladies are rare, like dead butterflies you don't see too many of them. Butterflies are like silk. Powdered to dust they vanish in the air. Dead men moulder. A man dies at seven in the morning by seven of the evening he is rotten meat.

That first day a body was brought in riddled with bullets. 'Sooner you cut and fill with lye the better, Hiram,' Simeon gave instructions to his helper. 'I'm taking our young apprentice on a tour of the shop.'

A showroom at the front and two rooms out back he towed Gabe around. An educated man, a doctor in Russia, he talked of clients not bodies. He said the business was small but it had a 'peccable reputation, the Parlour managed by people of fine sensibilities. He said he had excellent helpers in Hiram Abrahams and his wife. 'I trust them with my life as I trust them with the dead. Being a mortician is a privilege as well as a vocation. A last link to earth our job is to help make the transition easier for the living and the dead. It don't matter who they are! Here at the Valley Funeral Parlour everyone is treated the same. Innocent child or murdering drunk we send them on right.'

That said he got an apron from the cupboard and tied it about Gabe's waist. 'A last word, you may think dead eyes can't see. Trust me they can. Everything you do and say in this room is written in the air to be seen and heard forever. So mind your manners and roll up your sleeves.'

Gabe stumbled through that first year with his eyes half closed. Most of what he saw he didn't understand. Folks talk of the dead being at peace. There is nothing peaceful about the back room. Blood and guts and human shit, it smells awful though babies never stink nor do little kids. It's the grown that smell as though in growing they got stale.

Ugly gargoyles are trundled in and peaceful souls carried out. Mr Simeon does that, his knowledge and Annie-Lou's face powder.

It is at final viewings that Mr Simeon helps the living. Faces tight with sorrow mourners shuffle up to the casket. They peer down and then a soothing oil spreading through their veins they sigh and say, 'she looks like she's sleepin'.'

Gabe learned a lot from the Parlour and is grateful but come Monday he's seventeen and looking toward a new life. Tomorrow he goes to Charlottesville to enrol with the National Guard. A sergeant there whose mother the Parlour helped bury said he would propose him for the army. 'They'll take you,' he said. 'Strong and true, you're the kind of guy the army's looking for.'

So far Gabe's said nothing not even Ma. She' would beg him to stay but he has to get away. Nine years he's worked in the Parlour from early morning until late in the evening, in bitter cold winters, bodies stiff with ice and chilblains on his fingers, through to summer, a hot sun beating on the tin roof and flies buzzing.

Join the army and he is a man fighting for his country. Work for Simeon and he's a dummy with hands that stink of dead flesh.

Kids are mean to him. From the first day of school he saw no peace. 'Hey dummy!' they would holler. 'Where you plantin' your brains today?'

A couple of years back he quit going. An inspector came banging on the door threatening jail. Pa beat Gabe but he wouldn't go. What's the point? He ain't gonna learn anything. It ain't only school. People can be bullies. Hodge Templar is unpopular. Hell-raiser, thief and drunk he's upset more than a few. Ill-feeling gets passed on. Today Gabe carries the coffin ahead of the wagon. A crowd will gather eyes watching from under bowed heads and an ill wind blowing. They'll want him to trip and drop poor Becky.

He said so to Ma. 'Becos I'm stupid they expect me to act stupid.'

She brushed it away. 'It's a funeral. Folks are bound to stare. Your skin is too thin. You need to toughen up.' She said that then she hugged him. 'You ain't stupid. You're my bright and beautiful son and one day…!' She raises her hand as though swearing on a bible, 'Gabriel Howarth Templar will best them all.'

Gabe don't want to best anyone, he just wants to live. Maybe the army will make it happen. Then in time he'll get to do what he wants. Oak, and Ash and bendy Willow, working with wood is his dream. He wants to be a carpenter, to feel things growing beneath his hands, to make the dead wood live again.

He has another dream but such a dream it's best he stick with wood.

Wood is like the army, it's real, and it's here and now. You can dream of becoming a carpenter and work to make it happen. That other dream is so unlikely even to think of it in daylight he risks losing it; much better to save it for night and blue black darkness and the perfume of her hair.

Back in Bayonet Woods a hunk of lime has been fetched down by a storm. Later when Pa is abed he plans to hitch Shiloh and drag that stump to the barn. Weighing so heavy it'll be okay there. Pa can shoot logs off the river but he won't be able to mess with that.

Gabe loves the smell of wood. Walking among trees breathing fresh sap into his lungs, there's nothing better. Wood, animals, all free living things, two minutes alone with Shiloh, his pinto pony, and Daisy, the English Staffie and her whelp pups presently hiding out in the Eyrie and he too is free.

Other than Ma he's never cared for anything as he cares for animals. He understands them and knows when they're sick. If you listen a critter will tell you how to make him well. Gabe has nursed all kinds and believes an animal only dies when living is too hard. They don't want to die! They want to live and leap and run but comes a time when, soul weary, nothing can hold them back. Same with people, little Becky Ferguson didn't want to be here, the only thing that kept her these two years was love of her Momma. Her Momma knew that and so in the end gave her up.

~

Ceremony over and Becky in the ground along with the other babes Hiram took the rig back to the Parlour. Gabe stayed behind to fill in the hole. Once done he's visiting the Mizz Marches, Mizz Emilee saying rope burns on her dog's neck are infected.

Thinking to keep his jacket free of mud he hung it over a marble angel. If folks didn't stare he'd find pleasure wearing it. Ma can turn her hand to most things but antique velvet bought in Holland she worried over that.

'It belonged to my wife,' said Mr Simeon. 'I beg you cherish it.'

Tongue poking out, Ma traced the pattern. It turned out good. Mr Simeon was happy. 'It's a work of art, Madam, and your son a young Prince Onegin.'

Letting down sleeves and hems along the way she's managed five jackets out of that velvet. Now it's used up, the last enfolding Becky Ferguson.

Sun beating down Gabe shucked his shirt and set to. A little while later Bobby Rourke comes swaggering down the path and Sue Ryland with him.

Sue's skirt hiked up and him nipping from a flask they sat on a grave.

'Hey, big feller!' Bobby is grinning. 'That was some show you and the old Jew put on. Never seen so many folks! Who was you plantin' Greta Garbo?'

They sat laughing and drinking. Bobby held out the flask. 'That's a mighty big hole you're diggin'. Fancy a snifter to help it along?'

The earth hard and cold Gabe carried on digging. He knew enough not to accept. Time past he wasn't wise and thought this jackass held out the hand of friendship when all he held was a barb to puncture a boy's pride.

Baby Rourke the kids call him. Ma can't stand him. She says he has a filthy mouth. He sure can cuss. No word too dirty he can revile a man in every colour from blazing red to darkest blue. One year he got Gabe into trouble, Gabe mad at him, calling him a such-and-such son-of-a-bitch. Next day Mr Simeon was waiting. 'What's this I hear about you using foul language?'

Gabe had never seen him so riled.

'What is wrong with you?' says Simeon. 'This is America. Why foul your mouth with ugly words when you have such riches at your disposal? You have a world of literature at hand and none to say nay. You have Magic Lanterns, picture houses, theatres and poetry of your own in Sam Clemens and Walt Whitman. You have Shakespeare, Ibsen and Tolstoy, fine words stretching back to the beginning of time yet you soil your mouth with clumsy oaths contemptuous of love and scornful of a man and woman's body-parts.'

That day Gabe's head ached but still the tirade went on. 'Tell me where it's coming from! I doubt it's your mother or your father.'

Ma never cusses and Hodge Templar is all kinds of a bully but nothing heavier than blamed leaves his tongue. All that day Mr Simeon ranted. 'You don't hear Hiram or Mizz Annie-Lou cussing. They have newborn in Lemuel and wouldn't pollute his ears.' Then he lost patience dragging Gabe over the drain. 'See this?' He hefted a bottle of lye. 'We use it to wash stinking body parts. Cuss again and I'll wash out your mouth. Then I'll take you home and watch while your mother does it. You wouldn't work here again. Foul tongues come of foul minds. I wouldn't trust the dead to you.'

That shocked Gabe. He promised never to cuss again no matter the provocation. Seven years this Monday he's kept his promise though this feller Rourke, especially when he's with Sue, tempts beyond endurance.

At that, as if inside his head listening, Sue got up and slipping and sliding like warm molasses round a spoon took hold of Gabe's jacket.

'I like this. It feels good.' She buried her face in it. 'And it smells good.'

Bobby was chewing a blade of grass. 'What smell is that?' he drawls. 'Essence of hog shit with a touch of rigor mortis?'

'Nothin' of that,' she breathed the jacket in. 'It's of Gabe.'

'Yeah and I know why you like it,' Bobby grins. 'It's his dick you're sniffin'. That gigantic sausage you gals are always whimperin' about.'

'Is that what it is?' says Sue.

'That's exactly what it is. It's why he's here fillin' in graves. The bigger the dick the smaller the brain, everybody knows that.'

'Do they?' Sue hung the jacket back over the angel. 'Well then,' she says her glance on Gabe's naked chest. 'I guess that accounts for your little trouble. Back in class you was always voted the one most likely to succeed.'

Bobby laughed and taking a comb from his pocket smoothed his hair so sure of himself he didn't take offence. Gabe loathed the feller but envied him too. All that money there's nothing in the world he can't have. Everybody hollers after him especially now he's at West Point. His power is in Sue, one minute mocking the next shoving close her blouse dipping and offering an eyeful.

If there is unfairness in life it's this guy who willing to amuse his followers half chokes a dog to death and yet is still thought a gentleman.

'What you starin' at?' Grin slipping, Bobby shoves Sue aside.

'I don't know.' Gabe pats down the earth. 'I can't make up my mind.'

'Well quit it! I'm a costly guy. I charge a dollar a look and you can't afford me.' He brushed grass from his pants. 'Why, my laundry bill is more'n you get paid in a year. Same with my boots.' He scraped mud on a tombstone.

'My daddy gets them from Savile Row in London England. Gieves and Hawkes, hand tooled. Heard of them, have you? No, I didn't think so.'

All this talking and Sue yawning with her head thrown back! Seeing Gabe watching she licks her fingers and runs her hand down deep inside her blouse. She does things like that. Saturdays she works at the drug store. She comes back of the Parlour when he's cutting wood climbs inside a tyre on the tree and swings back and forth sucking a Popsicle. It sets Gabe's teeth on edge.

Annie-Lou reckons she is mischief. Annie-Lou don't know the half. Sue Ryland is a devil. Some nights she comes looking for Gabe with war on her mind, so far, though there's killing every time, she's won the battle but not the war.

Bobby puts his arm about her. 'We're done here, sugar. It's too warm to hang about. What say we find a cosy spot and get warmer?'

They walk away. Then Sue turns. 'Is there gonna be a marker on that grave?'

Gabe picks up his jacket. 'Not that I know of.'

'Shame,' she shakes her head. 'All those dead children and nothin' to say they lived? That's one sorrowful hole.'

~

Gabe is at the Eyrie feeding the dogs. Miss Emilee has said she'll take the pups. He'd take them home but Pa would likely drown them. Along with a chunk of army pay Gabe plans to give Daisy to Ma. If Pa's getting money for the dog he'll leave it alone. The money will go on drink but better that than Ma being alone. There's been thieving of late chickens taken and food from pantries. The shack is small but secure. Last year Gabe built a sitting room on for Ma and a cubbyhole in the rafters, the only way up by ladder. Pa's not good with steps. With luck one day he'll fall and break his neck.

The bible says honour your father and mother. Gabe will honour Ma until the day he dies but has nothing for Pa. What is there to honour? He is a coward. He bullies Ma saying she's old and ugly. 'Why did I wed you?' he shouts. 'I could've had anybody but I'm saddled with you, you dumb whore.'

When he calls Ma whore rage rises up in Gabe. Then a fist holds him back, a small fist but strong. 'Wait!' a voice whispers in his ear. 'It's what he wants! Don't be drawn. Let him die of his own making then you'll both be free.'

Gabe draws back into the shadows trying not to hear what's going on below. Having done his share of hurting Pa will slam out the door leaving Ma bruised. Then rage rises up and Gabe thinks 'if that's love, a man rammin' a woman against the table like a ruttin' bull you can keep it. I'd sooner live alone.'

~

The dogs fed and bedded down he leads Shiloh to where the Lime Tree fell. He has plans for that wood, some image in his head, a shape similar to a dream he once had about his little gal with her golden hair and eyes like diamonds.

She came to him last night about Becky's coffin. 'You made a nice job of that, Gabriel,' she says. 'I'm proud of you.' She never calls him Gabe, always the whole of his name. She says it's a true name and mustn't be shortened.

She has a funny way of talking. He laughs. 'You sound like you got a pip in your mouth and can't spit it out.' She gets huffy and slips away. He sits by the window wishing her back. 'I can't help the way I speak,' she says then. 'It's how I was born.' They sit together watching stars mate in the heavens. Just before morning she leaves. 'Is your back better?' she says. He fibs trying to keep her. 'It's still smartin'.' She takes his hand. 'Does it really?' When he can't lie no more she slips into sunlight a strand of her hair setting fire to the dawn.

This morning Ma asked who he was talkin' to. Gabe shook his head. He knows she doesn't really exist, that it's him making a friend of loneliness, and yet when her head is beside his on the pillow, and it's been that way since he could remember, then real or not he wouldn't be without her.

'Hey there, Gabe!'

A voice spoke out of the shadows and he nearly fell over. For one wonderful moment he thought she was here. But it wasn't her. It was Sue Ryland.

'Hi Sue.'

'What you doin'?'

'I'm bringin' this hunk of wood home.'

'That's heavy. You think Shiloh can handle it?'

'Uh-huh, if I hitch up with him.'

'I guess that would do, you strong as any horse.' A smell of blueberries in his nose and her hair spilling over his arm she knelt down. 'You need help?'

'Thanks, I got it.' Knowing it was a solid mass he came earlier attaching chains to the middle section. Now with him and Shiloh pulling it should move.

'Giddup!' There was a sudden shock of dead weight. Shoulders straining from the yoke collar about his neck Gabe bent to it. 'Come on Shiloh!' The lump of wood was slow coming and then the pony adjusting made a smoother path.

'That was some funeral today,' said Sue.

Gabe grunted. He needed every breath.

'I heard Mizz Ferguson was overcome with grief and jumped into the grave.'

'That's not true.'

'I didn't think it was.'

On they went through the undergrowth Sue pulling briars out the way. They got to the barn where he stores his stuff and shoved the wood inside. There was barely room. Whatever he plans on doing it can't be with a solid lump. The trunk will have to be sawn in half else it will make a hole in the roof.

Sue was panting.

'Thanks,' said Gabe.

'It weren't nothin'. If I'd known what you was doin' I'd have brought Sunny-boy. He's bigger'n Shiloh and would have pulled his weight.'

'Even so. You did help. ' She had a briar scratch on her arm. 'You got a scratch. Best see to it afore it turns nasty.'

She looked at the scratch and then held out her arm. 'You see to it.'

'What?'

She pushed her arm forward. 'You make it better.'

'Don't be stupid.' He dragged tarpaulin over the wood. It needs to be kept away from rain. Tomorrow he'll come back and take another look.

'Hey!' Sue pushed her arm under his nose. 'Kiss it for me and make it better.'

'I said don't talk stupid.'

'I ain't talkin' stupid. I know you can do it. Miss Emilee said so.'

'Her dog's not ill. Your fool buddy cut it about the neck. I did nothin' but clean it and bind it.'

'That's not what she says.'

'It's what I'm sayin'. And why are you still here? You should be home not hangin' about here causin' mischief. What happens if Hodge hears you?'

Eyes knowing, she smiled. 'He won't. He's been in the Hawaiian Bar drinkin' slops. Now's he's sleepin' it off. He won't hear the breath in his lungs never mind me and you in the moonlight talkin'. And who says I make mischief.'

'You're always makin' mischief.'

'Yes,' she moved closer, 'and you're always resistin'.'

Every time it's the same. She undoes his pants and then foraging inside she pulls him out and starts rolling him between her hands.

A man can be all kinds of thing and can endure all manner of pain. But at seventeen and busting out his body them fingers are hard to deny.

She gets him hard and then pulls up her skirt and no panties rubs him against her soft and slippery making mewing sounds. Why is she doing this? This same girl mocks when he walks by calling out scornful, 'hey there handsome, any sign of your brains?' Now she uses him like a tool, never taking him inside, just rubbing her face as pale as a corpse in the Parlour.

Then she's done and smiling slow gets down on her knees. That's when the mischief begins. Until that she was having fun. Now she is serious. She works at him sucking. He knows what she wants but damned if he'll give way.

Shutting her and her mouth out his mind his spirit flies to the Eyrie. Body shrieking demanding release he shuts his mind to everything but the attic. Once inside he is safe. It's over and Sue is doing nothing but pulling dead skin.

Realising that once again it's going nowhere she got to her feet.

Furious, she stared and then she slapped his face hard. 'You dummy! You lump of useless flesh! Why do I bother?'

Words, daggers, flash through her eyes. She's hunting for more to say, something real cruel to cut him to pieces, but in the end when there's nothing she can say that hasn't already been said she walks away.

Three
Tempting Fate

'I reckon she'll be okay now, Mizz Matty.'

Gabe grabbed his jacket and ran. He was supposed to be on his way to Charlottesville but got caught up with the Mizz March. It was Boo, this time, Mizz Matilda's poodle. 'There's somethin' wrong with her ears, Gabriel,' she says. 'She keeps flickin' her head back and forth.'

It weren't nothing but a hay seed. He got that out then they asked him to look at the churn the butter not separating. He fixed that and a tap on the water barrel and then took off for the station in time to see the train pulling out.

It's cold today yet bright the sun out. Gabe sat on the wall thinking about the Parlour. He told Mr Simeon he is leaving. 'I'm not surprised,' says he. 'It is time you moved on. But is the army a good choice? You were born to give life not take it. It's why you're here working your apprenticeship.'

Gabe couldn't see what burying corpses had to do with the army. Mr Simeon said by apprenticeship he meant the real reason Gabe was born. One minute a skinny old man with long fingernails the next a Prophet, Simeon Salmanovitz is always saying puzzling stuff. But then most things are a puzzle to Gabe. At times he thinks he is blind a fog between him and the world, the sky, the earth and the flowers, birds and beasts all hazy as though newly arriving.

As a kid he spent a lot of time rubbing his eyes. Ma said he needed specs. Pa cuffed him, 'he can see well enough. He's idle and should put up or shut up.'

Like logs off the river shored up behind his teeth Gabe put up and shut up for years, words and ideas stacking up until he couldn't open his mouth. Not that anyone expected him to speak. A nod or shake of the head was all he need offer. It got so folks didn't wait for him to try. They would grin as if he was a deaf mute. Gabe didn't argue and neither did Ma. 'Pay no mind,' she'd say. 'It's ignorance. You can't expect a hog to do nothin' but grunt.'

He tried not minding but wary of people it got so he couldn't talk when he was among them. Most kids of five or six are noisy, not Gabe, slipping between shadows he moved real quiet. Unless you looked you wouldn't know he was there. You'd think him a tree or a cloud passing over the sun.

People are a puzzle. You don't know what they are going to do from one day to the next. Take Sue Ryland? Why do that, why make a slut of herself? And why does he refuse her. Most guys wouldn't be so finicky. But he digs in. Same with Pa and the belt! No matter how hard it falls Gabe will not weep. The pain is there as are tears but he won't give way. It drives Pa nuts. 'Great lump, you don't have the sense to beg for mercy.'

Pride is a fault. Ma says one day pride will cost him dear. 'Don't be so sure you're always right, Gabe

Templar,' she says. 'Learn to bend; that way neither you nor those you love will need to break.'

~

Gabe was outside the station trying to figure the bus time-table when across the road a car screamed to a halt Baby Rourke grinning from an open-top Cadillac. 'What's up, big guy?' he yells. 'Missed your connection?'

'Seems like it.'

'Wanna lift?'

'No thanks. There'll be a train along soon.'

'I doubt it.' A guy pipes up alongside Bobby, a West Point Cadet lying back in the seat with his cap over his face. 'A wagon derailed back down the track.'

Gabriel's heart sank.

'Where you goin'?' says Bobby.

'Charlottesville.'

'Then this is your lucky day. I'm droppin' my buddy at the Academy. Get in!' He kicked the door open. 'And watch where you put your boots! I'm seeing Verna tonight. Any mess baptisin' them back seats is gonna be my mess.'

Gabe hesitated. Then knowing it was this or be late climbed in. The car shot away on to the freeway. For a while it was good, wind whipping through his hair and sense of freedom. Then Bobby adjusted the rear view mirror.

'Why Charlottesville?'

'National Guard.'

'You fixin' to be a soldier?'

'I'm hopin' so.'

'The National Guard, huh? I guessed it had to be important to bring you out from under the bodies.' Bobby nudged his passenger. 'Our friend here works in a funeral parlour.

'You don't say.'

'Indeed I do say. He lays out stiffs for a livin'.'

The West Pointer shrugged. 'Someone has to do it.'

'Sure as long as it's not me.' Bobby was quiet for a time but seemingly unable to settle started bugging his friend. 'What in God's name were you doin' last night, Ash, to make you so damned borin'? You ain't barely said a word.'

'I don't need to. You talk enough for both of us.'

'What's this, Birds of America?' Baby Rourke leans across reading the title of the book on the guy's lap.

'Mom got it for my birthday.'

'Since when were you interested in birds?'

'Since I was born.'

'That is some gift for a hot-blooded Yankee boy. It's as well I got tickets for Babes in Toyland at the burlesque or your R&R would be a washout. Long-legged gals struttin' in the nude has to be better than a book on birds.'

The car rolled on the two exchanging banter. Handsome with easy smiles and tailored jackets they were untouchable and sat relaxed and easy in a ten thousand dollar car with a dusty motorbike strung along the fender and no worries other than what to do on a birthday.

Gabe felt so alone. He was born knowing he stood outside a magic circle. He had thought he'd gotten used to it but in the car with these men it felt wrong, like he should be in the front laughing with them.

It was a bad feeling. It wasn't Bobby Rourke made him feel that way. To him Gabe has always been dirt to piss on. It was the other one with the cap over his face. Not once did he bother to lift it, the passenger not worth the effort.

Bobby lit a cigarette. 'So Gabe, my fine feller,' he says blowing smoke into the air. 'What's your take on this conversation?'

'What conversation?'

'The one I'm havin' here with Nature Boy.'

'I wasn't listenin'.'

'Oh right. Me and the Lieutenant were discussin' birthday gifts, what was best to improve the mind, a book on birds or tickets to a Burlesque show.'

'And?'

'And you don't have a preference?'

'No.'

'So a room full of naked girls, tits and ass wobblin' all over the place is not your thing? But then I guess workin' in a morgue for a couple of bucks a seat at a Broadway Show is beyond your field of vision... though hang on a second!' Bobby tossed the cigarette. 'You don't care to see nudes?'

'Not particularly.'

'Then you're in wrong job! For sure you must see nudes every day of the week and Sunday. Okay maybe the gals ain't exactly the Ziegfeld Follies, their flesh inclined to stretch a little. Even so it's still a freebie.'

Gabriel kept quiet hoping the guy would do the same but having found a chink in the armour he knew to niggle the knife. 'Sure,' he said his eyes hard in the mirror, 'I never saw it before but workin' in a mortuary a guy does get a new slant on the idea of naked. What do you think, Ash?'

'I think you should shut-up.' His friend yawned. 'It's eleven in the morning. I had a late breakfast and if it's okay with you I'd sooner keep it down.'

'It does heave the stomach some but you gotta admit the idea of our friend here gettin' his rocks off every day for free does tickle the imagination. 'Bobby laughed. 'I wouldn't mind a peek. Maybe next time you get a reasonable lookin' septuagenarian on the slab you might give me a call.'

He was still laughing when he dropped Gabe by the University. 'So long, soldier,' he yells, wheels screeching. 'Brace yourself for when them medics grab your balls. Hands cold as ice you're apt to come away with toothache.'

~

The meeting didn't go well. The Sergeant wasn't there. Another feller sat at the desk. 'Sergeant Keen doesn't do Thursdays. But now you're here buzz along to Medical Intake. They'll tell you what to do.' From then Gabe was passed from one desk to the next, questions about this and that until his head was spinning. Next he was told to strip off and hang his clothes on a peg.

It was Mizz Matilda March who gave the jacket. The two sisters share a house close by the Mission. When in need of chores they send for Gabe. Sweet ladies they always enquire of Ma and send fruit from their garden. Last week he confided in Mizz Mattie telling of his hope for the army. She and Miss Emilee fetched a pile of things from the closet. 'Our brother was killed serving his country,' says she. 'We kept his things but think maybe you could use them.'

Gabe took the stuff home. Ma had to burn most the moth got to them. She did salvage a jacket and though tight and smelling of violets it looked okay.

Among the stuff was a snakeskin wallet and inside that a fob watch. Gabe took it back. 'You should hang onto this, Mizz Mattie. It's made of gold.'

Mizz Emilee said, 'take it. You're a good boy and a great help to us over the years. Major Lawrence March served in the army. He'd want you to have it.'

Gabe should have left it at home. This is an open room no lockers. In the past, a trusting feller, he's been cheated more times than enough. Now stripped to the buff he must take the watch with him.

A Captain in a white medical coat frowned. 'What's that you got?'

'My watch.'

'Your watch?'

'Yes, sir.'

'That's a mighty nice watch for a farm boy. How d'you come by it?'

'It was a present.'

'Who gave it to you?'

'A lady.'

'What, your sweetheart? She'd have to come from a pretty close family to buy you a watch like that. Seems to me that casing is made of gold.'

Gabe didn't answer. He didn't think it fitting to discuss the March sisters.

'So why did you bring it in here?'

'I wanted it to be safe.'

'You didn't think it safe in the locker room?'

'I wasn't sure.'

'Gimme that!' The fellow set it on a table. 'I'm not sure about you either,' he pushed Gabe into line. 'Won't leave his watch in the locker room? Why that's tantamount to saying the US Army harbours thieves.' He turns to the line of the would-be rookies. 'Are you guys a bunch of thieves?'

The rookies snapped to. 'No, sir, Captain, sir!'

'I should say not.'

From then on Gabe was up against it and not only from the Captain, a couple of medics thought they'd have fun Gabe rolled up and down the line like a ball in a bowling alley and the rest standing by grinning. 'Bend down, stand up, cough,' God knows how many fingers was stuck up his ass. He came away from the medical wing with aching balls and doubt of the army.

Still the Captain wasn't done.

'Okay, Mister Universe, we've seen how bouncy your balls are now let's see if there's brain under that brawn.' He gave Gabe a paper to read. Having talked with the Sergeant beforehand he knew it was lines from the Declaration of Independence. 'They always trot that one out, kid. Learn it and you're in.'

Night after night Gabe practised saying it til he knew it off pat.

He read it but then another bit of paper was brought out.

He didn't bother to look. 'I don't know what is says.'

'Because you can't read?'

'No, sir.'

'I didn't think so.' The Captain sat on the table swinging his foot. 'I'm beginning to wonder whether you're our kind of guy. Seems to me a man who worries more about a gold watch than getting an education is not what this man's army is looking for.' He started on general knowledge questions: 'who was the current President and how many ss in the Mississippi.'

By this time there was a crowd looking on.

The last question was too much for Gabe.

The Captain was smiling. He'd had his fun and thought to give the farm boy a chance. 'Okay,' he says. 'You seem a good enough kid. We might be able to do something with you if only to use those shoulders pulling a tank. Answer this and we'll overlook the rest. How many feet in a yard?'

It's a basic question. Every kid in America knows the answer. The right words and Gabe was in the army but the man had rubbed him raw. Standing there with not a stitch on and all those guys watching it was cruel.

Gabe took his watch from the table. 'I don't know anythin' about no yard,' he says. 'The bank took ours. You'd best ask them.'

~

The Sergeant came to the house. 'Sorry, Gabriel,' he said. 'I should've said I wasn't in Thursdays. You got stuck with Captain Jerk-off Saunders. Right prick! Nobody likes him. But don't worry. Give it a year and trouble brewing in China they'll be after recruits. Meanwhile I got a job for you at Shenandoah Park.'

Ma was there listening when he said that. Her eyes lit up. 'A regular job?'

'Yes, ma'm. My youngest is foreman there. He said you can start next week.'

'Doin' what, Sergeant?'

'Helping out in the Park. It's a distance to travel every day. You could probably stay midweek to save on travelling. My boy would put you up and his wife is a great little cook. What do you say?'

Gabe's heart was busting. 'I sure would love to do that.'

'Okay then. Here's the address. Get there early as you can Monday.'

'I don't know what to say.'

'No need to say anything. You won't remember my boy but he remembers the kindness and dignity you showed to his Mom. '

Gabe was thrilled. The job of a lifetime and it is his. Ma was divided. He was to be away most of the week even so it was better than joining the army.

'What did I tell you?' she said. 'I knew you'd come out okay.'

'It ain't nothin' grand,' said Gabe, trying not to get too excited.

'It's a job with regular hours and pay. What more is there?'

~

News spreads fast in any town and Fredericksburg no different. Sunday morning Gabe went to the Parlour. He'd already said goodbye but they were busy so went to help.

Mr Simeon and Hiram were washing the rig. The glass-fronted carriage and the coal black horses are a big draw. See that rig rolling down the road and hairs on your head stand up.

Mr Simeon was pleased about the new job. 'Anything's better than the army. You wouldn't have lasted two minutes.'

Gabe was happy. The thought of being able to walk among the trees and not have to be with people and paid to do it is beyond a dream. Annie-Lou was singing and smiling happy for him.

It was a good day. Even Baby Rourke couldn't spoil it.

Eleven o clock he turned up flashing a new uniform.

'So big feller,' he leaned against the door. 'Where's your draft card?'

'There ain't none.'

'So I heard. That's somethin' ain't it bein' turned down by the army.'

Gabe carried on sizing wood. Here's another of life's puzzles. This guy always has a mob of kids trailing behind and every one anxious to hear what he has to say and yet he's keen to bring Gabe into his world.

'You don't seem sorry,' he says. 'If it was me turned down by the air-force I'd have gone crazy.'

'I thought you was at the Academy.'

'Nah, me and the Point didn't work out. Too many rules. I'm headin' for Langley and the Air Corps. The Point is my buddy's thing. Alex Hunter has army blue-blood in every vein and his pappy and grand-pappy before him. If you wanted the army it's him you should have seen not some two-bit medic.'

'I'm not bothered.'

'Seems not.' Bobby sat on an upturned coffin lighting a cigarette. 'So what does bother Gabriel Templar? What drives the motor and don't say buryin' stiffs 'cos no one believes that.'

'What d'you mean motor?'

'The life blood! The point of livin'! The thing you wake for in the morning, the crazy joy that sets your heart on fire. With me it's planes. There ain't nothin' else. Flyin' comes before everythin' to me even women.'

At that Gabe laughed. Baby Rourke, a guy in every girl's pants from here to the Appalachian Mountains giving up on women?

'I know.' He laughed with him. 'It does sound kinda dumb but I promise you given a choice pussy or flyin' there ain't no choice.'

'You want to be careful saying things like that, Mr Rourke, sir.' Annie-Lou spoke from out the shop. 'Sounds to me like you're tempting fate.'

Bobby flashed his teeth. 'Is that how it sounds?'

'It does.'

'Then I guess that is exactly what I am doin'.' He got to his feet and doffing his cap swept a bow a lock of hair falling across his brow. 'Okay then Milady Fate, on this day before God-fearin' witnesses I challenge you to do your worst! Send me the girl! Show me the plane! Let's see who comes out top.'

Then he turned to Gabe. 'Now it's your turn. If we're in the challengin' mood, and you laughin' the least you can do is tempt along with me.'

Though thinking it stupid Gabe felt so good he thought he'd take a risk.

'What am I supposed to say?'

'If I were you I wouldn't say anything.' Again Annie-Lou chips in. 'Words said in haste are often regretted. You had a tough start, Gabriel. Things are looking up. Why would you wanna mess with that?'

'Now, Mizz Abrahams,' drawled Bobby, 'don't be givin' him any of your voodoo slave shit. Gabe is a grown man. Let him make up his own mind.'

Yes, thought Gabe, let me make up my own mind. Seventeen tomorrow and a new life! He closed his eyes. Straight way he knew what he wanted. In he went. He didn't hesitate. He said it straight out. 'Alright then I got a challenge but it ain't for no Lady Fate. It's for my Pa's golden angel. My challenge is to bring my little gal to me so I know she's real and not just a dream!'

Four
Wallpaper

Pa came wanting money. He took the three dollars the Sergeant left for train fare. 'You don't need to pay,' says he. 'You ain't John D Rockefeller. You can ride the rail like everyone else.' Then he hung around the barn staring at the Lime. 'Whut's that wood you got there?'

'Lime fetched down by the storm.'

'I don't like it.'

'What's wrong with it?'

'It don't look right.'

'Look right?'

'Shift it. I don't want it here. There's somethin' bad in that wood as there is bad in everythin' you do.'

'What do you mean bad? It's just wood, that's all.'

'Then how do you explain it? One minute you got a lump of wood in your hand next you got a livin' thing. How do you do it? It's not like you had schoolin'. No one taught you how to carve so how does it happen.'

'I don't know.' Gabe shrugged. 'I see a hunk of wood then I see a fox or hare or whatever is in the wood. It just feels natural.'

'It ain't natural! It's some devilish thing you and whatever's inside you work together. But I ain't arguin'. I want it out of here and the other stuff with it.'

'I can't do it now.'

Pa clenched his fist. 'You tellin' me no?'

'I guess I am.' Gabe stared him down. 'I will move the Lime and the other pieces when I get back. I don't have time now.'

There was a moment, a fist wavering an inch from Gabe's face and then the wind dropping from his lungs Pa stumbled away. 'Move it,' he snarled, 'or I'll be movin' it for you.'

~

Hoping for time alone in the Eyrie Gabe slipped out around dusk. Time alone? The idea makes him smile. You can't be alone in that house. All sorts of critters bide there. There are mice behind the wainscot, squirrels in the attics and birds under the eaves, and every variety of bug that suck and build and breed and chaw! Close your eyes and you would think an army is on the move.

Miss Emilee says the house has been here more than a hundred years.

'It's akin to the old Mill. They were built around the same time. They were good houses once but you couldn't live there now, too noisy. They buzz, don't they, Matilda.' Miss Emilee says that and her sister, a little deaf, nods and draws a shawl about her shoulders.

Gabe knows what they mean by buzz. It's in the air and under your feet some cosmic power cable setting fire to the soles of your shoes. There are other noises. One time he heard a fiddle play and watched as pounding on the floor above caused dust to fall from the ceiling. Another time he heard people talking, nothing he understood, a drone no louder than pigeons cooing but yeah talking. Then out of the mass of sound a man called a name and a girl laughed light footsteps skipping from one end of the house to the other.

The first time it happened Gabe ran all the way home. It was hearing the name Rosamund. It made him sad like getting a message from a long lost friend. Over time he's gotten used to weird stuff in the way he got used to the Parlour, half-closed eyes, you might say, and the belief that dead bodies and dancing ghosts are no more scary than shrivelled spiders under glass. He knows it has to be that way because if he wants to keep coming he'd best mind his business.

Spring still hanging on it is chilly this evening the moon bright and a hint of frost. The dog, Daisy, came to meet him. Gabe will leave the pups with Mizz March on the way to the station. Pa said Daisy can stay if her keep is paid. 'But I ain't lookin' after her,' he said. 'One bitch to another your Ma can do it.'

With the job in Shenandoah Park Gabe won't get here so easy and so he's come to claim a keepsake. The top attic is his favourite place in all the world. Small, a maid's bedroom, it is his world. He knows every inch and can tell the seasons by the wallpaper, snowdrops for winter, daffies for spring, pink roses for summer and hawthorn berries for fall.

A long time ago a girl sat here feeling sad. She tore a flap through layers of wall-paper labelling them for the four seasons as she went and on the last piece she added a farewell note: '*To whomsoever finds this I wish a goodnight and goodbye from me, Rosamund Hawthorne, lost and lonely, perched in an Eagle's Nest, 21ˢᵗ October 1863.*'

He knows what it said because he copied the letters onto paper for Mr Simeon to read. 'A girl wrote this,' says Simeon looking at the squiggles, 'and a beautiful girl at that.' Gabe asked how he knew she was beautiful. 'It's there,' he replied, 'beauty and sadness writ in the letters.'

Gabe saw the ripped paper one winter and curious pulled and kept pulling bit-by-bit digging down through history until the note emerged, and finding it for some crazy reason he then fainted, falling to the floor and waking cold and scared hours later. He has no memory of fainting except he seems to think he was walking down a circular staircase but not in the dust of this century, in another time and that a girl in a tartan silk frock walked with him.

Sleepy like a half-remembered dream that walkabout is always in back of his mind as is the name Rosamund. He sees her as somehow connected with his little gal, his Other Self, and from then no matter where he is the memory of that strange day is in the rustling of silk upon the stairs.

Gabe was seven when that happened. Ten years on, he means to steal the memory. Part of him says leave it alone. It will be here when you come back. Another Gabe says no things will change, the world will turn and next time you're here there'll be a real-estate board in the yard.

Gently as he could he cut the bottom piece of paper, folding it inside Major Lawrence's wallet as a piece of history belonging to him and the Eyrie and Rosamund. Then weary and in no rush to get back to Pa and the inevitable beating he sat in the chair the dogs bundled about him.

It's warm in the attic. Outside a gale can be raging yet there's warmth and the soft susurration of those taking their rest. Two minutes and head down his arms crossed on the table Gabe is sleeping with them

Daisy wagging her tail woke him.

Someone was in the attic with them.

'Hello?' he said, nothing, no answer, only a sense of being watched.

There was talking in the room beneath, the long attic as he thinks of it where ghosts danced the polka and invisible boots shook dust on those below.

He crouched listening. There were three or maybe four fellers down there but other than an occasional word he couldn't get much. There was a mention of the Rappahannock River and of a pontoon bridge and a guy called Burnside.

Whoever they are the talkers are bone weary. One is hurt real bad, the back of his leg shot away. He's in pain! Gabe can feel it!

'Oh God!' The feller groaned and another whispered, 'hush up, for Chrissakes, Nathan, or we're dead men.'

Dead men? Gabe wonders if prisoners broke out of jail. But why hide in the Eyrie miles from anywhere? Is there trouble in town he don't know about?

Then as if to answer his thoughts there was the thunder of boots on the stairs and gunfire, four or five rifle shots, and sudden silence below.

Ear pressed against the floor boards Gabe leaned closer.

'I say, how very rude.'

He froze. A girl stood behind him, he could smell her perfume and see the toe of her shoe and tattered hem of her frock.

She spoke again. 'Do you usually eavesdrop on other people's conversation, sir, or is this a temporary lapse of judgement?'

It was her, Rosamund, the girl who laughed! He knew her voice.

Gabe wanted to turn and speak but held in some ancient vice couldn't move.

Rap, rap! Annoyed, puffs of dust rising she tapped her toe. 'Did you hear what I said or are you deaf as well as ill-mannered?'

Still he couldn't move. Eyes closed and paws flailing Daisy and her pups seem to be caught in the same dreaming vice.

Gabe struggled. What is happening and why is this familiar especially the wounded soldier in the attic below? I feel his pain. And he is a soldier! A Confederate! And the pontoon bridge they speak of and the man General Burnside are of the Battle of Fredericksburg!

It was all known, gunfire, the stench of cordite, her toe tapping and him fool of a man crouched on bare floorboards caught between incredible happiness and intolerable pain.

'I know this,' he said, words falling from his lips. 'I hear you and I want to turn and look but I know the moment I do you'll disappear.'

The foot was still. She was still, her hand drooping and the heavy green gem-stone on her finger flashing in the lamplight. 'Alas, it's true.' She sighed. 'If you were to turn to look I would vanish as if I never was and yet, Dear Heart, I am here somewhere, so please keep looking.'

Gabe turned.

She was gone.

~

From one dream he stumbled out of the house into a nightmare that was to last for many years. It was gone midnight when he broke through the woods. The lamp was lit in the barn and Pa was inside throwing things about.

Ma was by the door her mouth bruised. 'Where've you been?' she said.

'I fell asleep in the Eyrie.'

'You should've stayed asleep.'

'What's goin' on?'

'He's been to the Hawaiian Bar and come back loaded.'

'That'll be the train fare he stole from me.'

'It's more'n that. He took your watch and sold it for a quart of whisky.'

'Oh Ma!'

'I know and I'm sorry! He was up the ladder searchin' your bed. I couldn't stop him. I tried and got this for my pains.'

A gold watch for a quart of whisky, Gabe was bitterly disappointed. He had thought it tucked behind the loose shingles. 'I should've taken it with me.'

'It don't matter,' Ma sighed. 'He'd have found it sooner or later.'

Pa heard and came running. 'Yes and I shouldn't have had to take it! You should've given it to me as your duty.'

'You didn't need it. You had my three dollars.'

'Three dollars!' Pa spat in the dust. 'A man can do nothin' with that! I needed whut was owed to me as your father. And whut you goin' on about? You couldn't have worn it. You'd look real stoopid with a fancy watch hangin' on your vest. Same with the wallet and anythin' else you got hidden away! You ain't the man to wear them.'

'And so you're throwin' my stuff about lookin' for more to steal?'

'There must be more. Time you spend in that barn you could've hidden a dozen watches. And since when was it yours? Last I looked everythin' in this place is mine to keep and mine to trash startin' with that hunk of Lime.'

'Leave it alone!' Gabe pushed by him. The Lime tree is important, his heart tells him so. It is precious, a door-way into light and a glimpse of the future.

Heart sick, expecting bad damage he dragged the tarpaulin away only to find it exactly as he left it. 'He hasn't touched it.'

'Not for the want of tryin',' said Ma. 'Afore you came he was runnin' at it with an axe. He reckoned he chopped it a dozen times but like the scars on your back no sooner was it cut than it healed.'

'He is crazy.'

Ma shrugged. 'Drink has done for him.'

'It weren't the drink!' Pa yelled. 'It's the God's honest truth! The more I slashed the more it closed up. Same with the other stuff the birds and rabbits you done carved. I flung 'em against the wall but didn't make a dent.' He dragged Gabe outside. 'Go look! Find a single mark on any of it 'cos I can't.'

'You should lie down,' said Ma. 'You're sickenin' for somethin'.'

'I ain't sickenin',' Pa was almost weeping. 'I'm tellin' you I've seen the devil in them carvings. They're evil as is him that makes them.'

Ma put her hand out. 'Come on now Pa and lie down,' she coaxed. 'Get some sleep. Then maybe tomorrow we'll get a doctor to come look.'

'Yeah, you!' He thrust her back. 'You'd like that, wouldn't you? Some brain doctor lockin' me in a mad hospital? That would suit you. Then you and the dummy here would have a fine time on your own. Well, it ain't gonna happen.'

Eyes starting out his head he weighed the axe. 'If anybody's gonna need a doctor it's you, Marta May Applethwaite! You and your by-blow son that's been drivin' me crazy all these years!'

Wild-faced and foaming at the mouth he ran at Ma. He swung the axe and Gabe hit him dropping him to the ground.

The blow echoed around the yard, a flock of doves flashing upward in a swirl of wings.

Axe loose in his hand, Pa lay unmoving.

Ma knelt down. 'Oh Gabriel.'

She didn't need to say anything. He knew. All the years in the Parlour, so many dead people you can't miss it, a spark had gone out never to fire again.

They stood a while staring then Gabe went to the house for his coat.

Ma clutched his arm. 'Where you goin'?'

'I'm goin' into town.'

'What for?'

'I'm gonna tell them I killed Pa.'

~

They locked him in a cell. 'Sorry, son,' said the Deputy. 'I don't like doing this. I know what kind of a man he was.'

The Sherriff was good and mad. 'Damnation, Gabe Templar, why didn't you come to me first? It might've been an accident Hodge falling and hitting his head and you and your Ma getting peace at last. But no you had to come. Now I'm stuck between what's wrong and right. You behind bars for the next twenty years ain't right but it's where you'll have to be.'

There was conversation and phone calls. The Deputy brought Gabe a mug of coffee while the Sherriff sat other side of the bars endlessly cussing.

During the morning there was a steady stream of visitors. Mizz Emilee and Miss Matilda came and Mr Simeon and Annie-Lou. The Baptist minister came, the minister's wife asking the Sherriff why a nice young feller like Gabriel should go to jail for putting an end to a brute. 'You can't call that justice.'

The Sherriff said there was no such thing as justice. There is only the Law.

Before the minister left his wife took Gabe's hand through the bars saying he wasn't to worry she'd look after Marta-May. One after the other they came and Gabe ashamed knowing he'd always thought folks didn't care and here they are offering help and some only ever seen across a casket.

Sue Ryland was crying. 'I came to say sorry and that I promise to look after Shiloh and the rest of your animals.'

Annie-Lou wouldn't let her by. They argued, Sue angry, saying Annie-Lou was nothing but an ignorant slave and had no opinion in this.

Annie-Lou held out. 'Go your ways, Miss Sue,' she says. 'The boy's got enough to worry about without you meddling with his mind.'

~

Two days Gabe was held in jail every day bringing more visitors. Ma brought clean clothes. She said it was her fault and that she'd never forgive herself. Then Sergeant Keen came. He said he was sorry and that his son would be disappointed not to give Gabe the job. He said to trust him, if he got a chance he would speak up at the trial murderer or not.

The last to come was Baby Rourke who stood other side of the bars real quiet. 'I don't get it,' he says, 'why you and the real murderin' assholes roamin' free?'

Then he put his fingers through the bars almost but not quite shaking Gabe's hand. 'I guess I haven't always been the nicest guy to you but let me tell you it ain't over. You'll get through this and you'll be somebody. So stay chipper and don't let the bastards grind you down.'

The wagon came early next morning. The Sherriff told Gabe to get dressed. He wasn't to be tried in Fredericksburg. He was to go to Richmond.

'They think we're too friendly,' said the Sheriff. 'They prefer a neutral court.' Then he said he'd a message from Mr Simeon, would Gabe like to say goodbye to his father.

'I guess I'd better.'

The Sherriff put him in handcuffs, metal biting his skin, and led him across the street to the preparation room. Other than Pa under a sheet the room was empty. Seeing the Parlour for the last time so clean and quiet, the glass carriage shining bright in the sun, suddenly working there didn't seem so bad.

The Sherriff led him in. 'In a moment,' says he, 'I'm going to unlock these cuffs and then me and Mr Simeon will step outside leaving you with your Pa to make your peace. I'm doing this on a promise you won't run because if a man had a mind, if he were young and fit and knew the land, he could run and none could catch him. But he'd have to run hard and long. Don't matter if he is guilty or provoked into killing he'd have to run because once a man is on the run he's on the run forever.'

'Of course,' the Sherriff stared under his shaggy eyebrows, 'a man doesn't have to promise anything. He can take his chances. It's a matter of choice.'

An offer of freedom was being held out, Gabe knew it, Mr Simeon knew it, and probably Hodge Templar lying stiff and cold under the sheet knew it.

The key turned and the handcuffs released. The Sherriff stepped back.

'So what do you say, Gabriel Templar? Do I have your promise you won't run?'

Gabe sighed. 'Yes sir, you do.'

Five
A Saviour

Gabe was sentenced to fifteen years. He was taken from the courthouse to a basement building in the State Penitentiary where he was stripped of his clothes, hosed down with ice-cold water, had delousing powder thrown over him, given a mattress and blanket and locked in a cell.

Whistles blowing and prisoners marching back and forth, the Receiving Unit is run like an army barracks. There are rules about mixing with other prisoners, 'fraternising' the guards called it. There is to be no talking 'cept in the recreation yard and during work supervision and no body contact unless in supervised ball games.

The officer running the Unit, a guy they call the Lieutenant, was handy with a wooden Billy-club. Strong on back-chat and guys stepping out of line, he would whack offenders back of the knees sending them flying. He hit Gabe more than once said he was a dreamer and should wake up. 'You need to keep your eye on the ball, kid 'cos you never know when it's gonna drop.'

The prisoners worked every day of the week but Sunday. Gabe was assigned to the Wood Shop where they made office furniture. After a week of turning a lathe and drilling holes he was given apprentice to a Trusty by name of Pete working on a mahogany desk meant for the Oval Office.

A onetime accountant for the IRS Pete had been on B Block twenty years and never once granted parole not even when his mother died. 'I stole government money,' says he. 'It's why I'm still here. Murder and I'd be out by now.'

Familiar smells of wood tar and oak Gabe didn't mind the Wood Shop. Working all hours of the day was nothing new though he did hate the two mornings a week classroom with rows of guys sitting behind desks reciting the alphabet big letters and small taken from pictures on the wall.

Today's he's to be transferred to the main prison. Cell Block B is an iron birdcage where tier upon tier of cells raise both side a gangway and where the parrots, the canaries and vultures -twelve hundred at the last count- peer through bars at the latest captive to have his wings shorn.

Chained by his ankles and cuffs on his wrists Gabe shuffled along. The smell in there made him gag. It stank of blood and shit and fear.

The guards stopped at a cell. 'Opening number 45!'

Ankle chains unlocked and cuffs removed Gabe was pushed inside.

The door slammed shut. Into the sudden hush a voice called out. 'Hey there, young Gabe Templar, we hear you're good with wood. Come sit on my knee, sweet-cheeks, and I'll give you somethin' hard to whittle!'

There was laughter and catcalls.

'Shut up!' The Lieutenant rattled the bars with his club and laughter ceased.

'How come they know my name?' asked Gabe.

'Scum of the earth they know everything that goes on here and most of it filth,' says the Lieutenant. 'A good-looking kid like you is gonna find it tough. You need to remember what I said and keep your eye on the ball because they will be coming for you.'

'Comin' for me?' Gabe stared.

'Yeah, that's right. They're already fighting over your ass. Best thing you can do is get yourself a saviour and pay upfront. Fifteen years is a long time. You are fresh meat and the rats in here are ravenous.'

~

2000 hours and the cells are locked down for the night.

Restless, Gabe paced the floor. Ten days in B Block and every day his gut pulls tighter. There was a routine in the Unit: 0600 breakfast, 0700 til 1100 Wood Shop, half hour lunch and then work until 16000. Lunch and an hour recreation in the yard, 1800 supper, prayers, return to the cell and lights out 2130.

It's the same in B Block, same stony-faced guards carrying shotguns walking the walls. The difference here is that Gabe is the one being hunted.

He knows and throughout the day walks with toes jacked in his boots ready to run. Listening, all the while he's listening. Even inside the cell he's listening!

He is being watched. Everywhere he goes eyes follow him. They watch in the yard and in the showers and at night they are staring through the bars. He's seen that look in a fox hunting her prey, a natural craving, kill or starve. The hunger here is unnatural and never satisfied.

A lesser version of that look was in Sue Ryland's eyes. She was always hungry for something. Last week she came on the bus with Ma. They let Ma in but Sue not being family stayed outside. She's been to the house a couple of times. 'I don't know why,' says Ma. 'I've no real likin' for the girl. I guess she's lonely.' Gabe didn't tell of the night crawling. If Ma's getting company no point in airing troubles. As the Lieutenant said, fifteen years is a long time.

Fifteen years! God almighty! Gabe's head reels when he thinks of it. Fifteen years living in a twilight world, no space, no privacy and but for a couple of hours a day no sky. No wonder men go crazy.

When they took his clothes in the Receiving Unit he had nothing of his own. Other prisoners hang stuff on the wall of their cell, posters of movie stars and photos of family. Gabe has a sliver of wallpaper down the side of his boot, Rosamund Hawthorne's remembrance of loneliness in the Civil War. That piece of paper is all he has of life in Fredericksburg.

At night he sleeps with the wallpaper under his pillow. Not to dream of his little gal! No! He doesn't wish her or the ghost of 1863 anywhere near. He keeps all of that an arm's length. To bring anything feminine to B Block would be to tread snowdrops in shit. Even so she tries visiting, night-after-night tapping on his chest to come in. At times he thinks he hears her calling and crying as though something terrible has happened and her seeking comfort. But he won't let her in. Like him she must be patient and bide her time.

Fifteen years was the Judge's ruling. But for Sergeant Keen and Mr Simeon it would be a lifetime. 'They'll give you life for this,' said the Sheriff. 'D'you hear! You'll go in a kid and come out an old man. That's if you do come out! Judge Blake is a Killing Judge who'd sooner solve State problems with several thousand volts of electricity than let anyone off.'

Gabe could do nothing but let the Sheriff's frustration pour over his head. What was there to say? Pa is dead. He deserves what's coming.

The trial was the buzz of Virginia every bench in the courthouse taken. Some faces he recognized, the Misses March, the Minister and his wife, Hiram and Annie-Lou and Baby Rourke up on a balcony with his mother. The rest were row upon row of newborn calves with mouths hanging open to be fed.

The Judge had no love of sinners. 'Sons murdering their fathers!' He stared over his specs. 'What is this, a Greek tragedy? There is no discipline nowadays! Modern youth is allowed to run wild.'

Gabe thought of the belt behind the privy door and wanted to tell of years of discipline but words wouldn't come. The Judge said the jury should look at the size of him, 'a heartless, unfeeling brute without a shred of remorse.' He does have a heart but that is back in the Eyrie with the birthday boy who was almost happy with a job in Shenandoah Park.

The jury was out for hours and then suddenly back. Gabe was on his feet staring into nothing. It's likely at that moment he did seem like an unfeeling brute. Truth is he could only see Ma's eyes and only hear Pa's head hitting the ground in the squishing of a peach.

Mr Simeon and the Sergeant got the sentence reduced. They stood in the witness box, Simeon smart in best funeral suit and the Sergeant with medals polished, and hand on the bible told the truth as they saw it, Hodge Templar was a wife-beater and Gabe a quiet and well-meaning boy if a little slow.

His formative years spent burying the dead while his father was out carousing they said he never stood a chance.

They listed Pa's misdoings, the money owed, the wives spoiled and things stolen, on-and-on tearing him to pieces and Ma sitting with eyes downcast.

When they finally sat down the Judge didn't seem overly impressed but some truth must have got through and fifteen years the result.

Knowing it could've been worse the courtroom was jubilant, Miss Mattie waving her hanky and Mr Simeon his cane. Then Ruby Cropper got up on her hind legs saying the Judge was lenient, she wanted justice and quoted the bible, '*Exodus 21, verse 15, 'whosoever strikes his father shall be put to death.*'

A fight broke out, those downstairs hollering at those up. The Judge banged his gavel. 'One more outburst from the woman in the purple hat and she would be the one doing fifteen years.'

They led him away. His last glimpse was of Simeon Smith who stood with tears running down his cheeks. Now Gabe's in B Block and condemned to stay until his thirties. It seems an awful long time.

~

'Lights Out!'

The guard called out and all is dark. Then it starts, the whispering, men calling men, lovers calling lovers and threats exchanged, tough guys striking bargains, cigarettes for booze, a deal for a deal and a life for a life.

Gabe's name was mentioned more than once, filthy stuff, men saying what they were gonna do when they caught him. Up and down the block a dark river rolling it went on into the night gradually fading away until there was but one voice singing. Some voice! Deep and ringing out it gave Gabe chills, his skin bumpy as if standing in a draught.

'Deus meus, ex toto corde poenitet me omnium meorum peccatorum.'

Gabe recognised it as a prayer said every morning before work. He knew the words but had no idea what they meant. Respect for the dead as well as the living, a click back of the throat when angry and a loathing of cussing, he's picked up a lot from Mr Simeon over the years but he ain't managed Latin.

That old man was a mystery. He never talked of his past. Rumour had it his family died in a fire. One year the hotel on Clarke Street burned down and half a dozen bodies brought in among them children. Annie-Lou asked Gabe to work late that day. She said Mr Simeon couldn't manage it on account of his family, his father and mother, wife and daughters murdered back in 1919 in a resettlement issue in Minsk, their undertakers shop set on fire.

She said Simeon was away studying to be a doctor and came home to a family grave. 'His wife was brung up Catholic,' says Annie-Lou. 'It's why you hear a Catholic prayer though Jewish lips. He begs forgiveness for them that started the fire. He says he shouldn't be here in America. He should've stayed in Russia to mind their souls. It's why he does what he does here, guides the souls of strangers to their rest.' Then she hugged Gabe. 'He loves you. You are his family. Remember that for the future and keep a good heart.'

~

Exhausted by memories of the Parlour, Gabe slept.

Just before dawn a voice spoke in his ear. 'What is your name?'

Scared, he leapt away from the bunk to stand against the bars.

Someone was in the cell with him!

It came again, a deep voice with the rasp of a buzz saw. 'What is your name?'

He thought it best to answer. 'Gabe Templar.'

There was silence broken only by snoring from other cells.

The voice spoke again. 'Why are you here?'

'I killed my Pa.'

'Why?'

'He hurt my Ma.'

Again a long pause, information digested. Then: 'What did they give you?'

'Give me?' Gabe was on his hands and knees hunting the cell though at five foot by nine there was nowhere to hunt.

'How long a sentence?'

'Fifteen years.'

Gabe bumped into the metal toilet bowl sticking out the wall and knew the voice came from that. This was no ghost. This is a prisoner using the pipe as a telephone. He'd heard of this happening but didn't think to hear so clear.

He hung over the bowl. 'You talkin' through the toilet?' he whispers.

'Indeed that is so.' There was a rumble of laughter. 'I guess you might say I am talking through my ass.'

That was all the feller said. Next night he talked again through the can and every night for a week. Charlie was his name. He wanted to know about Gabe, where he lived and his history. An hour or more they talked their conversation ending the same way Charlie talking of the movies and Rudolph Valentino.

Charlie had a particular voice, educated, Gabe thought, and steady, every word thought out beforehand. He asked questions but said nothing of his own life no background or why he was in jail just a heavy Cane Toad croaking.

During the day Gabe would look for him in the Yard, searching faces, trying to fit a voice to a face but never able to pin him down and gained a picture in his head of a short feller with bushy hair and moustache like that Einstein always in the news.

~

Conversations with Einstein went on until Christmas and the Wood Shop when Gabe 'took his eye off the ball.'

Over the months ease had crept up. Pleased with the nightly chats Gabe forgot the Lieutenant's warning and began thinking he was among friends and that if he kept his head he might get through okay.

It was a mistake to think that.

It happened on Christmas Eve. Most of the afternoon was spent in chapel singing carols with the rest of the wing. Rules weren't relaxed, the same shot guns and batons, but seeing it was Christmas guys were friendly patting Gabe on the shoulder and wishing him Merry Christmas.

The last carol sung they went for supper. In the chow hall Pete, the Trusty carpenter squeezed alongside. He said Gabe was to go to the Wood Shop. There was a problem with the President's new desk.

If it had been another messenger-boy it wouldn't hurt so bad. Since being in jail this Pete had made a study of wood and knew everything from the splitting of rails to the refining of ebony. Gabe thought the old guy liked him. They seemed to get on and so he would tell of his carvings back home and the Lime Tree and his hope to one day he'd make something of it.

He'd come to think of Pete as a kindly uncle.

There was nothing kind about him.

Gabe never suspected trouble. They went to the Work Shop via the laundry Pete telling of his family, how Christmas morning they'd sing Tannenbaum with a glass of wine. 'It was a good life and would've stayed good if I hadn't tried auditing books to pay my debts. Do you gamble?'

'Nuh-huh.' Gabe shook his head.

'Then don't start,' says Pete. 'My father was a gambler. He bet on anything from a roll of dice to the colour of a woman's bush under her skirt. All day and every day he would bet. Most days he'd lose. Then knowing what was ahead he'd cry, saying nothing was worth risking the love of a friend.'

With that he shoved Gabe into the Wood Shop. 'Sorry, kid,' he rolled a barrel across the door. 'I am my father's son. Yesterday I made a bet about you and I lost.'

They came out of the shadows, three of them. Gabe would've run but there was nowhere to run. He crouched curling his fists.

The tall one, the leader of the pack smiled. 'Now then, honey-bun,' he says, 'no need to cut up rough. Play nice and we'll all get along.'

Sick at heart Gabe leaned into gloom. He knew them as Prairie Dogs always together in the Yard, a fat guy, a joker grinning, one they called Boss-man, wiry and mean, and a heavyweight bruiser seen lifting weights in the gym.

Boss-man smiled. 'I see you looking at Mac.'

Gabe stood tight.

'Like him, do you? I guess he is kinda handsome. He's got a great smile! Smile for the gentleman, Mac! Show him your teeth.'

Mac grinned, a great gap in front of his mouth.

'When he came here he had teeth front and back, didn't you, Mac, but they were big and horsey and didn't suit. So we took 'em out, one by one.'

There was tittering, the bruiser baring his gums, some sickly secret shared.

Boss-man reached down unbuttoning Mac's coveralls. 'Teeth are a problem, especially front teeth,' he hauls the guy's dick out. 'See, a man can get bitten in all the wrong places. You got nice teeth, young Gabe, straight and white. I see 'em this morning mashing your grits. I thought then I don't want 'em chomping my flesh. I'd want a smooth ride when I come in your mouth, a slippery ride, wet and woozy. I don't mind blood! Warm and wet I get hard thinkin' on it.'

There was more tittering. Then Boss-man drops Mac's dick in favour of a pair of pliers. 'This is the deal, your sweet ass eggs over easy or your teeth.' He grinned, his own teeth intact. 'You don't have to lose your looks. You can stay a movie star. I'm an obliging sort of guy. I can be won over. I know what I prefer but I'm open to trade.'

Gabe can't remember much of what happened then. There was no plan. Working on instinct he got between the lathe machines that way they had to come at him single file. He cast around for a weapon but there was only a sandbag. Roaring, he heaved that up and sprang forward driving the heavy bag into the bruiser's face pushing him and Boss-man back.

Cramped, there was nothing for it then but to get into a space. He vaulted a lathe landing on the joker who folded like a screen. Then Boss-Man hit Gabe back of the head with the pliers.

Stunned, he fell. Boots laying into his ribs they went to kicking him.

A boot took him in the head blood dripping into his eyes.

Boss-man laughed. 'Not so tough now, farm boy.'

Rage swirled in Gabe's belly. Years it had been simmering now like lava in a hot spring it heaves and spits, years of Pa and the belt, years of people laughing and calling him dumb, years of wanting to protect Ma and hearing her weep at nights and not being able to lift a hand, and years of working with the dead trying to be respectful and not once fighting back because he always assumed everyone was right and he was wrong.

But that was then!

Gabe was up and swinging and not caring where it landed. He swung and a jaw crunched under his fist. It felt so good he did it again mashing Boss-man in the mouth. A jab to the throat and the bruiser went down.

The joker leapt on Gabe's back. A little guy, legs dangling, he was a gopher clinging to a grizzly. Gabe ran backwards into the lathe, bouncing back and forth until the gopher dropped to crawl under a lathe.

The joker out for the count Boss-man hauled up and along with the bruiser, and Pete rushed forward. Waves of white washing the skylight it was snowing outside. Some Christmas Eve! Gabe wanted to laugh. It takes three not-so-wise men to put one Angel Gabriel down. They were on him and laughter turned to rage. Two whacks, left and right, and then there was only Pete who'd led him into a trap.

Hands about his throat Gabe squeezed. I'm gonna kill him, he thought. It didn't happen this way with Pa. Pa was an accident. This killing will be meant, the unfeeling brute without a shred of remorse has finally arrived.

Charlie appeared.

'Be gone, weasel,' he kicked Pete aside and reaching down grabbed Gabe by the hair yanking him back. 'Come away, *Shiye*. He's not worth it.'

Years later another man would get between Gabe and the need to kill and that for a far greater prize. This day, December 24th, 1934, B Block, Richmond Penitentiary, Gabe's saviour was not so much a man as a phenomenon.

The rat-pack clearly knew him and sank into shadow.

Straggly black rattail hair and pock-marked face a giant straddled the aisle.

'You must be Charlie,' Gabe panted.

'Yeah that's me, Charlie Whitefeather, *Hatali*, Navajo Medicine Man.'

Gabe thought he was tall but this guy is over seven feet and fat. Swathes of gut hanging over his belt and so many jowls you couldn't tell where the face ended and the body began.

Charlie Whitefeather? Gabe struggled. Who is this? What happened to Einstein with the cultured manner? The voice is there but that's it.

Charlie lit a cigarette. 'What are you doing here?'

'I was brung here.'

'Who brought you?'

'Him.' Gabe cocked a thumb.

'Ah yes, the book-keeper?' Charlie nodded. 'A wolf in sheep's clothing leading a lamb to slaughter, it figures.'

'I wouldn't have come but he said there was somethin' I needed to see.'

'And did you see it?'

'I did.'

'And it bothered you?'

'Yes!'

'Then I guess you won't be seeing it again.'

'Oh sure!' the Boss-man sneered. 'Like that's going to happen!'

Charlie yawned. 'Shut your mouth, glonni, and go lead your miserable pack of dogs back to their cage.'

'Don't you call me a dog! We know who's the dog here!' Boss-man pointed at Gabe. 'You thought we were trouble? You ain't seen nothing! This guy chanting Injun voodoo shit every night is the biggest ass-bandit this side of the Rio Grande. Ain't nobody safe when he's around. It's why he's in solitary.'

'I'm not in solitary.' Charlie pulled on a cigarette. 'How can I be in solitary when I'm here? It's Christmas and I am taking the evening air. As for Navajo voodoo shit that happens to be a Latin prayer of contrition I sing every night to save your miserable souls and belonging to your world rather than mine.'

'You shouldn't be here!' Pete pipes up. 'You're classified high-risk and should be in C Block but you got the screws so scared they turn a blind eye.'

Charlie turned. 'How's this for blind eyes! Skaaat!' He thrust his head forward, smoke coming from his nostrils that seemed in the half-light to be on fire.

'Agh!' Pete jumped back screaming. 'My eyes! What you done to my eyes!'

'Nothing that will be there in the morning if you leave now.'

They left, Pete limping between them and Boss-man having the last word.

'I'm sorry for you, farm boy. You don't know yet but this is the worse Christmas of your life. If Crazy Charlie spots you his bitch you ain't gonna have a moment's peace. Your ass will be paying the way every minute of every day.'

Gabe's heart sank. He held his fists high. I don't care who you are, he thought. Voodoo shit or not you ain't stickin' your dick in me.

Charlie frowned. 'Why are you squaring up to me?'

'I don't want any part of that.'

'You mean me an ass-bandit?'

'Yeah. I ain't into that stuff.'

'I never thought you were.'

'You didn't?'

'No. If I'd thought you were that way inclined I'd have left you to it.'

Fists still cocked, Gabe stared. 'Then why are you here?'

'I was sent to look out for you.'

'Sent to look out for me?'

'Uh-huh. There was some anxiety. It was felt you needed a friend.'

Anxiety? Friend? Gabe puzzled the words. They made no sense. Who in this Godforsaken place cared enough to send help?

'Did the Lieutenant send you?'

'Lieutenant?'

'The Unit man?'

'Why would he send me?'

'He warned me. He said I should keep my eye on the ball.'

Charlie laughed. 'Yes, well, if anyone knows about balls it's him. There's a bandit if ever there was one. No, it wasn't the Lieutenant.'

'Who then?'

'Tsohanai, the Sun Bearer.' Charlie ground the cigarette under his heel. 'Or in your parlance, the Lord Jesus Christ.'

Six
Short life
May 1942,
London, England.

'Christ sake, Ma, will you drop it?'

The phone kiosk is misted up. Bobby breathed on the glass rubbing a peep hole. This time of day office girls come out for lunch, some of them real lookers, he doesn't want to miss them.

'So Bucky died and you weren't married?' He leaned into the glass combing his quiff into place. 'What does it matter? You got the money didn't you?'

'I didn't get it! You got it, all one million dollars of it!'

Bobby yawned. 'One point seven-five million to be exact.'

'I don't care how much exactly! It should've been mine.' She was off again. 'I earned it. It wasn't you givin' birth. Nor was it you skimpin' and slavin' for years tryin' to bring a child up decent. I did that, not you.'

Bobby looked at his watch, if he's not careful he'll miss his date. This is his last day R&R in London for a while and a last shot at Lady Mildred Fenner, the cute red-head who works for the Foreign Office, drives an ambulance in her spare time and keeps a house in Knightsbridge. Mildred's husband has an estate in Sussex where he raises a herd of prize winning Friesian cows. A busy man, he don't get to town too often which leaves the wife free to entertain. This afternoon they'll repair to a hotel in the Strand where Bobby will present the bill. Tonight it's dancing at the Ritz, tomorrow it's goodbye London and hello boondocks in Suffolk where men chew straw and women shave.

What a waste of time calling home! He should be seeing the sights before his eyes and ears are closed forever. There was another raid last night the Thames on fire and the skyline again rearranged. Bobby believes it safer in the air than on the ground. It's why he wants to claim dibs on Lady M before the Luftwaffe thinks the same and splatters Lieutenant R E Rourke DFC all over London.

Three times he's wined and dined the lady and not once asked dibs. Time's up, milady, it's a room in a flea pit hotel and payment on the nose.

This line is so bad he can hardly hear Ma. Not that he needs to! Same old story, how she suffered bringing him into the world and how he's flown off to fight somebody else's war leaving his poor mother alone.

'I said to the parson, the sins of the father shall be visited on the son.' Here she goes again. 'Bucky Rourke was ever a sinning man. I prayed history wouldn't repeat itself but his son still follows in his footsteps.'

'What do you mean follow?' Bobby interrupted the flow. 'I ain't no Copper King. I'm one of the few who've never been owed so much by so many. I'm a hero. Winston Churchill said so. I've been awarded a DFC for gallantry so show a little respect, mother. I fly a Wellington. I don't dabble in ball-cocks.'

'And what good are medals when you're fetched home in a tin box or with a leg missin' and have to be looked after the rest of your life, tell me that?'

'Jesus, Ma!' He held the phone outside the box. All this yacking when she doesn't give a damn! He was never a son to Ruby so much as an investment. It's the only reason he was born. Bucky was not the marrying kind but he would stump up for a son and heir. Shame the old boy died. Bobby will miss him. They shared a few laughs. And yeah thanks for the money! 'Close on two million dollars,' said the lawyer. 'You can do a lot of good with that, Lieutenant Rourke,' Bobby had grinned. 'Yeah, and if I'm lucky a lot of bad!'

To be honest he's not bothered. Money was never the core of his life. Flying is his world and if he manages to survive this war and thereafter the dough keeps him in metal birds then hooray for Buckminster Copper. Until then it's Eighth Bomber Command and trying to stay alive.

'I'm going now, Ma. I got things to do and people to see.'

When she kept talking he mimed the pips. 'Pip...pip...pip! Sorry, we're about to be cut off. Goodbye! So long! It's been good to know you!'

Whack! He slammed the phone down and diving out of into sunlit air did a soft-shoe shuffle. A Wren in navy pea-jacket and a cute hat smiled, whereupon he whipped her up into his arms and danced her down Wardour Street the crowd parting to let them through: '*So long it's been good to know yuh! So long, it's been good to know yuh! So long it's been good to know yuh, it's a long time since I've been home and I gotta be drifting along.*'

~

Five in the afternoon Mildred is brushing her hair. Bobby lies on the bed watching. Girls and their make-up! You have to love 'em. Top-drawer or dime-store they sit at a mirror after sex repairing the damage. It's a tribal thing, a reconnecting with self, the girl that came in not the woman going out.

Look at her! How old is she thirty-five maybe or early forties and she's with the rest spitting in a box and blacking her lashes. Now it's lipstick, first a careful outline and then an emphatic rubbing back and forth with her pinkie.

War shortages and rationing meant cosmetics were in short supply, women scooping the dregs and walking about with permanently red pinkies. Certain of easy pickings Bobby came to Britain well equipped and not just with French letters. Boy was he ever wrong! When it came to lowering the drawbridge most of them gave the Big E, war or not they meant to hang onto to something if only self-respect.

It's why Mildred hung out. 'I hope you don't think I do this with every man I meet,' she said earlier her lips bruised from kissing. Being a decent guy he reassured her. 'Why Mildred! The thought never crossed my mind.'

To be fair she did her best. A tennis player and athletic rather than sexy she blew his best RAF socks off more than once and so earned a reward, which is why when she turns from the mirror and asks are they still going to the Ritz he'll smile and say, 'sure we are, honey. Why ever not?'

This is sex and nothing to do with love which is okay because after years of living with Ruby Bobby doesn't believe in love. He takes what's offered with a merry heart and a fleet foot. 'No thank you, milady. I'll pass on that.'

Mildred watched in the mirror. 'Pass on what?'

'Nu-huh, honey, just thinking out loud.'

'You do that rather a lot, Flight Lieutenant.'

'Do I?'

'You do. I think it is your way of laying down the rules.'

'I think you are right.'

'I usually am.' She patted her hair. 'Since we are thinking out loud can I ask why the RAF? You're American. Why not your own air-force?'

Good question. It's one he's been asking since '38 when he flipped over the border to Canada. Now with Pearl harbour and the 'great day of infamy,' all the humming and hawing can stop. It's official, the US of A is at war.

In '38 Miss Liberty was dragging her feet an anti-war lobby keeping Franklin D from honouring a promise. Suspecting war and thousands of planes soon to be let loose in the skies Bobby left Virginia for Alberta and the Royal Canadian Air Force. In '39 he was bumped to England and the real McCoy but not as he'd hoped to Fighter Squadron instead he got Tempsford and Bomber Command.

To say he's disappointed is to understate. Until then life was about being an eagle. Now he's a Dodo steering a dustbin full of bombs about the sky. He tried more than once for Fighter Squadron but soon understood it was about timing and the right accent and who you knew.

God knows why he should be disappointed. A fighter pilot is a one-way ticket to the Morgue. But then it's no different in Bomber Command. The odds of a short life and fiery death for all pilots are one in ten. He's had near misses yet so far has managed to bring his team home. Ponderous and with minimal guidance systems the planes aren't up to it pilots having to fly *into* weather rather than over. With so many killed the War Office has learned to keep statistics undercover so the ordinary man and woman won't take fright.

Now he's heading to Suffolk and night-raids over Berlin.

'In other words ABSS, another base, same shit.'

Mildred is looking at him.

'Sorry,' he grinned. 'I'm doing it again, aren't I?'

'It would seem so.'

'Okay then enough talkin'.' He got up off the bed and standing behind her ran his hands up her skirt. 'What say we make time for a quickie?'

'For heaven's sake, Bobby!' she tutted. 'I've just done my hair.'

'Don't worry about your hair.' He unzipped his pants and leant her over the sink. 'It ain't your head I'm aiming for.'

~

Food at the Ritz is passable but the guests take some swallowing. A rabid mix of long-haired poets in eye-shadow and displaced royalty sporting heavy-weight tiaras they're nightly here on the prowl looking for entertainment.

Bobby was propositioned three times crossing the vestibule.

'I say, what-ho!' In the can he gazed in the glass. 'Was it something I said?'

A guy from the band grinned. 'No, you're okay, Lieutenant.'

'Thank God for that. I was thinkin' I need to grow hair on my chest and lift weights. Say?' Bobby looked at him. 'Don't I know you from some place?'

The guy nodded. 'I used to play at the Blackjack Club.'

'That's it! You're the trumpeter. I knew I'd seen you before. Of course, a bomb put you guys out of work. Are they thinkin' of openin' up again?'

'I doubt it. It's more a graveyard than a jazz club.'

'Shame, I liked the place.'

'I know. You were a swell dancer.' The trumpeter dried his hands and smiled into the mirror revealing a decided inclination. 'Is your buddy in town these days, Lieutenant, the big army Major?'

'You remember him too?'

'Couldn't miss! A Ranger wasn't he, a real tough guy.'

'That's my buddy, born with a dagger in his mouth. Last heard he was at a commando base up North. I'm not sure where he is now.' Outside sirens wailed and ack-ack rattled. Bobby grimaced. 'You ever get used to this?'

'Do you?'

'No and I never will.'

Suddenly weary, he went back to Mildred. 'Sorry, honey, but we have to leave. I've got to be on the road early.'

They surfaced to clanging fire-engines. Bobby whistled up a taxi. 'Eaton Square for the lady and mind how you go.' A peck on the cheek and off she goes to her absentee Lord F, just another Ruby Cropper when you think about it but with better table manners.

~

Water mains gone and air thick with smoke he made for the Underground. Knowing he was going back that way he earlier left a bag at Liverpool Street Station. Trains are few this time of the night. If he's lucky he'll catch the 12-05 to Sudbury. Let's hope he doesn't have to wait. Underground Stations are a central point for the homeless. Scores of men, women and kids bedding down for the night the smell is worse than any hog pen.

Shoulders hunched, he picked his way between sleepers finding a spot against a wall budged up between two dough boys and their kitbags. From the high of the Ritz and a bottle of decent bourbon he was plunged into a blue mood.

It's the noise. It gets to you, the ripping of the eardrums as yet another piece of history falls. November 1940 he was in Norwich during a raid when a cinema took a hit. The walls collapsed outward revealing a row of seated bodies watching a screen where real flames flickered.

The sheer weight of destruction defies description. Forget the tub-thumping headlines, the clenched fist and 'Britain can take it' posters! A year or two of this and you begin to wonder if it really is the end of the world.

Bobby's lost count of bombing runs made since Canada. Most pilots score notches on the nose of their plane keeping track of kills. Not him. A civvie seeing the X counts it as one bomb and one child or man and woman killed. In reality the X is followed by a row of noughts, 10,000 or maybe 100,000. Bobby can't afford to care how many die. It's enough to get the plane there and back.

That he is still alive is the miracle. To hell with the Distinguished Flying Cross! Right now he'd give anything to be back in Virginny fucking Sue Ryland!

He grinned wryly. What's brought this on? Why so down? It can't be parting with Mildred. He has no desire to see her again. Maybe it's the trumpeter's keen interest in Ash. It's weeks since they were at the Blackjack Club and yet six foot plus of smooth muscle and bone you don't forget.

Winter of '41 Ash arrived from the States and was shipped to the Ranger base in Ireland. As he said when they met it was under the carpet. 'I'm not here. None of us are. We're figments of your imagination.' Bobby pulled the cork of a bottle of Krug, splashed it in a glass and slapped it into the figment's hand. 'Get that down your imaginary neck and I'll order another.'

He and Alex go back a long time. Alexander, or Ash, as he is known was always digging Bobby out of trouble. A reversed David and Goliath situation was the basis of their relationship. It was a joke among the Hunter clan. The General was not amused. He didn't get the connection and always answered Bobby's phone calls thus, 'it's what's his name on the phone, the fly-boy.'

A polite feller, Ash was embarrassed. 'Dad's not good with names.'

Bobby knows what it's about. It's Ruby and that she spread her legs by way of trade. It's some time ago but folks remember especially when she's thumping a religious drum. He tries keeping his distance. Friend or foe he never takes anyone home. She says to him, 'you never bring anyone.' He replies, 'what, so you can insult them as well as me?'

Ma will never soften. He got drunk once trying to explain her to a sweet sophomore she'd just trashed. He said as a kid she was left to fend for herself. The sophomore in question nodded, 'poor lady. It must be hard for her.'

Hard? Ruby is deep down nasty and the excusing by hard times don't cut it. Ash never comments, he has a natural grace that gets him through awkward moments. It's Bobby who finds it tough. He can't help comparing. Fresh flowers in the hall, and Mrs H with an apron about her waist the Hunter household is so well-ordered. They are so very civilised!

Ash laughs when Bobby says anything. 'We have our troubles same as everyone. We're better at hiding them.'

Ash is loved by his folks. You see pride in their faces. Look at Ruby and you see discontent. Before he died Bucky gave her a house and pension but it wasn't enough. It never is. As for the past if all that kept a son from loving his mother was her being a onetime whore then nothing would keep them apart. Bobby would love to be able to love her. She doesn't let it happen. The God she's forever quoting left a gap in her chest where her heart should be.

As a kid Bobby couldn't see it and bruised his own heart offering it to her. But for Ash and the Hunter household it might still be bruised. It's hard to believe but at one time he was almost a member of the family.

Red hair and fabulous eyes, Sarah, Ash's sister, is a goddess in the looks department. They dated. Bobby was thinking wedding bells. Sarah is bright. A Bryn Mawr gal with a mind of her own she wasn't overawed by the quiff and uniform. He had to work to impress her. One night he got fed up of trying and fell from grace with a softer option and bigger tits called Verna Hofstadter.

That betrayal nearly cost him his best buddy.

As a kid he wanted to be like Alex but you can't be another person no matter how much you love them. You have to be yourself. Ma reckons Bobby is a coward. She says he finds it easier being bad. She may be right. Though in terms of coward there's the DFC. You don't get that for playing marbles.

It happened one night after a strike over Bremen. The landing gear on the Halifax jammed and fire amidships he is proud of setting her down. Local newspapers had him a hero for hauling the navigator and front-gunner out. But what else was he supposed to do? Fuel tank blown and midsection on fire hesitate and there is no one to save!

The old codger of an Air Marshall pinning the medal said it could have been worse. Bobby plans to have that carved on his gravestone, 'it could've been worse.' It's likely certain women will disagree but you can't please them all.

Women are his weakness, he admits to it. Married, single, black and white, up or down, he don't care, come all ye unto him. Ash tells him to straighten up. 'Give your pecker and my nerves a rest, will you? When I'm out with you I'm forever looking over my shoulder to see who's on my tail.'

Though Bobby laughed he saw the comment as sour grapes. Ash may be the pride of the army but when it comes to women he's a dud. 'Leave me out of it,' he says when Bobby tries double-dating. 'I couldn't stand to watch you perform. It would burn my eyes.'

Bobby once worked a little magic double-dating Cathy and Debbie, a cute pair of Cockney usherettes at the Apollo Theatre who were more than willing to spend time with a couple of lonely Yanks. He was doing okay with his half of the duo, Cathy batting her lashes for a force ten gale. But sad-sack Hunter spent the evening telling Debbie about his dog, Sherbet, how he took it bird-watching back home on his motorbike. There was she wetting her drawers at the sight of him. All he had to say was roll over but no, bird-watching!

Talk about a waste! Bobby kept their number. Last month, Lady M unavailable, he gave the girls a call. Cathy was out so he asked Debbie for a date. 'Thanks ever-so,' she says, 'it was your pal I fancied.'

Amused and a little annoyed Bobby went on his way. Frozen out by a bird-watcher! Later that week he asked Ash if he was sorry he missed his chance. 'No,' says he. 'She was a sweet kid but not for me.' They argued, Bobby asking why he didn't make the most of it, that she was hungry for more than a lecture on the breeding habits of marsh birds. 'I'm not insensitive to the moment,' says Ash. 'I knew what she wanted and I wanted it too but not squeezed down an alley. When I fall I want it to be forever not for the moment.'

That was that. Steely, a man of principles, if Ash thinks he's right he'll stick with it to the end. He was like that about Bucky's funeral.

'Of course you should go.'

'Why should I?' Bobby says. 'He wasn't my Pa.'

'What's that got to do with it? His name might not be on the birth certificate but he's been there for you and your mother. You owe him.'

Bobby didn't see it that way. He liked the old guy and appreciated the money but didn't want to legitimize the relationship by appearing at the funeral. While he stayed away he was anyone's son not that of a pedlar. So only Simeon Salmanovitz was at the funeral and he died the following week.

What a difference then! Ruby went. Apparently it was standing room only. 'Such a crowd! The way they was goin' on you'd think that old Jew was somebody. I'll tell you who was there,' she says, 'that murderin' convict Gabe Templar. Tied up in chains he was with his mother and a feller in khaki. '

It appears Simeon willed the Parlour to Gabe. 'There wasn't any money,' says Ruby. 'He's been sendin' it to Russia. Thousands of American dollars gone out the country! Foreigners takin' what don't belong to them, it ain't right! Folks are up in arms about it so bear that in mind, Baby Rourke, and don't be bringin' a foreign girl back 'cos she'll get no help from me or anyone else.'

So Gabe got the Valley Rest Funeral Parlour! It's something when he gets out. Seven years he's been in the Pen. Shame! It didn't seem right him getting put away. The whole town knew Hodge was beating him and his mother. Sue Ryland as was, she's married now to Bert Willett, the baker, was crazy for Gabe. She told Bobby if'n she'd known he was gonna kill Hodge she'd have got there first and saved him jail.

Sue is one crazy female. Hot as a chill-pepper he used to have her every night and Sunday. That stopped when Gabe went to jail. Bobby tried picking up where they left off but she didn't want to know. A hot kind of love overruling all else he's never felt that way about anyone and wouldn't want to.

He's not like Ash, no need of a soul mate. Nice and easy is how he wants life, sex a-plenty and zero commitment.

Now think on this! Alex Hunter is super intelligent with a photographic memory, one look and it's in his head forever. Same with hearing! A couple of hours listening to a conversation in any language and it's mapped in his brain, the undercover OSS guys already on to him as a possible person of interest.

Some years back Bobby gave Gabe Templar a lift in his old Mustang. The guy was trying to enrol in the National Guard. Ash was on the front seat when it happened. Now, wouldn't you think he'd remember Gabe? He says he doesn't.

It is rumoured Gabe is getting out of jail. It seems that early this year the government started a campaign, 'serve your country serve your time,' the military recruiting able-bodied men from US prisons. Ma heard Gabe signed up for the Marine Corps. When Bobby told Ash he was noncommittal. 'The Corps are picky even in wartime and so a guy serving time for murder wouldn't be top of their list. If he is brought in then he has a sponsor and it's someone with clout. Good luck to the guy. Getting in via the back door he's gonna need it.'

When Bobby said Gabe was the guy they gave a lift to back in the day Ash seemed surprised. Bobby thinks that is odd. It sure sticks in his mind. He had a strong sense of déjà vu that day, like they'd done it before, three men bowling along to another army unit and another recruiting station.

At times Bobby looks at Ash and sees Gabe Templar. Grand piano in the drawing room or outside crapper the backdrop couldn't be more different and yet a thread of yesteryear unites them.

He admits to a twinge of envy. The Hunter clan are tight whereas Bobby feels the need to prove his worth. It doesn't matter that he has money. When it comes to class money doesn't count. That girl Debbie saw it in Alex and didn't give a hoot for Bobby, 'it was your pal I fancied.'

'Well fuck you Debbie! I didn't fancy you either.

Suddenly angry, he kicked out. So what if Sue Ryland and Cockney Debbie don't want him. He can have any girl he wants. Snappy in RAF blues, he has only to click his fingers and they come running. He's popular. Guys at the last base called him Captain America. They invited him out for beers and laughed at his jokes. He doesn't need a Cockney gal with bad teeth and ugly accent to like him. The girl he marries will be the Cat's Meow! She will be beautiful and gentle and good to hold and not a bit like Ruby. They'll have a home together with plenty rooms and the smell of baking in the kitchen. There'll be a yard out back filled with roses and kids will laugh and dogs will bark.

She'll always be there. 'Honey, I'm home,' he'll open the door and there she is smiling, a cold beer in her hand a kiss for his lips.

He'll know her the minute he sees her. Take that girl, the one in the train just pulled in, the one by the window, the blonde in the cute knitted hat?

Now that's a girl he could go for. Look at her, so lovely and with the face of an angel seen in an old painting. A girl like that would be the love of his life and no one would separate them.

'Shit! That's my train!'

Bobby lurched away from the wall. He'd been sitting so long he'd gotten sleepy and forgot what he's doing. That's his train! It says so on the front, Liverpool Street Station. If he doesn't get that he's another long wait.

'Get out the way!' Bobby hops between sleeping bodies, dancing from side-to-side, trying to get through but nobody's moving.

He has to get on that train! He has to meet that girl!

'Hey!' The warning buzzer's gone. The doors is gonna close.

'Wait up!' he yells. 'Someone hold the door!'

He yells and the girl in the window looks up. Now she's on her feet. 'Hold the door!' she's saying. 'Someone wants to get on!'

The door shuts. The train starts to pull away and Bobby is caught up in her eyes and apologetic smile. 'So sorry,' say her lips. 'Better luck next time.'

Seven
Cockroaches

The Sudbury train was in at Liverpool Street Station and the guard blowing the whistle! Adelia ran down the escalator leaping inside as the doors were closing. The 12-05 stops at every stop but at least she's made it.

What a day, she feels emotionally wrung out. She hadn't wanted to leave St Barts. After Aunt Maud fell ill she tried commuting but an hour and half each way, and that on a good day, it seemed more sensible to get a local job.

A horrible time! It's not the war so much neither is it the bungalow though run-down and piled high with junk that is horror enough. It's not the animals in the pens. It wasn't even Aunt Maud! It's that Adelia had to do everything alone. Now she says goodbye to friends known and loved for years.

Ahmed Sadozai, a five-year old brought in with spinal injuries after the dockyard bombing watched from his cot. 'Where you going?'

Adelia said she was needed at another hospital. He asked if she was coming back. She said she'd try to pop in now and then. He turned his head away. 'No popping Nurse Addy. You go far away or you die like my mummy.'

It's hard leaving. She's known most of the staff since training school. They will miss Adelia as she will miss them. Sister Edwards was rather stern but then she's probably wondering who will be next. There's been a falling away of nurses lately, especially students, their parents wanting them in the country.

Nowhere in England is safe but London is particularly dangerous. Last year there were raids every day friends killed just trying to get to work.

It is frightening. Death falling from the sky, there's nowhere to hide.

'I'm sorry to lose you, Nurse Challoner.' Matron wasn't at all pleased. 'We are painfully understaffed and nurses of your experience are hard to replace.'

'I'm sorry.'

'Yes, well these things happen. Let's hope you're safer in Suffolk. I understand you've found a new position?'

'St Faiths in Needham. It's only a bike ride away.'

'St Faiths!' A bad egg under her nose Matron grimaced. 'I know it well. I have had many a battle with their admin trying to find beds for patients returning to the area. The building is as old as Barts but not nearly so well maintained. Where will you be, what department?'

'I shall still be in Paediatrics. They've suggested the children's surgical unit for an introductory period and then a post later as Health Visitor.'

'Yes do work towards that. I can see you in Home-Care. You have a way with relatives as well as patients. But you could have done so much better. Far be it from me to criticize another establishment but in Queen Victoria's time St Faiths was more workhouse than hospital. Regrettably some of their more Draconian values prevail. You'll have to work hard to keep standards high.'

'I shall do my best.'

'I'm sure you will. I expect no less of a Saint Bartholomew nurse. As to that you may encounter resentment but remembering you from Nursing School I feel sure you'll manage.' She smiled, the battleaxe image dissolved. 'At least you're staying within the profession. Necessity draws you away rather than the charms of a serviceman as is the case in many hospitals. War, nurses and injured servicemen is a heady mix that doesn't always stand the test of time. Bear that in mind when you're out there alone. You are a beautiful girl with a beautiful heart. Try to stay so.'

~

The train pulled into Chelmsford passengers scrambling to get out. Finding an empty seat Adelia slept the rest of the journey. It's a pity the RAF pilot at Piccadilly missed his connection. She tried holding the door but at that time of night everyone is too tired to care. A charmer, he made a sweeping bow as the train pulled away. Judging the tailor-made uniform and brilliant smile he was an American, none of your British fangs and heavyweight serge.

Suffolk is teeming with GIs. Practically every base along the East Anglian coast has a branch of the US military aboard. Needham Air Base has a huge intake. Tanks and armoured jeeps rolling down the street you can't move for them. Public opinion is divided. Local business is delighted with shops and pubs doing a roaring trade. Among parents there is a sense of lock up your daughters. The daughters, on the other hand, keep a spare key; witness St Faiths for her interview, dances at the air-base and what to wear and whether to kiss on a first date the topic of conversation.

Another shipment of men landed yesterday. There'll be more now the USA is in the war though where they'll go heaven knows. Yesterday Adelia was in the yard feeding chickens when a jeep rolled up. 'Excuse me, ma'am,' a voice called, 'are you the owner of the house?'

'Sort of,' she replied.

'I see you have a realtor board. Are you for sale or renting?'

'Neither at the moment.'

'Pity,' the chap climbed back into the jeep. 'If it meant seeing you every morning I'd share with the chickens.'

Cheeky but fun is how she sees them. Aunt Maud was of another opinion. 'Marauders!' She would bang her fist on the bed. 'Loud and with awful manners, don't you bring one of those into my house!'

Anger from a ninety-year old spinster who as far as anyone knows hadn't set foot outside of Suffolk is a mystery yet even after a second stroke she held up her hand proclaiming a prophesy, 'thou shalt not let him pass.'

Sad the way she ended. Maud Challoner was once a beautiful woman. Adelia has seen photographs, a gorgeous heart-shape face peeping out from under a lace parasol. 'It's where you get your looks,' said Mother. 'Same heavy blonde hair and enormous green eyes she was the beauty of the family. That she wasn't swept off her feet was a surprise to everyone. Your grandmother said she'd had lots of offers. We suspect a dark romantic secret don't we, John?'

This was Mother reminiscing with Dad. They died in '34 on the road to Cambridge, their car in collision with a tractor. Now with Maud gone the dark romantic secret will remain so.

The storm last month finished the old lady. Adelia slept over that night. Thunder and lightning and winds lifting tiles off the roof she heard the outer door slam and found Maud face down in the yard, a bale of hay in her arms.

Tough, argumentative and really quite batty she died as she lived caring for animals. A compulsive hoarder she couldn't throw anything away. Empty boxes, bottles, tin-cans and newspapers she hung on to all hence the series of unsteady stalagmites rising in every room.

Mice droppings everywhere Adelia called pest control. The man said for a couple of quid he would take the rubbish away. One look at the tottering towers and the couple of pounds became ten. Adelia paid as she paid the Animal Sanctuary to take the animals. She wants her life back again. If St Faiths doesn't work out she'll sell the bungalow. But she won't go back to Barts. Little Ahmed is right there can be no popping back.

Matron wasn't keen on St Faiths yet one must work and it is within biking distance. Adelia has only what she earns. Aunt Maud spent every penny of her money on animals, and as Adelia was to learn the Challoner inheritance.

'I'm sorry,' the lawyer said. 'Over time it was frittered away.'

That there was any money was a surprise. A lecturer in Agricultural Studies John Challoner worked in Africa. He and mother were always hard up. Five hundred pounds with interest according to the lawyer the money was to be hers the day she passed her exams. He said he learned of this when taking over the practice and wrote to Maud. 'When she didn't reply I sent another letter. The week she became ill I received a note. This is it. *'I don't know who you are or why you're asking for money. I don't have any. I live hand to mouth and have done for years. I believe a sum was set aside for my Great-Niece. I remember withdrawing the odd amount and putting it in a safe place, banks going bust one must be so careful. I assume it's been spent. My niece does visit from time to time. Of course one of the goats might have eaten it, possibly Teddy, the yellow Billy-Goat. He always was a greedy beggar.'*

The lawyer begged Adelia's pardon and said hopefully the sale of the bungalow would go toward redeeming the figure. She looked at the bowed walls, sniffed the unmistakable smell of mould and thought not.

Before Maud became ill Adelia visited once a fortnight. She'd bring groceries and more often than not paid the baker's bill and the milkman. Though angry at the loss, she could have done a lot with a five hundred pounds, she chooses to believe Aunt Maud meant well her love of animals overshadowing all else.

But for chickens the pens are empty now. There is the dog, Lochie, an ancient chocolate brown Labrador. The vet said he should be put down.

'If an animal has no food value it should be shot. This dog is old with poor quality of life. You do it no service keeping it alive.'

Horrible man! Lochie is a nice dog. Adelia plans to give him the best if only for his last years. Besides, he's company. There is no one close by and so until she finds another place she and Lochie will tough it out together.

Father abroad and Mother with him, no sisters or brothers and years of boarding school, Adelia is used to being alone, even so she would like to settle and make friends. Any friend will do, she doesn't mind, possibly one of the nurses at St Faiths. They seem a nice bunch.

~

July '42,

So much for making friends! Two months she's been on Buttercup Ward and but for the ward maid, Nora Jackson, she knows no one.

She's tried making friends but they are not interested. The first day was hard but by the end of the week - seven twelve hour shifts frozen out by every nurse on the ward including Sister Forbes - it took every ounce of courage to keep going.

You might not call their behaviour bullying yet it seems like it. Every morning she is given a work schedule by Sister Forbes, mostly dirty jobs with the more difficult cases, beyond that the barest of words are exchanged.

The Grand Silence continues off-duty. Lunchtime she would take a sandwich to the canteen. Seeing an empty seat at the Buttercup table she'd ask if she might join them. A head would turn. 'Sorry, it's taken.'

Friday she was offered a place at the Registrar's table. Face burning, she sat. 'Don't let it get to you,' said one of the doctors. 'Smile and show your teeth.'

It did get to her and still does. Today is Theatre Day, three children for removal of tonsils, a baby with suspected intussusception and an emergency appendectomy. Up and down in the lift, fetching and carrying, wiping up sick and changing dressings and still she is ignored.

On her way home that evening seeing Nora trudging along with her shopping Adelia walked the bike alongside. 'Why the cold shoulder?'

'They're always like it with someone new.'

'Is that it? They are like that because I'm new?'

'It's their excuse.'

'For God's sake! I realise it takes time to get to know people but this is ridiculous. I catch them staring and I think what on earth did I do.'

'You were born, that's what you did. They're jealous! They want to scratch your eyes out and have done from the minute you walked on the ward.'

'But why? I'm no different to them.'

'You are.'

'How am I?'

'For a start you trained at Barts. Most of them trained locally. They think you're better than them, especially Fussy Forbes who came up through this dump with no qualification other than she was here first.'

'But that's silly.'

Nora sniffed. 'Silly it maybe but stuck-up cow is the word.'

'They think I'm a stuck up cow!?' Adelia was livid. 'That is so unfair. I've tried being friendly but they don't want to know.'

'That's because you're friendly with the wrong people. The Senior Registrar for a start, Mr Covington-Wright, and the others you sat with in the canteen.'

'I sat there because they offered a seat.'

'Nurses don't sit with doctors.'

'In Barts you sat where there was a seat.'

'You're not in Barts. This is Faiths where no one likes anyone especially beautiful blondes. They see you as competition. Every one of the doctors is fair game to our lot and you're putting their noses out of joint.'

'You are kidding!'

'I'm not. The offer of a seat at the doctor's table, and the fact that Buttercup Ward is suddenly popular with the male staff right down to the porters, is what it's about. As I said, you're competition. Lined up against you they haven't a cat's chance in hell and they know it.'

~

Adelia never sleeps well during the day. Noise and light keep her on the surface. She dreams more and today woke from a really odd affair, She dreamt she was getting married in St Giles church and as it was before it was bombed the East Window blazing over the altar.

A vivid dream, the church ablaze of light, long tapered candles set about the altar and tubs of red roses and the air heavy with a mix of perfume she wore a bridal gown of heavy silk a vile floating out in the air as though caught in a breeze. A man led her to the altar rail where they knelt on scarlet velvet cushions. She couldn't see the groom's face and didn't know his name and yet had seen him many times before in dreams even as a child.

Hands worn and callused, nameless and faceless he knelt beside her, unknown and yet loved until the end of time.

The service was delayed for the best man, a soldier away at war. Adelia was anxious. She seemed to know that if they didn't marry then they never would and so asked the priest to continue. The groom wouldn't be moved and gazed at cross on the altar as though he were the one crucified.

'We must wait for the best man,' he said.

The priest began reading from the bible, his deep voice intoning a psalm from the Old Testament, the Song of Solomon a poem of divine love.

Again she pressed. 'Why must we wait? Surely, we don't need a best man.'

'No, you mustn't ask it of me!' Golden hair flashing in the light the groom shook his head. 'It has to be the right way or not at all.'

Then with a terrible wailing sound a bomb crashed through the church roof and lay in the nave ticking.

'Please!' She was begging. 'You know how I feel. It's not a secret. I love you. Why won't you tell me that you love me?'

'I can't!' Eyes of silver grey he turned. 'I daren't! Don't you understand, the day I tell you I love you is the day I lose you!'

Boom! The bomb exploded blowing all in it to pieces. A last moment before waking Adelia was crawling through debris gathering bits of the man together only to find that he, the church and everything in it was made of feathers.

~

The dream stayed all week. It was scored on her heart, the sound of a bomb ticking and the priest's voice booming.'

Such feeling! Such passion! She'd never felt anything like it. There had been the occasional date but few and far between. There was a fellow she liked, a post-graduate at Queen Marys who went to the Congo with a Medical Team working with lepers. He did propose but Adelia didn't love him. Since then there's been no one. At Barts they called her the Snow Queen. Now at St Faiths she's labelled again and this time as a cow, a stuck up cow at that.

It's been quiet all week on Buttercup and then Thursday evening everything went mad. Staff cut down to three nurses per shift, and the senior nurse doling out pills for the whole wing, it's down to the other two to do the work.

Luckily, Adelia is paired with Nurse Maureen Jones who is filling in time before joining the Queen Alexandra's Army Corp.

Warm and full of fun Mo has made the difference. Adelia actually looks forward to work. Wednesdays are theatre days, the children still dozy from the anaesthetic the nights tend to be quiet. It's Thursdays that are difficult analgesia wearing off and pain setting in.

They were running about all night. No air-raids, thank goodness, and so far nothing coming from any of the Bases though the patient in the Broom Cupboard, a tiny private ward adjoining Buttercup is still being a pest.

An American pilot brought in from the Base with a broken leg a few weeks ago he is always wanting something, but as she said to Mo, thankfully, he is a male surgical problem and nothing to do with paediatrics.

It seems she spoke too soon. Two-thirty Thursday morning they had a call from Night Sister, 'when you've a minute go to the Broom Cupboard and adjust the leg-pulley. But be careful! That man has more hands than an octopus.'

This is the pilot seen in Piccadilly Circus some weeks back Adelia had thought to be charming but who is not at all charming. He is noisy and brash and in her opinion a disgrace to the RAF. So far she's managed to avoid telling him what he can do with the buzzer but if he keeps on she just might.

Mo was first to go to the Broom Cupboard. She returned red-faced.

'Night Sister is right, hands everywhere.'

'Damn nerve! You should've boxed his ears.'

Mo grinned. 'I would but he's a right cracker. I mean gorgeous! If I was that way inclined I'd be pulling out the stops.'

'And you're not?'

'I'm a girl's girl, if you get what I'm saying.'

'Oh.'

'Does that bother you?'

'I don't think so. I'm more bothered with that twerp ringing the buzzer.'

'He's not a twerp. He's a hero with a DFC. '

'Oh really? Bragging was he?'

'No not at all. He said anybody would've done the same.

'And yet he did it.'

'Come on, Dee, loosen up! He is doing his bit and you know America didn't need to come into the war.'

'I think they did, Pearl Harbour and all.'

'Don't nitpick. He didn't tell me about the DFC. I saw the ribbon on his jacket. I know about medals. I studied them for my interview with the Corps.' Mo laughed. 'He is a bit of a lad. He had me in stitches.'

'It's as well it was you.' Irritable and in need of sleep Adelia was beginning to sound like a sourpuss. 'He wouldn't have me in anything.'

'He wouldn't dare.'

'Why wouldn't he?' Adelia wasn't sure whether to be offended.

'You are extremely off-putting.'

'How am I? And don't say stuck up! You know that's not me.'

'It's nothing to do with being stuck up. It's about crossing a line. A man wouldn't try it on with you and nor for that matter would a girl.'

The buzzer went again, a red light shining over the door. Mo went to answer it but Adelia said to leave it. 'Hero or not we haven't time to humour him. Let him stew. See if it makes him even more heroic.'

~

The rest of the night was so hectic Adelia forgot about the pest until quarter past four when he was not only punching the buzzer he was yelling and woke Baby Morris who had just that moment gone to sleep.

Furious, Adelia stomped across the corridor. 'What do you want now?'

Leg entangled in the hoist, he was halfway out the bed. 'I want a piss and have wanted a piss for the last two hours.'

'Hold on!' She brought a bed pan from the sluice.

'What is that?'

'What does it look like?'

'Take it away! I want to piss not take a crap.'

Adelia ran the length of the corridor to men's surgical, grabbed a bottle and ran back. 'Here!' She slapped it in his hand. 'Now please stop yelling! I've babies in need of sleep. They don't want to hear you misbehaving.'

'I ain't misbehavin'.' Groaning, he peed into the bottle. 'I had to buzz. It was that or piss the bed.' On and on he seemed to pee forever. 'There you go, Warden.' He handed her the bottle. 'Pure unadulterated Scotch whisky.'

She emptied the bottle and trying to keep patience washed her hands at the sink, adjusted the hoist, offered a glass of water, straightened the cover and stepped back. 'Anything else while I'm here?'

He was a while answering and then he nodded. 'Yeah, there is somethin',' he said. 'You can marry me and come live with me in Virginia.'

~

Five o clock Bobby lay staring at the stars. Of all the crumby ways of meeting the girl you're going to marry that has to be the worst.

'Jesus H Christ!' He closed his eyes trying to block the image of Flight Lieutenant R E Rourke dick in his hand peeing into a glass bottle, while she - the Beautiful One, the

Swan with Golden Hair (**the girl on the train at Piccadilly Circus!**) stands with eyes averted.

'Agh!' He punched the wall. He couldn't believe it. How to screw up love before it's begun! 'Marry me,' he said, 'and come with me to Virginia!'

As if! Green eyes hostile she stared. He could read her glance, who is this creep with the filthy tongue and limp dick and why don't I slap him.

It's as well his dick was limp anything with life would've really rocked the boat but then what man gets a hard-on when ruining the chance of lifetime!

Embarrassed though she was she maintained her cool and placing the buzzer slightly out of reach said, 'try not to buzz again. You'll wake the cockroaches.'

Ha-ha. Funny!

There are cockroaches here. Last week he threw a shoe at one the size of the Hindenburg. Splat, it went against the wall. It lay for the count of ten then got up, shook itself, and sauntered off giving the claw to the would-be assassin.

Filthy things cockroaches, Bobby remembers reading that if the world fell down and couldn't get up roaches would rule. Right now he's a roach that's been hit with a shoe and doesn't feel like getting up.

'I mean, how do I get beyond that?'

Leg-hoist undone he hopped to the window. Five by nine, everything crammed together, it's more a monk's cell than ward. The hospital is a dump. Centuries old and everything falling apart, what's a girl like that doing here?

Talk about fate! The whole set-up, his broken leg and her being here is a mix of good and bad luck, bad luck him breaking his leg, good luck the Wellington he was due to fly that night was hit and everyone in it at the bottom of the North Sea! Bad luck that he just made such a fucking scene!

Why does he do it? Is he that much of a lost cause he can't keep his mouth shut even while she's standing in front of him?

Bobby sighed. He wished he knew what drives him. It's not as if Bucky was a bad influence, rough edges, sure, but he never cussed. Ruby's tongue is sharp. Given a chance she'll cut you down but she doesn't cuss. So why does he?

Maybe it's Wolfe Street and errands he ran as a kid, the looks he got and the invitations, the flashers and the groping hands, mud like that sticks to the soul.

In early days there were Uncles, maybe four or five a day 'Run down to the Hawaiian Bar, Baby, and tell Uncle Joe I'm home.' It got to be a pattern, a message for the bartender and the back stairs trodden by heavy boots.

Dark eyes and brown curls, Ruby was cute rather than beautiful. She must have had something because eventually the many were replaced by one who kept coming until Wolfe Street was history and Ruby a had a house on the Green same as General William Hunter.

Needless to say she was quickly out of there. Even Ruby hadn't the face to stick it out. She got Bucky to buy a place next to the Mission and closing the door on her old life took up the Lord God and His redemptive fury.

Bobby stared out the window watching sparrows strip a lavender bush. Life on Wolfe Street made him ashamed but he put up with it. Ruby's new hypocrisy was worse. Overnight she became set in stone Fredericksburg another Babylon and she the Judge.

A tyrant, she made it her business to root out sinners, little people, couples living over the hoof, or hobos breaking petty laws. Money to spend she bought into the Mission by way of the Minister and his wife. Soon she was arranging altar flowers and cleaning the church and supervising lay-people.

Everyone feared her, especially the Minister. One-by-one other helpers dropped away until there was only Ruby.

Pretending respectability she took up the name Rourke. Nobody was fooled. They knew who she was, and her son, what's his name, the fly-boy.

Contempt is what Bobby hears when the General says that. But Bobby hasn't helped. If he were to quieten down and become a citizen, get a wife and couple of kids and a house on the Green, then he would be someone the General could admire, the DFC pinned to his chest a head start.

Maybe that's what this war is about, thoughts flooded Bobby's mind, a clean page, a war hero arriving back in town with his lovely English wife on his arm.

Excited, he leaned toward the window and a new day. When he busted his leg he thought he'd really screwed up, that he'd be sent back to the States an all-time loser. Now he sees it a literal lucky-break. So he made a bad start with Nurse Adelia Challoner but he can make amends. And it's *Miss* Adelia Challoner! He's lain with enough women to know a virgin when seen.

Unchartered land he must go steady. No more mistakes! For this wooing he must swap places with a navigator and plot a route by way of the stars. He can do it! Yes he can, because for the first time in his life Baby Rourke is in love.

~

Exhausted, Adelia slept long into Friday afternoon. With no need to be on the ward until seven she lay watching sunlight play on the window. She'd dreamt of the wedding again, the same scenario, roses and perfumed candles and bomb ticking in the nave and again the bride begging to be loved. In this dream she knelt beside a stranger whose eyes were blue as the skies and who brought her hand to his lips. 'No need to ask. I do love you. I always have.'

Boom, then again the bomb exploded. She was again on her hands and knees collecting pieces of the dream and this time blue feathers and all the while as she scrambled about the priest read from the Song of Solomon; *'My beloved said unto me rise up my love, my fair one, and come away, for lo, the winter is past. The rain is over and gone. The flowers appear on the earth. The time of singing birds is come. Arise my love, my fair one, and come away.'*

Eight
Afterthought
July 1942
B Block, Richmond Penitentiary Exercise Yard.

Charlie Whitefeather sat against the wall warming his
bones. Gabe sat alongside. Midday it's too hot to sit in the
Yard, best keep walking, that way you're less of a sitting
target. Evening recreation is the best part of the day, the
sun going down and enough heat stored in the bricks to
ease aches and pains, and Charlie suffering from some
muscle disease is always in pain.

It's Gabe's last weekend in lock-up. 0600 Monday
morning a wagon takes him to Fredericksburg to say
goodbye to Ma and then on to Pariss Island, South
Carolina, and the Marine Corps.

'Are you sure you want to do this thing, *Shiye*,' says
Charlie, all this week asking the same question.

'It's this or stuck in here for the rest of my life.'

'How is it the rest of your life? Your sentence is fifteen
years. Seven from fifteen means you're halfway, less if you
get parole.'

'I won't get parole.'

'You might.'

'I'll never get parole, the guy said so.'

'What guy?'

'The Gunnery Sergeant Major! He threatened me. He said turn the Corps down after them makin' the gratuitous error of invitin' murderous scum like me aboard and I wouldn't live to tell the tale.'

'Gratuitous?'

'Uh-huh.'

'I doubt he meant gratuitous,' says Charlie picking grit out of his boots. 'I think he might have been confusing unwarranted with unnecessary. They don't mean the same, not in this context. Unjustified would make more sense, the means not justifying the end.'

Gabriel turned his face to the sun and let the rambling float over his head. This is Charlie Whitefeather, killer, scholar or bogeyman, take your pick. He likes words. He plays with them tossing them up in the air and watching how they fall. Clever, speaks other languages, so much learning crammed into a ton of pockmarked flesh the guy is a mystery. Here in the Pen they've built a legend round him. Real name is Hokee Chance, it's said he is one of only three American Indians to graduate from Harvard. No one really knows why he's here. It's said he hacked a bartender to death for raping an Indian girl, lawyers appealing against a death sentence close on fifteen years. Navajo holy man and Singer of Songs everyone's scared of him. They say the Warden cut him a deal, Charlie allowed to roam providing he keeps him ahead of what's happening. Gabe doesn't know what's real or fancy. Seven years of watching the guy slip and slide through walls and he's no wiser.

Whatever, he saved more than Gabe's life that day in the Wood-Shop.

Unsure of the price Gabe had stood his ground. 'I don't care who sent you. I don't need some guy seein' me his piece of ass. I don't do that with any man and I don't need protectin'. I maybe a kid but I ain't afeard of you.'

Charlie had laughed and lit up a smoke. That guy! You never see him without a cigarette hanging from his lip. It's the constant supply of smokes that feed rumours of him being a snitch. He's no informer. Links to the outside he can get all the cigarettes he likes and bottles of Jim Beam whisky for bribing the guards and opium for when his bones ache real badly.

All kinds of rumours, Charlie admits to nothing except being homosexual and on the hunt for a new flesh though never in seven years trying Gabe. 'Loving another of your sex is no sin,' says he. 'Navajo see such people as having two souls. I have many souls. I love all life and all life is lover to me.'

All life may love Charlie but it doesn't love Gabe. After the fight in Wood Shop Boss-man made life a misery even to putting shit in food. He worked in the laundry as did his rat-faced pals. That's where Gabe chose to make a stand.

Boss-man was quiet from then on. Gabe did think his fists brought that about. No way! The week he was in solitary Charlie sent a message through the wires; 'word to the wise. The next man to halt or in some way subvert my son's progress through this Vale of Tears is a dead man.'

Pete, the Trusty, says Charlie adopted Gabe. 'He calls you *Shiye* which means son. He says you are *diyin ya naa'a i* and must be allowed to live your life.'

'And what the heck does that mean?' says Gabe.

'Messenger from God.'

Gabe had to work with the guy that betrayed him. First shift Pete comes crawling. 'I'm sorry. Gambling is a drug. It takes me over. Even now talking to you it's best you don't believe a word I say.'

After nearly seven years stuck in here Gabe doesn't believe anything. He's not even sure about God. Shut away from air and trees and animals and all that makes life sweet there is no worst kind of Hell. The things that go on behind cell doors, the ugliness of it, the brutality, Charlie can talk of Divine powers and messengers of God but it's just words.

Pete's gone. Last year he got a busted appendix and died before they could take it out. He left his work tools to Gabe but he can't use them, they stick to his hands like bacon fat. The initial G burned into the handle he's got his own. The Pen makes office furniture to sell to high-class stores. These days Gabe is assigned special orders. Today he finished a bed for the Warden's daughter.

Spring of '35 Charlie moved into the cell next door. It was him came up with the idea of carving dolls. The Lieutenant from the Unit sells them as lucky charms and for trade hires porn movies to show in the Chow Hall. They lathe off-cuts of wood to a basic size and shape and Gabe finishes them in his cell.

A prisoner accused of murder you'd think the guards would worry about the knife. They don't seem to bother. Though mean as ever with Billy-sticks things trickle through now rather than swell as if the coming of a Medicine Man to B Block added a cushion to life.

Charlie suffers a disease that makes his muscles go into spasm. It gives him so much pain he can't sleep nights. It's why he sings. He reckons singing the only thing gives him rest. Last night a blackbird joined in his song. A feathery smudge glimpsed through the barbed wire the sound almost broke your heart.

The blackbird sang and Gabe thought on his little gal. It's years since he's seen her. He doesn't want her here among sweat and shit and men fighting and pulling their dicks. It's not a fit place. As he denies her so she denies him. The healing of bug's wings is a thing of the past. Gabe can get beat up all day long but cuts and bruises are still there in the morning.

He might reject her but she sometimes gets through. One time Charlie decided Gabe needed to learn to read. He got a book from the trolley, a French book called, '*La Belle aux Bois Dormant.*'

Asked how he knew foreign languages Charlie said he was schooled in an orphanage where the Sisters came from all over Europe. 'It wasn't difficult. Compared to my people's language French is easy. Nobody understands Navajo not even a Navajo.'

Gabe has trouble reading. Open a book and a door shuts between him and the words. Now the only book he listens to is in French. A girl with golden hair asleep on a bed he likes the cover. It reminds him of his little gal.

Every evening along with a Movie Magazine Charlie reads a page in French and then in English. Sleeping Beauty is a tale of a princess cursed to sleep a hundred years who can only be woken by true love's kiss. One night Gabe was listening and the cell bars melted. There was his gal grown and beautiful and looking straight at him; 'Who are you?' she said, 'What do you want?'

Somehow he knew the words weren't meant for him that she was talking to some other guy. It made him sad so he asked Charlie not to read again. Years on he misses the story but can't bear the idea of eavesdropping.

'You thought it was bad manners to listen in on her life.'

'What!' Gabe swivelled.

Charlie was still picking grit from his boots. 'You thought it wrong to spy on your Other Self.'

Shocked, Gabe stared. 'How come you know about that?'

'You told me.'

'I did not! I've never told anyone about her. I never would!'

'Then it must've been your mother.'

'No way!' Gabe was on his feet. 'Ma don't like me talkin' of my dreams. Wantin' the past to disappear she's put out of her mind as have I.'

'Sit down, fool!' Charlie flapped his hand. 'You're worrying the guards.'

The guy is a magician! It's not the first time he's been inside Gabe's head answering to thought. 'How did you know I was thinkin' of her?'

'You're always thinking of her. Night and day I hear the wheels grinding. You waste time trying to deny her. Push all you like but when a soul is part of you there is no separation.'

'She ain't a part of nothin'. She's someone I dreamt up.'

Charlie grinned. 'Really?'

'Yeah really!'

'Have it your way but she may not be a dream so much as a memory.'

'Of what?'

'Of when you wore a different body.'

'Don't start that with me!' Gabe flung away. 'I hear you talkin' with the padre when he comes bamboozlin' the guy about sky-walkin'. You can argue with him all you like. He has his faith to fall back on. I got nothin' and I tell you the thought of bein' born again to a man like Hodge I'd sooner quit before I start.'

'Then quit.' Charlie shrugged. 'It's nothing to me. Your life is your own. I'm not asking you to believe what I believe. Every man is entitled to his own thoughts. Just don't close your mind to other possibilities.'

'Like what?'

'Like the possibility that the love that burns in your heart and has since you were born is neither a ghost nor a dream, that the girl you call your Other Self is a memory of a life before or…!' he held up his hand, '…one yet to come.'

'A life yet to come?'

'Yes and already in the making, hence your dreams.'

'Lucky me!' Gabriel snorted, 'a life yet to come with the US Marine Corps fightin' Japs in the sunny Pacific. I can't wait.'

Thoughtful, the pockmarks in his face craters, Charlie climbed to his feet.

'It may be exactly that. The past is always trying to pursue the present. You are young and beautiful. Before this body I was beautiful. No butterfly, never that, but I had wings. Now I'm landlocked and ugly. People turn from

me, especially those I desire. *Ah ts' iid* ! It is my lot. I chose
this form and must continue with it, as you must continue
with yours. Your wings were given centuries before mine.
It's time you remembered how to fly.'

'You're talkin' trash, Medicine Man.'

'Maybe, but it's not me wishing he could read. You
thought you didn't need an education. We are born to
learn. Now that you're about to be tossed back into the
world from which you escaped you are afraid.'

'I ain't afraid.'

'You are. For years you've had your life laid out for
you, when to eat and to sleep and to shit. Now it's the
army and another set of rules.'

'Don't keep sayin' army. It's the Marine Corps and a
world apart.'

'So the man said yesterday.'

'The Gunnery Sergeant spoke to you?'

'Of course.' The klaxon was sounding time to fall in.
Charlie was already yards away. A big man but light on his
feet he could move like the wind.

Gabe went after him. 'Why was he speakin' to you?'

'Because I'm the one they came to enlist. You are the
afterthought.'

~

Afterthought? That the Corps didn't care to enlist an
ignorant farm-boy made sense. Being a Marine is a big deal.
They don't take anybody. Yet they did come to the cell last
week and the Warden with them.

'On your feet!' the guard had yelled. 'Someone wants to talk to you.'

For a while there was no talking only faces staring. 'What's this,' Gabe had snarled, 'a day trip to the zoo?'

When they carried on he got mad. 'What's the problem? If you're bored and lookin' to be amused I could always strip and swing from the bars?'

The guard rattled the bars. 'Shut your mouth!'

Barrel-chested and sprayed on uniform the guy in khaki grinned. 'Let him be. We came to be entertained and as it goes this kid is by far the most entertaining. So yeah, take off your shirt! Show us the goods.'

If Gabe had known what was on offer, a way out of the Pen other than in a wooden box he might've been more respectful but he was pissed off.

This place changes you. He's not the quiet unassuming guy he used to be. Inside he boils with such anger he cannot breathe! It's the lack of privacy and the constant staring. Morning, noon and night guys peer at you. You can't take a dump without someone watching. It's enough to drive a man crazy.

So fool that he is he took off his shirt and Charlie next door humming the Marine Hymn Gabe beat it round the cell like a Vaudeville stripper until the guy in khaki, and a chance of freedom walked away.

Charlie persuaded them to give him another chance. 'Don't let the muscle fool you. Gabriel Templar is a good kid with a good heart. Take him now while he has a chance of staying good.'

'Nah,' the Gunnery Sergeant had shaken his head. 'The Corps got enough murdering psychopaths as it is.'

'He's no murderer. He was brought in at seventeen. All he did was defend his mother. What man here wouldn't do the same?'

Still the Marine refused. 'He's got the build but I doubt he's the brains. We'll stick with the plan. We came for you, Hokee Chance. It's you we want leastways the guys in suits want you. Left to me you wouldn't get to sniff my ass never mind wear khaki. The idea of Injun low-life confusing the enemy with their bibble-babble is a joke and a bad joke at that.'

'Then you go back empty-handed.' Charlie had settled in the chair. 'Me and the kid will sit the war out. We don't mind. It's not our war. We didn't start it. Go ahead and fight and leave me and mine to work out our days.'

That's when the Warden spoke up. 'You don't have any days. Your last appeal was thrown out. Time's up, Charlie. The date is set. You're for the chair and early doors to your own personal Happy Hunting Ground.'

Gabe didn't hear Charlie's reply until '43 when Gunnery Sergeant JJ Emmet lay dying at Guadalcanal. Then he learned Charlie told the Warden to send him to the chair; '*much use a Navajo Code Talker will do you there.*'

Summer of '42 Gabe knew nothing of War Office plans to train Navajo Indians to create a code. Sure, he knew their language was set-apart. He'd been listening to it for years and thought it more grunts than words. Yet some clever guy had seen the possibilities and that a code using Navajo words and gestures was likely to confuse even the smartest Japanese Code breaker.

Ignorant of this he woke one morning to find the adjoining cell empty and other than a folded blanket nothing to say a man was ever there.

Charlie leaving cut deep. Gabe had grown to care for him, seeing him not-so-much a father as an elder brother. Now he's gone without a word as if seven years meant nothing and Gabe's alone again.

~

The Pen is on lock-down. A prisoner from C Block due to be executed nothing is going out and nothing coming in, all prisoners confined to their cells.

Restless, Gabe paces his cell. His protector gone he should be worried but finds he doesn't care. As he said, he ain't the quiet kid anymore and would take on all-comers without a thought, besides, routine slows the brain, men move in squares like zombies. If there are old wounds the cause is forgotten.

With Charlie to urge him on Gabe kept in shape, every day lifting weights or training in the boxing ring. In this place giving up is easy. A man falls into a pattern where what matters is gained by cheating and getting one over the hated screws. Meal to meal, cigarette to cigarette and jerking off late at night prisoners move inside a bubble survival an itch to be scratched.

Nothing about the State Pen is good but Gabe is scared about going out and wonders if signing for the Marines was a mistake. As Charlie said he's halfway there, might be better to finish his term. It's not as if he's nothing to go home to. Mr Simeon giving him the Funeral Parlour he'd have a place to work.

Gabe misses that old man and was glad when the Warden let him go to the funeral. Sergeant Keen, the army man swung that, he said Simeon was a father-figure and that Gabe needing to pay his respects.

It was a huge turn-out, that lonely old man with more friends than he knew. Being there Gabe visited Pa's grave. To mourn would be a lie. Ma tends the grave but like her son can't weep. Her weeping was done while Pa was alive.

Ma knows about the Marines, Gunnery Sergeant JJ Emmet told her. One minute glad and the next sad she said she didn't know how she felt.

'You could get killed. Marines are always first in battle. It's the code, Semper Fi, ever faithful.' There was pride in her eyes when she said that.

Gabe recalls a troop of Marines passing through Richmond. Relaxed and grinning they sashayed on knowing they were the best. Townsfolk knew it too and stood watching pretty girls hanging out of windows blowing kisses.

Tomorrow if the Corps hasn't changed its mind Gabe leaves for South Carolina. He gets fifteen minutes in the 'burg on the way. 'Make the most of it,' said the Sergeant, 'you've six weeks of hell in Pariss Island and then more hell in the Pacific with the rest of the grunts.'

Gabe didn't ask if JJ Emmet was based at Pariss Island. He didn't need to. The guy was another Charlie and read his mind. 'You bet your life I'm there,' says he. 'It's home-from-home for me and let me tell you as of 0600 hours tomorrow your ass in mine.'

~

Late into the night Gabe worked on a doll. The last one he'll ever make here in the Pen it needs to be right. If anything has saved him from going crazy it's these dolls. When first suggested he'd curled his lip. 'What's in it for me?'

Charlie had shrugged. 'I don't know but there's plenty for me.'

'Then you make them.'

'I don't have the skill. To me that's a lump of wood. To you it's a possibility. You see an eagle flying through the sky or a fox curled up in her den.'

He had Gabe. Dying of love for Ma and the Eyrie the thought of working with wood, even making trashy lucky charms was enough to set his heart racing.

Knowing this Charlie smiled. 'All life is possibilities. A man can work with trash until one day a stranger holds up that same piece of trash saying, 'I knew the guy that made this. Him and his Injun buddy used to push them out two dollars a chop. Now they're worth thousands.''

So they made dolls, every night Gabe dreaming of home until as Charlie said somewhere along the line the dolls stopped being trash and became art, selling at the last count upward of seventy dollars apiece.

This doll is not for sale. The wood was a gift from the Warden. He came to the Wood Shop one morning, smiling and asking Gabe to work on a four-poster bed. You don't say no to a Warden no matter how he smiles. Seasoned oak, a joy to touch the wood arrived. Specialised work requires specialised tools, Gabe asked and got. He got this too, a piece of pale blonde Ailanthus.

'It's not very big, Warden,' he'd said. 'What was you thinkin'?' The Warden said the bed was his interest Gabe could do what he liked with the rest.

This doll is special. More child in the making than doll the lump of wood progressed to become the beauty it is now. Hearing of it the Warden came looking. 'That wood I gave you,' he says, 'I hear you're working on it.'

Reluctant, Gabe showed it to him.

'My life!' He lifted his spectacles. 'That is the prettiest doll ever seen. Are you thinking of offering this for sale? If you are I've a mind to buy.'

Up pops Charlie. 'Sorry, Warden,' he says. 'That's already promised.'

The Warden screws his lip. 'Is that right?'

'It is so,' says Charlie. 'But if you're wanting one like it I imagine once the bed's finished there'll be time, won't there Gabriel?'

It was a testing moment but a sensible man and getting a state-of-the-art bed made on company time the Warden knew when to call quits

Now the doll must be destroyed. Two years he's worked on it. Guided by inner design he's taken his time, his fingers smoothing the high arc of a brow or the soft indentation of an upper lip until eventually the face appearing under the knife, so rare and lovely, was as familiar as his own.

It has to be destroyed! It can't be left here. The idea of some other guy holding it, say Boss-man or one of his filthy cohorts makes Gabe sick inside.

All night he's put it off until he can't any longer and snatching up the knife slashes at the face, the doll writhing in his hands as though screaming.

In that moment Gabe remembered Pa's fear of the Lime Tree. The hunk of wood is still there in the barn. 'I take care of it, son,' says Ma. 'Once a month I lift the tarpaulin to let it breathe. I do the same with the carved animals, though it ain't easy, folks seein' them and wantin' to buy and me short of cash. They'll be here when you come home.'

Now the doll is broken the face split in two. Good for nothing but the fire Gabe wrapped it in his jacket and shoved it under the bunk out of sight.

Then he lay down to sleep.

~

Three in the morning he woke to singing. At first he thought he was dreaming but it was Charlie alright singing a lullaby.

'Hush, little baby, don't say a word, Poppa's gonna' buy you a Mockingbird

And if that Mockingbird don't sing, Poppas' gonna buy you a diamond ring.

And if that diamond ring turns brass Poppa's gonna buy you a looking-glass.'

Gabe stood at the bars listening as did every other man. Their faces so many pale blotches in the gloom the whole of B Block looked to be awake.

Charlie sang on. Then, his voice soft as if he was in the cell, he began to chant a Navajo blessing. Gabe didn't understand a word yet listened with his heart rather than his ears and knew he was saying goodbye.

'Gabriel, my son,' said Charlie, 'the wind will shift and the sun will rise and your path will change but I, your Loving Friend, will be with you from this world to the next. Bear the sorrows that are to come, be strong and gentle on your journey. I bless you with the strength and protection of my ancestors. Fly, my brother, let the Great Spirit be the Wind under your Wings. Ahoa.'

The chanting stopped. The cell was silent.

One by one the men crept back their bunks.

Gabe stood a while holding onto the echoes and then as if someone took his hand he reached under the bunk. The doll was as she was, his Other Self, his little gal her face unmarked.

Lying beside the doll was the bit of wallpaper, Rosamund Hawthorne's message to the world. Years of handling it was worn thin and faded, nothing but the odd word: '…please …find…me…Rosamund… lost…in… Eagle's Nest…'

Gabriel took the doll in his arms, curled up, closed his eyes and slept.

Nine
Intruder
July 31st 1942
St Faiths Hospital.

The hairdresser squealed. 'Ooh, you are a naughty boy,
Lieutenant Rourke, and no mistake!'

Bobby glanced at the clock. Yeah, he thought, I am a
naughty boy and we've had our bit of fun – as the actress
said to the Bishop – now you need to quit messing with my
hair and get out. I'm expecting company.

Though always losing time the clock on the wall says 19-
30 hours, which by his reckoning means neat footsteps
heading down the corridor toward the kiddie's wing, a
door opening and Staff Nurse Adelia Challoner – *Miss*
Adelia Challoner please note, not Mrs, sweet,
straightforward, wonderful Miss – is in the building and
Flight Lieutenant Robert Rourke's day has begun.

'Okay then, sweetie. Ciao! Thanks for everythin'!'

Able to get about with a stick now the plaster-cast is
removed he bundles the hairdresser out the door. No
interruptions. It's got to be right. All week he's been
planning the scene. Paisley dressing-gown with velvet
collar, chin shaved and hair newly trimmed, chocks away
he is ready for action.

Forget black-market nylons! Nothing so vulgar! This is no wham-bang, thank you, ma'm! This is a lead-up to wedding bells. Never mind what happened before and the girls he's loved and left. This is the new-improved Baby Rourke.

Earlier he got the maid to give the room a once-over the bed changed and the nasty-looking medical paraphernalia cleared away. The maid is Nurse Challoner's buddy and by the sound of it her only buddy. She talks. He listens.

'The nurses here are a bunch of cows,' she says. 'If they don't like you they'll make your life a misery.'

'And are they makin' her life a misery?'

'They're not helping. But then you've seen her and you know why. She's beautiful, like that film-star though not so chilly.'

Ears on manual, Bobby kept her talking. 'So what do you reckon they're jealous of her?'

'Not much! The other day one of them asked if her hair was bleached. I told 'em straight, it's real, no bleach for her or your push-up bras. That got up their noses. They've always been wittering away at her but it's worse now since the old man sat her at his table.'

'Old man?'

'Covington-Wright, the Senior Registrar! He offered her a seat at the doctor's dining table. That really got to them. She doesn't go to the canteen now. She's in the rest room on her own or taking a quick bite at the Italian Bistro.'

'The Bistro, huh? Does she go there with her feller?'

'There is no feller that I know of. No family she was at Barts and living in the Nurses Home. But for her Aunty dying she'd probably still be there.'

'So where is she now?'

'At her Aunty's place. Gawd, what a dump! I wouldn't want to live there. Right out in the middle of nowhere I'd be scared somebody would break in.'

'Is that so?'

Dit-dit-dit-dot-dot-dot taking notes- no family — lives alone- no boyfriend!

'Alone, huh? You've never seen her step out with a Yank from the base?'

'No and I wouldn't tell you if I had, nosy sod!' Latching on to him the maid closes down. 'I've done your room. I'm on my way. If you want to know anything else ask her yourself! You Yanks have the cheek enough to do it.'

Over-paid and oversexed, et cetera, Yanks get mixed reviews in war-torn Britain and to be fair with certain credibility, Bobby a prime example, if it moves and wears lipstick fuck it, that's his credo.

Was his credo!

'Look out!'

That's her coming up the stairs. He'd know those footsteps anywhere. Later than usual she's running. Finger poised over the buzzer he was about to ring when he thought no, I'll give her time to settle.

Last night one of the babies died, doctors running in and out all night. Bobby was on his way back from the john when he saw them outside the Ward. The padre was with the family and Nurse Challoner with a bundle in her arms.

Remembering the moment Bobby closed his eyes. Her face! White as the baby's blanket she was but calm thinking of the parents.

As they passed he saluted. Thinking about it now it probably looked a pantomime but he meant it. It was such a little baby and the blanket was so big. Most people get him wrong. Because he's always joking they think him a heartless son-of-a-bitch. A son of a bitch he may be but not heartless. The things that make other people cry are the same for him. He doesn't like seeing people get hurt as he can't abide cruelty to animals. Okay, he did that thing with Miss Emilee's dog but that was because he was showing off for Sue. If Gabe Templar hadn't come and cut it down he would've.

'Stupid thing to do,' Bobby muttered. 'When I take Dee back to Virginia I don't want her hearin' of it. In fact I don't want her hearin' anythin'.'

Fat chance! What about Ma? If anyone's going to let it all out it'll be her.

Gloom descended. At the stage of his wooing he's decided it's best not to mention Ma. Nothing puts a bride off quicker than the thought of a cranky ma-in-law and you don't get crankier than Ruby.

An hour he sat watching the door. News came yesterday he's soon to be checked out of here and in for a transfer to another Base and low-level bombing and Avro Mosquitoes. 'There is one out there with your name on it, Flight Leftenant O' Rourke,' said the Wing Co. 'So get your leg mended, there's a good chap, and leave rounders where you found it.'

Rounders? Condescending bastard! That guy is always getting his name wrong as he's forever using the old-fashioned Leftenant instead of Lieu. Typically old-school type he is so up his own ass he can see daylight. O'Rourke might have been Bucky's father's name but he left the O back in Ireland years ago.

The Wing-Co doesn't like Yanks and doesn't mind showing it. He's not the only one. There is plenty tension between GIs and the local guys and usually to do with GIs wearing smarter uniforms and being paid more and stealing their girls. Bobby doesn't have any trouble. He gets on with well with everyone especially Fighter Squadron. They know he's wasted at the wheel of a Wellington dustbin. 'Never mind, Yank,' they grin. 'The way things are going, a chap shot down every sortie, you'll have your chance to go the same way.'

~

Ten o clock and he's at the mirror checking his shave. Irish roots again he has five o clock shadow at two and always in need of a shave. Ash swears by a cutthroat razor. Water swirling over his shoulders and steel flashing Bobby can see him now in the shower. A man's man is Alexander Stonewall Hunter, early cave-man type but a gentleman at heart.

Now if Bobby was taking Dee home via the Green and the Hunter clan he'd be a happy man. You can have faith in a family like that. Mizz Ellen is a classy lady. She knows who she is and who she wants to know. Ma wouldn't get across the threshold and not because of her shady past but what she is now.

Bobby sees trouble ahead. A girl like Adelia, shy and withdrawn, Ruby will give her hell. Any young bride hoping to find comfort in the family bosom needs to think again. But then who needs Ma? Bobby's bride won't need to lean on anyone but him.

But listen! Someone is coming! There are footsteps out on the corridor!

There's a knock on the door.

Trembling with excitement he is on his feet and combing back his hair.

'If that's my favourite Nurse I hear knocking on the door you can walk right in!' he calls. 'Contrary to what folks say I am perfectly decent.'

The door opened and a fist slammed into his gut.

Talk of the Devil! Ash Hunter stood in the doorway.

'Hi Bobby.'

Truly, Bobby thought he would faint. Waves of nausea rocked him. He must have looked pretty sick because the guy came running.

'Sit down, pal. You don't look so good.'

'I'm okay.' Knees quaking he sat. 'I guess I got up too quick.'

'I guess you did. Wait! I'll get you a glass of water.'

'Don't bother. I'm okay. It was the shock of seeing you.'

And my God it is a shock! Bobby had forgotten how much space one man can fill. It's not the size of him though that's enough it's the man. Lieutenant Alexander Hunter – no wait a minute check the ribbons and pips – pardon me

Major Alexander Hunter has presence. He has a kind of lustre. You see it in certain people. Franklin Delano Roosevelt has it. Ike has it. No doubt Napoleon had it. This man has it in spades.

'You shine, Ash.'

'What?'

'Nothin'. Forget it.'

Greatcoat laid aside the man is revealed in immaculate khaki. 'It is warm out there. I probably didn't need this coat.'

'No.'

'Are you sure you're okay?' Ash is frowning. 'You seem a tad confused.'

'No, not confused, just a little surprised to see you.'

'I know. I heard you were in dry-dock and thought to check you out. I didn't bother with prior warning because I wasn't sure I'd make it. How are you?'

'I'm chipper, thanks.'

'Chipper?' Ash grinned. 'You latching onto RAF slang now.'

'Yes, sir, I am. Jolly good show and all that.'

'It suits you, especially with the silk cravat. You are all very Noel Coward.'

Bobby shrugged. 'Got keep standards up. So what do I owe the pleasure? What brought you scuttlin' down here?' *And what is gonna send you scuttlin' back 'cos buddy you ain't staying! You can't! She's mine! I saw her first!*

'Why are you here?'

'I'm here because in ten days from now I'm across the English Channel taking a late Continental break with the rest of the boys.'

'You mean Dieppe and then onto Italy.'

'Oh gee!' Ash rolled his eyes. 'So much for secrecy!'

'I did hear a rumble. Ten days furlough and yet you came all this way to see me? I'm flattered. How did you get here?'

'The bike.'

'Of course the bike, what else.' Bobby couldn't help grinning. 'That bike. You didn't by any chance bring the dog with you?'

Ash grinned. 'You're never going to let me forget that.'

'Sure I am, when you're knee-deep in sex and don't need any pointers. But look, buddy, as good as it is seein' you for Chrissakes don't let me get in the way. Ten days isn't very long. You've better things to do than chew the fat with an old crock like me.'

'What things?'

'I don't know. Girls? No future Mrs Hunter Junior lurkin' on the horizon?'

A shrug of the tailored shoulders. 'Not that I know of, but hey, I'm open to offer. This is a hospital. Is it possible there is one pretty nurse somewhere here in Suffolk who has held off the entire Allied frontal assault?'

Bobby fists tightened. 'I very much doubt it.'

'Man! Where did they all come from?' Alex laughed. 'I didn't know there were so many guys in America.'

'We are makin' our presence known.'

'I'd say so. The air is thick with cologne and spearmint toothpaste.'

'Indeed it is true. England is under siege.'

'You're not kidding. This is a real pretty county but so weighed down with GIs I feel I want to pick it up and carry it away to safety.'

'Yes, we have the effect.

'If I had the time I'd take a look around.'

'But alas you haven't. Like me you're eager to be up and runnin'.'

'I don't know about eager. I'm not so eager a spell of R&R in a country cottage wouldn't hit the spot. Scotland is wild and beautiful with tremendous wildlife but I spent too many days hanging my ass from a cliff to appreciate it. Anyway forget about me. It's you I came to see. What's with you? What are you doing with a busted leg? How did you get that another attempt at a gong?'

They talked then, Bobby telling how it happened, how he tripped on a pothole fielding an out-ball and how his leg was pretty much mended now, thanks ever so. It was a weird conversation. Ash was his usual calm self interested in the world and his friend and the damaged leg, whereas Bobby was on thorns torn between love and the need to tell him to fuck off.

Eleven on the dot Dee makes her rounds. Him quick on the buzzer his door is always first to be checked and of late, him keeping her talking, the last. Busy, busy, she's never keen to stay but well-mannered never looking at the fob-watch on her beautiful breast, simply stands on the toes of her well-polished black lace-up shoes.

Now there's this guy emitting streams of glory. One look at him and like Debbie, the Cockney usherette from the Apollo theatre, Nurse Dee will be out for the count.

Good God! Bobby realises he is jealous of Ash.

There was always a niggle but he thought that was more to do with envy of his family. This gut-wrenching ache is about the man, the smooth skin and the blue eyes, the smile and the heart honest and uncomplicated. Yeah and the body! Don't forget that Baby Rourke! Six foot plus of muscle and bone, he embodies the US Army.

A thought popped into Bobby's head. 'Say, guess what I heard? That bozo, Gabe Templar got out of jail signin' up for the Marines.'

'So you said.'

'Did I?'

'Uh-huh, you mentioned it last time we spoke.'

'So I did. Strange, I see you and I see him.'

'You said that too.'

'Did I? Bloody hell! I must be gettin' old.'

'Yeah, you do talk about him some.'

'And yet you don't remember him.'

'I remember the car and that a guy was trying to enlist but as for face and manner nothing particular impinges.'

'I find that odd. You are the Camera, Mister Memory-Man. It's well-documented that you have the memory of ten elephants. You'd think a guy like Gabe would stay.

'I do have blank spots.'

'First I heard. I thought it was once seen never forgotten.'

'Maybe I didn't see the guy.'

'No, but you must have heard him speakin'. I find this very odd.'

'Not as odd as you keep asking.' Ash's gaze was straight. 'What is your interest in the man? No, belay that, what is the obsession?'

'I'm not obsessed. I recognise oddities and one elephant refusing to see an elephant in the room is more than odd.'

'Okay then. So it's odd.' Click! Discussion over. 'How is your mother?'

Change of subject! Not only does he not remember Gabe Templar he doesn't want to talk about him and calls Bobby's interest and obsession. As Lady Mildred would say, Freud would make much of this.

They talked then but a stilted conversation and Bobby's impatience showing.

Ash is a sensitive man. Red tide staining his cheek he's clocked the fact that he is not welcome. This sticky situation needs to end. Best thing Bobby can do is suggest he is tired and needs to rest.

'Hang on a minute!' Another thought pops into his mind. 'I've just realised visitin' hours are from two til four. How did you get in at this time of night? The Matron here wears iron corsets. She wouldn't change the rules for love or money, so how come you got in.'

'I told her I'd come down from London and that I had a day and then to get back to Southampton.'

'Southampton, huh?' Bobby nodded. 'You sailin' from there? So, yeah, I guess you do have to get straight back.'

'I guess I do at that.' A flash of irritation pinged the calm exterior Ash's lips thinning. 'It would seem there's nothing here to keep me.'

Bobby tried smoothing it over. 'So Matron let you in without a struggle? And here's me thinkin' you need lessons in how to operate. What an ass! You're a real smooth operator, Ash. I can't think where I've been lookin' these years.'

Alex shrugs. 'Natural charm, buddy.'

A pause and then Bobby stuck out his hand. 'Yeah, well, it was good to see you, pal. I am feelin' kinda tired.'

'Sure, I get it.' He shrugs into his greatcoat. 'Message received and understood. I am on my way out.'

He was hurt, Bobby could tell. What the hell! Here's a guy about to go to France to fight and maybe never coming back. Surely after years of friendship they shouldn't let a girl come between them. Bobby knows he needs to repair the damage but try as he might he can't give the guy a hug, his arms like his mouth are clamped shut.

'Okay then.' Ash turned. 'Good luck with whatever's going on here.'

Ever the gent he reached down to shake hands.

Bobby got up out the chair, leaned on the bed for balance, and hit the buzzer.

'Beep! The buzzer sounded. A red light blinked above the door. The room was still, both staring at the buzzer knowing they should stop it but neither trying.

Beeeeeeeee!' It is so very loud.

A door opened. Clip, clip, footsteps sounded, angry footsteps, frustrated, sharp and determined.

'It's okay!' Bobby can hardly speak. 'False alarm, honey. No need to bother!'

Too late, the footsteps march on.

Both men turn to the door, Bobby with a double sense of loss, of saying farewell to a friend and to a dream.

Alex Hunter on the other hand stands to attention. Blue eyes blazing, back straight and hands to his the sides he seems to know that whoever is coming through that door will change his life forever.

Part Two
Pigeons
Alex

Ten
Once Seen

'No, really I couldn't.' She blushed, her cheek stained red.

Alex dug his hands in his pockets. 'I don't mind waiting.'

'I'm afraid you'll have a long wait. I'm on duty all night.'

'That's okay.' He nodded. 'However long it takes.'

That was six hours ago now sunlight clipping the horizon he shares a mug of overly sweet tea and consolation with a grieving night-watchman.

'I'm sorry. It must have been tough watching your house burn.'

'It was bloody awful.' The night-watch man shook his head. 'I wouldn't want anyone to go through that. They took everythin' I had, the bastards, my wife, the house and a coop-load of racin' pigeons. I loved my birds. Years I'd been workin' with them. Good birds, brave and hardy like my missus. Last year my racer Alexander the Great took top prize in a local Derby.'

'Alexander the Great!'

'Yes I know it's a bit much but the name suited him. He was a brave little bugger. Now look at him a clump of feathers on a taxidermist's table.'

'You're having the bird stuffed then?'

'I am. Ten years I had him reared from a chick. My wife doted on him. He would take seed from her mouth. I don't like seein' him stuffed but I got to have somethin' to remind me of better times.'

Bizarre conversation! The night-watchman's house was levelled in a bombing raid. Now he lives with his daughter but unable to sleep gave up the day job to work the night-shift at the hospital.

Weary and undoubtedly lightheaded stuck with the thought of being perched on a mantelpiece with kapok shoved up his ass Alex is fighting hysteria. There's nothing funny about the guy losing his wife and his home but still laughter bubbles in his chest as though a cork pulled on a bottle of champagne.

It's the girl! It's Adelia! One look was all it took!

'I'm sorry!' Feet made of lead they were passing in the corridor. Awkward, he jogged her arm. 'That's all right soldier,' she said walking on. 'No harm done.'

But oh brother, there was harm done, massive harm from which he hopes never to recover. It's why he is here squatting in a night-watchman's hut.

'Forgive me,' he said aware of the guy frowning. 'I'm not usually this crazy. I met a girl, and not just any girl, you see, the girl.'

'Oh I see!' A flask was produced, more tea poured and this time brandy added. The watchman passed a mug. 'Sit down, lad, and tell me about it.'

What is there to tell? Simple really, the buzzer buzzed, the door opened and there she was. 'You rang?' she queried, irritation in her voice and the alarm still beeping.

When neither he nor Bobby answered she stopped it. 'Is there something you want, Lieutenant Rourke?'

Alex left them to it and nerves jangling waited in the corridor. When she came out he barred the way his hand held up like a fool directing traffic.

'May I have a word?'

'What is it?'

'Can I buy you a cup of coffee?'

'I offered to buy her a cup of coffee.'

The watch-man nodded. 'Nothin' wrong with that.'

'It was a dumb thing to say. On night duty, in uniform, her hair scooped back in a veil and mask over her nose why would I offer coffee?'

'You were nervous. We all say daft things when we're nervous.'

'I was nervous.' Alex pushed his fingers through his hair. 'I still am!'

'It's alright. ' The guy patted his arm. 'I was the same with my Ada, gabblin' like a monkey. It's a wonder she didn't run in the opposite direction.'

'Gabbling is right. I'm normally a calm guy. I don't get het up about anything but this girl blew me away.'

'Well you need to calm down. You don't want to carry on like a crazy person. You'll frighten her away.' The old guy started reminiscing about how he met his wife at a dance and how they'd been married nearly fifty years and both their daughters married with kiddies. 'We're grandparents twice over. May next year would've been our Golden Wedding.'

Alex felt for him but could not suppress the joy in his heart. It was the look in her eyes, wonderful eyes, green with flecks of gold and long lashes, a look of recognition, 'Oh, it's you, my darling! I wondered where you were.'

Ridiculous! Why would she look that way? She doesn't know him. More likely she was wondering when he'd leave and take his noisy pal with him.

'Can I buy you a cup of coffee?'

'A cup of coffee?' Her eyes were wide over the cotton mask.

'Uh-huh.'

'I don't think so.' She'd started to walk away. Then she paused pulling the mask away revealing the rest of her lovely face. 'But if you're looking for refreshment the canteen is probably open.'

'I d...don't want coffee.' The words stuttered out. 'I want you.'

That's when, face aflame, she walked on. He said he'd wait. Well, he's waiting and he's gonna keep waiting until she knows his name. He knows hers! Click, click, the Camera homed in on the name tag, Adelia Challoner. Nice name. Adelia Hunter would be a million times nicer.

'And it would please my folks.'

The watchman frowned. 'What's that you're saying?'

'I'm thinking my folks will love her.'

'What you're thinkin' of taking her to America?'

'Affirmative.'

'Here, hold on a minute! You're a bit premature, aren't you? If as you say she's a good looking lass she's probably already got a bloke. Maybe two or three! There's plenty of 'em around, especially your lot. The town's overrun'

Of course! Overwhelmed by the truth of it Alex sat down with a bump. As the man says it's likely she has someone. 'She didn't look like she had anyone.'

'What d'you mean?'

'She looked, I don't know, untouched.'

'Untouched?'

'Uh-huh, like made of glass.'

'Ooh, mate, you have got it bad!'

'I guess I have.'

'Well you need to be careful thinkin' like that. Untouched? No, mate! This country's been through hell. No one can go through what we've been through and not be changed. She's a girl not a statue. She's flesh and blood, bless her heart. She'll be warm and alive and wanting to laugh and be happy like my Ada. If you think of her as glass take my word it'll be you that breaks.'

Sobered by his words they sat in silence. Then the old boy got to his feet. 'I got to do my rounds. Take this.' He offered a key. 'This is to the gent's lav. You've got your kitbag so go have a wash. Wake your head up, like. Then come back and sit and think what you're going to do. Maybe as you say you were meant to meet. If that's the case nothin' not even war can get between you. Then again you may be ships in the night and this time tomorrow not worth a memory. Sit 'til she comes out and if you feel the same then cling to her and never let go. It's what I did with Ada. I knew she were streets above me so I clung like mad. But for a bomb I'd still be clingin'.'

~

A kid under tutelage Major Alexander Hunter washed and shaved. It helped to clear his head. He hadn't meant to come. There didn't seem time and then Mom's letter, Bobby in hospital and according to his mother at death's door.

Hogwash! There was nothing death's door about him. Spiffed up in a dressing gown he was up to his tricks, a girl at every base, maybe a nurse, maybe Nurse Challoner though that didn't seem likely. He wasn't at all friendly. He was offhand to the point of rudeness. 'I don't want anythin',' he'd turned his back on her. 'Clear off back to your bratty kids! All I want to do is sleep.'

Baby Rourke is right! Such a goddamn kid! Usually his nonsense passes over Alex's head but not with her. Anger flaring, he could've knocked him down. No, she's not the one. She's not Bobby's type. He likes the more obvious, the bigger the breasts the less effort.

Sarah maintained he led with an inner tape-measure anything less than 40 double D he wasn't interested. Back in the day she had it bad for him. They talked marriage until she learned he was double-dealing with a hat-check girl. It's as well they broke it off. He wouldn't have got by the General especially after the hat-check girl.

That betrayal almost killed their friendship. Bobby leaving West Point and joining the Air-force put space between them long enough for his sins to be understood if not forgiven.

'It's not his fault. He had a lousy start.' Alex has been saying that since kindergarten. The General gets mad, 'poor beginnings are no excuse for bad behaviour.' They weren't an excuse they were an explanation. Bobby has had it tough. No one will know how tough though him. He never talks of how shoeless and skinny at five-years old he ran messages for his mother at a local cat-house touting two-dollar Uncles to share her time.

Half starved and looking to make a buck the kid hustled day and night.

Alex has a memory he'll never share with anyone especially Bobby. Veteran's Day they had been to church, Dad taking the salute. In the car on the way back Alex saw him on a street corner doing a soft-shoe-shuffle, baggy shorts and skinny legs going crazy and folks tossing in the odd dime. It hurt to watch.

That was during the depression. So many whores in the area they fought for business. A strip routine or some lewd trick they all had gimmicks.

Bobby was Ruby's gimmick. It's as well the Copper King arrived on the scene, the kind of men she serviced it's likely he saved Bobby's life.

Ruby Cropper is a bitter woman. Her son tries pulling away but is never far enough. A brave guy awarded the DFC hopefully this war will be the making of him. Flying is his life. An eagle with ten foot wing span he should have been born a bird. Then Buckminster Rourke accepts his son and Bobby gets a plane and works the air-circus flights over Chesapeake Bay three dollars a flip.

'What do you see in the guy?' The General would shake his head. 'You have nothing in common. Can't you find a better friend?' There are times when Alex asks the same. He can be so crude! A door to the past will rattle and his mouth will scorch your ears. There's a hard surface to him a layer of thorns that if you were clumsy would cut you deep. He can be brilliant company. A clown, he finds humour in everything. People like him. Alex has been at West Point gatherings where the ice was so thick you daren't fart for fear of breaking silence. In comes Bobby and the place is swinging.

Good-looking and with an easy smile the girls adore him. He doesn't have to try. Alex used to admire his nonchalant ease and wanted to be relaxed and easy that way but couldn't the Camera sees too much.

People think eidetic memory is a gift. They ask the same question, 'is it true once seen never forgotten?' Some look to party tricks. His maths tutor was a whiz at that, opening a book at random, showing a page, and then closing the book expecting Alex to remember. As a kid he took up the challenge. Now he would deliberately make a mistake that way he wouldn't ask again.

It is true once seen never forgotten. It's equally true of sound, a conversation of up to three people and he can repeat it word-for-word his inner ear processing sound. With sight he sees, closes his eyes and click, the word, the diagram, the face or the picture appearing on an inner blackboard.

No trick, no rabbit pulled out of a hat, the Camera.

It's been that way since he was a kid. Certain languages give him a problem, a heavy dialect takes a while to disseminate as does conversation between more than three, arriving as a wedge of sound it needs time to be peeled away.

Friday he was trying to explain the process to General Sam Jentzen of Army Intel. 'A group of people talking at once sound interweaves and needs time to be unravelled.'

The General didn't understand. That's okay, Alex doesn't always understand plus he's no desire to join Intel and work behind the lines.

The Camera has an upside, Miss Adelia Challoner for one, a face he will never forget.

'Attenhut!' Alex is up and on his feet. 'She's here!'

She stands in the doorway blinking in the early sun. Then, swirling a cape about her shoulders - red-lined for danger – she walks on.

Alex follows.

Adelia is hopping mad. The fellow has been here all night and with nurses peering out of windows and porters taking bets on how long he'd wait. There have been complaints. Night-Sister phoned. 'Is that man waiting for you?'

'I hope not.'

'Yes and I hope not! Soldiers hanging about the grounds 'til the early hours of the morning, how do you think it looks?'

'It's nothing to do with me! He is a friend of the American air-man in the Broom Cupboard.'

'I might have known. He's another with no sense of propriety. Well, whatever the situation if he is waiting for you tell him not to do it again. It does nothing for the reputation of the hospital or you!'

Adelia ground her teeth. So much for making headway! On night duty and out of circulation she saw a softening of attitude, a couple of nurses actually smiling! There was an invitation from one to see *Gone with the Wind*, the latest movie at the Gaumont. Now there's this!

'I say, Miss!'

He's right on her heels! A big fellow she can hear him panting. And, Oh my word, here comes Fussy Forbes on her bike! Wouldn't you credit it! That's it then! She'll tell everyone on Buttercup and for a whole weekend they'll be trashing her name. Lovely! She might as well not bother going back.

'I say, Miss, wait up a moment!'

She spun on her heel. 'What!'

Stopped in his tracks he stepped back.

She said it again. 'What do you want?'

'I thought I might buy you a coffee.'

'Thank you, I don't want a coffee. I've worked non-stop from seven yesterday evening until seven this morning. Any break I had was to gulp down a cup of coffee, dreadful coffee too, Camp Coffee, if you've ever heard of it, no coffee at all, chicory to help wind up the nerves. I should stick with cocoa or tea, really, or maybe gin. Yes, gin! I've heard it's good for overtired nurses. So no you can't buy me a coffee. To be perfectly honest I wouldn't care if I never saw another cup of coffee again.'

She stomped on and then turned. 'As for hanging about the hospital I hope you know you've done me no good service. This is a rotten place filled with miserable people whose only delight is making everyone else miserable. My reputation was in tatters before I started. Knowing this I've tried keeping my head down and silly me did think I'd succeeded enough to at least feel daggers sliding down my back as opposed to sticking in! Now thanks to you and your idiot friend former suspicions are proved and there are daggers enough for this night and many more to come. So well done, thank you and good night!'

Adelia stomped on again and then thinking about it turned. 'Sorry. I didn't mean any of that. I'm tired and you out here all night must be the same.'

'Whoah!'

She was about to walk on when he caught her sleeve. 'It's me should be apologising. I don't know what's happened to make you unhappy but if I've added to the problem then I am sorry. I didn't mean for that to happen. I wanted to get to know you.'

'There's nothing to know. Please excuse me. I have a long bike ride home and things to do before I can sleep.'

'I could give you a lift.'

'I don't think so.'

'My motor bike is in the parking-lot.'

'It's alright. I don't want to keep you. I'm sure you've other things to do.'

'No! I've nothing to do, absolutely nothing at all but to get to know you.'

Taken aback by the urgency in his voice, she stared. 'Why?'

'Why?'

'Yes, why?'

'Because you matter to me.'

'How can I? You don't know me.'

'I do know you. I've always known you.'

'Don't be absurd! We've just met. Yesterday you didn't know me. Tomorrow you won't know me again.'

'Oh, I will know you!' He grasped her hand. 'Believe me, today, tomorrow, and forever I will know you.'

While not exactly mocking she smiled. 'You Americans! You push all before thinking you can work miracles. Shame you weren't in the war earlier. I dare say it would be over by now. But this is no miracle! We are not *Gone with the Wind*. This is a car-park in the grounds of a second-rate hospital in Suffolk. It's not a mansion in Georgia. You're not Rhett Butler and I'm certainly no Scarlet O Hara. This is real life, soldier, not the movies.'

'I never thought it anything else. I know who you are, Adelia Challoner, and I know who I am.'

'And who are you?'

'Major Alexander Hunter, Ist Battalion US Rangers in transit. I saw you in Bobby's room and I knew I had to be with you if only for a day.'

'A day?'

'Uh-huh.' Eyes so very blue he smiled. 'I have forty-eight hour's left of a ten day pass and half of that already used. So, in terms of movies I lean more toward *Cinderella* and chimes at midnight than the Civil War. And though you're right I'm no Rhett Butler I was born in the South and all that it means. So please, lovely girl, humour me and spend a little time with me. '

It was then Adelia felt she did know him. It was his eyes. Blue as the skies, she'd never seen eyes like them and yet knew they'd smiled at her before.

How silly. This live now pay later war mentality is catching! He says he's known me forever and suddenly I know him, the handsome face, the determined nose and chiselled jaw. I know the man, the whole man, the depth of character and courage under fire, his conflicting self, shy modesty fighting a stubborn heart. This is the man and to argue about being on the back of a motor-bike is waste of time because knowing him he will never give in.

She sighed. 'What a pity. I think I would've enjoyed being with you but I can't. I have to get home and feed my dog.'

'Where is home?'

'A couple miles out of town.'

'Then let me take you. You'll get there a whole lot quicker.'

'Very likely,' she said conscious of eyes staring out of windows. 'And a whole new story to tell the troops.'

He followed her gaze. 'I sure am sorry about that. People will talk and I guess when it comes to gossip a hospital is the same as any other place.'

'Yes they talk and say foolish things.'

'I should've thought about that.'

'It's not your fault. It is the way it is.'

'But I could've found another way.'

'Maybe there isn't another way.'

'No! Maybe this is the only way.' The grip on her hand tightened. 'And the others, the miserable people who delight is making others miserable, maybe the damage is already done.'

Adelia nodded. 'I was thinking the same.'

'So what harm can it do to follow through?'

'No harm whatsoever.'

'Then come with me.' He took both her hands. 'You to feed your dog and me to hang onto a dream.'

'A dream?'

'Yes. You are my dream.'

Then she remembered white angel-feathers and blue eyes and promises of eternal love gave her hand. 'And you are mine.'

Other eyes watched the motor-bike pull away from the hospital.

Bobby wept tears of rage. Two minutes and he was dressed and in the lift on his way down. No way was he letting this go without putting up a fight! Alexander Hunter is not having this one. This is no Cockney Debbie! This is Baby Rourke's lifelong pursuit of happiness and where she goes he goes.

The lift down he limped out into the foyer.

'Good morning, Lieutenant.' Matron was at the desk.

'Mornin' Matron.' He wiped his eyes. 'I'm goin' out for a quick gasper.'

'Don't be too long. You're due to see Mr Covington-Wright later and with luck on your way out.'

'Signed off? Hallelujah! I can't wait to get out of here.' Teeth clenched he smiled. 'Not that I haven't enjoyed your company. It's been a gas!'

A mean old bird she wise to his games. Her face didn't crack. 'Make sure you're back on time. I don't want to have to send out a search party.'

'Don't worry, I'm a man of my word. When I say I'll do somethin' I do it. You carry on oilin' the hospital motors like the good slave you are.' He saluted. '*Per Ardua Ad Astra*, God save the King, and all that!'

He was out and heading back of the laundry to an army jeep always parked there. Boom! First touch it sprang to life. Soon he's out on the road. Needless to say there's no sign of the love-birds. They had a head-start. That's okay; Bobby knows where they're going. He knows everything about that girl right down to her early morning feeding of chickens.

He swung the jeep onto the main road not that there is a main road in Suffolk, narrow winding lanes is what you get so if you're backed behind a tractor tough, you've had it.

Today it wasn't a tractor slowing him down. It was a convoy of tanks, GIs grinning and giving him the finger. 'Pull over, you ignorant slobs!' he yelled. 'Give a guy some room! No wonder the locals think you're shit-for-brains!'

Shouting didn't help. He crept along until ahead he saw level-crossing gates about to be lowered. Quickly, he pulled out and to a barrage of cat-calls overtook the convoy narrowly missing the 8-10 express to Cambridge. Heat from the locomotive singed his ears but a clear road ahead it was worth it.

Now that must be some way to go! 40,000 lbs of horsepower ploughing into your guts, you wouldn't know much about it. It would be over so fast you would keep going a grizzled mess up front of a non-existent jeep.

It's been said that that does happen, that with sudden death folks carry on with their idea of living not knowing they are dead. Bobby remembers being in a pub one night and the locals discussing ghosts, how Roman Legionnaires can sometimes be seen marching down the Watling Street.

A Spitfire pilot said what about rumours of Von Richthofen and his Albatross C, how he is was seen circling Amiens after he was shot-down.

It started a conversation, '*if you had a choice where is your heaven.*' Bobby pipes up; 'As long as I get time off for bad-behaviour and a cuddly dame with big bazoomas for company I don't care where I go.'

They laughed at that Bobby with them. He's not laughing now, everything he once believed including cuddly women with big bazoomas up for question.

There was nothing cuddly about Nurse Challoner last night. Boy, did she go for him! That stupid buzzer! She leaned across to switch it off then waited while Ash was out of earshot before firing both barrels. 'You selfish man! You only think of your own comfort. There are only two nurses on our Ward at night and some very sick children. You are selfish and disrespectful! That dreadful display the other night! Saluting when little Baby Thompson died? What a way to behave and his poor parents in tears. I was ashamed of you.'

He tried getting a word edgewise, how he never meant to be disrespectful. Eyes flashing she tore him a new ass. It wasn't anything he didn't deserve, every sin duly noted, he just wished it wasn't her pointing them out.

Wouldn't you think being bawled out like that would knock her off her perch and him taking his heartfelt longing elsewhere? Not a chance! Her anger only served to turn up the rheostat on his heart so that where once was a pleasing warmth, there is a raging inferno.

When calm she is a doll of sugar pink icing. Enraged she is a Goddess. But forget dolls and sugar icing the Army is in town.

God! If he'd known Hunter was behind that door he'd have hung a death's skull on the handle, 'No Admittance on Pain of Death.' Instead, a thief in the night he stole her away and Bobby will never give her back

~

Alex was staring at the bungalow. 'You live here?'

'I know. Dreadful isn't it?' Chickens squawking, she shook corn through wire-netting. 'But right now Lilac Tree Cottage is all I have.'

He grinned. 'Lilac Tree Cottage? That's a real nice name.'

She laughed. 'Yes very nice. I don't know who chose it but I'm guessing it was tongue in cheek. Right, that's done!' She slammed the coop door. 'Now there's only Lochie and me to feed. Thank you for bringing me. Now at least I can get on with my weekend.'

'You're welcome. I guess I'll be on my way.'

One waiting for the other to speak they stared at the ground.

'I would feed you, Major Hunter,' said Adelia, 'but I've only a couple of eggs in the pantry.'

'It's okay. I can't say I'm hungry but eggs would do....unless I take you to breakfast. The Italian place back in the village looked okay.'

She shuffled her feet. 'You saw that, did you? I do sometimes eat there.'

'We could try it.' He shrugged. 'Italians do have a way with food.'

'They do.'

'So what do you think?'

'Would you wait while I change?'

'Take all the time you need.'

Pulling clothes from the wardrobe trying to find something that didn't smell of damp she ran about like a mad thing. In the end she settled for a cotton dress, white cardigan and sandals. A bath is out water levels in the tank so uncertain it would take forever to fill. With no other choice she stood in the bath pouring jugs of tepid water over her head stopping now and then to peep through the window wondering if she'd imagined him.

There he is leaning against the bike! Alexander Hunter. It's a good name. Oh God! She hugged herself. Such a beautiful man and it isn't only his looks, it's a feeling of knowing him and the things he likes, his family and birds and sketching, and things he hates, liars and those that would hurt the defenceless.

She looked in the mirror. A pale creature with frizzy hair looked back.

Nothing for it she plaited her hair pinning it on top of her head, tonight when unwound it will go crazy but better corkscrews than dragging about her face.

She scoured the remains of a make-up bag for what was left of a Coral Peach lipstick. Lochie sat watching. 'It's alright for you,' she said applying mascara. 'You have naturally dark eyelashes. Mine need help.'

The dress is creased. She ought to run an iron over it but the thought of losing even a minute with him hurts! One day is all they have. Tomorrow he goes back and she may never see him again.

Thank God for new underwear! You can get anything black market from cold cream to a fur coat all you need is coupons and not too many scruples. Though not above stealing Adelia's inheritance Aunt Maud had a million-and-one scruples but even she would baulk at turning away lace knickers.

Label torn away they were clearly under-the-counter but still Adelia crossed her fingers and offered Aunt Maud's ration book. This is war! Coupons are what the spiv wanted and Aunt Maud is hardly able to disagree.

'I wonder if there'll be a lot of blood.'

Aware of what she was doing, the decision she was making viz-a-viz virginity, a pain cut through her heart. This day, the first of August, 1942, is the true beginning of her life and all that went before and all that comes afterward, the repercussions of her choice, she will accept with an open heart.

'Perhaps I ought to wear a sweater. Oh for God's sake!' She tossed the dress into the basket and took a fresh uniform from a hanger. 'What does it matter what I wear!'

Dressed she snapped the silver buckle at her waist. Yes, she thought, this is me, Nurse Challoner. A navy linen cape, blue frock with white collar and cuffs, it's a suit of armour I have worn forever. Why change now?

Knowing they might not find anything to eat, the Bistro possibly closed she made a sandwich with the last of the cheese.

Lochie was still watching. She knelt down. 'Don't worry about me. I never wanted to be a girl that gave love away easily. I always wanted to wait for the right time and the right man. Well, I've found him, or rather he found me.'

'Be a good dog.' Leaning down, she kissed the soft fur pate. 'Don't bother staying up. With luck I shan't be home until midnight.'

Eleven
Promises

The Bistro was open. Crossing the road Alex took her hand and in his heart no matter what followed, the horror and the pain, he never let go.

It was a small hand dainty yet work-worn from caring for babies and feeding chickens. Thinking of that dirt shack where she lived he wanted to take the hand inside his heart and keep her safe.

They found a table. He asked if she'd always wanted to be a nurse. She said it was more progression than choice, her parents out the country months at a time she went from boarding school to Nursing College and on to the wards.

'It probably wasn't what I would've chosen. What about you? Were you always going to be in the army?'

An image in his head of the General and Pappy Frobisher and the medals and ribbons and bull-dog jaws Alex offered a cut-down version of schooldays. 'My father, my grand-pappy and great-grand-pappy were Academy men. It was natural for me to follow on the same.'

She asked about the Academy, it sounded a studious sort of place. West Point studious? That's not the word that springs to mind. How do you describe years of non-stop drill and the crunching pursuit of excellence that is West

Point to a tender-hearted girl? It can't be done. 'Perhaps the easiest way would be to liken West Point to Sandhurst your own British Military Academy.'

'I see. You went to boarding school and from there to the army. Is that it?'

'More or less.'

'Both boarded-out from an early age and visiting or visited high-days and holidays I imagine your schooldays were not so different to mine.'

'High-days and holidays, that sounds kinda of lonely to me.'

'Does it?' She paused, her lovely face thoughtful. Then she nodded. 'I think it was lonely. Yes. It was.'

He grasped her hand. 'Are you lonely now?

'No.' Her hand closed within his. 'Not at this moment.'

'That's good.' She smiled and his heart rolled. 'I'm real glad I came to Suffolk.'

'Me too but do let's eat then perhaps we can get out and about. There are places I'd like you to see. There's a church by the park where my mother and father were married. It's a ruin now, a bomb last February, yet it is still a holy place. I'd like us to go before you leave.'

'Whatever you want.'

Click, click, the Camera is on double-time settling on her hair, the glint of gold, and her liquid green eyes and her lips, such lips he wants to kiss.

Click, she's laying her cape aside the scarlet lining a brilliant backdrop to the blue frock and the white of her skin.

Click! The silver buckle on her belt is shaped like a butterfly.

Click! Her left hand is bare, no rings!

Click again! She's known here and turns smiling as the owners of the Bistro come to ask what they would like to eat.

Click! He's on his feet being introduced; 'This is Alex. He's here for the day and then must rush back. We haven't eaten. Perhaps we might see the menu and then perhaps Luigi a pot of your delicious coffee.' She turns to him. 'Alex is a coffee enthusiast. He sees it as a cure-all, don't you, love.'

He grins. 'In this case, yes I think I do.'

Head whirling, he sits down. She called me love! What does that mean? Britishers are an odd bunch. God, King and Country, they mock the things they hold dear in a shocking fashion and yet one-to-one are buttoned-up to the point of zero-gravity. They don't like us Yanks. They think as they thought of the last war that we came too late, London a case in point. Squads of bowler-hatted gents march through the City umbrellas in their hands and sneers on their lips. No one has a good word for us and then out of the blue a charlady will smile and call you Dearie.

Now this girl calls me love. Am I her love or is it merely the British penchant for saying what they don't really mean.

'Is that it?'

'What?' She's turning giving him her hand to hold.

'Did you mean that?'

'About the coffee? No, I was only teasing.'

'Not the coffee! You called me love! We're you teasing about that too?'

A blush rolled up her throat rising to the roots of her hair.

He asked again. 'Were you?'

She shook her head.

'You meant to say it?'

'Yes.'

He bent forward, his mouth against hers. 'Then say it again, love.'

~

'Oh Jesu!' Bobby is parked opposite. They are sitting in the window, she's smiling and now he's kissing her.

The bottom fell out of his world. How did this happen? When we came to this country we're told to mind our manners because your average Brit is unfriendly. Every GI is shown a Mickey Mouse movie on what to say and do but it don't mean a thing because the folks here are a bunch of liars.

Look at this girl! Stuck up cow they call her. He's heard them. 'Okay now, Yank?' They were grinning last week. 'Happy now you've got Nurse La-di-da Challoner singing you a lullaby?' But look! She's kissing a guy that twenty-four hours ago she didn't know existed. Where's the stuck up cow now?

Last week he was happy. She was single and available. A bit sniffy regarding overuse of the buzzer and still inclined to slam the door but he hoped given time she'd see the light. So hopeful, he thought to invest in property.

According to the maid Adelia Challoner has a cottage to sell that no one wants to buy. Hearing this Bobby poked around learning that Lilac Tree Cottage was up for a pittance. Until last night and the Hero of Mafeking storming the barricades he was on the point of making an offer; nothing nasty, no bribery and corruption, just keeping an eye on things, which is pretty much what he's doing now and will continue to do until he's sure it's a hopeless case.

Fact is that while he's based in Suffolk and Hunter is heading for France Bobby has room to manoeuvre, and so flying under the radar is the order of the day. Forage hat pulled down he sits and watches and waits.

The other night in the pub discussing ghosts and the best way to die he got to wondering what happens when he does dies. All that about Roman centurions haunting Watling Street and the Bloody Red Baron pedalling a diaphanous plane over Amiens is junk. When you're dead you're dead. Bobby has no belief in the afterlife but men dying every minute of the day it makes you think.

The real story here is one point seven-five million dollars and who will benefit if he is killed.

It's a lot of dough. He could leave it to Ma. Like hell he will! Can you imagine her the millionairess! Would she an avowed Christian donate her worldly goods to starving kids in China? Yeah right! She wouldn't give the drippings off her nose. Hat on head and palms together her religious duty would consist of a daily pilgrimage to the bank vault to gloat.

'No way!' He punched the wheel. 'I'd sooner put a match to the lot!'

Maybe he should make a Will leaving Nurse La-di-da Challoner 1.75 mill. He would never tell her. Bobby would carry the secret to his grave. It would just arrive through the post one day, a letter on the mat, one point seven-five million, a gift from a reluctant angel.

'Stand-by!' Bobby hunkered down in the seat. 'They're on the move!'

They are out on the sidewalk, Alex tucking her arm through his. They stand close together in some discussion about where to go. Then the big fellow gestures and leaning down rests his forehead on hers.

Briefly, Bobby can't help but be glad for him. Look at him big pussy cat! Usually he fights shy of girls but look how he wraps his body around her like covetous wings. A good guy Ash doesn't always have the best of times. His dad is hard to please. He demands the best of his son and devil take the cost.

It would be great to see him happy.

Bobby wants him to be happy.

'But not with this girl.'

~

'This was a beautiful church.' Adelia is picking her way through fallen masonry. 'All this mess I realise it takes some imagination but trust me it really was lovely. The stained glass window over the altar was a Gothic masterpiece. It was of the Annunciation, the Angel bringing good news to Mary. It was quite well known. People came from all over the world to see it.'

'I imagine it was something to see.'

'It was.' She turned to him. 'Did you know that in the fifteen-hundreds and before stained-glass windows were known as a poor man's bible?'

'I didn't know but I get the connection. In those days if you were poor you didn't get to read. Books were for the wealthy.'

'Exactly! Worshipping at St Giles you didn't need to read. The word of God was there before you. This particular window was predominantly in gold and silver, though strangely the Archangels wings were of blue. Do you see the Latin inscription, *Omnia Vincit Amor?*'

'Love conquers all.'

'Yes, love conquers all. It was thought to be the work of John Thornton, the artist who designed the Great York Minster window.

'It must have been quite a sight.'

'It was. When I was little I was in the Brownies. Easter Sundays were special. We would come to sing hymns under that window, me in my brown dress and hair in pigtails and my mother and father in the congregation.'

'You said your people worked abroad.'

'Yes, part of an Agricultural programme. They couldn't get always get home but were here for Easter Sunday. Naturally I was on my best behaviour.'

'Naturally.'

'We were all cherubs that day, my Brownie friends and I standing under the window, golden light streaming down giving us all temporary haloes.'

'Cherubs?'

'Why are you smiling? Do you not see us that way?'

'I see you exactly that way.'

She laughed. 'Sorry to spoil the image but we were actually horribly mercenary little beasts. We paraded through town and sang hymns and smiled and behaved like angels but with one thought and only one thought in mind, the chocolate Easter egg at the end of the service.'

'Shameful!'

'Indeed, a black mark against my soul forever.'

'Did you to get to join the grown up league?'

'I'm afraid not. There were similar things in boarding school but nothing like that, and nothing at all like this church. Did you know St Giles is the Patron Saint of the Outcast?'

'No, but I guess if anyone needs a saint it's them.'

'There used to be a statue of a deer here by the altar, St Giles' emblem, but that was destroyed.' She sighed. 'I loved that window. The angel was so real I felt I could touch His feathers. Seeing it now I wish we hadn't come.'

'Why did we come?'

'No reason. Me being sentimental I suppose.'

'Oh come now, Nurse Challoner!' Alex frowned. 'Is that you telling the gospel truth or is this former Brownie failing in her duty to come clean?'

She looked at him.

'You had a purpose.'

'Why would you say that?'

'Because you did! You don't do things just to be sentimental. You had a purpose in coming here and I'd like to know what.'

'It was nothing. It was me being ridiculous.'

'Tell me why we came and I'll judge the ridiculousness of it.'

'It will sound silly.'

'Tell me.'

'Oh!' She put her hands to her head. 'Well, I thought that if we came together we could ask, or rather *I* could ask the Angel to bring you back safe. Not necessarily to me, though I would be so glad to see you! I thought He might bring you safe home to the world in general.'

'I love you.'

'What?'

'I love you.'

'Oh don't!' She covered her ears. 'You mustn't say things like that.'

He pulled her hands away. 'I love you.'

'You shouldn't say things you don't mean.'

'I do mean it! From the moment I saw you I loved you. I am pretty sure I was born loving you.'

'That's a very big thing to say and cruel if you are playing games.'

'I'm not playing games.'

'Really?'

'Really.'

'And you mean it?'

'Affirmative. I love you and it's my belief you could learn to love me. Isn't that what you meant when you called me love in the cafe?'

'I did call you love.'

'And did you not mean it?'

'I meant it.'

'So what are you going to do about it?'

'I don't know. What can I do?'

'You can marry me.'

Her face is white and drawn. 'You mean wait for you and then marry?'

'I mean marry me today!'

'How can we? These things take time and you don't have time!'

'We have this! We have the church and the window and your angel. You said it yourself. 'It's a ruin now, a bomb last February and yet it is still a holy place.' That's what you said, didn't you?'

She stared. 'I did say that.'

'Then that's enough!' He slapped his chest. 'It's enough for me. I love you. I want you for my wife. What more is there to say? You said you think of this as a holy place. Does that mean you believe God is here?'

'Yes.'

'Then marry me! Stand up before what's left of the altar and give me your love and in turn I will promise that whatever lies ahead I will come back to you.'

'Really?'

'Really and truly.'

'Then yes I will marry you.'

'We should kneel. Hold on.' He spread his greatcoat in the dust.

They knelt.

'Do you know the words?'

'No! Why would I?' She was trembling, a curl loose from her braid quivering in the light. 'I think it could be along the lines of to love, honour and obey, and possibly to cherish unto death. Words like that.'

'That'll do. Give me your hand.' Inexpressible need pushing he took her hand. 'I Alexander William Stonewall Hunter take Adelia Challoner for my wife. I will love and honour you and keep you safe from harm now and forever til death us do part No! Hang on!'

Startled, she pulled away. 'What? What's wrong?'

'I take that back.'

'What do you mean, take back?'

'The death parting us bit. I won't say that because it's not going to happen! Not now not ever! Where you go I go until the end of the world and that's my solemn promise.'

Silent tears dropping she began to cry. 'I ought to say something.'

'Yes, you should!'

'I Adelia do take thee Alexander William…what's the rest of your name?'

'Stonewall.'

'I take thee Alexander William Stonewall Hunter as my husband. I promise to love and honour you and…' a tear slid down her cheek, 'cherish you forever.'

'And you won't marry some other guy.'

'I won't marry some other guy.'

'Wait a minute. We're not done.' He tugged at his class ring. Squeezing it over his knuckle took a layer of skin but he didn't care. For it to work, for the promises to hold, he has to give her a ring. 'Here you are?'

It hung on her finger a dead weight so that when she tried closing her fist it skidded away in the dust. Alex snatched it up. He knew he was rushing and that she was crying but he couldn't stop. This means something! This moment in a ruined church before the defunct altar is a sacred talisman. Soldiers know these things. They recognise the moment and the power of protection.

Most soldiers carry an amulet to keep the wolf from the door. It won't be a gun that brings Alex through the war it will be his promise to this woman.

'Give me your purse.' Unzipping a centre pocket he dropped the ring inside. 'There, it's official. You are my wife so kiss me.'

It was a tearful kiss. She was weeping and damn it so was he.

Sunlight poured through a roof open to the sky. Ancient blackened walls shook under the rumble of planes heading out across the North Sea, planes meant to drop bombs on another church. And she, his beloved, face puffy and smudged with tears, the moment was seared upon his soul.

'Don't cry, honey,' he held her close. 'I know it's not how it should be but when this is over we'll do it again. Orange blossom, bridesmaids, a guest-list long as the Declaration of Independence, you name it, it'll be yours.'

'It's alright. Nothing we do will ever match this day. I feel utterly and completely married. Besides,' she pointed a shaky finger. 'We have a guest.'

He turned to look. 'We do?'

'A field mouse sitting on what's left of the altar.'

'Well, I'll be!' He laughed. There it was a tiny little critter nibbling a bit of stale bread. 'That is great.' With a feeling of blessing and of vindication Alex hugged her. 'And you feel properly married, Mrs Hunter?'

'I do and so we should celebrate.'

'Sure. What had you in mind?'

'Bed.'

'Bed!'

'Yes, bed and then possibly sleep. I am exhausted and you must be. '

Heart pounding, not quite sure how to take this, Alex waited.

She glanced under her lashes. 'I know a place.'

'You do?'

'Yes a hotel near the Air-Base. People go there when they want to be alone.'

He frowned. 'And you know this how?'

'Everyone knows. It has a reputation.'

'And you want to go there?'

'If you'll come with me?'

'This is something you want to do?'

She scrubbed her face with a hanky. 'It is.'

'You're sure?'

'I'm sure.'

'Hold on a minute!' He held up his hand. 'Let me get this right. I mean, I am getting this right aren't I? You do mean bed? I'm not picking up wrong signals.'

'No you're getting it right. And we are married, aren't we?'

'Affirmative. We are married.'

'So what do you think?'

'I think I need to breathe. You are a woman of surprises, Mrs Hunter. You make my heart leap, you scare me, and I have a feeling, my God, a hope, that fifty years from now I'll be saying the same thing.'

Twelve
Black Swan

Bobby yawned. 'Do me a favour, Mac, and change the friggin' record. If I have to listen to that tune one more time it'll be you gettin' a kick up the ass!'

The guy flipped him the finger, dropped another dime in the slot and out it rolled again. '*I get no kick from champagne, mere alcohol doesn't move me at all, so tell me why should it be true, I get a kick out of you.*'

'Yeah, that's right!' Bobby snarled. 'Crawl back to your fat momma and keep tellin' yourself you don't mind she's ugly.'

He supped his beer. He should shut-up. One more crack and he's in trouble but pissed out of his brains he doesn't care. They are in the Lounge-Bar. If he peers over the counter he can see them huddled together in the back room by the piano a glass of beer between them and star-dust in their eyes.

If he felt bad before it's nothing to how he feels now. The Black Swan, or Mucky Duck as it's known on the Base, is a British version of a cat-house where you can get what you want with a pint of warm beer on the side.

Guys coming through this door have one thing in mind. First day on the Base he was tipped the wink. 'You wanna a cheap room and a girl to match that's the place to go.'

Needless to say he has taken advantage of mine host's generous accommodation more than once. But that's him, Baby Rourke. What happened to bring the clean people? What magic word cut through the red tape? Surely not a ruined church and a voice from above, 'Go forth, my son, and multiply, and do it now before you get your balls blown off in Dieppe.'

Ash still no fast-mover they hold hands and gaze at one another while the clock ticks. It drives Bobby crazy. He thinks what are you doing? Get up the stairs and do your bit for Uncle Sam while you still can. Then he realises what he's thinking and hauls it back. 'Keep your sorry ass glued to the seat! No fraternizing with the locals. Go back to the army as pure as you came.'

What a difference a day makes. Yesterday he and Bobby were life-long buddies. Given the need it's likely one would have died for the other. Now's there's frail flesh and blood between them and friendship is done.

Bobby is so down he's not sure he'll ever get up. The atmosphere doesn't help. In the back room, the Twilight Lounge as they call it, they play a wind-up gramophone and unlike the idiot here go for smooch tunes like *Always* or Glen Miller's *Moonlight Serenade,* romantic music great for holding a girl close and breathing the perfume of her hair. They have danced, if you can call it that. Ash is a handsome guy, elegant in a darkly brooding manner but with no sense of rhythm. Now if it were Bobby he'd be showing his moves.

'Fat chance!' He tossed the beer down his throat. 'Same again, bartender!'

This must be his last or he'll do something dumb. A shrink back home reckons Bobby has an obsessive nature aggravated by alcohol. Right now he's so aggravated he could leap the counter, pull Ash's pistol and shoot the guy dead.

'What now?'

Still hugging the shadows he stares across the counter. What's going on back there? They're going to the desk? Yes! Ash is collecting a key! Finally they are on their way upstairs leaving him an outcast with a bottle of beer.

What a waste of time! He should be signed out the hospital and on with the business of the war and Second Tactical Air-force and a de Havilland Mosquito and low-level bombing. To hell with this! Stalking a buddy is not why he joined the RAF.

This is women! They are the root of all evil starting with Eve in the bible and on to Sue Ryland. A woman can turn a man's head so he doesn't know which way he's going. She can force him to compare man with man. Once it was Gabe Templar bugging him now it's Alex Hunter, though after two decades of hero-worship it ain't easy.

Sarah reckoned Bobby loved her brother more than her. 'A chromosome to the left,' she said, 'and you'd be a raving queer.'

Bullshit! Bobby knows who he is. This is a temporary adjustment. He needs to hold on for the morning.

~

'Oh well.' She gazed about the room. 'I suppose it's functional.'

Functional? Dirty looking black-out drapes and tape criss-crossing the window, rusty taps at the sink and a grubby bed-spread? It's a dump.

'Negative!' Alex opened the door. 'We're not staying.'

'It's alright.' She laid her cape on the chair. 'We can manage.'

'I don't want to manage. Come on!' He took her arm. 'We're out of here.'

'It's alright.'

'It's not alright. It stinks! I don't want you here.'

'I do.' She locked the door. 'I don't want to be anywhere else.'

'This is wrong. Why don't we forget about this and trust in tomorrow. I can live with waiting for you if you can live with waiting for me.'

'Of course I can live with that.' She took his great-coat and spread it on the bed. 'Knowing you love me I can live with anything, but..,' she slipped her shoes and unclipping her belt began unbuttoning her dress, 'I'd sooner live knowing I loved you as I wanted to love.'

'Adelia?' He took her hand. It was ice cold. She was scared. But then so was he. 'You really want to do this?'

'I really do.'

'Then let me help.' He took over. Buttons small and his fingers suddenly thick he struggled. One-by-one they came undone until the dress slid about her ankles. Taking her hand he helped her step out and watched as she hung it over the chair, pretty little thing, lovely little thing, in white lace underwear and stockings.

Bang, bang, his heart was thrashing. He kicked off his shoes. 'Now me,' he said croaking like a frog. Lips trembling she unclipped his tie and started on his shirt. Three maybe four buttons went and the belt to his pants but then the soft silk of her breast and gold-tipped lashes on her cheek were too much.

'Oh my Lord, I do love you!' He swung her up in his arms, kissing her lips, tasting her tongue, lemon shandy with a touch of panic. 'Pretty baby,' he whispered, 'pretty girl, are you gonna stay mine forever.'

Hands digging in his hair she kissed him back. 'Always, darling, Alex, always and ever.'

Discarding bobby-pins left and right he undid her hair. Golden molasses spread on his great-coat it didn't seem to matter then that the bed-cover was beer-stained and wrinkled or that the pillows had cushioned too many heads. She was in his arms beyond that nothing mattered.

Pants down and kicked away he was rocket hard and pushed against her. Clumsy, hurting her for a while there was no entry, a thought flashing though his head, the night-watchman hinting of untouched glass. Then the glass splintered and he was inside her and there were no thoughts, only the sweetness of his wife.

~

Later he got it wrong. The first time, though her body was driving him nuts and had since he saw her, Alex tried keeping his wits sharp. 'Come on, soldier! Don't let the lady down.' Though there had to be a breaking-in he tried being gentle and giving what she needed, and eyes wide open and silent scream of pleasure she seemed to appreciate his effort.

Full on sex is as new to him as the blood on his coat proves it so for her. There were fumbles in college but nothing important. This is important. He had to do it right. Having found her pleasure he sought his own, groaning like a wounded man yet again with his mind on the future pulled away before any damage.

'I was unprepared!' It's as he said later when music drifting up from below they danced cheek-to-cheek and then lay on the bed sharing a squashed cheese sandwich; 'If I had known my sweet baby was gonna be at the end of the rainbow I'd have bought out your Boots Chemist.'

Eyes sparkling, yet still covered up and shy, she laughed. 'Good old Boots. What would we do without you?'

'Life-saver,' he said, 'it's like this old coat! I'll never complain about it again.'

'Did you complain?' She was playing with the dog-tags about his neck.

'Sure I did. Eighty in the shade out there and me with this on my back I must've looked a complete idiot.'

'You could never look an idiot. You are far too handsome but since you mention it I did think it heavyweight for the time of year.'

'It's the bike,' he said. 'If I was going to get back to Southampton in time for lock-down I needed to travel from Achnacarry through the night.'

'That was asking a lot.

'As I learned after the first fifty miles and stopped to bum a lift. No way am I going through that again. Joe

Petowski, a buddy of mine from the same outfit takes a truck back tomorrow, me and my bike are going with him.'

'Joe Petowski! What a wonderful name, thick and growling.'

'Thick and growling!' Alex laughed. 'That's Joe! Maybe not thick but growling alright. A great guy, he is my God-father. I would trust him with my life.'

'You'd trust him with your life?'

'I sure would.'

'Then I shall remember Mister Petowski when saying my prayers tonight.'

'You mean Sergeant Major Joseph Aaron Petowski! A fussy guy, one button out of place, and you're likely to be on a charge.'

She kissed him. 'Will I be on a charge if I forget your title, Major Hunter?'

'You bet your life you will.' He pulled her onto his lap, 'confined to barracks forever and physical discipline employed.'

'Ooh that sounds scary,' she shuddered deliciously. 'I can't wait, but back to Sergeant Petowski. He sounds a sensible man. From now I shall pray that he helps keeps you sensible. No schoolboy heroics. You're to be an honest soldier, my darling, be brave and true but not too brave.'

'Call me that again.'

'What, darling?'

'Uh-huh.'

'Darling.'

'And again?'

'Darling, darling…'

They made love again and this time it was love rather than speed. Easing in deep and slow Alex took his time, arching over her so that he might see her face and kiss her lips, delicious lips, waiting, touching, kissing and loving, until she would scream again.

Fingertips clutching his back she cried out and he was on the point of coming and thinking not taking chances went to pull away. That's when she did it, held onto his back rising off the bed with him so he couldn't get away.

'No, baby, don't!' he yelled.

Too late, he was emptying into her and no way back. She let go of him.

He rolled away. 'What happened there?'

She gazed at him. 'I hung onto you.'

'I know you did but why?'

'I wanted to.'

'But, honey, that was dangerous. You know, close like that, I couldn't stop myself, and well…anything might've happened.'

'I hope it did.'

'You don't mean that.' Anxious, he crouched on his haunches. 'What if the worst happens?'

'What is the worst that can happen?' She was talking, explaining her feelings, saying she wanted this. That she hadn't exactly planned it. It was nothing as cold as that but that it was what she wanted.

Windows rattling and bed shaking, scores of heavyweight planes passing overhead he couldn't get what she was saying. She laughed and covered her ears. Alex wasn't laughing. He was downright scared. What if it was a bad mistake, what if she gets pregnant and is left alone to manage?

'How would you manage?' Planes moving away into the distance the words leapt out. 'You got nothing but a shack to live in and a job that makes you unhappy! You've no real security and no family to turn to! And what about collateral damage, bombs ripping this country to pieces and people dying and who knows me getting the same? Who's gonna take care of you then?'

Mimicking deafness, she tapped her ears. Then seeing he wasn't happy her smile faded. 'Are you angry?'

'No, not angry, out my head with worry!'

'Why?'

'Why? Because this is happening too fast! I can't get my head round it. One minute I'm seeing a buddy, next I'm meeting the most beautiful girl in the world. Then we're making love and I'm giving my heart and soul. Now there's this and the thought of you struggling alone will drive me nuts!'

'I won't be alone,' her smile was gone. 'I shall have part of you with me and so I'll never be alone again.'

'Oh honey!' Struggling, and not particularly tactful, he sat on the side of the bed. 'That sounds okay but it isn't. How can I be with you when I'm thousands of miles away sticking an M16 down some guy's throat! You said be sensible and keep it real, this was no movie, you were no Scarlett O Hara and I was no Rhett Butler. You're right. It isn't a movie. It's two people coming together in war, one staying and one going away. I love you. I was always going to worry but you've added a whole new dimension, and frankly the thought of you and a babe struggling is one worry too many.'

Her face dropped. 'No need to be concerned. I can take care of myself.'

'I'm sure you can but things can change.'

'Things do change and people with it. I took care of myself yesterday and I can do the same tomorrow. And what's more…!' She raised her hand forbidding speech. 'If there should be a new dimension I can take care of that too.'

So saying she took up her clothes to dress.

'No you don't!' He snatched her back. 'I'm not letting you take offence and swish off out of my life, lady. You're here now with me in this shitty room and you're gonna stay while we have the time.'

'Let go of me.'

'Uh-huh, like that's gonna happen.' He hauled her onto the bed and sat with her between his knees. 'You're gonna sit while I tell you how much I love you. Then I'm going to hug and kiss you, and then we're gonna try grabbing some sleep because we're both tired and talking rot.'

She struggled against him but with no real heart. It was as he said. High on love and fear for one another they were both exhausted.

'Come on, sweetheart,' Conscious of time he lay down with her fast in his arms. 'We need to sleep. Then in the morning even if it means going AWOL I'll find a padre and make you and me and a possible new dimension official.'

It took a while. She wasn't giving in and muttered of conceited Americans who thought too much of themselves. Then she slept and so did he.

~

'I get no kick in a plane, flying too high with some gal in the sky is my idea of nothing to do, but I get a kick out of you, oh what a kick, I get a kick out of you.'

Bobby heard the air-raid siren but sodden with booze and accustomed to the sound ignored it. The same record on the juke-box rolling on it felt like he was partly-awake and partly asleep. Flying jacket for a pillow and feet on the bench, his body is in the Black Swan here but his soul is back home in Virginia gazing at a broken-down Mill and thinking the blind-covered windows looked like so many sleeping eyes.

Sails broken and rooks nesting in the roof, the tower sent out a message, stay away Baby Rourke! Once through these doors you're never coming out.

There was a garden and there were roses. Such roses! So many colours and varieties the air was sticky with scent and the sound of bees humming. As the house appalled so the roses thrilled.

Sunbeams warm on his head Bobby strolled through the garden. Down by the willows the glass panes of a greenhouse were blue with condensation. A peaceful place, he thought it would be good to sit in the greenhouse drinking a beer and smoking a cigarette and with maybe a dog for companion!

The greenhouse felt good as did the rose-filled garden but the Mill house with its sleeping eyes scared him so much he thought best to leave.

Light spilling the door opened. Dee Challoner stood there, but not the prim and stuffy nurse of July 1942, an older woman ravishing and infinitely softer.

She called out, 'come on in, Captain Robert E Rourke DFC. Don't be afraid. There is a place waiting for you.'

No ma'm, he wasn't going in! Too much sadness in there!

Then she held out her arms. 'Come on in, dear boy, and rest!'

He began to run and panting crashed through the door into warm darkness and sheltering arms.

'Chrissakes!'

Heart going rat-ta-tat, he sat up. 'What was that all about?'

'Ah shut-up!' The doughboy necking a girl in the corner yelled. 'Moaning and groaning half the night, there's somethin' wrong with you!'

'What you talkin' about?' Bobby stretched his leg hurting. 'I wasn't moanin'! It's you with your tongue halfway down her throat. You sound like hog at a trench. It's enough to put a guy off his feed.'

Talking of food what time is it. He screwed a look at his watch. Two in the morning! No wonder he feels bad. Maybe he'll take a quick malt whisky; a hair of the dog might make him feel better.

But for a lamp over the till it's dark in here. License laws in England are tight, 2230 hours last orders, 2300 everyone out but this is wartime and rules don't apply. All these thirsty Yanks spending their hard-earned dollars? No way, honey! As with the Windmill Theatre the Black Swan never closes.

There was no sign of the other two. Top floor, Room 11, Bobby checked it out, they'll be down soon. Ash needs to be on his way which means Bobby needs to get out. The last thing he wants is to be found down here skulking.

A siren began to wail, a bombing raid anti-aircraft guns pounding over the coast. Such a noise for a minute Bobby didn't know where he was here in the Black Swan or back in the dream with giant bees humming.

Ten minutes and folks are heading for the door.

The doughboy is stuffing his shirt into his pants. 'I don't like the sound of that,' he pulls his girl to her feet. 'It's too close for comfort.'

Hackles stirring Bobby leans over the counter. 'Hey!' He shook the bartender. 'You need to sound general quarters and get everybody up and out!'

'It's nothing!' The bartender yawned. 'We hear this all the time. It'll pass.'

It didn't pass. '*Yow, Yow, Yow, Yow*! A siren started up, an eerie high-pitched whine that Bobby knew only too well. Then machine-guns started rattling.

'Get down!' He dived under the nearest table. 'Everybody take cover!'

Later he learned the pilot of a crapped out Stuka 87 mistimed a run over the Base and veering away jettisoned what was left of his load over Needham.

'Boom!' The first explosion shattered every piece of glass in the bar, folks ducking as lethal shards flew every which-way.

'Boom!' The second bomb hit the distillery next door exploding the furnace and ripping gas-pipes apart. A wall fell and fires sprang up.

'Everybody out!' The guy who owed the pub and his wife and kids still in their pyjamas came barrelling down the main staircase. 'They got the brewery next door. This place will go up any minute.'

Caught in the general panic Bobby was carried out and along into the cool night air to cower, shocked, as a series of smaller explosions rocked the hotel.

'Oh my God!' A girl screamed. 'The place is on fire!'

'So it is! It's the lounge bar where we were only a minute ago!'

'Look at the first floor balcony!' The same girl, hysterical now. 'Those two climbing out the window? That's Milly Prior from the cafe and her guy Phil.'

'They're stuck!'

'They can't get down!'

'Someone call the fire brigade!'

'There are ladders round the back! I saw them earlier.'

'Let's go get 'em!'

The bartender was close by. Bobby grabbed his arm. 'Where is it?' he said.

The guy stared. 'Where's what?'

'The fire-escape, you moron!'

'There is no a fire-escape.'

'You're kiddin' me!'

'We were putting one down the side but the guvnor said it wasn't worth it.'

'Not worth it! What about the kids on the top floor? How do they get out?'

'I don't know.'

A few minutes before that Adelia was asking the same question.

'How do we get out?'

'Don't worry about that,' said Alex. 'Just get dressed.'

It was the chunka-chunka of anti-aircraft that woke him. With the alert siren wailing and a raid right on top he figured it was time to scram. She lay still and quiet, her fingers looped onto the band on his shorts.

'Wake up, honey,' he touched her shoulder.

Snap, she was up. 'Is it a bombing raid?'

'Affirmative. You should get dressed.'

No argument she was out and pulling on her underwear. 'It sounds close.'

Knowing it was too close he didn't answer. A man split into several parts, one Alex was zipping his pants, another cussing and blaming sleep, thinking he should've heard the siren, and a third, the soldier, was checking escape routes and wondering if Joe Petowski was caught up in this.

Another aspect of Alexander Hunter, the cold, clinical eye of the Camera, was busy taking life-shots of everything he loved wrapped up in one woman.

Click, head bent and hands behind her back she struggled to fasten her brassiere.

'Hang on.' Click, he is behind her scooping her hair from her neck, counting the bones of her spine and fragile shoulder-blades.

Click, no time for socks he's stuffing his feet in his shoes.

Click, she's doing the same minus stockings.

'Hurry up, honey.'

'I'm comin.'

'Leave your bag.'

Click, eyes big and frightened she is looking at him. 'I don't like this.'

Neither did he! Above the roar of guns there is the wailing of a Luftwaffe banshee. Alex knows the sound. He's trained to hear it, and as we know, once heard never forgotten. It's a Stuka Bomber, the propeller driven siren known by the British Tommies as Jericho Trumpets, the sound of death in the sky.

She was searching her purse. 'I must get my ring!'

'Leave it!' He held out his arms. 'Come on! Run!'

Hand outstretched, she was turning toward him.

'Boom!' The door blew in, Adelia was tossed over the bed while Alex was thrown across the room to slam up against the window.

From then on memory takes over, goddamn memory, the tragedy viewed from another day and another year in the slow-mo replay of a horror movie.

Bright light pierces the darkness. The room is frosted with ice.

Arms outstretched as though soothing the air Adelia is held upright.

The silver buckle on her belt flips open.

The blast is shredding her clothes, first the dress, the uniform so proudly and lovingly worn, and then the brassiere white lace petals shrivelling.

Alex can't move. An invisible hand forces him back against the window.

Zip-zip, the pane of glass is splintering, sharp slivers piercing his back.

Boom! The room is tinged with red.

Then Boom again with orange, a scene from hell.

Click, click, the Camera is in overdrive, frame after frame recorded.

Now he wants to gouge his eyes out putting an end to this picture-parade.

Boom! Some unseen force lifts Adelia twirling her gently round.

Poised, she hangs in the doorway a ballerina treading air.

Another twirl and she is a scarlet clad angel, her lion's mane of statically charged hair flying in the up-draught.

'Alex.' She is speaking to him.

Blinded by tears he shakes his head. The blast ringing in his ears he is deaf, not a word gets by yet he hears what she says because he is saying it too.

'I love you. I will always love you.'

Boom! A Giant Hand, a greedy hand, cruel and unloving, hundreds of pounds of pressure becomes a fist.

The window frame shatters! Alex is sucked through the opening to fall down to the ground into darkness.

Thirteen
A Plan

'Move, will you? Get out the way!'

Bobby is running. No fire escape but there is a way in through the cellars. He knows that because before his leg went bust he and Patsy, the barmaid, made a quick exit one night when her old man came looking.

Panting, leg aching, Bobby is scared. They're not out among the survivors, neither of them, and that can only mean that Ash is disabled.

It has to be that. This is your Iron Man, your West Point Double Major Cadet. Upper floor on fire or not if there was a way out he would find it.

This cellar hatch is open and smoke pouring out. Scarf over his nose, Bobby is down the hatch and through the cellar and up the back stairs.

'Hey!' A couple are coming down the girl's face a bloodied mess, the guy all but carrying her. 'Many more up there?'

The guy nodded. 'Plenty, but I don't know how they gonna get out. A midsection of the roof collapsed and the front landing blocked.'

'Then why are you hangin' about? Get back up and get 'em out!'

'I have to get Jane down first. She has glass in her eyes.'

'Okay, but come back!' yelled Bobby. 'And bring others with you! If we don't move fast there's gonna be a lot of dead people in this place.'

Someone was screaming. Bobby pushed the door open. It was the barmaid! She'd got under the bed to hide and the ceiling had fallen on top of the bed.

'Help me, Bobby!' she calls.

Part of him wants to keep looking for Dee but he couldn't leave Patsy trapped. Heaving the bed aside he grabbed her hand.

'No!' she screamed. 'Don't pull! I think my arm's broken.'

He drags her out by the armpits. 'Can you make the stairs?' She nods and he's off running to the next landing.

There it is, Number 11. The door is off the hinges. Dee is alive but unconscious a lump back of her head size of a duck-egg.

'Lie still, honey! I'll get you out.'

Where the hell is Ash? His greatcoat is there but not the man.

The casement window askew Bobby leans out but can't see for smoke.

Boom! The building shifts and with it a sense of skin being sucked off your body! Cracks appear across ceiling the air alive with smouldering debris. Then as though bowled by a giant hand the dresser rolls across the room!

'We're out of here!'

Keeping low to the floor Bobby wraps Dee from head to toe in a sheet. Pausing to stuff what was left of her bra in his pocket he slings her over his shoulder and makes for the stairs.

People are calling for help. 'Hang on!' he yells. 'I'll come back for you!'

Eyes streaming, barely able to breathe, he manages both set of stairs and back through the cellar splashing through Piper's Best Bitter.

A slow-roasted rat he pops up through the hatch

The sky is red and roaring. The police are here and fire-brigade.

An ambulance trundles toward the gate the bell clanging.

'Hey!' He flags them down. 'I got a girl here.'

The driver shakes his head. 'Sorry, mate, no can do.'

'What d'you mean no can do?'

'This is not the only place to catch it! The village has been hit. Now with those we got from here we're stacked to the gills. '

'I don't care! You're takin' her.' Bobby pulls open the door.

The guy wasn't lying, the van is packed.

A woman squats on the floor with a child in her arms.

'Her name's Dee!' Bobby sets Adelia down. 'She's a nurse at St Faiths. This is hers.' He passed the brassiere. 'If you get a chance put it on. She's a good girl. She don't need to be seen any other way.'

He shuts the door and the ambulance pulls away.

No time to waste he heads back down the hatch and up to the second flight.

A girl with half her hair missing and shoulders burned is crawling along the landing. He carries her out and then he and the doughboy grab hatchets from a fire-wagon hacking their way into more rooms.

It was bad. One guy, a kid from Kansas, a mechanic seen on the Base, was dead but with not a mark on him. Bobby carried him out. He thought on the babe at the hospital. No parents here to weep for the Kansas kid but that's alright he is weeping for him.

Sick to his stomach he asked the doughboy. 'What the fuck is all this about?'

The doughboy shrugged. 'I couldn't tell you, Lieutenant. I stopped asking that a long time ago.'

Two more desperate runs and then, exhausted, he could do no more. Fire on the first floor taking hold the police are keeping everyone back. People from nearby houses are out with blankets and hot tea plus and guys from the Base are pitching in. Good guys, guys you'd like to know as buddies.

'Talkin' of buddies…?' Bobby gazed about. 'Where is Ash? Why isn't he here doin' his bit?'

An uneasy thought crept into his mind. Maybe he lost his nerve and left Dee to save himself. There was a drainpipe running down the side of the window. He could've shinned down that.

No! Impossible! Bobby shook the thought away. Ash wouldn't leave anyone. It's not his nature. He'd sooner die with her. But the thought kept creeping back, if he didn't leave her then where is he?

'My head!' Alex lies in a wheel-barrow tomato plants rearing above as oversize grapevines. He has a pillow under his head and a blanket over his knees. Weathered face and gumboots, a woman squatted beside him.

'Oh thank goodness! I was beginning to worry.'

'Where am I?'

'You're in my garden. I tried getting you to the house but couldn't manage so I thought best to leave you.' She took his hand. 'How are you?'

'My head aches.'

'I'm not surprised. You've a nasty cut on your forehead but considering you fell two flights I don't think that's too bad.'

'Two flights?'

'You landed on a compost heap. You won't smell very nice but it probably saved your life. My husband's a fireman. He saw you fall and thought to get you away from the hotel.'

'Hotel? My God, Adelia!' Alex was up and running except there was nowhere to run the Black Swan ablaze with flames piercing the sky.

'No, No, No!!' So scared, he can't think. Survivors, bedraggled men and women in various states of undress stand about the square. Frantic, he stumbles from one group to the next. 'Have you seen my girl? Her name is Adelia. We were together last night.'

Mute, they one and all shake their heads.

He ran to another group and another but they all have the same shocked expression and stare as though his questions make no sense.

Then he saw a face he recognised, a heavyweight doughboy seen in the john last night. 'Hey!' He grabbed his arm. 'Have you seen my girl, a blonde by name of Adelia? We got separated when I fell out the window.'

'You fell out the window?'

'The blast forced me out. Have you seen her?'

'I can't say I have. A couple of girls were brought down from the second floor but I don't remember your blonde.'

'Were the girls okay?'

'Both dead. Say, Major? Did you say you fell?' The guy was frowning, a look Alex was to see again. 'How come you're in one piece?'

'I don't know. Did they get everyone out?'

'No and they've given up trying.'

'They can't give up!' He ran to the hotel entrance.

'Hey you!' a firemen yelled. 'Get back from there!'

Alex kept going. If she is in there he is going to find her. The front desk and most of the ceiling lay across the stairs. The only way in was up and over.

The palms of his hands sinking into molten leather he vaulted the desk. If there was pain it didn't register, the thought of her overtaking all else. Then he was scrambling on the stairs and going nowhere, hands dragging him back.

'Where the fuck do you think you're going, Camera?'

'Joe!' Straight way he knew who it was. 'My girl's in there! Let me go!'

'Like hell I will.' Joe Petowski hauled him back. 'There's nothing you can do up there so leave it alone.'

'No! Please, I'm begging you! Let me try!'

'Hey, quit struggling!' Joe was having a job holding him. Then a fireman came to help and still Alex fought like a trapped animal.

Joe threw a fist. Whump Alex was out. He laid him on the grass. An RAF pilot was stood by watching. 'Say you, wing-nut, come give me a hand!'

'What's the trouble?'

'Hold this guy! I need you to keep him quiet.'

'What was he doin' back there tryin' to fly?'

'Seemed that way.'

'A girl, I guess.'

'Yeah, a girl. Do you know who?'

Bobby shrugged. 'It could've been anyone. It's that kind of place.'

'She wasn't anyone. His hands are burned to the bone. Whoever she is she meant a lot and those hands telling the tale for the rest of his life.'

'If you say so.'

Joe looked up. 'What d'you mean?'

'I don't mean anythin' except you have to ask if she meant that much why is he out here, and she's in there.'

'Where this kid is concerned I don't have to ask anything. This is my Godson, Major Alexander Hunter Ist Battalion US Army Rangers. If he wasn't in there with her there's a damned good reason.'

'Godson?'

'Yeah, why what's it to you?'

'Nothin'. I was only askin'. I didn't know Ash had a Godfather.'

'Well he does. He has me. You know him?'

'He's a friend.'

'Then you know this boy wouldn't leave a fucking mouse to burn let alone a girl. Now do yourself a favour and keep your thoughts to yourself, or you and me will be having a little wall-to-wall counselling, you get me?'

'Yes, Sarge!' Bobby saluted. 'I get you.'

'Make sure you do. I came with a bunch of guys. I'm going back to the Base to collect my wagon. While I'm gone get a medic to look at his hands. If his C/O sees them like that he'll be up on a charge.'

'Will you be long?'

'Will I be long?' Joe stared. 'Are you sure you're a buddy?'

'Sure I'm sure.'

'Then why the rush to get away?'

'I've got things to do.'

'Yeah, well he's got a broken heart and that takes precedence. Stay with him and be a real buddy.' With that Joe was off thumbing a lift back to the Base.

~

Bobby lit a cigarette. Two minutes, that's all he'll give then he's off back to St Faiths. He had thought to be gone by now but like everyone was caught up in the tragedy. Ash's face! Blood running into his eyes, he'd staggered about the square like a drunk. 'Adelia,' he was yelling. 'Where are you, baby?'

A woman standing nearby was in tears. 'Here listen to that bloke, Dot,' she said to her friend. 'You'd think he was calling his dog.'

Ash usually so calm and controlled it was hard watching. Bobby ached to put him out of his misery, to say, 'it's okay. You're girl's alive and safe.'

He wanted to do it, to bring comfort to the guy's heart but another Bobby - the dark and dangerous Baby Rourke - wanted the girl more.

Truth is, he can't believe he watched a friend suffer and didn't try to help, AND as he watched a plan began to grow in his mind - a dumb plan, dark and dishonourable. Then Joe Petowski arrived dragging Ash back from a suicidal fight with fire and the idea was still dishonourable but not quite so dumb.

Hold on! Ash is coming to.

Torn between right and wrong Bobby wavered. He had a few seconds where he could make it right, a small window in time to decide what he is going to do. Then he saw Dee's face and the plan was on.

He knelt down. 'Hold on there, buddy, everything is okay.'

'Bobby!' Alex struggled to his feet. 'You're here.'

'Yeah, I'm here.'

'Did you see her?'

'What?'

'Did you see her?' Panting, mouth opening and closing, his head filled with fear, it was all Alex could say.

'Who are we talkin' about?'

'Adelia! I was here with her.'

'Who?'

'Your nurse! I was here with her.'

'My nurse? You mean the kiddie's nurse from the hospital? You were here with her? Good Christ, I didn't know that!'

'Uh-huh, last night. There was a raid and I...I...so you haven't seen her?'

'No. My God that's awful! I'm so sorry. I was at the Base gettin' new orders. Then with this raid I thought to swing by to see if I could help.'

Alex stared at the flames. 'No one can help.'

'I hear the whole of the upper floor is gone, fire-fighters waitin' til mornin' to retrieve the bodies. But say, how did you get down here?'

'I was blown out of the window.'

'Blown out of the window? Gee, that's tough! And you were with Nurse Challoner. I sure am sorry. She was a good kid.'

'She was.' Hope flared in Alex's heart. 'But then I heard some had been taken to hospital. She could be one of those, couldn't she?'

'Of course she could! You know what they say, hope springs eternal!'

'Joe stopped me going in.'

'He saved your life. You wouldn't have got far.'

'I guess not.' Alex was finding it hard to string thoughts together. He was invisible and the fire and the sound of flames crackling heard by another man.

'You're sure she wasn't brought out?'

'Buddy, I'd love to tell you I'd seen her come out smilin' but from what I hear casualties are high, mostly the upper floors, bodies that are brought out so badly burnt they can't tell who's who.'

'Oh Jesu, my poor baby!' Alex swivelled, vomiting into a plastic Wishing-Well, a chalked sign, *'Penny for your dreams,'* making mockery of heartache.

Again and again he retched. It's not true. His lovely baby is alive somewhere in the world. She's scared, he knows that and she is asking for him. He can hear her, 'where is my darling, Alex? Where is my husband?

'We got married.'

'What!'

'We got married in the church.'

'You need to sit down. You're not right.'

'I know I'm not right. I'll never be right again.'

'Come on, old sport!' Bobby put his arm about him. 'Let's go find your gorilla pal and get you squared away to Southampton.'

'Negative!' Alex shook him off. 'Until I know what's happened to her I'm not going anywhere.'

'But what good can you do? Surely it's best left to the fireman.'

'My hands hurt.' Puzzled, Alex gazed at his hands. 'I guess they got burnt.'

'They need dressing. Let's go see what a medic can do?'

'No, I've got to keep looking. My hands can wait.'

'They can't wait! You go see the medic. I'll ask around.'

'It's okay, Bobby. Thanks for the offer but it's me she needs. She's here somewhere and she's looking for me. I know she is.'

'Say, Alex!' Suddenly afraid of what he had begun, the enormity of the lie, Bobby held on. 'You're not makin' sense. You fell down two flights. Your head's bleedin' and you've burnt your hands. You're not in your right mind.'

'I'm not in my right mind, Bobby.' Alex was walking in circles. 'I'll never be in my right mind again. She is here somewhere. I gotta find her. She'll come if I call, I know she will. Adelia!' Hands held out as though a blind man seeking help he blundered away. 'Sweetheart, where are you?'

'Hey, medic!' Bobby called out. 'Can we get some help here?'

Ash looked terrible, if he didn't sit down soon he'll fall.

Knees buckling, he did fall.

'Jesus Christ!' Horrified, Bobby crouched down. He was out cold. What have I done? Have I killed my best friend? 'Come on now buddy!' He rubbed Alex's hands. 'Don't give in! She may be alive. Someone may have got her out.'

No response, nothing. Eyes empty and staring, it was awful seeing him.

Bobby struggled. There's a way round this. He can make it right. All he needs do is say she's alive. He squeezed Ash's hand. 'Wake up, buddy! I got good news to tell you!'

'Hey you, what's-your-name, fly-boy!' Joe Petowski pushed his way through. 'I thought I told you to keep him quiet.'

'He is quiet.'

Joe knelt down. 'Whad'you say to him?'

'Nothin' he didn't already know.'

'And what did he already know?'

Bobby got to his feet. 'His girl is dead.'

'Is she dead?'

Bobby shrugged. 'I heard a rumour.'

'Okay. Say medic!' Joe yelled. 'Give me a hand! Help me get this guy into that wagon.' The medic came and between them they shuffled Alex forward.

'Let me stay,' he was trying to put one foot before the other but the ground was buckling. 'Let me stay, Joe.'

'You can't do anything,' Joe was urging him on. 'It's done now and you need to get back to Base and get better. Your buddy will search for you, won't you?'

'Sure I will! You don't need to ask.'

They pushed him along. Alex went because there was nothing else to do. 'When you find her, Bobby, tell her I love her and that I'll come back for her.'

'Sure thing.' Bobby is patting his shoulder. 'I promise the minute I get news I'll call it through. You can count on me.'

'I know that. You always were a good friend.'

Stumbling, falling, Alex was almost in the wagon and on the way to Southampton when a fire-fighter chose to inject humour into the day.

Smoke-stained and weary, the fire-fighter was rolling a length of hose onto a spool. Years later looking back on that day, Alex remembers fatigue and the fire-fighter's red-rimmed eyes and the British habit of making light of pain.

He remembers and is sorry.

Click! A Cockney voice rings out. 'Cor blimey, Yank, what happened to you?'

Alex remembers rocking on his heels, Bobby Rourke beside him promising to search for Adelia, to 'make it right,' and Joe Petowski - good old Joe, honour to the core - hauling Alex along.

The fire-fighter laughed. 'Ah, the good old Mucky Duck! What a place! A bed, a bottle of beer and a dirty little girl it's tailor-made for you Yanks. You can love 'em and leave 'em and none the wiser.'

Stupid remark! Casual and cruel it was a match to a fuse. Adelia burned to death in that stinking room and Alex to blame for letting it happen!

They had to claw him off the fire-fighter or there would have been another body in the morgue. As it was Joe

Petowski couldn't stand anymore and whump the lights went out. This time for good

Fourteen

Ordinary
August 2nd '42
US Marine Corps Recruit Depot
Parris Island, South Carolina

'And what the fuck d'you think you're doing, asshole?' The Corporal stood alongside the Chow Hall garbage cans.

Gabriel came to attention. 'Returnin' my mess tray, sir.'

'Why is there food still on the tray?'

'Can't eat it, sir.'

The Corporal took a pencil from his top pocket stirring the mess of congealed eggs. 'What d'you mean can't eat it?'

'Not feelin' hungry, sir.'

The Corporal tossed the pencil in the bin and hands on hips leaned forward, the stiff brim of his campaign hat scraping Gabriel's forehead. 'What has feeling to do with it? Since when did your feelings matter?'

'They don't, sir.'

'That's right, asshole, they don't and never will.'

Gabriel wasn't the only recruit at the garbage pail with food left. A dozen or more guys with a similar problem stood alongside the wall but they're okay, they enlisted through the right channels and not via the State Pen.

'Now listen up!' The Corporal strides centre of the Mess Hall. 'Though a mystery to me and always will be the Marine Corps loves you assholes. It's why the Corps goes to the trouble and expense of providing a healthy, nutritious breakfast. After so much trouble we expect you same assholes to be grateful and eat the nutritious breakfast. Am I right or am I right?'

'Aye, aye sir, you are right, sir!' Guys juggling rifles and mess-trays jump to.

'You bet I'm right. In this time of war you should be grateful for any kind of food never mind leaving it!' The Corporal heads back to Gabriel. 'And what do we find joining us this morning, some murdering ex-con brought out of Virginia Correctional Department and given a chance by the Marine Corps to serve his country instead of his time. Guess what? He's refusing to eat his food on account of he doesn't feel hungry. Now what do you other assholes think of that? Wouldn't you say that was against the spirit of the Marine Corps?'

'Aye, aye, sir, yes, sir, we would, sir!'

'That's what I thought. Now the British too long alone in this war have a poster going round that says waste not want not, give your leavings to the hogs. Seems to me the hog in question is here in this Mess Hall. So line up, assholes, and when the hog has finished his leftovers feed him yours.'

They lined up, the Corporal baring his teeth. 'That's it! By the time you're done this will be one sickly hog. He may never leave a morsel of food again.' He nodded to Gabriel. 'Okay, start with your own leavings.'

Gabriel picked up his fork.

'What are you doing?'

'Eatin' my leavins, sir.'

'Who said anything about a fork? I never mentioned a fork.' Enjoying himself, the Corporal turned to the queue. 'You assholes hear me mention a fork?'

'No, sir!'

'And why didn't I mention a fork?'

'Hogs don't use forks!'

'Correct. They slurp. So eat up, asshole, slurp up every fucking crumb.'

Gabriel slurped. Three trays later heavy with slimy bacon and other guy's spit he was gagging. Lucky for him the next recruit in line laughed.

'As you were!' The Corporal jabbed the guy. 'You find this amusing!'

'No, sir.'

'Bet your life you won't. Since you feel like laughing the rest of you assholes can down forks and slurp your own crap. Then every Man-jack will accompany me to the yard and rifle at port arms join the hog doubling round the square chanting a little song, 'I am not a man, I am not a Marine, I am a fucking hyena, an animal that laughs at things that aren't funny. This is the sound a hyena makes, Ha-Ha-Ha-Ha!'

~

That was Gabriel's first meal on Parris Island. The Corporal was right about one thing, he never left food again. No matter how bad the chow his mess tray shone. Not that trying to toe the line made a difference. First to last he is a pariah, a murderer judged to be dodging a rightful term in jail.

Pariah! Until Parris Island he didn't know what the word meant. Gunnery Sergeant Major JJ Emmet set him straight on the way to Fredericksburg.

'It's you,' he said. 'I don't want you in the Marine Corps. Current rookie assholes don't want you in the Marine Corps. Marines long dead and those still to die don't want you in the Marine Corps.' So saying he pulled the jeep to the side of the road. 'So why don't the guard undo the cuffs and then you can drag your ragged ass any direction other than to South Carolina.'

Seven years ago Fredericksburg's Sherriff made a similar offer. Gabriel didn't run then as he wouldn't now, and not because the guard accompanying them had the flap open on his holster. He refused because he's not a quitter.

The prison guard fastened the holster, Gunny started up the jeep, and on they went to Fredericksburg and Ma.

'How you holdin' out, son?' Face lined, Ma looked older than remembered. No use telling her how bad it's been. Always a good heart, how was she to know he was swapping one prison for another.

She'd made a pot roast. 'Pull up a chair,' she said to the guard. 'I didn't know there'd be two of you with my boy but that's alright, I made plenty.'

Gunny getting a whiff of pork and grits went along with it and had the guard remove the cuffs. 'Thank you kindly, ma'm, we'd be glad to set awhile.'

Poor Ma, a mix of fear and pride, her son joining the Marines she rattled away asking questions. 'Does this mean he'll never go back to jail?'

Gunny spooned his grits. 'The answer to that is in his hands.'

'But he's a good boy! His Pa was an awful brute. Nobody knows what he had to contend with. He should never have gone to jail.'

'Good or evil we all pay for our sins, ma'm. There can't be any choosing.'

'But him bein' a Marine, does it mean he's fightin' in Europe or someplace back of the world nothin' to do with you and me or any other American?'

The guard was too busy filling his face to comment. Gunny Emmet remained polite allowing Ma to keep her dreams, Gabriel was grateful for that.

'War is thrust upon us here in the USA as it was to other countries, Pearl Harbour saw to that. Whatever the situation rest assured the Marine Corps will take care of your boy as one of their own.'

That first morning slurping other guy's saliva Gabriel knew he'd replaced a jail sentence with a death sentence and if not by Japanese in the Pacific then at the hands of fellow recruits.

Parris Island was worse than the Pen. For a start there was no Charlie Whitefeather to soothe his pain. Awake night-after-night, his hands covered with blisters from sanding a deck Gabriel saw Charlie for the Guardian Angel he was. It's what he said that day in the Wood Shop. 'It was felt you needed a friend.' Asked who cared for a seventeen year-old kid he had smiled. 'Tsohanai, the Sun Bearer cares, or in your parlance the Lord Jesus Christ.'

At the time it made no sense, it still doesn't. For sure Private Gabriel H Templar needs someone to care. Gunny says he brings dishonour to the Corps. Rookies sharing the hut agree and after a week of paying for his sins took revenge with nightly Blanket Parties, ganging up when Gabriel was in his bunk and dragging him out across the floor.

Furious, a trapped animal kicking and scratching, seeing them no better than Boss-Man and crew, Gabriel gave as good as he got until they dropped back.

Faces battered they circled him. 'Why are you still here?' says one, 'when it's obvious you don't want to be?'

'Yeah,' said another. 'Do us all a favour and run because with you here this hut will always be in the shit.'

0345 hours the following morning was the usual bunk-junk inspection. Nothing was said of newly acquired black eyes. Silently endorsing the nightly attacks the Corporal carried on as before, every man's rifle the filthiest ever seen, what were they but a bunch of clowns, consequently they were all to 'join the Corporal on the square imitating the action of a duck,' which meant squatting, rifle braced back of the neck and waddling from one end of the square to the next.

A fortnight of that it's a wonder the rookies didn't Deep-Six Gabriel into Ribbon Creek. Were it not for Gunny's pony they might well have.

Billy-Bob was a rundown hack with no other purpose than to hobble up and down howling with toothache. That was some abscess! Gabriel could see the poison bubbling and feel the pain zigzagging from the donkey's jaw to its brain.

The noise brought complaints. Officer's wives and their young babies kept up nights Gunny was forced to take a gun to it.

That say guys were hanging out windows cheering. 'Hooyah! That fucking pony is finally gonna get it!' Gabriel was doing push-ups in the square, first in combat gear and then in states of undress carrying a rife and chanting, 'my rifle is my best friend. I am a miserable sonofabitch, God have mercy on my soul.'

Gun cocked, Gunny was lined up ready to fire.

'Hey!' Gabriel came running. 'You don't need to do that.'

Eyes popping, Gunny turned. 'You talking to me, asshole?'

'Your pony's got a rotten tooth. It's why he's yellin'!' Gabriel prized the pony's mouth open, put his hand in and pulled. Out came the biggest, rottenest stump. 'I don't know why no one saw it. It's been drivin' him crazy.'

Gunny was scarlet. Mortified, he snatched the tooth. 'And you, asshole, are driving me crazy! Get back on that square and drop another fifty.'

That night everyone slept including Gabriel. Next day he was called to the office Gunny fiddling with a pen. 'How did you know about the toothache?'

For a moment he thought of lying but then shrugged, how much worse could it get. 'Billy-Bob told me.'

'What d'you mean told?'

'He told me of his pain. I heard him.'

'And how did you do that?'

'I don't know, sir. I always hear it with critters.'

'They tell you when they're sick?'

'And where.' Gabriel tried to explain. 'I hear it and I see it as smoke hangin' over the pain. I see it with people too, like the Corporal's guts ache.'

Gunny sniffed. 'The Corporal is a guts ache.'

'He's got ulcers. He should go see the medic before they explode.'

Hustled out, Gabriel didn't get beyond that. A week later it was rumoured the Corporal was in hospital with a busted ulcer. The following day Gunny Emmet sent for him again. 'Front and centre, asshole, you're coming with me.'

Next he knows he's in married quarters looking down at a tiny little woman curled up in a chair. 'This lady is my wife,' says Gunny. 'She heard about you and Billy-Bob and wants to know if you can tell what's wrong with her.'

Gunny held up his hand. 'And before you open your trap you should know you're here against my wishes. I'd sooner shoot you than have you coming through that door but my wife is ill and so for the next ten minutes you're a person not an asshole. After that it's Hut 23 and an asshole again. Breathe a word to anyone about this and you're a dead asshole.

'What do you want me to do?'

'I want you, if you can, to tell me what's wrong with me, Private Templar,' says the wife, 'and don't worry about JJ and his mouth. He's just scared for me.'

Gabriel didn't know what was going on but thinking she is the same as anyone else leaned down. Her so tiny and him so tall it was a heck of a way to lean so he got on his knees. 'Where did you say the pain was ma'm?'

'Here.' She touched her breast. 'I wake up with it and I go to sleep with it. Maybe you can set my mind at rest one way or the other.'

Gunny breathing down his neck Gabriel reached out. A hard grey lump crawling out from under her left arm he could see the problem.

'Is it okay if I touch you here?'

'You go ahead.' Behind him Gunny opened his mouth. Mrs Emmet flicked him a look. 'One word JJ and I'll never forgive you. I have to know what it is even if it's not good news. So hush up and let the boy concentrate.'

Gabriel didn't need to concentrate. It was cancer octopus. He's seen them before in a dog's leg and another time in a lady's stomach. Nasty things, they're darn near impossible to shift but occasionally if he can get a tentacle loose the rest decide to leave go for a while.

'Can you see it?' she says.

'Yes, ma'm.'

'Is it what I think it is?'

'I think so.'

'Oh, dear Lord!'

'We could try pushin' it back awhile.'

'Pushing it back?'

'In time.'

'In time?'

'Yes, ma'm.'

'You mean it would give me more time?'

'I hope so.'

'How far do you think we could push?'

'I don't know. Maybe ten years?'

She smiled. 'Ten years would be wonderful.' She closed her eyes and Gabriel closed his and gave his hands to whatever bit of God might be listening.

~

No one asked where he went that day or why but something was said and from that day on, the dummy in Hut 23 being some kind of ghoul, distance between him and other rookies was impossible to cross.

They quit beating him out his bunk at nights and there was a general easing up of sanding decks but the silent treatment continued.

A hut full of men, none better or worse and yet Private GH Templar was alone. Always a quiet boy now he is the silence existing within a wall of anger. Muscles rippling, his body couldn't be more honed. Running, boxing and shooting he did what Marines do and with nothing else to take his attention was better than most. Cut off from his feelings and with no one to talk to he was no more than block of wood.

Maybe that's how he came to help Mrs Emmet, all feeling locked up inside she gave a place for it to go. Fortnight later he found a note in his locker. He was staring at it when Gunny marched in, snatched the note from his hand, and read it out the rest of the hut with gaping mouths.

*'Dear Private First Class Templar. Thank you for the
consideration shown to me and my husband. You behaved like a
gentleman. I have felt better this last week the octopus lessening
in size. I don't know if this is due to you or as Gunny Emmett
insists lucky coincidence, whatever way I believe the new and
un-hoped for ten years may well be achieved. I understand your
unit is due to leave soon for places unknown. I wish you well
and hope you come through this terrible war sound of mind and
body. Yours faithfully, Jean Emmet.*

PS. Congratulations on your promotion.

Gunny then set fire to the note, watched it burn and then
ground it to ash under his boot. 'What the fuck are you
assholes staring at!' he roared. 'If gawping at a man's
private mail is all you got to do I suggest you get out on the
square and start pumping. As for you, PFC Templar, you
are to proceed to utilities where you will collect certain
changes to your attire. Once you've done that you will
rejoin the assholes out on the square.'

~

PFC Templar? Private First Class! Promotion coming out
the blue like that it took Gabriel's breath away as did
Gunny Emmet reading the letter out loud. It was a weird
thing to do, kind of like nailing his colours to the mast.

The rest of the hut were not happy and didn't miss a
chance to let him know.

Thursday, knowing they're soon to ship out Gabriel sat
on his bunk cleaning his rifle. A good shot even as a boy his
scorecard on the Ranges was A-1 and better by the fact he
aimed at a paper target rather than flesh and blood.

A rookie, a bit of a tough guy, stood watching. 'Say, Templar!' He moved closer. 'You are some kind of weird guy healing donkeys and all.'

Gabriel ignored him.

'Now you're promoted Private First Class.' The guy pressed on. 'D'you ever wonder how you got this far.'

Still Gabriel sat quiet.

'Private First Class in six weeks? Wow!? Keep that up and you'll be sporting pips before the year is out. Seems to me you might need to learn to read then or at least sign your name. How else will you know to draw your pay?'

'Seems to me you need to mind your own business,' said Gabriel

The rookie leapt back. 'It speaks! What do you know, all this time and us thinking it mute! It must be true. The Marine Corps makes the man!'

The words were no more than an irritating buzz in his ear but then the rookie stretched out his finger pushing the rifle barrel aside. 'Say, dummy, I'm talking to you. I'm trying to understand how out of all us sharp-shooters you're the one gets promoted. What did you do to get it? Did you suck Emmet's horny dick? There must've been something got you through.'

Still Gabriel sat quiet but he kept on pushing. 'I'm wondering if it was the love-letter Gunny Emmet's old lady sent. What d'you do that she calls you gent? Did you give her the finger of fun up her dried up old crack?'

Gabriel hates pointing fingers. They remind him of Pa.

Wrenching the finger back he threw the rookie down. Then stepped on him and boot planted deep in his chest aimed the rifle between his eyes.

'What was that you were saying?'

Nobody moved.

Gabriel's finger hooked about the trigger. 'I asked you. What was that?'

The rookie on the floor daren't speak.

'Let him up, buddy,' a guy mutters. 'It don't need to go this far.'

'What did you say to me?' Gabriel didn't lift his head. 'Did you just address Private First Class Gabriel H Templar as buddy or did I imagine it?'

Silence. Gabriel's finger tightened.

Palms upward, the speaker stepped away. 'No excuse, PFC Templar.'

'None at all?'

'None.'

'And you on the floor? Somethin' you want to say?'

The guy rolled his eyes. 'No, PFC Templar.'

'Anythin' you're might be sayin' in the future?'

'No, sir, nothing.'

'You sure of that?'

'Yes sir, PFC Templar, sure and certain.'

Gabriel sat down at his bunk and began stripping the rifle down again.

~

That night he lay gazing up at the ceiling wondering if he'd ever be happy. Seven years in jail and now this! Simeon Smith used to say we live the life we've earned. Gabriel can't think what he did to earn this. Last night he dreamed he was outside the Eyrie and his little gal inside wandering from room to room calling out for help. He wanted to help but the Eyrie locked him out. He couldn't get in and all the while he could hear her stumbling about inside.

He'd never been so scared! 'Stay put!' he yells. 'I'll come and get you.' But every door locked and barred he couldn't help her and woke shivering.

Stupid dreams! This world or the next he'll never find that girl because she doesn't exist. He's here in this world alone and that's all there is to it.

He sat with his head in his hands. Somehow he's got to stop being seen as weird. Healing hands, Billy-Bob's toothache and Mrs Emmet's cancer, that kind of stuff gets him into trouble. Same with his love of wood! So he whittled dolls and animals that folk said looked as though they were alive? It doesn't mean anything. He is a dumb asshole and always was. The sooner he gets used to that the sooner he gets through this war.

He misses his little gal. She's always on his mind, him feeling as though he is seeing through her eyes and feeling her joy and pain. It's like he has another pair of eyes that are able to follow wherever she goes.

But what's the use of that? It doesn't help. She doesn't help! She never has! It's best she leaves now and never comes back!

With that he leapt from the bunk and ran out into the square. Head back and arms outstretched he looked up to the sky, the heavens ablaze with stars.

'Go away, Little Gal, and never come back!' he yells. 'I don't want you! I never wanted you! I was born alone and I'm gonna die alone!'

Then he went back to his bunk and slept.

......and dreamed he was on a ship heading into harbour, sunlight striking the Statue of Liberty making a living fire of her torch.

In the dream he stood at the rail with other passengers. He was seeing through a woman eyes and thinking her thoughts and feeling her heart beating. Scared and excited she was gazing down onto the quay looking for her man. There were other women aboard kiddies holding onto their skirts. They did the same, looked down at the many faces as those on the quay gazed up.

A band is playing and flags flutter in the breeze, the Stars and Stripes flying alongside the British Union Jack. Then suddenly he is one of the men gazing up and it's him Gabriel, kitted out in best blue Marine jacket, and cap under his arm running his hand over his head checking the buzz-cut.

A wave on an ocean, he shifts back and forth with other men, a thought running through his head, I'm here! Look down and see me!

His little gal is on that ship but she doesn't see him. Beautiful, her face pensive, she is searching for another. Gabriel's not the reason she is on that ship anymore than he was the reason she was on the Tall Ship, sails billowing, that brought her to America so long ago.

Groaning, he turned in sleep and again he is at the Harbour and again in uniform, but this time a different uniform, a grey swallow-tail jacket embroidered with gold braid and he's carrying a sword.

Anxious to look his best he removes his cap and smoothes his hair.

She looks down toward the quay and sees him and curtseys.

'Rosamund,' he says. 'I thought you would never come.'

'I know,' she said, the dream fading. 'I told you I was here and that you needed to look. I'm still here but you don't want me and so I'll say goodbye.'

She was gone slipping away into night.

'No!' Realising he's made a mistake Gabriel shouted out in sleep, 'Come back! Please come back! I miss you so much!'

She was moving away, the ship and the girl retreating into distance until they were a tiny gleaming dot on the horizon.

'No!' Fear grabbed him. 'I can't let you go!'

He knew if the ship kept going, if the dot blinked out, he would never find her again, and with that fear raging he rolled out his body and began to run.

Another Gabriel stayed behind, the flesh and blood asshole who all his life wanted to be like everyone else slept on. An ordinary man, now he is like everyone else, he has a single heart where once were two.

Fifteen
Bobbie's Girl
Annexe: St Faiths Hospital.
Needham, Suffolk

What a week! Bobby's been running around like a fool.

After the wagon hauled Alex and the Polack away he stole the abandoned motor bike and took off to the hospital. The doctor wouldn't let him in, 'if he wanted to help he should check on Miss Challoner's dog. She's calling for him.'

The dog was dead the cottage hit in the raid. It was never much of a place. Now it's rubble. Poor critter, the dog was under a table among the remains of the kitchen. The chickens copped it too but a fox got in and with only feathers left Bobby buried the dog and then tried retrieving some of her belongings.

Back he went to St Faiths to a basement lock-up filled with gaga old women.

Pale as death, a mauve orchid bruise blooming behind her left ear she lay staring into nothing. But for the lump on her head you would think she was okay. Two minutes and you knew she was anything but.

One moment a beautiful, intelligent woman, the next a crazy person talking to shadows, there had been a splitting of personalities.

She knew Bobby. 'Hello, Lieutenant Rourke.'

He couldn't bring himself to mention the dog. She knew anyway, saw it in his eyes. 'Poor Lochie! I wish I'd been there with him.'

She enquired of Bobby's leg. He said forget his leg, how was she? Tears in her eyes, she said, 'I wish I could tell you. I don't seem to know.' They hustled him out after that. When he looked back nurses were fitting safety rails to her bed.

Back at the Air-Base war was ongoing. It was three days before he got to visit again. He dropped by that evening to a bit of a fuss. Her bed was empty. She'd gone walkabout in her nightclothes and he learned not for the first time!

'She's looking for her feller.' A woman in the next bed pipes up.

'Lookin' for her feller?'

'Her husband. It's why she goes to the church. They were married there.'

Guessing the old woman meant St Giles he went looking. There was she was sitting in a broken pew gazing at a gap in the wall. He sat alongside. It was a warm evening but she was trembling. When he draped his jacket about her shoulders she turned eyes like the moon. 'Isn't it a wonderful window?'

There wasn't a window. There was a patch of sky with stars shining through.

'It's the work of John Thornton,' she says. 'He designed the York Minster window. See the Latin inscription, *Omnia*

Vincit Amor? 'Love Conquers All' That says it all, don't you think.'

Bobby saw the emptiness in her gaze and thought if he had any hope of winning her love then he must conquer the devil.

~

Today he's away early from the Base and made straight for the Annexe. The nurses were making up an empty bed. One of the old ladies had died a sheeted corpse being lowered into a tin box and trundled away.

Dee was asleep and the safety rails round the bed still in place.

He asked at the desk if she was any better.

The nurse sniffed. 'Your guess is as good as mine.'

'What does that mean?'

'It means if she isn't better it's her own fault. She will keep wandering off. It's why we put up rails. We haven't time to keep watch on one patient.'

'Why does she wander?'

'I don't know! Maybe she's looking for her reputation.'

Bloody hell! Bobby was furious. What a thing to say and Dee lying there!

Seeing his face and sensing trouble another nurse spoke up.

'Adelia was upset earlier. She remembered her dog had died.'

'Has the big guy been to see her yet, Covington Wright?'

'Mr Covington Wright is away.'

'Has no one else seen her? No specialist?'

'The psychiatrist was with her yesterday talking about the Black Swan.'

'The Black Swan!' The bitch nurse sniggered. 'You mean Needham Knocking Shop, don't you?'

'What is your problem?' Bobby rounded on her. 'What does it matter what the place is called? People died there! And if some guy hadn't got her out she would've died. I know. I was there.'

'Were you?' The bitch eyed him. 'Then you probably saw him.'

'Saw who?'

'The Yank she was with.'

'I saw lots of Yanks!' He was cagey then, minding his words and trying to look ahead. 'Who do you mean in particular?'

'The one who left her to die.'

'Left her to die?'

'It's what's being said.'

'And is it what Nurse Challoner said?'

'She doesn't say anything. According to her she doesn't know anything. He's a Mystery Man, the Yank that never was, who didn't take her to the Mucky Duck and who didn't have his way, and who when the bomb fell whoosh,' she flicked her fingers, 'vanished in the morning mist like a wonderful dream.'

'You find her situation amusin'?'

The bitch shrugged. 'I'm just saying she doesn't remember him.'

'You shouldn't be saying anything.' The other nurse intervened. 'You don't know what happened and shouldn't be making assumptions.'

'Damn right she shouldn't!' said Bobby. 'Bad-mouthin' the girl as she's lyin' there with no one to defend her? You ought to be ashamed.'

'Well, I'm not,' says the bitch. 'She's the one making assumptions thinking we would swallow her story. Amnesia my foot! That girl really fancied herself. She thought she was a cut above us and that's why she's making such a fuss. She got caught with her knickers down and doesn't like it.'

Though aching to slug the bitch Bobby held off. Something was coming and he needed to know the facts. 'Are you sayin' she's suffering from amnesia?'

'I'm saying what she's saying, that she doesn't know what happened, not the chap's name or what he looked like or how she got there. It's all gone.'

~

Amnesia was the case. A block of time has gone awol in Dee's head beginning 31st of July with the buzzer beeping in the Broom Cupboard door and ending with her regaining consciousness here in Faiths.

How his conscience wrestled with that! Is this a gift from heaven or what? Is the Good Lord – or the Devil depending how you see it – offering a pot of gold at the end of an extremely dodgy rainbow and is the plan still up and running?

Bobby began to dig his fortifications. He started with Dee's friend, Nora Jackson, asking her to do a little shopping for a robe and other female bits.

Nora wasn't keen. 'Why are you doing this? What do you hope to gain?'

'I want her to like me.' He tried telling the truth for a change. 'She lost all her stuff in the raid. She needs to get better and lyin' about in hospital nightgowns doesn't help. You don't have to say I paid! You can say you bought them.'

'That won't do,' says Norah. 'She knows me and Bert don't have the money.'

'You could say you won a bit the pools.'

She laughed and then strong on old fashioned values she frowned. 'I don't like telling fibs but if it helps to make her better I suppose it's okay.'

As it turned out the win on the pools gambit grew legs and trotted round to Christmas '45 to be useful. In the summer of '42 Bobby saw it a way of helping them both. Next time visit she wore the new robe and her hair had been washed. She looked her beautiful self. She was also strapped to the chair.

'What is this?' he asked the bitch nurse. 'Why is she locked in?'

'Because despite the rails she wandered away again last night and came back with her feet cut to ribbons.'

'Christ!' Things are beginning to look bad. 'Where did she go?'

'The Aunt's cottage or what's left of it. The police fetched her back. She needs to get a grip. Keep this up and they'll lock her away.'

He stayed most of that day. She seemed quite sensible. Then she said she'd seen her dog. 'I went for a walk last night.'

'So I heard. You need to stop that Dee or they'll think you're crazy.'

'They already do.' Shoulders thin under the nightgown she shrugged. 'I saw Lochie. He was in the meadow chasing a ball.'

'Dee!'

'Yes, with Aunt Maud.' Tears flashing she smiled. 'It's alright, Lieutenant. I'm not crazy or rather I'm trying not to be. I did see him but a young Lochie and a very young Maud with roses in her hair so I think it safe to say I dreamt it.'

He took her hand. 'Better yet say nothin'. This isn't the kindest of places.'

'Bless you.' She squeezed his hand. 'You are a good man. And brave too! I saw you drag those chaps from the plane. Such a courageous thing to do!'

'What!' How he stared.

'The undercarriage was jammed and the fuselage on fire wasn't it and yet you stayed to get your radio operator out.'

'How do you know about that?'

'Didn't you tell me?'

No way! No goddamn way did he tell her anything about the crash! So how does she know? Baffled, he shrugged. 'Any guy would've done the same.'

'Yes but not everyone did. And there was the poor girl in the Black Swan with her hair and shoulders so terribly burnt. You got her out.'

Bobby was reeling. No one knows about that girl as no one knows it was he that got Dee out. Continually covering his ass he hasn't told anyone.

How does she know these things? Then eyelids fluttering and fists clenched as though trying to force her way up through mud she fell back on the bed, symptoms he learned to recognise as the sign of a seizure.

'Where was I?' Then, her glance anxious she frowned. 'What were we talking about, Lieutenant?'

'Nothin' much.' Wanting to calm things down he moved the conversation to safer ground. 'Say Dee, now that positions are reversed, you the patient and me the Doc, do you think you might call me Bobby?'

'I'd love to. Thank you, Bobby.'

That was the final hit of Cupid's Arrow. If he was in love before the sound of his name on her lips and his heart was hers forever.

He rode back to the Base knowing it didn't matter how this tangle came about or the lies he needed to tell, he would do what was necessary to keep her.

Now most mornings returning from night raid he heads for the Annexe and soon if he's not pushing trolleys and feeding the old ladies he's walking in the gardens holding Dee's hand and trying to stop her floating away, because say the word and she would float, and no one, not even the man she forgot would be able to pull her back.

They walk and other than offer comfort to her soul he doesn't say much.

Yesterday brought comfort to his soul, news filtering through how at 0800 hours Ash Hunter was on his way to Dieppe and who knows another bomb.

It's been tough keeping him away. You wouldn't credit the phone calls. The latest call was to thank Bobby, 'and to ask if something should come up, anything at all, you will let me or my folks know.'

The man doesn't get it! He just doesn't seem to understand that as far as Alex Hunter is concerned - no more Ash, too familiar and too close to home —the woman is dead and buried!

So many calls and if not from him then from Petowski! The clerk at the Base was for putting Bobby on a charge. 'Don't you Yanks read notices? What does it say up there? No personal calls going out or coming in!'

Every day was the same, first from the hospital where Alex was getting the burns to his hands treated and then from the camp in Southampton. It's like he was deaf and couldn't, or wouldn't, hear what was being said.

'No point in coming down here,' Bobby would say. 'I told you, bodies brought out from that wreck were burned beyond recognition.'

'Then how do you know it was her?'

Bobby improvised. 'By the butterfly buckle on the belt she used to wear! I recognised it. It was scorched black. It looks like she was trying to get dressed when the hotel was hit again.'

'Oh, my God, my poor baby!'

His voice! You'd think his belly had been ripped open and his guts dragged out. A dangerous moment! Overwhelmed by guilt Bobby wavered but God or the Devil intervened again and time's up, the operator cutting them off.

Every day a call! Bobby thought he would go crazy. He had to answer every one! If he hadn't Dieppe or not the guy would've come down. As it was Alex was getting Petowski to ring every hospital within a hundred miles asking if they had a patient by name of Adelia Challoner.

Naturally, his first port of call was St Faiths. Then it only needed one person to say 'she's here' and it would have been all over. It didn't happen. Once again mystery intervened in the miserable face and shape of a Night Sister.

Bobby heard about it from the ambulance driver. The morning of the bomb he was making his way into the hospital when the driver recognised him.

'Hey, mate! I dropped your girl off earlier!'

Bobby said he was trying to locate her.

'You'll find her in that shit-hole in the basement. Night Sister put her there,' he says. 'Miserable cow! If she's an angel of mercy give me the other kind.'

The driver went on to say that when he and his ambulance arrived A&E was a madhouse. 'Doctors running about and dead and wounded everywhere it was mayhem. I carried your girl in. Then some woman runs after me waving a bra and wanting to put it on your girl. Bloke's eyes popping it caused a traffic jam. Then old misery guts loses her temper and tells a porter to take your girl away. She didn't bother properly admitting her, didn't write her name down or anything just shunted her along to where they keep the old folk.'

That's how it went, Dee hidden where no one could find her. It's possible they meant to move her but seeing the luck of it Bobby fought to keep her there and overnight became a nurse's helper fetching and carrying for his girl.

His girl! The ambulance driver referred to Dee as Bobby's girl so that's how he sees her. Why not? She is his girl. He saved her from death, no one else!

Now with Hunter out the picture he plans to get her moved to a private hospital. She needs specialist help. Forget the cost! What's money for if not to help his future wife.

Bobby sighed. Every day he's knocking himself out trying to find out what she knows about that night and yet it seems she genuinely doesn't remember.

It's strange. People have told her she was with a GI. Bobby being another GI you'd think she'd enquire of him. She doesn't ask anything. It's as if she can't bear to speak of the man fencing him and the day off in her mind as sacred.

They say you only fall in love once that the rest is a copy. Bobby doesn't plan to be a copy. That maybe okay for some but not for him. It does seem he's making ground, the bombastic Lieutenant of yesterday who pissed in a bottle and kept babies awake becoming a thing of the past.

The making of a New Man is not that hard to do. Due to her injury Dee often loses small amounts of time, people and things sucked away into nothing, and so she is never too certain of anything. On the right day he could say the moon is made of blue cheese and she wouldn't argue.

He's been asking around about amnesia. Is it short-term and can it last forever? The history of WW1 is everything about amnesia and shell-shock and how whole personalities were wiped clean overnight.

God forbid that happens to Dee. While he'd love the day in question to stay lost to lose more of the essential woman would be a loss indeed.

Ducking and weaving takes its toll. Though consumed by Dee he's still Baby Rourke and still rampant. Last night the Base ran a concert in the commissary, guys dressed as women kicking their legs in the air, and Oh Yummy there she is, a new NAFFI girl behind the bar.

Cute and with perky tits Bobby moved in and after much persuading managed to get her number. He wants Dee like no other but the right way and that means marriage. He can't take liberties. She's too fragile. They walk together her arm through his. He aches to kiss her but keep off the grass is the thought. Now with this new barmaid, and/or Lady M in tow he can siphon off excess energy.

Incidentally, there is something up with Mildred. She talks a lot of the future '*and what they're goin' to do in America.*' She says if she were to leave Lord F wouldn't fight it. 'Ronnie is first and last a gentleman. His family don't do divorce and so he'll probably quietly hang himself.'

Naturally, she was joking but he isn't taking chances. His dick maybe leaning toward her but his feet are definitely pointing in the opposite direction.

~

Friday lunch time he is again at St Faiths feeding mush to an old girl when the Big Chief and his entourage appear. Bobby asked if he might have a word.

The guy gave him the fish eye. 'And who exactly are you?'

'A friend of Dee's.'

'Dee?'

'Miss Challoner. I met her when I was in with a busted leg.'

'That was you, was it, the noisy chap in the Broom Cupboard? I didn't recognize you. It's the uniform and the gold braid. It does blind one so. And how is the leg? Are you still upright?'

'Chipper thanks.' Sarcastic old sod! 'It sticks now and then but it'll do until I get Stateside and decent Medicare.'

'No doubt. So you want a word?'

'If you don't mind.'

He nods and the entourage fades away. 'You're not he that decamped are you?' he says, suspicious. 'Not returned to survey the damage?'

'No, sir, I am not! Last I heard the guy was on his way to France.'

'Ah yes, American GIs, the bold and the brave intrepid seekers of new frontiers. What would our poor little island do without you?'

Bobby was tempted to say you'd probably sink but he kept quiet. This is the Big Man around here. If he's to get Dee out of Faiths he needs him onside.

'It is our pleasure to serve, sir.'

'Mm, yes. And the other chap? I understand he was an American.'

'I heard a rumour to that effect.'

The Doc stared over steel-rimmed specs. 'And did you hear that this particular specimen of the bold and brave leapt out the window of a hotel leaving that girl to burn to death?'

The contempt stung. The thing is Bobby takes what happened personally. It shook his soul. Alex was always the good guy. If it should turn out he did abandon her it would be like being let down by Abraham Lincoln.

Covington Wright sniffed. 'I'm told you spend time with Miss Challoner.'

'I come when I can.'

'You'll have to excuse me. I see the pretty badges on your jacket but have no idea what they mean. What is it you do exactly?'

'I'm with Eighth Bomber Command. I steer Wellington heavyweights above and about the German skies exactly.'

'Dangerous work.'

'As you say dangerous.'

'Well, I can't talk to you. You are not a relative and therefore not entitled to know. More importantly I have been in London and am new to the case. I can tell you the blow to her head was severe and that such trauma is likely to have long-term ramifications. Does she have family?'

'Her parents were killed in a motor accident in '34. There was an aunt but she died. She has friends at Barts.'

'You seem to know a little of her history.'

'We pass the time of day.'

'And in passing does she ever mention the man in question, name, rank and serial number?'

'Not to me.'

'Nor to anyone. When asked she declares a memory block. As yet I haven't had chance to speak to her and can't say yay or nay to anything other than the old adage time alone will tell. Did you know the man?'

Guessing the old boy figuring on sending out a search party Bobby played dumb. 'He wasn't anyone I knew. A friend of a friend, I heard.'

'Not that you'd tell me if you did know.'

'Why wouldn't I tell you?' Bobby was miffed. 'I hate the way she was left! I couldn't have done it. I'd sooner die.'

In that moment Bobby's feelings showing there was a softening of attitude, the Doc recognising an ally. 'She's going to need a lot of care. There's bound to be complications some of which will lay hidden for years. She needs support which I'm sorry to say she doesn't always get.' He peered around. 'It's certain she can't stay down here. It's completely the wrong atmosphere. '

'Damn right she can't! I know this is an old hospital but come on! She deserves better.'

The man's face tightened. 'We all deserve better! Believe me, had I the funds I'd tear the hospital down never mind the Annexe. But this is wartime and unlike your Country we've been at war some time, and as you pointed out we don't have decent Medicare. We do the best we can with what we have.'

'And is this the best you can do for Adelia Challoner?'

'It is not! And a situation I hope to rectify!' Then thinking he'd said too much Covington Wright shut up shop. 'Very well then.'

Entourage gathering he was on the move. 'Stay in touch, Flight Lieutenant. ' He paused at the door. 'Keep up the good work over Germany and here at St Faiths and you'll get your reward, whatever that is.'

~

Bobby has seen a way to get Dee out of St Faiths. Nora Jackson has friends looking to rent an apartment above their shop. He went along to view and by greasing a few palms, paying key money and adjusting the rent, got a promise on the Let.

Poor visibility Monday meant all bombing raids were off. He nabbed along to the Annexe. They've gotten used to him there. They see him always cracking jokes and they think nothing gets him down. Well, sometimes he's up and sometimes not. Truth is he's worn out and should be in his bunk right now getting some sleep but another night of listening to guys farting and crying in their sleep is too much. Feet on a stool and flying jacket wrapped round his head he'd sooner sit in the Annexe listening to old ladies doing the same.

It's a shitty place but companionable and while he's here Dee can't go walkabout. If she's to get signed out she doesn't want to be visiting ruined churches. Covington Wright is not keen to sign her out. He suggests she has a room in the Nurses Home for a while.

Bobby said okay then two weeks there and after that she's an apartment waiting. 'It's above a bakery. Fresh bread every day and normality.'

The guy hummed and hawed and then finally agreed. 'But keep a close eye on her. The majority opinion is that she should be sectioned and undergo psychiatric treatment. I am against it but I am the only one.'

Then he'd stared at Bobby. 'Of course if you two were married we wouldn't be having this conversation. She'd be out of here and the situation entirely in your hands. A responsibility, wouldn't you say?'

Bobby does say! A special licence could be managed but look at her staring into space. She's dreaming of her errant lover and while that happens it's too soon for anyone to talk of marriage and judging Alex's ring forever squashed in her fist it may be too late.

His only hope is that Alex Hunter, and for that matter every other male on the planet will sooner or later find a stray bullet.

Sixteen

Unresolved
October '42.
Needham Village.

Adelia dreams she is getting married. It is a familiar dream
and pathetic in that she always seems to be begging for love
and with a choice of men!

While dreaming she knows everything about them and
adores them both. She wakes and they are gone and sanity
with them.

After the air-raid the dream changed, the same wedding
dress, roses and scarlet cushions, but now the blue-eyed
man has wounds to the palms of his hands. As for her silver-
eyed lover he no longer kneels at the altar but a
Michelangelo statue rather than a person he stands apart.

The church too is different. It used to be pre-war St
Giles the window blazing in the sun. Now a Madonna
stands before an unknown altar, her painted face cracked
and worn.

Surfacing from such dreams is torment. She crawls
through red-hot lava and wakes to hostile faces and to the
general opinion that she is 'putting it on.'

She would love to tell them to try living with the pain in her head and to see how they like it but knowing they don't give a damn she stays quiet.

It's not all bad news. Today instead of waking to a poster warning that 'talking costs lives' she wakes to a window overlooking a cherry tree and canary yellow curtain fluttering in the breeze. Nora Jackson found this little haven. Two rooms and bath over a bakery in the High Street it is small but after a fortnight of shouting and slamming doors anything is preferable to the Nurses Home.

She moved in last week, not that there was much to move, most of her things lost in the raid. The flat comes furnished and with Toby, the cat as sitting tenant. 'Chuck him out if you want. We won't take offence,' says Edna James, a lady with a sweet smile and a kind, if a little inquisitive, manner whose husband, Ted, bakes bread at five in the morning sending a gorgeous yeasty smell up through the floorboards.

'You'll be alright here,' says Ted James. 'We won't interfere with you. Just keep an eye on the shop at night and make sure the bugs don't bite.'

Immaculate counter and scoured ovens there are no bugs. Such things are back in the Annexe where before the war bodies were wrapped for the morgue. Awful place! Ten minutes and one is desperate to get out, a feeling of being in an abandoned bus-shelter waiting for a bus that will never come.

The porters have a name for it. They call it the Bin. 'It's what you do with rubbish,' said Mrs Samuels in the next bed. 'You chuck it away.'

Damp and poorly ventilated it is more a store-room than a hospital ward, the beds pushed so close together your nightmares are your neighbour's and vice versa. Every night Adelia relives the bombing of the Black Swan waking every morning to a mind swept clean. Sometimes she shares dreams that don't belong to her. They belong to corpses so long forgotten they needed a ticket on the toe to be recognised; they and their memories of home ride round and round the ceiling like aging children on Hobby-Horses.

The word is once in you don't get out. The old ladies sit gazing into nothing. One can't help feeling they, poor dears, need tags on their toes so St Peter will know them when they arrive.

Adelia said as much to the Senior Registrar when he sprang a surprise visit. Mr Covington Wright is known for arriving on a Ward any time of day or night. Nurses dread his visits. There is a tale of him dressed as Santa Claus in red wellies and white beard scrubbing Theatre sterilising units on Christmas Day.

He came to Buttercup once. Two in the morning Adelia heard a noise and saw polished brogues sticking out from under a cot, CW mending the brakes.

The day he came to the Annexe she was nauseous and about to vomit lurched up to a bowl shoved under her nose. The curtains were pulled but missing several hooks they sagged heavily. It was too much for Adelia. She burst into tears. 'Why don't you just drop a bomb on us,' she cried, 'then you won't need to pretend you care!'

CW drew a chair alongside. 'I care.'

'What?'

'I said I care.'

'I'm sorry about shouting,' she said. 'I meant to think that rather than say it.'

'So I gathered.' He folded his arms. 'What are you doing here?'

'I was hurt in an air-raid.'

'And?' Eyebrows raised he urged her on.

'That's it. That's all I know. It appears I am somewhat confused.'

'Indeed.' Though smiling she could tell he was livid, the Annexe the bane of his life and skewed curtains one indignity too many.

'Right,' he said. 'I've been away but I'm back. So let's sit awhile and take stock, you endeavouring to be less confused and me catching up on details.'

She apologised again. He tutted. 'Forget apologies, stick with the day and simple needs like a clean nightgown and a change of bed linen, and curtains that swish and the safety rails on this bed removed immediately!'

'Excuse me, sir,' a nurse hovered. 'Matron says they are to stay. The patient might wander and fall.'

'And has she wandered?'

'Yes, sir.'

'And did she wander far?'

'Yes, sir, once to St Giles and then to the village and then....'

He cut her short. 'And in any of her wanderings did she fall?'

'Not that I know of.'

'Then the rails come down.'

They came down. Caught between Matron and CW the nurse couldn't win and afterward made her feelings known by clattering bedpans.

Adelia's standing in the hospital was never high. After his visit she was on the bottom rung. He complained, saying as a nurse she should've been shown the respect due to a member of the nursing team and if not given a private room then a Ward matching her situation. Now, resented by nursing staff, especially Matron who sees all criticism as a personal slur Adelia is up against it.

Nora says she needs to forget St Faiths and get a new life. Lieutenant Rourke agrees. 'Look ahead, honey. The future is what counts.' She would like to oblige but is boxed in by questions. What kind of man takes a girl to a hotel for sex and dumps her in the middle of an air-raid? And why did she go with him?

So many questions crammed into twenty-four hours no wonder she searches for answers. Mr Covington Wright says she will get her memory back one day. But does she want it? Men and women burned to death and she left to burn with them it would be a kindness to forget forever.

Mrs Samuels, the patient in the next bed says she's blocking pain. 'You're blocking the man you love and will keep blocking until he is forgiven.'

That first day regaining consciousness Adelia tried sitting up in bed but hadn't the strength. She asked a nurse what had happened and how she got there and received a withering reply. 'I haven't the faintest idea.'

Clara Samuels was more kind. 'You were hurt in a raid.'

'A raid?' Adelia was confused. 'When did it happen? Was it on Buttercup Ward? Were any of the children hurt? Was it near my Aunt's cottage because if so my dog is there! Has anyone heard of my dog?'

Again, so many questions! Mrs Samuels knew the answer to some.

'I'm sorry to say your dog was killed.'

'Oh no!'

'Yes, the chap that visits you, an American pilot who's always here, said your house was flattened and the poor dog killed.'

'He told you that?'

'Yes and you!'

'Me?'

'Yes, several times. It's not your first day in this hell-hole, dear. You've been here a while but you keep forgetting.'

Adelia loses track of time. Whole days disappear. One moment it's Wednesday and then Friday and no remembrance of what went between.

So it was that day she learned the bungalow was gone and Lochie dead.

'That's it, my dear, have a good cry,' said Mrs Samuels. 'The way this war is going we'll all be crying soon. My husband is dead and me with cancer. I shall be glad to get out of it.'

Poor Mrs Samuels! She liked to knit and to talk. Knit one purl one, chat-chat hour after hour, no particular garment emerging only endless rows. It's a hobby Adelia ought to consider, it might stop her wandering.

Even here above the bakers she wanders. The other night she woke in the ruined church sitting talking with a tramp, the keys to the flat in one hand and a cheese sandwich in the other. 'Here you are, Miss,' the tramp offered a mug of cocoa from a Salvation Army stand. 'It will help.'

That tramp? Face unshaven and long hair tied back in a knot she's seen in St Giles and also at the ruins of the Black Swan. Yesterday she went looking thinking to offer him a bath but couldn't find him. The Sally Army woman didn't remember him. She said people like that don't come out in the day, 'they are unresolved creatures of the night.'

Aware that she too is considered such a creature Adelia returned to the flat praying she would never wander there at night again.

The first time she went walkabout the pilot, Bobby Rourke, fetched her away. He said he was acting as chaperone. 'Don't worry,' he took her arm. 'We'll get through this and one day we'll look back and laugh.'

So far she's seen nothing remotely funny.

Bobby Rourke? She feels awkward using his Christian name. Time has moved on for him but for her he's still the ill-mannered Yank in the Broom Cupboard.

The day he was brought in it was said that though obviously in pain he laughed and cracked jokes. His bad behaviour came later when his leg was in plaster and he was bored and unable to fly.

'I was a holy terror then wasn't I, Dee?' is what he says now. 'I'll bet you were glad to be rid of me.'

She stares. 'I don't remember you leaving.'

'No,' he says. 'I guess not.'

'I remember your buzzer.'

At that he smiles and peeling a peach brought from the Base commissary offers her a slice. 'My buzzer is always goin'. I'm that kinda guy.'

Adelia doesn't know what kind of guy he is. Foul mouth and brooding anger, first impressions linger. The rest of the staff adores him. When he strolls through the door flying jacket slung over his shoulder and brown eyes flashing, waists are sucked in and breasts shoved out.

'What a cracker!' Mrs Samuels would giggle. 'Those white teeth and that smile! You'd think him a film star.' Adelia is beginning to like him. He visited when she was confined to bed. Asked how he managed to get to the hospital early in the day he said his tour of duty was about night-bombing.

She asked if he had local digs. He said no, he hunkered down at the Base.

'That can't be comfortable.'

'It's a bed,' said he. 'When I get back from a raid, if I get back, it's usually around 0500. I shower, change and then I head out here.'

'You mean you don't sleep?'

'Sure I do.' Face suddenly closed, he nodded. 'I sleep when you sleep.'

Adelia was puzzled. He forestalled her. 'I like to keep an eye on you.' When she frowned he said it again. 'I like to keep an eye on you.'

Most people want to know about the raid and the Yank who ran out on her. They test her memory asking if he was he tall or short, dark or fair, were his eyes brown or blue.

A nurse who saw them at the Bistro said he was 'gorgeous with deep blue eyes and dark hair.'

Adelia remembers nothing of the time but as blue eyes are the best guess she goes with that. Not the man who left her! She chooses the man in her dream. His eyes were blue. She might as well be loved if only by a dream.

~

Adelia was up early Tuesday. She has an appointment with a doctor at 9-30 and then another appointment with Matron at St Faiths.

Aunt Maud's property didn't sell. It was requisitioned for military use by the MOD. As next-of-kin Adelia received an interim payment of fifty pounds a further payment of fifty deferred until a later date.

What a disappointment! She has to get a job. She had hoped for work at the bakery but with shortages they are only just managing. Now it's beginning to look like St Faiths or nothing. She doesn't think Matron will take her.

'Sure she will!' says Bobby. That old battleaxe will love the idea of you havin' to beg for work. But don't do it. I'll stand any dibs you want.'

She doesn't want him standing dibs. She wants to work! If she was alone blitz or not she'd return to Barts. But she's not alone and can't deliberately walk into danger not now with a baby to consider.

A baby! It's why she's seeing the doctor confirming what is already known.

Adelia regained consciousness certain she was pregnant! It was the one thing she did know as though she'd had a chat with the baby. 'Alright then, Baby, you and me will be on our own. But that's alright. I'm not afraid.'

She isn't afraid! If a child is the result of that day so be it. And she will manage and she will be strong! Amnesia or not nothing on this earth will keep her baby from her.

Eleven o clock, her cheeks on fire, Adelia hurried from the surgery.

Horrible man! She shouldn't have gone to see him. That he was Aunt Maud's GP ought to have been warning enough. So he's fed up of seeing girls who in his words have made a mess of things, need he be so cruel?

'Not another one!' Two minutes into the consultation and he was rolling his eyes. 'What's wrong with you girls? Keep on like this and Suffolk will be overrun with Yankee babies. Sort yourselves out! If you can't manage birth-control at least cross your legs!'

Beast! Furious, Adelia snatched up her bag and walked. He followed to the door. 'Young woman! It's never a good time to bring a fatherless child into the world!' he bawled to a waiting room full of patients. 'But babies do thrive even in wartime. Stick with it and who knows around May of next year you'll have come to terms with this and be making the best of a bad job.'

Best of a bad job!? Poor little baby, what a way to begin life!

Of course, Matron will have to be told. Pregnancy is not a secret you can keep. Hopefully, she'll be discreet and keep information to herself. The thought of yet more fresh meat being thrown to gossips is too hard to bear.

It's as she said to Nora. 'I don't know who I am anymore.'

Nora shrugged. 'It's that feller. You loved him and he hurt you.'

'I must have loved him fool that I am.'

'Maybe not such a fool, he did give you his ring.'

Ah yes, the ring. It was in her hand when she was brought in.

'We had to leave it,' said a nurse. 'You wouldn't let go.'

It's a man ring and too big to wear but along with the baby helps keep her sane, for while it is there, a tangible object, she can believe he cared.

Adelia doesn't talk about her feelings, not even with Nora.

Nora doesn't encourage conversation. 'Least said the better. You need to keep quiet and not walk about at nights or people will think you're peculiar.'

'Hush! Keep quiet! Don't make a fuss. People will think you're mad!'

It's all she hears! So hard! How do you prove you're not mad when you partly believe you are? Doctors already have reservations as to her mental state. She's seen the notes, *'query psychological trauma.'*

If she were alone it wouldn't matter. It's wartime and everyone is crazy. Bombs will flatten whole cities, hundreds of people will die, yet now that a baby is on the way a woman sharing a sandwich with a tramp in the early hours of the morning is seen as definitely crazy.

~

The secretary poked her head round the door. 'Take a seat, will you, Nurse Challoner? Matron is busy right now.'

Minutes ticked by. Adelia sat regarding her one and only pair of boots. Black leather with a Cuban heel they came via the bank and two pounds of the land settlement. She told the bank manager she needed shoes. 'If I were you, Miss Challoner, I'd make that two pounds last a very long time.'

An hour later Adelia sat with her head down, a penitent child listening to a catalogue of her failings and learned that her days as a children's nurse were over, if she worked anywhere in Faiths it would be the Annexe.

'Aren't I needed on Buttercup?'

'Not especially.' Matron adjusted her cuffs. 'I have other nurses able to fill your shoes and capable nurses at that. And what's wrong with the Annexe? Old people deserve the same care.'

'Indeed they do. I saw that while I was there.'

'What do you mean saw? Do I detect criticism?'

'No, Matron, not criticism, only that the Annexe is at the end of a busy line and because of that patient's needs are often rushed.'

'What needs are rushed?'

'Meal times mostly. Being slow the ladies need more time. It's the same with dressing. It seemed to me a little more patience was needed.'

'So you are being critical?'

'Not too critical I hope.'

'And I hope not since any criticism from you at this point of your life would be seen as pot calling kettle black.'

I bet, thought Adelia. And the old me, the forelock tugging student conditioned to thinking you're God wouldn't dare criticize. But you asked and I see no point in lying. 'Why can't I work on Buttercup?'

'You're not up to it.'

'Because I'm pregnant?'

'Not particularly. If in the usual way you were pregnant you'd do as most nurses work until the seventh month, and if as you say you are beginning your third month you should be able to do the same but not with children.'

'Why not?'

'Because you're unfit! And that's not only my opinion. It's the ruling of the Hospital Board. Wandering about at all hours of the night talking with all kind of odd people! Good heavens, girl, you ought not to be anywhere near sick children. Indeed, you should think yourself lucky you have a job at all.'

'Is that why you kept me in the Annexe?'

'What?'

'Me being unfit? Is that how I came to be there?'

Matron shuffled papers. 'One thing has nothing to do with the other. You asked for work, I'm offering work, night duty in the Annexe. Of course, if you don't want it fine. No one can say I didn't try.'

Bobby Rourke was right. This is not about work. This is pay-back, the setting down of a cheeky bitch of a nurse who had the nerve to complain.

'I didn't complain to Mr Covington Wright.'

'I beg your pardon?'

'Mr Covington Wright came to see me.'

'And why did he come to see you?'

'To talk, I suppose.'

Matron was puce. 'And what did you talk about?'

'Mostly about getting well. He said the amnesia may be a temporary condition. When things are back to normal I'd be able to get on with my life. But things aren't back to normal and never will be though it's not for want of trying. I am ill, I know that, but being called liar and treated with contempt doesn't help. If anything it makes me more ill. I wonder you don't see that.'

She should've kept quiet. Matron lost her temper, raging of modern girls, how they can't be trusted one day to the next. If not ducking responsibilities they are sneaking out at night with every Tom, Dick and Harry at the Air-Base and coming back heaven's knows what time. 'We've had to put porters on the door of the Nurses Home and bars on the windows to stop men climbing in. Outrageous! You modern girls have no moral values whatsoever.'

Adelia could hear her shouting. She could hear people taking in the corridor and a mower cutting the lawn. Then suddenly she couldn't hear anything, Matron was a faulty ventriloquist's doll, mouth opening and closing but nothing coming out.

Then sound rushed in, but a dark voice heavy as oil dripping on stone. '*You gotta pull yourself together, Camera! While you focus on what happened in Blighty you're a danger to yourself and me, so get a grip!*'

Crack! Crack! There was a sound of rifle fire and of shells bursting overhead.

Adelia thought it another raid and hid behind the desk.

Bang! Matron's voice rushed back. 'What are you doing down there?'

'Isn't there a raid?'

'Get up, you stupid girl! There's nothing happening here other than me wasting time talking to you. I don't know.' She waved her hand. 'A slip of a girl, you come complaining of other nurses and inviting doctors to interfere in the running of my hospital? The cheek of it! I don't know how you've the nerve to ask for a job. But then I don't know how you've the nerve to be in Suffolk! You must have the hide of a rhinoceros. Made pregnant by one American service-man and kept by another, I couldn't stand to be the butt of such gossip.'

'I…I beg your pardon?' Thinking she might faint Adelia held on to the chair.

'Oh no!' Matron shook her head. 'It's too late to beg anyone's pardon. Shallow and hysterical and utterly without morals, I've no time for you.'

'Off you go!' She flung open the door. 'Time you returned to your *pied a terre* over the baker's shop and the generosity of the US Air-force. I tell you, *Miss* Challoner, you're lucky to get a job. If I had my way you wouldn't be within a hundred miles. But then while there are silly apes like Covington Wright who only see blonde hair and red lips and who have no idea how to run a hospital, you will manage. Your type always does. Well, I could care less who's pleading your case. One wrong word and you're out on the street where you belong.'

~

Mrs Samuels is dying. Adelia heard and went to sit with her. Even gasping for breath the old lady needed to talk. 'I'm glad you're here. I felt so alone.'

Adelia took her hand. 'You're not alone now.'

The woman lay quiet for a while and then as though afraid to be silent started up again. 'Do you believe in heaven?'

'I'm not sure.'

'Me neither. I so want to see my darling husband again. He's all the heaven I want.' She slept and then she opened her eyes. 'Be careful of that chap.'

'What chap?'

'That feller Rourke. He's besotted with you.'

'Oh, I don't think so.'

'Oh I do think so! He's really gone on you but you're not gone on him.'

'I like him.'

'He doesn't want like. He wants it all.'

'Maybe.'

'Be careful. He has secrets.'

'You make him sound exciting.'

'I don't know about exciting, risky I would say. Forget him and keep your eye on the other one whose ring you wear.'

'I don't wear it.'

'Yes because you're afraid to lose it!' Mrs Samuel's eyes were strangely bright. 'It was his gift and you don't want share him with anyone. So you keep him locked up in your head and every night you go looking for him.'

Adelia opened her mouth to speak but it was too late to say anything.

'Oh David!' Arms open wide, Mrs Samuels sat up in bed. 'Is that you?'

Then slowly she subsided onto the pillow and smiling died.....

... Or so Adelia thought until the dead eyes flickered and opened.

'Yes, be very careful.'

Seventeen
The Road
North Africa
February '43.

Alex kicked in the window, his boot through the pane, the wooden frame splintering and shards of glass exploding outward. Then to his horror the glass reformed around the frame until the window pane was whole again.

'Hold on, baby!' Desperate, he punched again and agin but every time was the same. 'I can do it, honest I can! Give me a chance and I'll get us both out!'

Chest wringing wet he woke shouting. No one was up on his elbow asking what the hell's wrong with you. As usual any shouting is inside his head.

Every time is the same. He's once again embroiled in the last few frantic moments at the Black Swan. He sees her in the glare of incendiary fire, her hair flying in the up-draught, and now as though made of fire she floats toward him. He's holding out his arms and calling, 'come on! Run!' She is running on air. And it's still okay! They can still get out. All he has to do is open the window. He tries but can never get it to stay open, the glass closing up until he's forced to punch it out again and again and...

'Oh God!'

Every night! Whiskey or prayers it doesn't matter how he tries blocking it, every call for help fall on deaf ears. So he tells himself it is okay! It was your fault. You should never have gone there. You deserve to pay and if it takes the rest of your life, Alex Hunter, you will suffer as she suffered.

Heart broken anew he sits staring at his hands. The wounds on his left hand have opened up again. Last August his C/O in Southampton wanted to put him on a charge. 'What the hell were you thinking? Can you actually do anything with those hands? Seems to me you'd have trouble picking up a match never mind a M16! I ought to put you on a charge for being unfit for duty.'

It was a week before he could close his left hand without blood dripping. If it hadn't been for Joe Petowski and early martial arts training it would've taken longer. His Godfather's gift to Alex on his sixth birthday was a bucket of sand. He remembers Joe hauling into the gym. 'You got girl's hands,' he says. 'If you're gonna get anywhere in this you need to get stronger.'

He then proceeded to introduce Alex to the art of Jari Bako strengthening hands and finger joints at first pushing through soft sand and then onto rice and to pebbles and weights and padlocks and anything that the he, Joe, the Master, the Sensei, would think to use. From that he moved to strengthening the arms and upper body and down through the torso and the legs and feet. Now, almost two decades later while nowhere near Joe's level he is able to hold his own with higher ranking Bu, an official 'tough guy' as Joe would say only now his hands, and his heart bleed for the love of a girl.

~

It's mid afternoon and all around him men of A Company, Ist Battalion US Rangers, sleep on makeshift bunks in huts on the Mediterranean shore.

A night raid is scheduled. Men grab what sleep they can, their souls flying homeward to the wives and children they may never see again. As for Alex his body is here while his soul roosts among pigeons in a ruined church in Suffolk.

They got married that day, there wasn't a priest to ask of solemn vows yet their promises were real enough. Alex gave Adelia his class ring. He'd like to think it buried with her but guesses it was found by workmen rebuilding the site and is worn by a brickie laying the damp course of the new hotel.

Last time Bobby Rourke called to say they were rebuilding the Black Swan. A four day pass last December Alex did think to visit Suffolk and visit her grave but lost his nerve and settled for Achnacarry and Scotland. The heartache of searching cemeteries at Christmas time just couldn't be borne.

The good thing about eidetic memory is that you can recall a memory at any time. A Thanksgiving party in the old homestead, kids at Halloween in crazy get-ups, or gathered about the Christmas Tree, click, click, it's all there for you to enjoy again. The bad thing about is that you can call up any picture any time. Click, and here it is again, the girl you love burning to death.

There is no hiding place. As you sought the memories so they now seek you, and that one, a narrow grave covered with snow he dare not keep.

Another year into the war and he fights on. Nightmares weigh down the man but they don't cripple the soldier, if anything they sharpen his teeth.

Joe says he should move on. 'It happened and I'm a sorry for you but that was then. You gotta move on.' When in response Alex stays mute he gets angry. 'Trouble with you, kid, you're stuck up your own ass. You make up your mind about something and won't budge. I always thought your father a stubborn mutt but you take it one step further. In deciding that girl is the only one you could ever love you have secured a padlock about your heart.'

Knowing his Godfather anxious Alex would let the words roll over his head.

'You're too much of a good guy,' Joe in Aunt Sally mode continued. 'You think life is about honour. You want to kill them that killed your girl but you want to do it through the rules of war and King Arthur and a fucking non-existent Round Table and it's that way of thinking that nearly got us killed in Dieppe.'

He's always harping on Dieppe. Alex knows he didn't nearly get them killed.

'I saw what I saw, Joe, and reacted to it.'

Joe explodes. 'Reacting is all you do. You're a machine. Can't you let go of your brain for once and get physical? You're a great-looking kid. There are girls out there that would give their right tit for a squeeze from you. It's time you started squeezing.'

Sergeant Major Joseph Aaron Petowski is so sure of his opinion he squeaks when he walks. Army Phys Ed allied to West Point and martial arts expert, the only Westerner conferred 10th Dan by the Kadoka, the rest all Japanese

judoka, he knows a lot but he can't know everything.
There are girls out there, pretty girls, Alex sees them here
and knows they are for sale but that's all they are.

That day in Suffolk was the best and worst day of his
life. He gave his heart and soul. It was plenty physical hence
he not only dreams of Adelia dying he dreams of them
fucking and then fucking again.

So many words to tell but no one to tell them to! Until
Adelia there was no one special. Like any other guy he
went on dates and though the girls were bright and
beautiful they were not her. It was like he was waiting for
Adelia to walk through that hospital door and into his heart.

Before Suffolk he was a virgin Virginian who never put
his dick in anything other than the palm of his hand. Bobby
Rourke would laugh, 'what's wrong with you, Ash? No
lead in the pencil?' In many ways Joe is right! In those days
he was Army bullshit crazy. West Point and war-craft was
his world. He thought Robert E Lee a second God and a
Southern Cotillion the way to romance.

Joe likens him to a machine. He says he doesn't talk
anymore, that he is silent. But what is there to talk about?

Alex stared out over the sea. I gave her all of me. I
wanted her to remember and ache as I knew I would ache
for her. So I thought on guys like Bobby and went the other
way. I was tender where he would've skipped anything but
his need. I watched and let her eyes teach me. Given time
there's nothing I would not have known about her because
to know her was to know myself.

And anyway what is physical? Who decides the
demarcation? Where does love end and the physical begin?

The thing is she understood him. That's what Joe and the others will never see. Adelia Challoner saw beyond the soldier to the man and knew what made him tick. It was there in her eyes, 'Oh there you are, my darling. I was wondering when you would come.'

Here's something else Joe Petowski doesn't know; Adelia may be dead but she sure won't lie down. She's here every step of the way! And not only in the click of eidetic memory! She's here now. Her perfume is in Alex's nostrils. Her breath in his ear! Her skin one touch away!

Part of him takes comfort from her ghostly presence, the rest, the Christian son and broken heart cries out, 'Go away! You are killing me!'

Maybe dying is what it's about. She knows he and the rest of the team are pushing their luck and a Romeo and Juliet pact is waiting for him.

'Don't do it, sweetheart,' he whispers. 'Romeo was a hasty guy. He should've waited to die because Juliet wasn't dead.'

Anger rises up in Alex. Knowing what he knows now he wants to move back in time to the Suffolk in the hospital car-park. He wants to snatch her up and get on his old bike and run and keep running until this war is over.

'But alas, poor Romeo, this is real life and she burned.'

The raid was reported in a local newspaper. Bobby sent a cutting from the East Anglian Gazette: '*A difficult time for relatives identifying loved ones, many such bodies brought from the hotel burned beyond recognition, identification made possible in some cases only via personal effects.*'

'Like a belt buckle shaped like a butterfly.'

A butterfly! How right is that? Back home Alex has a book on birds Mom bought for his birthday. In it there's a coloured plate by Martin Johnson Meade of a White Magnolia, a luscious blossom opening up to the light. That was Adelia, silken skin on blue velvet, rare and exquisite, one minute sweet and shy and the next seductive calling him 'my darling…'

'Darling? Darling Alex, where are you.'

Sometimes he thinks he hears her calling. Then he's scared because he is in hell and wouldn't want her looking for him there. He'd sooner she look to the day they shared. They didn't do anything special. They went to a Bistro and to a park where kids played on a swing and a guy threw a ball for his dog.

'You had a dog,' she said. 'What was your dog called?'

He said he was an Old English sheepdog by name was Sherbet.

'Sherbet?' She laughed. 'I love that. It makes me think of lemon dabs, the ones you stick a straw in and they're all fizzy back of your tongue.'

She was the fizz is his heart. They walked together in the park. There was a street photographer with a monkey. He took a shot of her holding the monkey. Knowing he wouldn't be able to collect Alex paid for the roll and stuck it in his pants pocket. Later in Southampton he had the film processed.

Only one shot in the whole reel came through. The chemist wasn't surprised. 'They don't really take pictures. They prance around clicking the shutter but only bother when someone shows interest. The rest is smoke and mirrors.'

Smoke and mirrors? Alex knew what the guy meant but also knew the photo was meant to survive, that she was meant to smile at him forever.

~

'I get no kick from champagne, mere alcohol doesn't move me at all, so tell me why should it be true, I get a kick out of you.'

Four in the afternoon and he's remembering a tune they played back room of the hotel. It's stuck in his brain. Now, whatever is ahead, rifle fire or thud of guns on the battery that tune will remain. Thinking he'll go mad if he doesn't talk to someone Alex took time out and went to confession.

There is no confessional booth out here, there's a box-crate, a bible, and a black barrage balloon of a man called Franklyn Washington Bates.

Frank is padre to the division. It's not the first time they have talked together. 'No wonder you feel bad,' says Frank. 'You met heaven and hell in one day, Major Hunter. That's enough to knock any guy for a loop.'

'Sure, but I can't help thinking it's my fault.'

The padre seems to be experiencing problems of his own and sits, morose and heavy, with the prayer book loose in his hands. 'How is it your fault?'

'If she hadn't been with me she'd still be alive.

'Didn't she agree to go with you?'

Did Adelia agree to go with him? Click! Alex is back in St Giles sunlight pouring through the roof. Beyond the outer walls and broken pews there's very little left of the church. As Adelia said it's hard to imagine how it was before. A sense of holiness prevails, and also regret, the Lord God staring down through blackened rafters at the mess Adam made of Eden.

Whole villages destroyed and families torn apart and suddenly here among the ruins a moment of beauty, in a shaft of sunlight a field mouse sits upon what's left of the altar nibbling a crust of bread.

Adelia loved that mouse. 'Oh look, darling! He's come to bless us.'

One minute sighing over a mouse and then looking under her lashes, here she is again, a White Madonna lily a mix of woman and girl.

'Major Hunter? You still with me?'

Alex rejoins the world. 'Yes, she agreed to come with me.'

Frank shrugged. 'Then her death is not down to you. She died because a bomb dropped.'

'So why do I feel like a murderer?'

'You need someone to blame and you're the obvious target.'

'I can't come to terms with it.' Alex shook his head. 'She is always on my mind. And not just the pain! It's the sweetness of it, her arms about me and lips on mine. She is so close I can feel her heart beating. But why am I telling you? You're a padre, a man of God. You don't want to hear this.'

'Why don't I? What am I here for if not to listen?' The padre sank further in his chair. 'I do little else. I am a man of God but I'm flesh and blood too, no saint and never likely to be. A woman's kisses matter to me as they matter to you. We are told the Lord God delights in love. It's why we are created, though seeing what's going on all around us, the slaughter and endless suffering, you have to wonder what exactly is His idea of love.'

'No way!' Alex had to stop him. 'I'm not going to wonder about that! I'd sooner not think on God. I have no great faith in Him right now.'

'We all have our doubts.'

'What, you too?'

'Oh yes!' Frank nodded. 'Like you I'm looking for someone to blame and the Lord God was ever an easy target.'

'I don't see that blame helps,' said Alex. 'It doesn't help me. Lately I'm likened to a man without feeling. I don't know that it's true. I do what we all do to stay alive, eat, drink, shit and sleep. I live because lives are entrusted to me and I can't let them down but beyond that being alive is no great thing to me, which, as was pointed out in Dieppe, is not good news for a soldier.'

Franklyn Bates scowled. 'Dieppe was a nightmare in itself. You want to feel guilty about something, feel guilty about that.'

'No, sir! Again, with respect that's not for me! That is your domain. I can't do my job and feel that kind of guilt. I have to believe, or at least hope what we do is for the greater good. But that's not it. I miss her, you understand?'Alex stared out across yesterday. 'I miss the sound of her voice and the dent top of her lip and the colour of her hair and the way it felt to my touch. I knew her less than twenty-four hours and yet she's in my heart and won't go away!'

'Then I envy you, Major, as well as pity. We should all love like that, to the heights and depths of our soul. Love is offered but all too often we're looking to see what else is coming round the bend and miss what's under our nose.'

'Okay, padre!' Alex was done. 'I need to get on.'

'The Lord bless and keep you, my son.' Heavy hand upon his head the padre blessed him. 'You are on the Road and will be until set free.'

'And what road is that?'

'The Road to Calvary.'

~

It is dusk. They're in trucks destination Tunisia, objective to raid Italian defence positions at Station de Sened. The aim is to surprise. Alex's Team will be dropped some miles from the enemy camp and go the rest of the way on foot which is why they don't carry packs just water and armaments.

US Rangers have been based in Oran since November of last year. By rights they should be on R&R every man sick of constant training. But the Allied Army has the jitters. The raid on Dieppe didn't go down well. It was a fiasco closely followed by Operation Torch where no one knew who the fuck he was fighting, whether it was De Gaulle and the Free-French alongside the Allies or Petain's pathetic crew, the Vichy French, cuddling up to the Germans.

Two heavyweight mess-ups so close together put the fear of God into every man from the top Brass down to the humble dogface. Everyone was looking to blame someone including Joe Petowski so that in November '42 when a

French kid tottered toward their dugout with a clapped out WW1 service rifle in his hands Alex hesitated and Joe blew him away.

After years of training Alex is first and last the professional soldier. Never mind what he is thinking and feeling, doesn't matter that he's got toothache, or that he has a hangover or the Cavaliers lost the ball game, or even that one night in Suffolk, England the girl he loved was burnt to a crisp, he is a soldier, the boots and battledress are in control and a switch deep in his subconscious overriding all else. It has been that way for years. It was that way in Dieppe.

Joe shot the kid and afterward aboard the Landing Craft tore into Alex. 'What was that about? What were you going to do wait til he had you stuffed and mounted on a wall to show his buddies, Alexander, the Not So Great US Army Ranger shot while having his mind elsewhere?'

Alex said it was okay.

'It didn't look okay.'

'Maybe not but I had it covered.'

'How did you?'

'You saw him, Vichy France and fifteen if he was a day.'

'So?'

'So, I gave him a chance to change his mind. Plus the clip on his magazine was buckled. He couldn't have shot anything with that other than himself.'

Joe was quiet then. 'I didn't see that.'

'I know you didn't. Not that it mattered. The thug coming up behind had a Springfield rifle stolen from one of ours. You took them both out.'

'I did but I didn't spot the magazine.'

'So what? Would it have made a difference if you had?'

'No. Even so I should've seen it.'

Thinking he'd messed up Joe worried about that buckled magazine. Now he's behind the lines in Salerno in covert operation preparing for the next fuck-up and has other things on his mind. Alex misses him. Aunt Sally or not it was good having him as back up.

~

The transport stopped about four miles before the Sened Station. They crept the rest of the way. US Rangers are good at creeping. Back in Achnacarry, in Scotland, creep and abseil down mountains was all they did.

The first day in '41 he along with twenty others left the bus for a fourteen mile trek to Fort William. The camp CO marched along with them. He thought it amusing to see how Yank commandoes would manage.

They managed then. Now it's North Africa and they're still managing. Cammo-blackened face and woollen skull caps, loose tags taped down and leathers oiled to eliminate noise they wait the signal to advance.

Just after nightfall they moved out Alex heading A Company. It was a still night. Even though they moved real quiet the Italians got wind of the approach and started firing. It being dark they had no real idea of the target and shot over the Rangers heads enabling Alex to spot the gunner's position.

It was dirty fighting. These were no Vichy French cowards. The enemy were of the best Italian Centauro Division and elite Bersaglieri Mountain troops.

Rangers are trained to make a lot of noise when moving in. Coming as they do out of the darkness screaming like banshees, it has the blinding effect of a bomb exploding. Though taken by surprise the Italians quickly reformed. Soon it was hand-to-hand fighting, Colonel Darby and his Company slicing through the middle while Alex's team managed gun placements.

The guards were quick and slippery but finally went down under bayonets.

As he said, dirty work, nothing to brag about when it is over.

The objective was to take prisoners and information on the movement of German troops passed back to HQ. Mission accomplished they buried the Italian dead and carrying their own wounded began the returning march.

One Ranger killed and twenty injured the raid was considered successful. Any screw-up came later with a heavy ocean swell and an overweight and deeply troubled Man of God.

~

Weary and on a battle-low Alex wanted to get back to the camp and sleep but the weather turned. Rain lashing down and tricky underfoot they had to take their time climbing down. The sun was up by the time they reached the shore. Radio messages were waiting. Two prisoners, an Italian Captain and his Lieutenant were to be transferred directly to a destroyer, Alex, fluent in Italian and German to accompany them acting as interpreter. Also, as one of the

EX O aboard was thought to be ill they were to bring the padre.

The sea was heavy. Alex would sooner have waited and judging the padre's face so would he.

They went out on an ancient mechanised landing craft. An uncertain beast it rode through the waves rather than over. Once aboard the cutter Alex was taken to officer's quarters. A cup of coffee, a slug of rum, and interrogation began but was soon brought to a halt with the Italians pleading fatigue.

An hour and they were heading back and the padre with them. It appears the Executive Officer had a bad case of dysentery but was coming through.

'I guess he felt better seeing you,' Alex clambered into the LAC.

'I don't know why,' muttered the padre.

There is something hugely amiss with the guy and not only a case of *mal de mer*. Rumours back in Oran say he's drinking and missing communion and that he seems more comfortable now behind a rifle than a pulpit and has been that way since Dieppe.

He told Alex he was questioning. When asked what he was questioning he said himself. 'I was brought up in poor conditions but always trusted that one day I'd be able to bring my hopes hope to men. I was wrong. There is no hope.'

A toad in bilge water he sat slumped in bottom of the LC. Years later Alex would ask Frank if he meant to die that day but getting no reply would never ask again.

They were moving away from the Destroyer approaching the inlet. The wind was high and landing craft rocking. They were almost in dock when a wave shook the LAC so that it all but overturned. It almost threw the guys overboard. All held on but for one. The padre removed his helmet, made the sign of the cross, and slid over the side.

All that gear, the heavy BDU, he dropped like a stone.

Maybe he couldn't swim. For sure he didn't try. Down he went and once hitting the bottom stood upright, hands down and boots planted in the sand like a stone relic of a sunken city.

There was a moment of stunned silence. Then Alex grabbed a rope and jumped in. He hit bottom. Fighting heavy swell he forced his way forward a coil of rope in his hand.

The padre saw him coming and raised his hand as though warding him off.

No way! Alex was determined to get him. The man mattered! His association with God mattered! Having taken Alex's confession he was the one sacred link to Adelia and the bastard was not gonna funk out now.

It wasn't easy. Alex had to move against the tide and pressure of water. It was tricky! Never mind Bates he could've drowned!

The padre didn't struggle but neither did he help only stood defying survival eyes bulging and a thin stream of bubbles coming from his nose.

Who knows why he did it. Maybe he was testing his faith, hoping St Michael would lean down and pluck him out.

After much cussing, Alex was able to get the rope round his neck. He might have been rustling a steer. Franklyn

Washington Bates is huge. Five hundred pounds of solid meat he was a polished Buddha minus the smile.

Alex dug deep and hauled. A sailor jumped in and then another, all leaning toward the shallows. There was momentary resistance, the rope stretching, and then realising he might cause others to drown the padre surrendered.

They got him out. He lay on the shale coughing with Alex beside him throwing up salt water. Nobody said a word all too damned exhausted.

They took him back to camp and from there airlifted to hospital.

News drifted back of him running amuck though the hospital grounds waving a machine gun. Though none came to harm he was invalided out as having a breakdown. The latest message was that he'd left the church.

That was Franklyn Washington Bates.

It would seem both he and Alex walk the Road to Calvary.

Eighteen
Rules
St Faiths Hospital
March 22nd 1943

Adelia dragged the trolley into the sluice but got stuck midway between the door and her belly. 'Oh for crying out loud!'

'What's up?'

'I'm stuck.'

'So I see.' Captain Mo Jones is on leave from the Queen Alexandra Nursing Corps and presently lugging a stirrup pump in through the back door thinks Nurse Challoner's antics funny.

'It's not funny.'

'It is from where I'm standing. Great big belly and skinny little legs, you look like a pregnant frog.'

'Yes and if I have empty another mucky bed-pan I'll be a sick pregnant frog. That's the fourth in the last hour. What's wrong with the ladies tonight? They seem to be extra fidgety.'

'Is this different then? Aren't they always this shitty?'

'Not at all. Most sleep though and if not there's always largactil. But you've moved on. What do you know about mucky bed pans?'

Mo grinned. 'I don't. I leave the dirty work to underlings.'

'Lucky beast!'

'What about largactil? Do you really give the old dears that muck?'

'Not if I can help it. CW prescribes a tot of sherry every night. He says largactil causes nightmares. He's right. I know because they gave it to me.'

Mo was shocked. 'They gave you that?'

'Yes, a couple of times when I went walkabout.'

'Bloody hell!'

'I know. They thought I was mad.'

'And are you?'

'I have my moments.'

'Not too many I hope.'

Adelia secretly crossed her fingers. 'It's better than it was.'

'It needs to be! I get what you've been through but you know what Welfare is like. If they think you're not the full shilling they'll take your kid away.'

'I'd like to see them try.'

'Yes, well as I say be careful.' Mo shuddered. 'Get a job in a cafe or someplace cheerful. Working down here in this dump is not good for you.'

Adelia hosed down the sink. 'It's not good for anyone.'

'I'm serious. It can't be doing you any favours.' Mo lit a cigarette. 'Largactil? I've a good mind to report them to the Nursing College.'

Adelia flapped a towel. 'I've a mind to report you for fouling the atmosphere.'

'I don't need to foul anything in here. It's pretty rank as it is. Try a puff. Might clear this sluice and your head, silly goose.'

Adelia took a puff and started coughing. 'That is vile!'

'Vile nothing! My Jimmy loves French fags, if you'll pardon the expression. She's got a mate on Harbour Patrol who nicks the odd bit of contraband.'

'Maureen Jones!' Adelia smiled. 'You are a truly wicked woman!'

Mo grinned. 'You don't know the half. Short life and merry is what I say! But come on, get out of this dump.'

'It's not that bad and I don't have to work here. It is my choice.'

'Some choice. I bet it's all they offered. You should be with your babies.'

'I should but I'm not. They won't let me, not with my medical record. Oh, my back!' Adelia stretched. 'I think I'll sit for a minute.'

'Do. I'll keep watch.'

'It's good of you to help.'

Mo shrugged. 'I didn't want to take leave but the QA are sticklers about that.'

'You're happy there.'

'Best thing I ever did especially now I've met Jimmy. So what if I give a couple of hours to my beautiful idiot pal? What's that in the scheme of things?'

'You're a God-send!' Adelia kissed her cheek. 'I tell you, when you walked through the door the other night I could've cried.'

'Me too with your belly blown up like that! I thought my life had changed but it's nothing compared to yours.

I'm glad to help out. Even so, if I find you still here at the end of the week I'm putting you on a charge.'

Adelia saluted. 'Aye, aye, Captain!'

'I mean it!' She hugged Adelia. 'You don't have to prove anything to me. You loved the bloke or you wouldn't have gone with him and whether there's a side of the story that we don't know, or he's just the biggest swine going, it doesn't alter the fact you loved him.'

That was Mo, bless her. She was with Adelia all week making sunlight of winter. Had she lived she would've been Godmother to the baby but shortly after rejoining her unit the Hospital ship, HMS Newfoundland, came under fire and Captain Maureen Jones among the casualties.

~

It snowed throughout March. Toward the end of April the sun came out. This was meant to be her last day at Faiths. Then Night Sister asked if she'd work til the end of the week. She should've refused. It took a tougher guy to do that.

Bobby Rourke comes around a lot these days. Adelia used to think him an arrogant bully. She was wrong. There is nothing arrogant about him. He is funny and kind and generous. The latest gift is a blue teddy bear.

Edna James saw it. 'The Yank again I suppose.'

'Yes and I wish he wouldn't. It's too generous.'

'I wouldn't worry. You'll get the bill soon enough.' Edna said that with such a twist to her lips Adelia struggled not to take offence. It was a look she'd seen before; a suggestion the bill was already being paid.

Adelia is not deaf. She knows what's being said around the village as she knows what Bobby wants but she's not ready to commit yet to anyone.

'It is kind of you to buy for the baby but really I wish you wouldn't,' she said the following day. 'As I said, I can't think beyond the day. It's too soon.'

'I know,' he said, 'and I don't want to push you. I want you to see us as a possibility and that with you bein' unwell it might be the best for all concerned especially the Bump.'

The Bump? Adelia told him of her pregnancy as soon as she knew. That he cared was obvious, it would have been wrong not to tell. In any event he took the news on the chin. 'Are you okay about it?' he said.

'I don't feel I have a choice.'

'I guess not.' He sat playing with his cap. 'Life can be rough.'

'It can though I don't see the baby as a tragedy.'

He'd stared. 'You don't?

'No! I see it as a wonderful thing.'

With that he'd smiled and flung his cap in the air. 'Then so do I.'

~

For a time afterward the he stayed away. One day she saw him in the Bistro.

'How are you?' she said. 'I haven't seen you in a while.

'I thought it best. You livin' alone I didn't want people talkin'.'

'That was thoughtful.' She stirred the teapot. 'Anyway, let's share a cup of tea and to hell with talk!'

From then on he called at the shop most days, joking with Mr and Mrs James, casting his usual spell. It was Christmas before he spoke of love and that with the blue teddy bear.

He set it on the kitchen table. 'I thought the babe might like it.'

'I'm sure she will.'

'You think it's a girl?'

'I do.'

'Ah heck! And here's me got him lined up for flying school.'

'That's alright. You never know she might be into flying.'

'Could be! Gals are feisty nowadays. Look at you! How feisty can you get?'

When she laughed he took her hand. 'You know that I would do anything for you, Dee, and by you I mean you and the babe.'

'I do know.'

'So will you give me a chance to prove it?'

Really she should have said no, her heart was empty and only her baby able to fill it but he seemed sincere and so she said nothing. No doubt she was wrong to do it but it was Christmas, damn it! Who else cared enough to slog through snow bringing a gift to a child?

The blue teddy changed everything. Though nothing was said, a promise neither sought nor offered from that moment there was tacit understanding that if they got through the war Adelia and her baby may well be his.

Rules came into place, his rules, no visiting after seven, a bunch of roses every Saturday delivered to the bakery and lunch twice a week at the Italian Bistro, Luigi allotting them the coveted window-table.

They were soon seen as a pair. Much was whispered but no one enquired out loud, certainly no one at St Faiths, to them she will always be the lying slut who concocted a story about amnesia.

Bobby wanted her to stop working there but she was determined to keep her word. 'What word is that?' he said.

'To finish what I started.'

~

Of late the Air-Base has been busy, scores of Bombers taking off every night. She hadn't seen Bobby in a while and when she did she was shocked. Razor thin and rings around his eyes he looked terrible. That same day she was stopped by another pilot. He said Bobby had flown forty-six ops and was in danger of burn-out. 'The Doc at Group is thinking of pulling the plug. He needs to stand down. We wondered if you might have a word. He'll listen to you.'

'Bullshit!' He didn't listen. 'I'm fit as the proverbial so don't you worry about it.' When she pressed he lost his temper, thin lips and buzzer blaring, the old Bobby arriving. 'Burned out my ass! Don't talk about things you don't understand! I'll quit when I'm ready.'

Friday night brought a disastrous raid over Germany, the Base suffering heavy losses of men and planes and only a couple of Lancasters returning. Bobby came to the Annexe around midnight. Still in flying suit and heavy boots and smelling of whisky he laid a bunch of roses on the drainer.

'I thought you were done here?'

'They're short of staff.'

'Short of staff nothin'! Get your coat. We're out of here!'

'I can't leave yet. But you go. You look worn out.'

'I am worn out. I am dead beat, dead as buddies over Essen. Dead meat! *Fried* meat, crisp and crunchy! Get your purse, we're leavin'.' He kicked the trolley. 'You shouldn't be here! This is a drop-off point for the world's leftovers. Someone should put a match to it.'

'Hush!' she hissed. 'Don't make such a racket!'

'Never mind racket!' He took her arm. 'You're comin' with me.'

'Stop it!' She shook him off. 'You're scaring the patients.' She tried shoving him out but he wouldn't budge. This wasn't about her, this was about him, Flight Lieutenant Robert E Rourke, DFC, crashing and burning.

'Wake up leftovers!' He went from bed to bed rattling the frames. 'Why are you alive and takin' up space when young guys are dead? 'Cos they are, you know! They're all dead, Johnny-in-the Sky burnin' like a candle!'

Arms wide and head thrown back he stood centre of the Ward singing a kiddie's hymn. '*Jesus bids us shine with a pure clear light, like a little candle burnin' in the night. In this world of darkness so let us shine, you in your small corner, and me in mine.*'

Face so empty, it was awful watching him Adelia wanted to weep.

'Say look! A kite! Let's see how she flies!' He dragged the trolley from the sluice and leaping on the bar scooted up and down the Ward still singing.

'*Jesus wants me for a sunbeam, a sunbeam. Jesus want me for a sunbeam, I'll be a sunbeam for him.*'

Night Sister arrived. 'What is going on?'

'Stand by your beds chaps, bogey at four-o clock!' He leapt off the trolley and arm outstretched pointed at Sister. 'This woman is the cause of it all. It's her fault. If she'd signed the register as she should none of this would've happened. The secret would be out and we'd all be free again especially me.'

'*I can laugh when things aren't funny, oh, oh, oh, happy go lucky me!*'

Still singing he grabbed Adelia waltzing her between the beds. Then he swooped down kissing her hard on the mouth. 'Receiving me are you, Nursey? A phone call to the front desk and all would be revealed!'

Adelia hadn't a clue. She took his arm. 'I'll take him home.'

'Yes and don't bother coming back!' Sister was livid. 'I think we can safely call your position at this hospital terminated.'

'Hospital?' Bobby scoffed. 'This ain't no hospital. This is a Labour camp. Hitler couldn't do better. It's child labour, skivvies takin' up the slack while people like you sit on your fat asses. Well tough! You'll have to pull your own weight now. You don't quit Dee. She quits you. Come on, sweetheart!'

Sister sniffed. 'And I should think so too!'

Bobby had to have the last word. 'Tell me, Sister, if this girl had been a skinny bitch with a face like stewed prunes would you've treated her the same?'

She folded her arms. 'Here at St Faiths we treat everyone the same.'

'Then God help the patients is all I can say.' He tore Adelia's apron off and grabbing her hand marched her out giving the finger as he went. 'Good night and goodbye sweet ladies! Get your free pardons on the way out!'

~

He dropped Dee at the bakery and roared off into the night. So he shouldn't have frightened the old girls but making Dee work like that the old cow of a Sister had it coming. And why does she work there? It's not like she has to. He would willingly pay dibs. But no she must earn her pathetic little stipend.

Pisses him off! Why can't she be more manageable? Why insist on doing things her way? Okay, she's still grieving over the Mystery Man but why not name the day then they could be married.

Truth is he has never actually proposed. It's on the edge of his tongue but he can never spit it out. Every time he does he sees Ash's ring on her finger. She's had it made smaller and wears it all the time even when working.

The big guy was at the camp in Achnacarry at Christmas. He phoned Bobby to say hi. And do you know what, she wasn't mentioned. Not a word! It was him broke the barrier. 'Sorry, buddy, nothin' to tell on that situation.'

There was silence and then, 'I didn't think there would be.'

It's obvious what has happened. Unable to live with it the Hunter steel-trap mind has slammed the gate. Dee as a topic is done.

Bobby should feel relief but doesn't. What he feels is guilt. And man, such guilt! It's the same with Essen! Why is he alive and others dead? Why 47 ops and other than his brain skewered he is still in one piece. What's God playing at? They were decent guys. Where's the Justice? Where's the eye-for-an-eye and the tooth-for-a-fucking-tooth!

Foot down, he raced through the night. A seventy-two hour pass, it's Knightsbridge and Lady M for hot sex and sweet relief. No good looking to Dee for favours. A bump the size of a zeppelin she's not giving and he's not asking.

Christ! A thought comes into his head that almost had off the bike laughing. What after all this they get married and she turns out the meanest lay he's ever had? You know, one of those tight-assed bitches who are so afraid to give they wouldn't lick the end of your dick if you paid them.

What if she's like that?

The thought gave him pause. Then he remembered her with people, the tender touch, and knew she wouldn't be that way with the man she loved.

'Except I am not the man she loves.'

Miles flashed by but sobered by the thought he eased up the throttle. This war is costly. It's losing him friends. Ash was the biggest loss, Dee coming between them. Naturally, the guy doesn't suspect Bobby of lying. Who in hell would? Even so, she is the elephant in the room no one wants to see.

It touches everything. The Registrar, Covington Wright, nabbed him the other day asking when he was going to do the right thing.

'What do you mean right thing?' Bobby was indignant. 'What am I doing that's wrong, and don't say sleepin' with her 'cos I'm not.'

'Excuse me!' The guy froze him with a look. 'I'm no gossip leaning on a fence. I have no interest in your affairs other than natural concern for another human being. By right I meant marry the girl and remove her to better treatment than this country can provide! Don't be fooled by her apparent serenity, Lieutenant. She is not well! Do you understand?'

Bobby understands. He's been there and seen it with his own eyes.

You think she's okay. You think she's dealing with it but Noh! One minute she's talking and then she's crumpling and falling on the floor.

Christ! The first time it happened he thought she'd died and was going to ring for an ambulance. She came round smiling but not the girl that had fainted, a stranger looked through the smile.

It freaked Bobby out. It's like that butch army nurse, Mo, said, 'One foot in this world and another in Hell, get her out before they lock her away!'

With that job, night-shift in the Annexe, Matron did Dee a favour. Stuck in here five nights a week she can't go walkabout, her professional self won't let her leave the old ladies. Bing, bong, bing, her days however are spent gliding through a magical triangle. She wanders about Needham so pale and so silent and sad if you didn't know she was alive you'd think her a tourist.

This is her itinerary: seven in the morning she leaves the hospital. She goes to the flat, showers, changes her clothes and then to the Bistro for egg on toast. From there it's the ruined church. Rain, snow or hail she sits staring at a non-existent window. Then it's back to the flat for an hour and again to the Bistro and the window-table for a pot of tea, Luigi and his wife looking on.

'Every day she come for breakfast and afternoon tea,' Luigi told Bobby. 'We don't know what to say. She smile but she not here, she dreams of some other place. My wife worries. She says bambino when it comes is not safe.'

Bobby sat a whole hour one morning on the motor bike in full view of the window but she didn't see him. She doesn't see anyone and yet appears to be sane, pays for her food and leaves, but as Luigi says there's no one there.

The two nights she is off-duty it's a dawn stroll to the Black Swan to stare at yesterday's ruin. He's never seen her there. By the time he's done at the Base she's always back at the flat. The police have brought her home more than once. 'I shouldn't worry about it, sir,' says a cop. 'She don't get into harm. She sits on the memorial bench. And she's never alone.'

Bobby asked, 'what do you mean never alone?'

'A bloke sits with her, a tramp. It's alright, he's harmless.'

Harmless! It drives Bobby nuts. Wandering out in the middle of the night talking with hobos! It's like she's in a trance. One lunch time he sat for twenty minutes opposite her in the Bistro. Then he called her name. She blinked.

'Hello Bobby,' she says. 'If you're having breakfast I recommend the omelette.'

Holy shit! What can you do with a situation like that? Your hands are tied. You can't say pull yourself together, girl, because she seems normal. You go along with it. You order an omelette and then she tells you she's pregnant!

Honestly, when she told him that it took every bit of nerve not to run. Sick in the head and havin' Ash's baby!? That's a heavy load for any guilty man to carry. Why should he do it? Why not find a girl without all this angst? There's no shortage. There's the one in the NAFFI and there's Lady M, and if need be there's Sue back in Virginia, although she has troubles of her own, her husband, Herb, losing his arm at Guadalcanal.

Now he's off to see to Lady M and her rounded vowels. But who wants that. It's as he said, second-hand love is no good to him.

Brakes screeching, he turned the bike. Forget Knightsbridge and sex on the Grand Piano. It's too far out in every way.

It was almost light when he parked the bike. The lights were out in the bakery and the upstairs flat in darkness. He stood looking up at the window and suddenly tears are running down his cheeks.

It was the guys in Charlie Three. He saw them fall, a 109 Focke-Wulf Fighter can-opener slicing through the midsection of their Lancs and the cockpit opening and the two guys, Muggy Danes and Willis, his co-pilot, tumbling out.

2145 hours it happened, Bobby could see his watch in the searchlights.

Over and over they fell! He will never forget it. So fucking small against the sky he could've swooped down and caught them like fish in a net. But they kept falling and he had another 109 on his tail.

God, it hurt seeing that! It hurt so much he can't stop crying.

Now look! The light is on and she's at the door, bless her, so tiny in her nightie with her belly poking through.

Still he's crying. She has him in her arms and all but carries him up the stairs. She undoes his boots and covers him with a blanket. His nose is running. Mother hen with a chick she wipes snot away. He wants to stay and he wants to hold her but can't because a face gets in the way. And not the one you'd expect! Not Ash Hunter, the suffering soul! The other one, Gabe Templar!

Nineteen
Cutting Wires
May 1943,
Marine Camp
Tahiti Bay,
Wellington, New Zealand.

'Do you take sugar with your tea, Corporal?'

'No, thank you, ma'm.'

Gabriel sighed. They say never volunteer for anything. He surely didn't volunteer to take afternoon tea with ladies of the Women's Guild in the grounds of Government House yet every other guy in the billet rushed at it. Why? What's so great about having to wear best blues on a warm day and stand about making small-talk? An hour later he understood. It is a tea-party. It's local people and USO volunteers promoting the Welfare of Soldiers. It's men in smart button-downs and women in pretty hats and a harp playing and tea-cups rattling. It is also a pick-up service for anyone on the prowl.

Yesterday Captain Ridges came to the hut waving a bunch of invitations. 'Now hear this! I need some of you baboons to go meet and greet tomorrow at Government House. The Governor General's wife expressed a wish to mingle with everyday Marines. So saddle up, you everyday Marines and mingle. Who knows, mixing with decent people you might learn something.'

That said he tossed a bunch of invitation cards into the air. There was a stampede, guys fighting for tickets.

Gabriel stood by open-mouthed. The Captain grinned. 'So how is it with you, Corporal Templar,' he said. 'How come you're not fighting for one of these?'

'Are they worth fightin' for, Captain?'

'Depends how you see life in the Corps, the disadvantages *and* the often quite spectacular advantages of being a US Marine.'

'Advantages?'

'That's what I said.'

'Pariss Island, Guadalcanal and a hole in my shoulder?' Gabriel grimaced. 'I'm gettin' wise to the disadvantages but so far I don't see the advantages.'

'Then you're not looking. There is a particular advantage to being in the Corps that has nothing to do with rank. It's there for the lowly jarhead as it is for a four-star General. It's a matter of recognizing what's being offered and then of knowing what to do with it.'

'I don't follow, sir.'

'Then it's time you did. I was told you were a man in need of education. Gunny Emmet said that, though I doubt if even he knew how much of an education and in what area. Take this.' The Captain shoved an invitation down the front of Gabriel's vest. 'Come to the tea-party 1500 hours tomorrow and learn.'

He came and stood for the last hour juggling cup and saucer in one hand and plate in the other while trying to melt into the background. The other guys are okay wolfing cake and making eyes at waitresses. It's him that's awkward. Talking with fine ladies in expensive hats is his idea of hell and so he's pitched his tent back of a rose arbour with an overweight spaniel for company.

The dog reminds him of Daisy. Ma wrote saying the old dog's arthritic and can hardly get around. 'You got the same likes you two. She spends most of the day in the old house Orangery where it's warm.'

The Orangery! Along with the attic it's his favourite place in the Eyrie. In summer the scent of wisteria climbing the wall drifts all the way back to Grandma's house. They got one here at the Governor's residence, not as well-established and yet one sniff and he's home.

'Lottie seems to have taken a fancy to you, Corporal.'

'Beg pardon?' Gabriel snapped to.

A woman was smiling. 'Sorry,' she said. 'I interrupted your day dream.'

'It's okay. Is that the dog's name, Lottie?'

'Well actually it's Princess Charlotte Louise of Saxon-Coburg and Gotha, Crufts Champion English Cocker Spaniel 1938.'

'Crufts?'

'You don't know of the show?'

'No, ma'm.'

'It's *the* dog-show, a kind of Kentucky Derby for thoroughbred hounds. It's held annually in London and a dog that's any kind of dog is bound to attend. Lottie won in '38 and to our way of thinking remains the unofficial champion.'

'Unofficial?'

'It's okay. It's a family joke.' She reached down tickling the dog's ear. 'There hasn't been a Crufts since '39, London considered too dangerous, plus of course so many pets having to be put down.'

'Folks had their pets killed!?'

'I'm afraid so, some nonsense about taking valuable foodstuff. Not me! I wouldn't put Lottie down! She is my friend. We share what we have hence as you see she is a little overweight.'

Gabriel knelt rubbing the dog's belly. 'Yet still a winner.'

'Yes, a winner!' The woman smiled. 'My husband says not being entered at Crufts was a technicality. She would've romped home.'

'I bet she would. How old is she?'

'We're not sure. We think eleven. We had her as pup not long after our daughter was born and Kate will be twelve in June.'

In straightening up Gabriel jolted the table the cup and saucer rattling.

'Let me rid you of those.' The woman beckoned a maid. 'I've been watching you. You've been hanging onto them for ages and as pretty as it is the china looks so absurdly tiny in your hands.'

Colouring up, Gabriel stuck his hands behind his back. 'I guess they are on the big side.'

'They look to be extremely competent hands.'

'They have their uses.'

'I'm sure.' She took a cigarette case from her purse. 'Do you smoke?'

'I don't.'

'Very wise. It's a filthy habit that will no doubt lead to a filthy disease. Would you mind?' Cigarette in her mouth she offered the lighter. Hand on his sleeve she leaned close. He flicked the lighter and she pressed closer the top of her dress gaping revealing breasts like ripe melons.

She exhaled. 'Are you in Wellington long?'

'I doubt it. Just waitin' on orders to move out.'

'And where do you suppose you will move to?'

'The Pacific is a mighty big ocean. There's plenty places still to go.'

'I understand you were recently in the Solomon Islands. Was it as bad as they are saying?'

'What are they saying?'

'Heavy casualties.'

'It was bad.'

'I'm sorry. I heard you were wounded.'

'What me?' He didn't know whether to laugh. 'You heard *I* was wounded?'

'Yes and that you acted with great courage at Henderson field.'

Acted with courage? He didn't know where to look. Who in this corner of the world has ever heard of Gabriel Templar never mind that he was injured or acted with courage. It has to be some kind of joke.

'No really, there's nothing we don't know about.' She smiled wryly. 'We are a small community yet where gossip is concerned our post-bag is international, particularly since you gentlemen camped here. So how is the shoulder?'

Last October Gabriel was part of a detail laying explosives in a cave. When the charges blew he took a piece of shrapnel in the left shoulder. It aches and probably always will but is nothing compared to other guys.

'It's mended now, thanks.'

'Good, I'm glad,' she said. 'My husband is with the Royal Navy. He was wounded in '39. He'll probably never walk straight again but he's up and doing in the Pacific, though where I don't know. It's all so very hush-hush.'

'I guess it needs to be.'

'I suppose so but it does mean waiting on news. Good or bad one is forever hovering on a thread. But there it is.' She drew the brim of her hat over her eyes. 'It's the price one pays for being a sailor's wife. Do you have family?'

'There's my Ma.'

'Just your mother?'

'I have cousins in Baltimore.'

'No sweetheart pining for her handsome Marine?'

'No.'

'What a waste. I can't believe you haven't been snapped up. There's no accounting for taste. Whereabouts in America or is that hush-hush too?'

'Ma is in Virginia.'

'Oh Virginia!' She closed her eyes. 'I love the Southern States. We were in Baton Rouge in '35 with the Mandevilles. Such fun! Do you know Henry and Lillian Manderville? They have horse stud there.'

'I don't.'

'Yes, such fun. I look back on that time and remember America as hot summers and cool mint julep.'

Gabriel thought on Parris Island and the State Pen and made no comment.

'Is that not you?' she said. 'No bougainvillea over the door?'

'Nu-huh.'

'Pity.' She stubbed the cigarette out and selected another, her nails the colour of blood. 'You do so fit into the image.'

'What image is that?'

'The image you convey with your clean and competent hands of the romance of the Deep South, of soft summer nights and perfumed air. Gosh, it's warm out here don't you think!'

She took off her hat lifting the fall of her hair from the back of her neck.

'Our bungalow is across the cove, a secluded spot not thirty minutes from the camp. We have a glass veranda. Warm in winter and cool in summer I spend a lot of time there sometimes all night wearing nothing but the night. Do you sleep so, Corporal? So much more natural I always think.'

Thinking he stood on the brink of trouble Gabriel stayed mute.

'Light me will you?' She licked her lips and straight away he saw Sue Ryland outside the Parlour sitting in that rubber tyre sucking a Popsicle. Wellington or Fredericksburg, shop-girl or sailor's wife the invitation is the same.

And he liked it! Boy did he! Standing so close together he got to see a lot, her sweating, the silky material of her frock clinging to her curves and the freckles on her left breast as a scattering of glittering sand.

She smelled hot and sweet as summer in a field of poppies.

Knowing the effect she was causing she tipped her head and smiled, a world of promise in her eyes. Dick throbbing between his legs, he ached to get the zipper working on that frock so it fell to the ground and he could take hold of those melon-shaped breasts and make her do more than smile.

'So do you sleep naked?' she said softly. 'A big fellow like you, so much muscle, I imagine that's a sight to behold.'

A grenade with the pin pulled her lighter was heavy in his hand. Such noise, glasses clinking and people talking he couldn't think. Through a haze of sunlight he saw guys locked in similar battles their backs turned and arms outstretched repelling boarders. And Captain Ridges! Hand under a woman's elbow he was on his way out. At the gate, as if answering a question, he shot a look. 'It's your choice, Corporal,' said his eyes. 'You either do or you don't.'

Gabriel's gaze carried on by the terrace windows. Long slabs of glass they reflected a Marine in Class A uniform, a Corporal, big guy, buttons gleaming and blonde hair shorn, and a woman with a cigarette between her lips, an offer in her eyes and a wedding ring on her finger.

'Excuse me, ma'am.' He bowed and sticking his cap under his arm moved on. 'I believe I'm wanted elsewhere.'

~

That evening he was told to report to HQ. The Colonel nodded. 'Stand easy, Corporal. I received a letter this morning from Gunnery Master Sergeant Emmet's wife thanking us for carrying his body home to South Carolina. The letter was addressed to me with a message for you.'

'For me?'

'Yes. Mrs Emmet asked I might read it out.'

'I see.'

'Do you see?'

Gabriel shook his head. 'No, sir, I don't.'

'Okay, well, neither do I but Jean Emmet is a close friend of my wife and Jim being about the best man I know I'll read the message. It says; 'Thank you, Gabriel Templar for the extra years. I am grateful for the thought but find that now my Jimmy's gone time has no meaning, years stretching into the night as an unlit road. So again I'm asking for your help. Cut the years to days, Gabriel, and Jimmy and I will bless you. I don't know how you will do this but am trusting that you can. Jean Emmet.''

It was quiet in the office, a blackbird singing out on a tree. The Colonel folded the letter. 'Having heard the message does it now make sense to you?'

For a while Gabriel couldn't speak. Then he nodded. 'Yes, sir.'

'It does?'

'Yes, sir.' Heart sinking, thinking here we go again, the freak-show, Gabriel opened his mouth to explain.

'Belay that!' The Colonel raised his hand. 'It is a personal issue of great importance to the Emmets and I'll enquire no further. If those two good people thought you worthy of trust it's enough for me.'

'Thank you, sir.'

'You were with Gunny when he died.

'I was.'

'I understand he died hard.'

'He died like Master Gunnery Sergeant JJ Emmet.'

'As I would expect.' The Colonel came round the desk. 'I guess you heard he recommended your latest hike up the ranks.'

Remembering sidelong looks and resentful whispering that accompanied every promotion Gabriel gritted his teeth. 'I did hear talk of that.'

'Yes and idiots suggesting you not worthy. Well, I can set you straight about the last hike if not the idiots. Gunny Emmet did recommend you for promotion while deployed in combat but I carried it through. I was at Henderson Field. I saw you set the charge and I saw you haul that young Lieutenant to safety when he took a hit. You saved lives that day, Corporal. '

'Wasn't me so much as the Lieutenant. He got the idea to haul it up there.'

'Yes and a fool idea it was! It ought never to have been attempted! Lugging explosive up the side of the hill, it's a wonder you weren't both killed.'

'Maybe so, but beggin' your pardon, sir, it did work.'

'More by luck than judgement as I shall inform the Lieutenant in question who happens to be my nephew. I shall tell him he was damned lucky to have you aboard. Most guys would've kicked his ass never mind carried him back. Fool kid! One of these days he's gonna break his mother's heart. Even so, as you say it worked and though I expect nothing less of a Marine I saw what you did. So forget what you hear from *Girenes* with nothing between their legs but pebbles. Stick with what you do know. Ex-con or not you are a first class Marine and worthy of recognition.'

~

Gabriel went back to the hut. That he's no longer seen as dead weight is okay but it doesn't take away Gunny Emmet's death. If killing Pa was murder then Gabriel Templar now stands a double murderer.

When he said JJ Emmet died a Master Gunnery Sergeant he told the truth but with half his chest shot away the man was in agony and would've died howling had Gabriel not cut the wires.

October 24th saw Marines in battle at Eniwetok defending the airport from Japanese attack. 1600 hours advancing through undergrowth their unit came under fire. Gunny was hit and Gabriel took shrapnel in his shoulder. They hid in a culvert hoping help would come.

You had to be there to see it! The side of his face and half his chest blown away, Gunny knew he wasn't going to make it. 'Leave me,' he says. 'Go get help for your shoulder.'

Gabriel wasn't leaving anyone, not after yesterday and the torture of Big Bo Ambrose. 0250 Bo was shot and dragged away screaming and kept on screaming until 0450 when Gunny couldn't take it anymore and lobbed a grenade over the palisade. It killed Bo as well as the Japs. 'That's okay,' says Gunny. 'He was going to die anyway. Better dead than howling.'

It was those words out the horse's mouth that Gabriel tried to remember when it was Gunny's turn to scream.

They were hunkered down in the culvert, mortar fire raging, and Gabriel trying to staunch the blood.

That's when he said it. 'Lob a grenade for me.'

Gabriel kept on mopping up blood.

'You heard what I said,' whispers Gunny. 'Give me opposite of what you gave Jeanie.' Gabriel knew what he was saying but thought to wait. Dug into a hole the size of a kiddie's sandpit, blanket fire and dead Marines everywhere, it felt to be only a matter of time before they were all dead.

'No way!' Gunny picked up his thought. 'You're not meant to die like that. See your shoulder blade poking through? You're meant to know how it feels to be human and to hurt but not to die. Him upstairs has other plans.'

'You're ramblin'.'

'I ain't rambling. The pain is bad. I'm hurting in my soul but I know what I'm saying and so does Jeanie.' He clutched Gabriel's arm. 'Cut me loose, son. I know you can do it. Remember Billy-Bob? The way you stuck your hand in and pulled that tooth? That's what I need you to do for me. Stick your hand inside my chest and pull my aching heart!'

'You don't know what you're askin'.'

'I do know and God won't mind. It's why you're here. You were born to help us lesser creatures in situations like this to put us out of pain. So Semper Fi, Angel Gabriel, be faithful! Cut the wires and set me free! '

Gabriel wasn't sure what he meant by cutting wires but knew what was meant about being the pain; he felt it as his own. 'Like still and save your strength,' he tried pacifying. 'Help may come.'

'Sure, help will come but not for me. No surgeon in this world can sew me back together. But you and your hands can set me on my way. So don't falter. It's too late to hold back. Be brave. Do what you came here to do.'

There could be no faltering. It was already happening. The minute Gunny asked so one-by-one wires were being cut. Gabriel didn't need to do anything but smooth the path, so smooth he did putting his hand into the gaping hole.

Bang, bang, that good old heart beat against his palm like a netted bird.

Eyes closed, Gabriel prayed that the pain would stop. And sure enough as though bathed in white light Gunny's face evened out.

'See! Oh Lord!' says Gunny. 'I said you could do it.'

Eyes wide open and smiling he lay against Gabriel's knee, a babe thinking on sleeping. 'Did you know the JJ in my name stands for Jim and Jeanie? When it was plain J I was a sinning China Marine with no hope of love. Then I met my Jeanie. She was like a song, the melody in my heart. We were one person. We are still. What she feels I feel and vice versa. Right now she's grateful.'

Gabriel had ached to tell him to hush up but the words wouldn't come.

'That Navaho injun said you were a Becoming Angel. That was his words, capitol B capitol A.' Gunny sighed. 'I don't mind telling you I laughed. I said what, like the cherubs you see in the bible with rosy cheeks and pudgy knees? The Injun shook his head. He said cherubs look nothing like that. That's man's idea of a Becoming Angel. So I said what do Becoming Angels look like? Do you know what he did? That Injun poked my chest. 'They look like you, Master Gunnery Sergeant!''

'Quiet now.' Gabriel tried to stop him talking.

'It's okay. I ain't got no pain and I want to tell you what I'm feeling. That Injun said you was his son in spirit. That he was sent to keep an eye on you to make sure no harm came to you. Now me and Jeanie always wanted children. I tell you if we'd had you for a son we'd be proud. '

'My Jeanie!' Colour fading like an ancient photograph Gunny was dying but shone with his love for Jeanie. 'I was a bum til I met her. She taught me so much. One day a Jeanie will come for you and teach you.'

Tick...tock...tick...tock, the heart in Gabriel's hand was barely beating.

'Well lookee-here! It's old Billy-Bob!' Smiling, Gunny lifted his hand and commenced stroking a donkey only he could see. 'Hello old boy! I'm real glad I didn't have to shoot you. Seems you made it over here anyway. That's okay.' He closed his eyes. 'Let's you and me set awhile and wait for Jeanie.'

~

That night Gabriel couldn't sit still. Unable to bear the hut and guys talking of the tea-party and the women they'd fucked he pulled on sweats and took to the beach running himself weary. He needed to settle the day, to forget the letter and Mrs Emmet asking the impossible. There was no miracle. Gunny died because half his chest was blown away. Nothing miraculous about that.

The moon hung over the sea a lamp washing the world with silver.

Gabriel kicked off his sneakers and ran. The sand felt good between his toes. It felt of life and flesh and blood and nothing of Navajo voodoo.

Head down, he ran knowing until this morning's letter guys had pretty much stopped seeing him a freak show. It happened in Parris Island, a ripping of his soul from his body, Gabriel leaving camp a different man with new freedom but also with a sense of loss.

The loss is hard to put into words; it's like being hollow, all special feelings emptied out. It's his own fault. In Parris Island he ordered his little gal to back off and she did the magic if not gone then a million light years away.

Today he was given an education in how it feels to be a Marine, the advantage of uniform and razzmatazz. At the time he turned the offer down. As Captain Ridges said, you either do or you don't. Well, ordinary guys do. Gabriel Templar is ordinary and means stay so.

Stopping for breath he took out the invitation card.

All evening the woman was back of his mind, the scent of her smelling of poppies. She was ordinary and talked of his hands but nothing about cutting wires and setting souls free. No freak-show required, she was clear in her wants. She wanted body warmth. Tonight that's what Gabriel wants.

The bungalow was set back of the trees. The light was on in the veranda.

She is there! He could see her pale shape beyond the glass. What's more she had seen him and getting to her feet slid back the door.

That she'd guessed he would come brought shame. Was he that much a giveaway? Then she slipped her robe over her shoulders and stood naked in the dim light and he didn't care what she thought. He let his body do his thinking and climbing the rise stripped so that by the time he reached the veranda he was as she said wearing nothing but the night.

~

It was around five when he left so weary he could hardly lift his feet. It was that kind of sex. Shoving and pushing, no kisses or sweet words their meeting the loneliness of war. It gave the body release but left the soul ashamed. That she felt the same was clear in the way she turned away as he was leaving.

It's okay. They are not likely to meet again. New orders cut Gabriel and his unit are soon to be back in the fray, talk of an Island hopping campaign across the Pacific. She will be fine. She'll get through this and be with her husband. Meanwhile there are other Marines with competent hands.

'Pity you're not in uniform,' she'd said grasping his balls. 'It's so incredibly sexy.' He had a mind to say, 'hold on, I'll run back and get my cap then we can take turn and turn about, you can wear it and you can fuck me.' But that would've been cruel. She was lonely and she was kind and she loved her husband enough to turn his photograph face down on the dresser.

The sun was a band of gold streaking the sky. Gabriel stood thinking on Gunny Emmet and his Jeanie and the quality of their love. No grappling in the dark with strangers for them. Lonely, ill or dying they would be true to the end.

Gabriel closed his eyes, held his hands up to the sun, and an ordinary man that he is sent out a prayer that when he fell in love it might be with the same enduring passion. That said, recalling his duty, and not wanting Gunny to be lonely he one-by-one cut the wires that held Mrs JJ Emmet to the earth.

Twenty
Peculiarities
St Augustine Private Clinic.
Bury-St-Edmonds, Suffolk
May '43

'Phff! Phff! Phff!' Adelia is panting.

'That's it, honey!' Bobby takes her arm. 'Keep breathin'
nice and relaxed and you'll be okay.'

'God's sake, Bobby!' She pulled away. 'I am in labour
and have been for what seems forever! Please stop telling
me I'll be okay.'

'Sorry honey, I guess I'm repeatin' myself.' He pulled
out a chair. 'Sit down a minute and I'll give you a back
rub.'

'It's me that should be sorry.' In tears, she flopped into
the chair. 'I am a selfish bitch full of my own concerns and
you with the transfer on your mind.'

'Forget the transfer! It's not on the cards yet. And if the
change does come about it's only along the coast so not that
far away.'

'Good. I wouldn't want you far away. I would miss
you.'

'You don't have to miss me.' He took her hand. 'I'm here and plannin' on stayin'. Selfish bitch or not you're stuck with me at least until our little Bump is brought safely into this world.'

Weary, she nodded. 'Yes, our little bump.'

A nurse took Dee away. Bobby sat in the waiting room confident that after months of trying to pin her down his plan is actually coming together.

Guys at the Base take their relationship for granted. 'How's the wife Captain America?' they say. 'She dropped your sprog yet?'

He laughs and says, 'it's no good askin' me. I don't know how these things work. I'm just the father that's all.'

They slap him on the shoulder. 'Bet you never thought you'd come away from this scramble with a wife, a sprog, and a DFC!'

'The thought never entered my head,' he says, 'though now you mention it I guess there's time to add another gong if not another sprog.'

'Jammy sod!' they say envy in the eyes. 'Talk about lucky!'

He grins. 'I guess I am lucky at that. But quit with the Captain America stuff, will you? You'll have me in trouble with Group.'

They need to drop it. Last time out the Wing Co gave him a bollicking. 'Quit the in-flight chat, O' Rourke! Your crew should maintain radio silence not arse around calling one another fancy names.'

The crew do arse around but that's because they're young and fresh out of training and scared. Humour gets you through. But they should quit harping on Bobby's luck.

Coming up fifty ops and still in one piece let's not rub Fate's nose in it. Others haven't had it so good. Most guys he flew with in the early years are dead. Same back home. Ma wrote that Herb Willet, Sue Ryland's husband, shot himself. Ma was almost gleeful. '*Put a gun in his mouth and blew his head off. But then he always was a whining kid.*'

Lately Bobby's been dropping hints suggesting he's coming home with more than a medal on his chest. While not wishing to poke the hornet's nest he wants to pave the way. Ma pretends she doesn't get the letters, 'I ain't had nothin' in months. I was thinkin' you'd forgotten your dear mother.'

Dear mother! It should be her blowing her head off. Herb Willet was missing an arm, she is missing a heart. The streets made her hard. Thirteen years old, Pa a drunk and mother in Western State asylum hard was all Ruby had to sell. Never having known love she doesn't know how to give love. Bobby can't recall ever being hugged. Muffled tears and the stink of spunk there's nothing of his childhood worth remembering.

It's the future that counts. Ma can declare Virginia a no-fly zone but the moment Dee says yes she and the babe are on the first plane out. Most folks think they're already married and with a transfer in the wind he needs to make it formal. He would have done it already but for Gabe Templar's miserable face always back of his mind. Last night Bobby put the problem to a bartender and told what happened in '42.

'It's the name Gabriel.'

The bartender stared like he was a nut.

'It's true though, isn't it?' Bobby had protested. 'Most folks think of angels when they hear the name Gabriel.'

The bartender had shrugged. 'I wouldn't like to say.'

'Go on say!' Bobby pressed. 'If I did that, if I stole your girl from under your nose and said she'd died wouldn't you sic an angel on me?'

'Never mind angel!' The bartender slammed the bar door. 'Cheat me out of my old lady I'd sic the Devil and all Hell on you!'

Bobby must propose. The new Base is not that far away yet with Dee still inclined to wander near is never near enough. He spoke to Covington Wright.

'I thought bein' pregnant would stop her. It slowed her down but that's all.'

'You're using your own sense of logic,' says the old guy. 'Adelia inhabits two worlds, the world of now and of yesterday. Her rules are not the same.'

'You make her sound crazy.'

'In my opinion to prefer the past to the present is far from crazy. We all wish we lived in more innocent times.'

'You mean she lives in the past?'

'I wouldn't say lives, more that she hankers after what the past meant. Wasn't it you said she visits St Giles to talk of a non-existent window and the architect who designed it?'

'The cop who sometimes walks her back to the apartment says she talks of the window and of a mouse sitting on the altar eating bread.'

'There you are! It's what she and her lover did. They visited St Giles and while they were there a mouse ate a crust of bread. Rather sweet I'd say.'

'I don't know about sweet! Do you think she wants to remember him?'

'I think her wandering is her looking to remember. She feels a double loss now for herself and her fatherless child.'

'The babe doesn't have to be fatherless.'

'I suppose not.' Covington Wright then looked at Bobby. 'I don't know who you are, Lieutenant, but I believe you do care. I wonder if you care enough to weather the storms that will inevitably accompany her.'

~

Quarter to ten and Her Highness reluctant to be born there is still no change in the baby department. The doctor poked his head round the door.

'Your wife said you should go home.'

'You mean it's a false alarm?'

'Contractions have stopped. They will start again but for now she is resting.'

'Nothin' wrong is there?'

'Not at all! A strong young woman and healthy heartbeat in both mother and child, it's the father who looks exhausted.'

'Can I see her?'

'She's sleeping. You should do the same.'

'Fat chance! Wanna slip me a bottle of knock-out drops, Doc?'

'Yes if it would give you rest! We have a visitor's suite. You could stay there.'

Bobby laughed. 'Do I look that bad?'

'As a matter of fact you do. When was the last time you slept, Captain, I mean *really* slept?'

'I don't know. It feels like a very long time ago.'

'Then considering the dangers attendant to your profession you should rest. It is your bed. You're paying for it.'

Thinking on the size of the hospital fees Bobby nodded. 'Ain't I just! But I'll pass, thanks, and go check the flat see everythin' is okay. Give my love to Dee. Tell her I'm rootin' for her. By the way, I'm with Bomber Command. They don't believe in Captains.' He picked up his jacket. 'And they don't believe in sleep.'

~

Motorbike fading into the night Adelia breathed a sigh of relief. 'Finally.'

The nurse smiled. 'Was your husband fussing?'

'Fuss isn't the word.'

Edna James was always saying it. 'My God, the man feeds on you. I don't know how you stand it. I would feel I was choking.'

'Bobby is kind man.' Adelia chose to defend him.

'I'm sure he is but can't you find a lonely British Tommy somewhere in this world who is as kind but not about to whizz you away to America?'

Adelia had laughed. 'I'm not going to America. England is where I was born and it's where I plan to stay.'

'Then you better say so! All the gifts and the flowers and baby-stuff, if you're not going to be with him it's not right to keep him hanging on.'

Adelia does say. She's always saying. Beyond writing 'I do not love you' in blood on the wall she doesn't know what else to say. As for flowers and baby stuff it's his way of wooing. No doubt he woos other women the same way.

He does see other women, his love of flirting common gossip and one of the reasons Adelia holds back. The pressure to give in is enormous and would overwhelm her if she wasn't careful. She tries paying her way with money from sale of the land but can't keep up with him, her stay in the clinic a case in point, booked and paid before she could say no.

It had to stop somewhere and Thursday and the gigantic pushchair was it.

'Oh, Bobby, you shouldn't have!'

His face had fallen. 'Don't you like it?'

'It's lovely.'

'I got it through the USO. I've been waitin' weeks.' He polished the handle. 'Accordin' to the sales-pitch the Burlington is the Rolls Royce of buggies.'

'It is wonderful but you must let me pay for it.'

'Don't talk of payin'! It's a gift for Chrissakes!'

'I know but I can't keep letting you do it!'

'Forget it! You don't want it?' He picked up the pushchair and threw it down the stairs. 'You don't get it.'

She heard it went into the canal. Shame! He was so proud of it and she was clumsy in refusing. Now, cutting her nose to spite her face she's had to get another and one not nearly as nice from the pawn-shop under the viaduct.

Losing his temper like that brought the former Bobby back. It made her think she's best alone. She hates being dependent! Thinking for herself is how she got through college and nursing school. Now with the War dragging on and the baby due, and this damned illness, she is afraid to trust her own judgement.

Mr Covington Wright likes Bobby. 'You could do worse. He seems to care and let's face it, Nurse Challoner, not everyone is sympathetic to your plight.'

As she is learning! Last Monday the doorbell rang. Two women stood on the step for more than an hour lecturing her on children's rights. They left and Edna James came running. 'What did those two old biddies want?'

Adelia said she thought they were raising money for war-orphans.

'War orphans my eye! They're from the Christian Morality League.'

'Christian Morality League? What do they want?'

'I don't know but it'll be St Faiths doing. Matron is Secretary of the League. They must have heard something they don't like and come sniffing it out.'

Adelia had laughed. 'You make them sound like the Spanish Inquisition.'

Edna wasn't amused. 'I wouldn't be too giddy about it if I were you. The older woman is a Justice of the Peace and sits on the local bench. Tough old girl, you wouldn't want her rooting through your private matters not with your little peculiarities. Not everybody is as broad-minded as me you know.'

Adelia spent the night wishing she could root through her own private matters then she might learn something. She knows less about said 'little peculiarities' than anyone. Nora and Edna James and Mr Covington Wright and the psychiatrist have all at some time voiced an opinion as to what and why. Nobody worries more than Adelia but with no answers can only wonder why the Christian Morality League are knocking at the door.

'Ooh!'

As if to answer a contraction racked her body and Adelia knew that being regarded as 'not quite right in the head' is why they knocked.

The psychiatrist says that when Adelia is unwell another woman emerges.

'I believe it to be a protective mechanism, Nurse Challoner that when you are feeling weak or unwell a personality stronger than the everyday you arrives to pick up the slack.'

'And who are you talking to now, doctor?' she'd asked. 'The everyday me or the pugilist?'

He'd smiled. 'I'm not sure. A bit of both I'd say.' He attributed the seizures to the blow on her head. 'You sustained physical damage which in turn led to psychosomatic pressures. It is my belief you sleep through much of the day.'

'Do you mean as in sleep-walking!'

'Well, something of that nature. Not perhaps sleeping so much as operating from a safe distance.'

'I don't know what you mean by operating at a safe distance.'

'I mean that there is a lot of undercover activity in your psyche and the fainting and the so-called wandering are part of that activity.'

'Doctor, this undercover activity sounds rather dangerous.'

'Your condition is not without dangers though thinking in terms of actual sleepwalking the subconscious alerts the potential walker to trouble as it alerts you hence you cross roads and dodge traffic and walk round walls rather than into them using the inner radar that all sleep-walkers possess.'

He was smiling when he said that.

Adelia was not amused. 'But anything could happen!'

He smile died. 'I'm not saying otherwise. War or not, a woman wandering the streets alone at night is bound to be in danger. I confess that having read your notes I'm amazed you got off so lightly.'

Much of this was said when she was in the Annexe with her wrists bound and tied to the bed. In answer she had held out her hands. 'You think this, me being treated like a wayward child is getting off lightly?'

'I'm sorry,' he'd apologised. 'I'm sure this is painful for you.'

'You have no idea how painful. I have no real memory of what happens and because of that I am called a liar and a whore and told that the best thing for everyone would be for me to be locked away.'

When asked if this horror will ever stop the psychiatrist says every case is different, that most patients displaying such symptoms will have suffered physical trauma but that given time her memory should return. He says this while prescribing chlorpromazine, a knock out drug so strong it gives her vertigo so that even during the day she staggers like a drunk.

Each night before bed she prays not to do anything silly yet around three in the morning another Adelia - who clearly doesn't give a hoot for drugs and those that prescribe them - slides out of bed and into St Giles Church keeping a rendezvous with a tramp.

She is the talk of Needham. A policeman who sees her home tries to make her smile. 'We're going to have to stop meeting like this, Missy. You're close to popping and I'm no good at delivering babbies as my wife would tell you.'

Adelia shakes her head. 'You must think me an awful pest.'

'I don't think anything of the sort,' says he. 'But you need to be careful. This War has shaken all kinds of rats out the woodwork. There's them that would take advantage of a woman in your circumstances and there's the good sort.'

Then the kindly father-figure is overtaken by an officer of the law. 'The bloke that sits with you in St Giles, the big feller? Known him long, have you? Only I'd like a word but he disappears when I arrive.'

Knowing these are questions she can't answer Adelia smiles and closes the door. To be known as the local eccentric is enough without being suspected of romancing a tramp. Anyway, he is asking the wrong person. It's the other Adelia he wants. She has the answers to everything. This everyday Adelia only remembers a frayed cuff on the tramp's sleeve and the soft American drawl that thanked her for a share of a cheese and tomato sandwich.

~

Dee had her daughter at precisely four am, Bobby knows because he was there watching the hands on the clock go round. While he wasn't exactly in the delivery ward, not pacing the floor or holding her hand, he was there.

It was around 2200 hours when he left the Clinic, too late for the pubs but okay for the Pink Flamingo. The Pink Flamingo Casino is known to guys at the Base. You can bet on anything there from a blackjack shuffle to the gaps in the stripper's teeth.

The stripper tonight wasn't all bad. When she finally quit fannying up and down the stage and got down to the buff she was more wrinkled than she should be even so she was worth a grapple in an upstairs room.

Five quid it cost him. Five quid! No way was she worth that! For a start she smoked cheap *Players Weights* ciggies, her breath like a sick horse. 'Christ!' he says, pushing her head down to the lower levels. 'Don't bother with a gas-mask, honey. Smoke those and you'll make your own sulphur.'

It nearly knocked him out. But never mind. Like all broads who've seen better days she made up for it oral fashion, two minutes and he's a spouting whale.

So he paid and came out smiling. The smile didn't last and that because he dared to grab a couple of winks in Dee's bed.

It was a mistake. A man should never sleep in a girl's bed unless his reasons for doing so are virgin pure. It leads to nightmares. Having been relieved of a load in the Pink Flamingo all he wanted was sleep but as he said to the Doc, sleep and Captain America don't go together.

A key to her apartment he opened the door to heaven. Clean? You could have ate off the floor. She'd spent the better part of a week getting it ready. It is tiny yet cosy with colourful drapes and lavender smelling bed-linen.

You don't get clean sheets in barracks. You get a blanket and a biscuit for a mattress. Back home if didn't do his own laundry then sweaty sheets would be all he got. Same with cleaning the house! Ma's not into housework. She does her own rooms but that's all so once a week Bobby pitches in.

Radio on and him boogying about with a broom he used to quite enjoy it. He never told anyone he kept the house clean and neither did Ma.

Three floors plus a top attic most of the rooms are unused the furniture hung with dust sheets. Bobby is fussy about his things. Open his closet and you see neat rows of Brooks Brothers' coveralls. In Dee's apartment the smell of fresh bread drifts up the stairs while lavender wax drifts down. Small but tidy it suits his soul especially with the baby stuff. He got the cot from a market dealer. Britain is broke so most of Dee's stuff got is second-hand including the buggy.

He was angry when he kicked the other buggy down the stairs. She didn't like his anger. It made her wary. She was right to be wary because in that moment it was her he wanted to kick down the stairs.

Penny-pinching shit! Why the fuss? Why not accept and be happy?

It's a bad thing about her. He sees it as delaying tactics keeping him at a distance. While she does that, promotes independence, she keeps offers of marriage out his mouth and his dick in his pants.

~

The bed looks comfortable and he is tired. He kicked off his shoes. A combination of baby powder and Dee he lay breathing her in. Then a dark cloth descended and he slept. Later, thinking about what happened he wondered if he's a sex maniac. Only an hour before a stripper had given him a decent blow-job but sleeping in Dee's bed he dreamt of seeing her naked.

A strange dream, hot and dirty it made his heart pound. Towel draped about her she came out the bathroom. Not the tiny tub here! This was a great lolloping bathroom, gold-plated faucets and all.

He was lying on the bed thinking she was even more beautiful now she's older. Then in the dream she drops the towel and breasts caressing his chest slides across him and he's dying of love and desperate to get inside her but can't get it up his dick flopped against his groin as a broken bird.

And he's weeping! Actual tears running down his cheeks! And she's hugging him, 'it's alright,' she's saying. 'Don't worry. We can get through this.'

Jesus! He lurched up in the bed. What was that about?

Nerves shrieking, he scrambled for a cigarette. He's had nightmares before when drinking but nothing like that and never about being impotent.

It was so real! Even now he can see the rose-tips of her breasts and feel her arms about him. And the pain! His heart was being torn to pieces.

No fucking way!

He tossed the cigarette. This non-romance has to stop! If this is what it does, makes him question his abilities she has to go. Shocked, he lay back on the pillow. Got to get his breath back! He can't go to the Clinic feeling like this.

Maybe it was thought of the Clinic that took him there. Next he knows he's asleep again and in the delivery ward. And he's not alone! Tall and silent like stone carvings the other two are there.

It came to him then as it had so many times before how alike Alex and Gabe are in build and purpose, the Sun and the Moon, good men, honourable men, a lie never passing their lips, the Light of truth shining about them.

Bobby's always known them to be the good guys. It didn't matter what fantasy he spun, Gabe a moron and Alex Hunter a stick-in-the-mud. Those two shone bright as any stars. What he hadn't known or even imagined was that he too shone with the same Light.

There they were grouped about the bed, three men linked together in a circle encompassing the woman and her babe, and all five held in a luminous glow that throbbed with the beating of his heart.

Joy filled his soul. Love of Dee and her babe and the other two filled his heart. Such a love! It was a holy thing from God. He'd never felt anything like it before nor would again.

He woke, dressed and slipped away. Bobby didn't need to ask about the Light nor why the silent watchers were there. Like him they were joined in the same battle and the same love and always would be.

Part Three
The
Cuckoos

Twenty-one
Baptism
October 31st 1943
St James the Less Church
Needham

Adelia frowned. 'What do you mean concerns?'

The Vicar coughed. 'As I said, while I am only too delighted to welcome Sophie into our flock here at St James-the-Less there are issues we need to discuss.'

'Such as?'

'Well, such as God-parents and their commitment to Sophie.'

'I told you. Mr and Mrs Albert Jackson are to be Godparents. They offered and since I have no one else I was glad to accept. They are good people. They love Sophie and she loves them.'

'I'm sure they do. Sophie is a delightful child. Who could not love her?'

A telephone rang in the next room. Visibly relieved, the Vicar hurried away leaving Adelia wanting to punch his nose. Ten o clock was the appointed time. It is now gone eleven. Three quarters of an hour she waited in the Vestry among dusty hymn books and sweaty robes. On view is the only way to describe it, heads popping round the door, the curate and cleaning lady with offers of weak tea and other piddling excuses to gawp at the loose woman.

Loose woman, an absurd expression that but for another poisonous note through the letter-box she would dismiss as absurd.

Red ink scrawled across unlined paper, the author missing the A off Adelia, it's the third of its kind; '*One Yank down Delia and another sniffing your skirt there's a name for loose women like you. You should be ashamed. What's your little girl going to think when she hears how her mother runs her life?*'

That was the basic tenor of note and with it, as with every note, a day-by-day listing of the week, where Adelia had been and what she had done, small things such as missing church last Sunday and dashing down the road to catch the milkman and the door on the latch and Sophie inside,' *where anything could have happened! The place set fire and the baby burned to death.*'

A war crashing about them you wouldn't think anyone would bother to detail her life yet someone does, probably another to add to the list of those in the past who never thought to speak but now insist on calling her Miss and always with Sophie in tow. The butcher's wife manages at least three Misses when passing the weekly chop. Then there's the Librarian who defied her own ruling to shout that 'the new Doctor Spock is in, Miss, if you've a mind to read it!'

Last Sunday the Vicar's wife bent over the push-chair; 'Good-morning to you, *Miss* Challoner, and how is poor dear Little Sophie today?' Adelia managed to resist saying, 'thank you, Mrs Tarrant, poor dear little Sophie is well. As yet Satan hasn't dropped in for tea but if he does I'll be sure to give you a call.'

Such retorts stay in the head rather than on the lips. While not exactly numb to the situation Adelia goes with the flow sooner than argue but this third degree when trying to arrange baptism is a bit much.

'Sorry for keeping you waiting.' Red-faced and mumbling he's back. 'Being at everyone's beck and call is my lot these days as I'm sure you appreciate.'

Adelia stared, silence growing he continued. 'It's like this, Miss er... Challoner, I am not sure of your marital status.'

Still she stared. Damn it, she thought, you created the situation deal with it.

'One hears so many things, and because I don't know if you are legally married I'm not sure whether the child I baptise is of legitimate parentage.'

'Does it matter?'

'Maybe not so much from a point of law but from the churches canon yes! Perhaps you'd enlighten me as to your status. It is my understanding you're not married and Sophie born out of wedlock.'

'Yes.'

'Oh!' He blinked. 'You are not married and Sophie born out of wedlock?'

'Correct. I am not married and Sophie was born out of wedlock. Shall I say it again or perhaps write it so that you have it in black and white?'

'There's no need to take offence. I'm trying to establish the truth.'

'And the truth is I am single with illegitimate daughter.'

'Dear me! You are aggressive and if I may say unnecessarily so.'

Embarrassment giving way to indignation he leaned back in the chair. 'Think of it, Sophie born of one American and you currently involved with a pilot from the Base who claims you as wife is it any wonder people are confused.'

'People? What people?' Furious, she dug in. 'I don't care about people! Who are they to be confused? My life is nothing to do with them or you for that matter other than you helping me bring my daughter into the church.'

'I hear different stories.'

'There is only one story. I am not married nor ever have been. Sophie is mine and mine alone. That's it. Or is it not facts you want so much as gossip.'

'If there is gossip, Miss Challoner, you've only yourself to blame. Your unhappy life provokes speculation. Your affairs are none of my concern yet are continually brought to my door as are your late night wanderings.'

'Ah, so you do listen to tales! What a pity! Had you enquired of me I could've told you that my unhappy life, as you refer to it, is hardly worthy of gossip. I rent a flat above the bakers. I have a small sum of money left from the sale of my Aunt's land that enables me to pay my rent. No one foots my bills! I pay my own way. It's true I have a friend in the pilot you thought fit to mention and being a friend he likes to bring Sophie gifts. I can't stop him doing that. Why would I when he enjoys giving and she receiving?'

'I say, Miss Challoner, there's really no need to continue.'

'Oh but there is as I learned this morning opening my mail! I had what you might call a poison-pen letter and not the first I might add. It seems people worry about the way I live though if they knew me they'd see it nothing out of ordinary. My mind troubles me and there you are right to call me unhappy, a bomb in '42 making me so. But that is my burden and I must carry it, not you.'

'Mea culpa! I'm sorry!' He held up his hand. 'You are right to chastise. I did hear rumours and as shepherd to the flock should have learned from you instead of listening to others and for that I apologise. As for you being here today I meant well. My concern was for you and your daughter.'

'Never mind! It's done now.' She took up her gloves.

'And the Christening?'

'I'll get back to you.'

'As you wish.' Uncomfortable, he hovered. 'I understand there's a Halloween party at the Base this afternoon.'

'Yes, we're going.'

'Halloween?' He rolled his eyes. 'It's an American thing. I understand that people need to laugh and be happy but being of the cloth I think on the sanctity of the occasion rather than trick-a-treat. All Hallows Eve is a special time where we should mourn those we have lost.'

'And most of us have plenty to mourn.'

'Indeed.' Anxious, he looked at her. 'Will you come back and see me?'

'All being well we'll be in church on Sunday.'

'Miss Challoner, Adelia?' He took her hand. 'When I heard you wanted Sophie baptised I was glad and would have done it no questions asked. I thought while you were here I might warn you that your life is a source of interest to the wise *and* the foolish and that in time of war people say and do ugly things.'

'As I am every day finding out!'

'Very well then. Please know you are always welcome at St James. We are a small community yet we try to take care of our own. I shall pray for you and ask that you do the same, committing your life and troubles to the care and safety of the Lord Jesus Christ, especially at night.'

Adelia put on her gloves. 'Thank you, I have already done that and am assured He is there for Sophie and me day and night.'

~

Men at the Base put on a Halloween party for local children. Fairy-lights hanging from the roof a wind-up gramophone and trestle-tables laden with cake and soft drinks, it's quite an affair. Ladies from the village came to help Adelia among them. Now at gone six the party is coming to a close.

Worn out, Sophie sleeps. Nora has the pushchair outside in the cool evening air. 'It's time she went home. It's too noisy in there.'

It is noisy. Adelia wants to go home but must wait while the last few children shriek up and down the Hangar trying to pin the tail on a donkey, the donkey in question Flight Lieutenant Bobby Rourke dressed in dyed pink camouflage overalls and woolly ears.

'Good evening, Mrs Rourke.' The Air-Base Commander sat down beside her. 'I guess this trick-or-treat rag is new to you here in Suffolk.'

'We don't usually celebrate it.'

'It gets a little rowdy but it's only once a year and if kids are not making a racket they're not happy.'

'You speak from experience, Squadron Leader?'

'I do, though it feels more like from memory. Two years since I was home and both my boys growing up fast, I reckon they'll be making a whole new noise.'

'How old are they?'

'Johnny is coming up ten and Benny seven.'

'Such a long time away you must miss them.'

'I do. I miss them all, my home and my dogs and horses, I don't like being away. Things happen when you're not close by. Mistakes are made and nothing you can do about it.'

A true remark and so close to home Adelia chose to bypass it. 'The decorations are jolly. Your men put in a lot of effort.'

'They had a tough task-master in your husband. He kept them at it.'

'A born ring-master Bobby loves any kind of circus. I wouldn't like to say who is enjoying this more him or the children.'

'He sure likes to put on a show. The guys here appreciate him but as of tomorrow he belongs to Bradwell and Avro Mosquitoes. He'll like it fine. It is as you British say his cup-of-tea.'

'He is looking forward to it.'

'But not you, Mrs Rourke, I imagine.'

Adelia weighed her answer. 'It's not too far and he must do as he is bid.'

'As must we all. Good evening to you, ma'am.' The Squadron Leader tipped a salute and wandered away. Another who calls her Mrs Rourke. Bobby's Commanding Officer knows they are not married but a courteous man he goes with the party-line rather than embarrass.

On reflection Adelia feels sorry for the Vicar. He did mean well and what he said about gossip being her fault is true. Dithering has helped no one. Certainly Bobby thinks so, his concern for Sophie funny if wasn't sad.

'You're doin' her no favours. Next thing you know some kid'll be callin' her dirty names.' He clenched his jaw. 'Better not do it when I'm around.'

As if that will happen! Sophie is an angel. No one would ever say anything nasty about her. Skin like milk, dark curls and bluest of eyes she is beautiful and such a joy to own that every day no matter her beginnings Adelia thanks God for the man who brought such treasure to the world.

According to Edna James the American soldier had the same amazing eyes. '*They say he was a real dish.*' Then there's Luigi in the Bistro: '*Why he leave you, Miss Addy? He stare like he want to eat you more than my omelette.*'

Sophie smiling through the bars of her cot every morning the amazing eyes cannot be denied. But that is old news. Last week Sophie had a cold.

A healthy baby she wasn't ill for long but it scared Adelia. It made her see that despite friends like Nora Sophie is utterly dependent on her mother, that there is no one else to help her through.

Strange how a little thing like the common cold can change the world. The need for independence is all very well if you are able to carry it through. If you can't then you shouldn't take chances. If after Christmas Bobby Rourke still wants them, then it will be a new year, a new name, and a new country.

Sophie adores him. She would be happy to have him for a daddy and yes America would be good for them both but it is wrong, so wrong! They can go to America. Adelia can try to make him happy but how can she succeed when she believes the hole in her heart - that no matter what he says or does Bobby cannot fill - will one day be filled, that the door bell will ring and a man with blue eyes will say, 'it's me. I've come back.'

~

Bobby transfers to Bradwell tomorrow. Adelia plans a going away present. Seven o clock that evening Sophie is tucked up asleep and the table laid for dinner. Eight o clock he rang the bell. Perhaps she should forget the wine for though smiling and seemingly relaxed Bobby's clearly been drinking.

'Hold it!' He shoves a camera round the door. 'That's it now smile, you gorgeous creature.'

Adelia bared her teeth.

'Jesus, not like that! You look like you're about to eat me.'

'No, I'm not about to eat you.'

'Shame, I would love for that to happen. Now smile properly. You know, like the big, blue-eyed bruiser is marchin' through the door.'

Adelia smiled.

He clicks the shutter. 'That's more like it.' Tanned and handsome, he leans against the dresser. 'So how are you, honey babe? Did you and the parson settle the baptism baloney?'

'You think it baloney?'

He shrugged. 'Does it matter what I think?'

'Yes.'

'Really? Well, that's a first! But never mind, if you're seriously askin' my opinion then I'm seriously sayin' it's bullshit. There ain't nobody up there lookin' after anyone down here just as there's not too many down here lookin' after anyone down here.'

'Oh Bobby!'

'What do you mean Oh Bobby! It's a fact. Nobody cares if we live or die. It ain't the nature of things. I'm damn sure nobody cares about me. The Kraut that strafed my Lancs yesterday didn't care. All he wanted was me and the rest of my crew spinnin' down to earth screamin'. But then that's what I wanted for him. Kill or be killed, honey, it's the way it is.'

'It's not the way. There is love in the world and always will be.'

'Love?' he scoffed. 'You kill me you really do. Here you are in this poky apartment, no room to swing the proverbial, bombs droppin' and half the country in ruins, you and your kid alone 'cos some guy walked out and you're thinkin' love? What are you some kind of nut?'

'Probably.'

'I mean, who does that? Who speaks of love when they've nothin' to back it up? You can't be talkin' of blue eyes. The guy left you for dead and you with fire in the hole! Where's the love in that? And you surely can't be referrin' to this town when all you got is hypocrites spoutin' gospel and dirty minds callin' your daughter a bastard!'

'There is love. You just need to see it.'

'Then I must be blind 'cos I don't see it. I see the world at war and folks livin' hand to mouth who'd sooner shoot than smile. The parson is right. You need to watch out. People *are* tricky. If they don't like you, if you upset them, if you start stirring the primeval mud they start wavin' pitchforks.'

'Primeval mud! Bobby, you do exaggerate! This is Needham not Salem. I'm not a threat to anyone.'

'How do you know?'

'What do you mean?'

'Like I said, how do you know you're not a threat? Sittin' talkin' with people that ain't there about a window long since blown tohell isn't exactly sane. You worry people. You have them questionin' their sanity never mind yours.'

'Don't be silly.'

'I ain't bein' silly. You got any recollection of sittin' talkin' with moon dust.'

'You are being silly.'

'No I'm not. I'm askin' if you remember what you do when you go walkabout. Do you come back here knowin' you spent the mornin' talkin' to shadows about a window that isn't there? Do you recollect doin' that?'

'I don't remember everything I do but then who does? Do you remember everything said and done when as you say you are wishing a Kraut dead?'

'As a matter of fact yes. At such moments I'm firin' on all cylinders, adrenaline runnin' hot. I see it now. I can reach back to the moment when the tail-feathers on the Kraut went and he, poor shit, tried turning into the wind when there wasn't one. It was calm over the North Sea not a ripple. I can tell you the last thing he saw before he died because I saw it too, trillions of stars and suns and moons, the unimaginable backdrop that the God you believe in hangs out every night and has done since the beginnin' of time for murderin' thugs like me and the Kraut to look on as we die. That's how vividly I remember.'

'Well, I don't kill people and so I don't recall such things. It's true I'm not always sure of what I've said and done but I don't believe I'm dangerous.'

'You're not! You are an amazingly beautiful woman, the queen of my heart who happens to be crazy as a loon so that the danger, if there is any, is for me and no one else. And that's it! Bye-bye Baby!'

A sharp crack echoing he slapped his hands together. Next door Sophie whimpered. In he went scooping her out the cot, smiling all traces of anger gone. 'Well, lookee who's awake and smilin'.' He buried his face in her neck. 'Did your nasty old Da-da wake you?'

'Da-da.'

'Yeah that's right!' Jubilant, he crowed, 'I am your Da-da, the one and only. See?' He turned to Adelia. 'She called me Dada!'

'I heard.' Adelia took Sophie and brooking no argument laid her down again in the cot, 'though at six months she doesn't speak at all. She parrots you.'

'She don't parrot! This is one bright child. She hears a thing and gets it straight away. I know. I've been watchin'. It's a memory thing.'

'You think so?'

'I know so.'

'Memory or not it's time she was asleep. It's market day tomorrow and rumours of fresh fruit. Also,' she looked up. 'I've made dinner.'

'Ah!' He nodded. 'So that's the delicious smell. I did wonder.'

'I got beef from the butcher and made pot-roast.'

'How did you do that? Was it a case of partin' with more than money?'

'Possibly an extra flash of the teeth.'

'I hope that's all you flashed. I know that butcher. He has the hots for you. But then he's not alone. The whole Base has the hots for you.'

Adelia sighed. 'I don't care about the Base. I care about you and me and Sophie. As for the butcher we have pot roast and wine. Not very good wine, I'm afraid, but wine nevertheless.'

'Wine, huh?' He picked up the blue teddy and holding it over his face mimicked the teddy speaking. 'So what's up, Doc? What are we celebratin' other than me movin' on down the coast?'

'What would you like to celebrate?'

'I'm not sure. This invitation is makin' me nervous. Usually you can't wait to get me out the door. Now I'm gettin' new vibes.'

'Do you like the vibes you're getting?'

'Like them! If they're the vibes I'm thinkin' you bet your life!'

He was leaning down and though smiling his lips were tight.

Adelia was ashamed. This is his life too! How dared she think she could play with it? She put the teddy in the cot. 'I did think we might celebrate.' She took his hand. 'It all depends on whether you still have the hots for me.'

~

He left around two, the door closing. Adelia lay staring at the ceiling. At four-thirty she got up and going to the wardrobe took out the red waterproof cape seen in the pawn-shop last week. Corded velvet, it is lovely if rather worn.

Abe behind the counter wondered. 'Why would you buy this, lady? It was good once but like me has lost its glory.'

The Other Adelia, the glamorous girl, likes it because red is her favourite colour. The miserable one, the sad-sack, sat all last week sewing rips and wondering why she'd bought it. She had it dry-cleaned. Now though still water-marked it smells less of mothballs and more of the lavender bag in the pocket.

Sophie adores the cape and plays peek-a-boo with the hood. It's how they go out for their special walks, Sophie in the pushchair in pink rabbit pyjamas and the hat with tiger's ears Bobby bought and Adelia in the raincoat.

Tomatoes are why they're up early. They always take a sandwich on walkabout. It's why they're after tomatoes.

They grow bits but they are soon used up and so they are for the market, but first St Giles and the window.

Adelia loves St Giles. It's the one place she feels safe. It doesn't matter what's going on outside, the world could be dissolving yet here under the Great Window nothing can hurt them. She knows that because the tramp said so.

She hasn't asked his name. Rough beard and tangled fair hair, he's always here in the shadow of the pulpit, long legs shoved out and boots down at heel.

Bobby says he doesn't exist. 'No one but you has seen him. He's another shadow you talk to.'

It's not true; a policeman on the beat has seen him. He's not a tramp. He is down on his luck that's all. It's why she brings a sandwich. They don't talk. She tells of the window and he listens. He smells as though he lives in a warren. She wanted to offer a bath but the thought of Edna's face put a stop to that.

Edna James is protective of Sophie. 'If you feel the need to go out I'll always baby-sit. Me and Ted love kiddies. We can't wait for when our daughter has hers.' Then she passes a loaf. 'I've put rusks in the bag. She can suck them. Much better than the sweets your Yank brings. They will ruin her teeth.

Edna worries about her lodger's state of mind. Nora is another always hinting of danger. Adelia knows they care. She also knows if things were to go wrong, if Sophie was to get hurt, they would be first taking up a pitchfork.

What is it they see? Is she that much of a problem? It's true she used to go out at night but that was before Sophie was born. Now if they go out at all it is early morning and sunlight breaking over the horizon, and the birds singing and the horror of war somehow softened.

The psychiatrist believes she makes these trips when she's had a shock. If that is true then the poison pen letters do not help. Red ink trickling across the page they are malevolent. There was another waiting this morning. '*If I were you, Delia, I'd watch what I was doing. Entertaining that Yank until the early hours, it's disgusting. You should be locked away in a place for mad people.*'

She showed it to the psychiatrist. He didn't seem surprised. 'People are quick to judge.' He didn't say if he thought their judgements were right. He made notes in her file changing the original diagnosis of post-traumatic stress to 'a chronic condition where in emotional turmoil the patient suffers blackouts.'

Blackout is the right word. During such an event Adelia moves on automatic pilot. At some point she'll wake. It might be seven in the evening, Sophie asleep in her cot and everything normal, yet what happened during those seven hours she couldn't say. She listens and learns taking her cues from what is given. Nora might talk of the day. 'Wasn't Sophie funny today? All those ducks pecking at rusks! I thought she was going to fall in the pond.'

There it is, Sophie feeding the ducks in the park! Given the right clue a memory will rise and like am embroidered fan the day will open.

Words are what Adelia needs. Supply them and like the ducks she'll quack.

But it is so wearing! It is exhausting. She can't think anymore. She leaves thinking with the Adelia who knows it's wrong to marry Bobby. If she didn't leave it, if there wasn't another to carry the load, both Adelias would go mad!

Take last night! She had planned to have sex with Bobby. There was sex but a sensitive man beneath the flamboyance he saw the wine and pot-roast as payment for tickets to America and offended he held back and what should have been a mutually loving affair became delicious punishment.

He didn't stay. Jaw taut he stood at the door. 'Soon as I'm settled we'll talk marriage.' She didn't argue, after two raging orgasms she couldn't. No turning back, it'll be a quiet ceremony so that when the butcher's wife calls her Miss Adelia can wave a wedding ring under her nose, a small triumph yet satisfying.

It is a beautiful morning, sunbeams shining on the wreckage of a world war. In the Other World of Happy Adelia the window is as it was before the war, the blue of the Virgin's robe illuminating the white of angel's wings.

The stained glass reflects down onto the nave, the angel appearing to fly upward out of the stone. Sophie asleep in her arms Adelia kneels in the dust.

'I'm sorry Nora and you Bert,' she whispered, 'you would've made wonderful Godparents but you're here in Suffolk and we are to be in America. It is enough that I cheat Bobby. I can't cheat God and I can't cheat you.'

A breeze wafted through the church, a door opening. The tramp is here!

Adelia continued with her prayer. 'Dear Lord, this is my daughter, Sophie Emma. Please accept her into Your care. Please love her and keep her safe through this world and this life for evermore. Thank you. Amen.'

The tramp kneels beside her in the dust. 'Amen,' his deep voice echoing the prayer. It is only when back home hanging up the red cape Adelia finds a single white feather caught in the sleeve of the cape that she remembers a dream where she knelt at the altar with a man whose eyes were blue as the sky and where another man stood apart and a bomb fell through the roof white angel feathers scattering.

Twenty-two
Primrose Alley
February 1944.
Rome.

The kick-start happened at a bottleneck near the Via Di
Anna, a narrow alley running down a side-street beside a
cafe. Alex knows that alley. He remembers it from ten
years ago when he and Mom and Sarah were on the
European Tour. It stood out in his mind because of a waiter
kissing a girl. She was sitting top of a stack of beer crates
with her arms about his neck. Tanned knees and raspberry
pink skirt, Alex can see her now as he can hear the waiter
laughing.

No laughs today. There's the sound of feet tramping and
a trigger-happy guard barking commands, beyond that it's
eerily quiet, a crowd of on-lookers watching in silence.

What a difference in a decade! Dad deployed to Manila
in '34, Mom was free from his control, Sarah a teenage
beauty with fiery hair and temper to match, and him a
college kid with braces on his teeth. They were happy that
day and carried cameras and Baedekers. Rome is an
amazing city. They toured the Coliseum necks aching from
gaping upward. They shuffled through St Peters Basilica and
onto Leonardo da Vinci and the Sistine Chapel. Heavy with

history the city numbs you into awe, even Sarah was subdued.

Today acting Lieutenant Colonel Alexander Hunter, Ist Battalion US Rangers, returns again to the Holy Roman City but this time under guard, a prisoner captive to the German war machine.

But not for long.

Streets, rivers and mountains, all information is noted and stored from his last visit. He has no need of a Baedeker. As for a Camera he brings his own deluxe model which according to a former C/O in Achnacarry is currently being closely monitored by US Intelligence, the message, 'we'll be in touch.'

What is he supposed to make of that? Is he meant to say, 'Golly Gee! How exciting! Hang on, sir. As soon as I've quit this war I'll join yours.'

Spook bullshit! Until his latest promotion is ratified he remains a humble Major under US Army command and has neither the power nor the wish to change that, all former hopes and aspirations swept away in the loss of love and the death of hundreds of men Joe Petowski among them.

If anything has made a bitter world colder it is Joe dying. Men like Joe are not supposed to die. They are made of iron. They eat raw meat, drink bat's blood and shoot sparks when they fart or so we believe. It turns out they die same as everyone else though in Joe's case - this at least expected- with courage and a last chance to instruct his Godson. 'Quit blaming yourself. Go find the, dirtiest whore and fuck until memory of that girl is obliterated. Do it and I'll die happy.'

Nothing of that was said that day yet it was felt in the grip of his hand. So there in puddles of blood and rain Alex promised to try to forget.

One day he will try but not today.

Today is about an alley here by *Campo de Fiori* and a farmer leaning on a dung-cart who is desperate to get through the crush and on his way because no sewage on the fields means no food on the plate.

Alex spotted the cart as they turned the corner. A four-foot high layered pile of horse shit and piss-sodden straw he could smell it never mind see it. The farmer was running left of the road trying to find a way through barricades but hemmed in came to a gradual halt until now, resigned, he leans on the wagon watching six hundred men march by.

Thinking of Joe dying and six hundred men a poem comes into Alex's head that his father, the General, loves to quote in praise of courage under fire, a poem about the problem of men under orders to incompetent leaders.

It wasn't the Charge of the Light Brigade on Anzio's Yellow Beach yet similar foolish mistakes caused a similar outcome, two battalions of Rangers cut down as they ran, slaughtered, cannons to the right and the left and such ferocious returning fire from the awaiting army it brought the whole of the Fifth Army to a standstill, the Germans far better prepared than anyone had thought.

Joe was one of the first to go which is ironic since coming over on the Landing Craft all you heard was him telling guys to duck.

'Don't fire until I tell you,' his voice was a drone against the rumble of distant bombing. 'Some of you are new to this and might hold philosophical ideas on the goodwill of all men. Nazis are not men. They're devils that rape cows and stick babies with bayonets. So stick them but not in the chest. Go for the soft parts, the belly or the throat. Get in and get out! You get me?'

There was buzz then of weary bees, 'yes, Sarge, we get you.'

The night was cold, and the sea rough, and they were afraid. Chin strap swinging, Joe was not so much a man as a figure-head on the prow of Viking long-boat. He wanted to save them, to reach down and cover every one of those young helmeted heads with his own brand of four-letter blessing.

Fifteen paces into the Ditch he stepped on a mine.

'Remember what I said.' Even when falling he is talking and GIs running and dodging bullets and skipping over wounded buddies are listening. 'It's your life or theirs! Don't be afraid to kill and don't be afraid to die.'

For a while Alex considered hiking him over his shoulder but Joe got angry, spitting blood. 'Stow it, fool! I know what you're doing. You're thinking you don't want to leave me like you left her.' So Alex set him down, pocketed one of the dog-tags, covered Joe's face with his helmet and moved on.

It was all he could do. Nothing made Joe madder than pointless sacrifice.

This walk of shame in Rome would've killed him again. We should have hung on. If those in command hadn't lost their nerve men would still be dead but the main thrust would've broken through. As it is after days of running and shooting and killing and being killed Alex brought what was left of his Company to a farmhouse a hundred yards from the road. There, exhausted, they settled to taking long-range pot-shots at whatever popped up.

Radio links broken, no communication to the South, he was about to give the order to retreat when Second Lieutenant David Furness, a massive hole in his gut, stayed his arm. 'Don't bother, sir. It seems we're quitting.'

And my God we were quitting, Allied troops coming in from every direction with raised hands!

Stunned, they sat watching until Furness took out his pistol. 'Enough of this,' he whispers, tears in his eyes. 'If I surrender to anyone it'll be the Lord Jesus.'

Pistol in his mouth he fired. Snipers now alerted to their position, Alex snatched Davy's dog-tags and ran toward the forward line.

Men scattered as he ran. To keep fighting and not to give in was no empty gesture! He meant to go on. Alexander Stonewall Hunter was not of a mind to surrender. Like Davy Furness he'd sooner sing his own tune. He didn't get far. Pinned down by machine gun fire he crawled into a barn and up into a loft. There was shouting and the rumble of wheels, a four-man crew turning a self-propelling gun toward the barn.

Alex leaned out the window, dropped a grenade down the spout and ran but was butt-stopped at the door.

From then on it was about being moved from one place to the next until herded into a farmyard along with a bunch of Canadians. For a while, a heavyweight Mauser pointing it seemed they would be shot. There was a dispute between a young *Oberschutze* and a tired looking *Feldwebel*, the Private pointing to the Canadians and waving a fistful of Nazi wing emblems torn from German field jackets, 'scalps' some guys like to collect.

The kid stood haranguing the *Feldwebel*. He wanted them all dead. '*Nein. Wir werden warten.*' He got a shake of the head. This parade is why the *Feldwebel* waited. Some quick-thinking Nazi had spotted the propaganda value of such a situation and wanted to make the most of it.

It's why newsreel cameras are here and GIs being trucked in from other areas of Italy. It's also why there's not a single wounded prisoner, guys with missing limbs and other battle scars shot or shipped off elsewhere.

Lined up ten abreast and evenly spaced, armed guards every third row, we are meant to be seen as hale and hearty, not a bruise in sight, cowardly Yanks who gave in too easily. It's why the crowds are quiet, an order gone out, no disrespecting the prisoners, no spitting or throwing stones.

This is History in the making, a morale boost and with the Italian army already under Armistice to the Allies a shot in the arm for the beleaguered Third Reich.

It's quite the parade. If we were stateside there would be tickertape.

Machine guns either side the road a man would have to be crazy to try making a break. So many eyes and itchy fingers he would have to know exactly what he was doing *and* where he was going, in other words a plan.

Alex doesn't have a plan but he does have 3-D memory that once on the run will keep him so. Dark hair, dark blue eyes and fluent Italian he'd be able to get around. He also speaks German too but without a uniform that's no help.

Forget being shot as a spy! That can wait until peacetime and US Intelligence. For now it's the dung farmer he wants and if it is still there the cafe, *Chiaro di Luna*, and Primrose Alley running alongside.

If Alex is to do it he has to get the timing right. As more people gather to watch the spectacle so the bottleneck draws tighter the crocodile of men compressed and lines pushing together. Right now they are approaching the square. An Oberleutnant calls halt. There are to be speeches, more opportunity for their statesmen to offer oily if shaky grins.

Alex edges along the line. There's only one guy now between him and the far left and he seems to know Alex is planning a break and taps V for Victory on his thigh. It is Buzz Knowles, 1st Rangers. A good guy. If Alex was to run with a partner it would be him but this is a one-man stunt, two will get them killed, Buzz knows this and when a moment later he reaches down to relieve his boot of a non-existent stone Alex calmly steps round him.

Now he is at the outer edge. Ahead a flag bearing a silver moon flutters. It is the Moonlight Cafe, paintwork peeling and shutters broken yet it's still there alongside an alley that leads to the market and a honey-comb of smaller alleys and the Holy Mother of Mary Church and hopefully sanctuary.

Alex knows the priest there, Father Benedict Brandt, or rather Mom knows him. Aunt Clary, mother's youngest sister, is married to Claus Brandt, Father Benedict's brother. Though not kissing cousins he might push Alex in the right direction and then again coming from Bavaria he will have divided loyalties.

Joe Petowski had a similar problem. A black belt ardent follower of the martial arts this war really pissed him off. Having spent much of his childhood in Japan, his mother a teacher in Kanagawa, he saw the assault on Pearl Harbour as an act of betrayal. He said Admiral Yamamoto aboard the Japanese flagship delayed declaring war which held back Emperor Hirohito's statement for three hours giving Japanese bombers time to get to Hawaii and sink ships like the *Oklahoma* and with a thousand men on board.

'It was a dirty trick and against Bushido Code.'

Godfather to Alex and Phys-ed tutor since Second Grade Joe took his paternal duties seriously, making it his business to enquire into his Godson's life and choice of friends. He thought Bobby Rourke a hustler and when with burned hands Alex was confined to barracks in Southampton he wanted details.

'What are you doing with a guy like that for a buddy? Who is he and why haven't I heard of him before?' The long answer to that was 'you're a second father to me. A guy doesn't take his Pa when out hunting girls.' The short answer was closer, 'I knew you wouldn't approve.'

Bobby is a hustler, especially where women are concerned, he is also brave and loyal and did everything he could during the Suffolk Situation.

The Suffolk Situation is how Alex sees the events of '42. Such feelings, so much to say and no one to say it to the memory weighs him down. In confining the tragedy to two simple words Alex tries giving himself distance.

Frank Bates, the former padre, says he's kidding himself. 'You could run to the Moon and you will still remember.'

Rumour had it Bates reenlisted working as a mechanic in the motor-pool. Chances of running across him were slim yet there he was in a Bar on the quay the day Alex was due to leave for Italy, a chauffeur to the General.

Seeing him that day stirred up memories of confessional conversations and of the raid on Sened Station and of Bates' aborted suicide attempt.

If Alex was uncomfortable with the meeting he was the only one. A wrench in his top pocket and oily hands, Bates seemed comfortable in his new role. Always a big fellow he'd lost nothing in weight and smiled if not at peace with the world then reserving his struggle for the servicing of jeeps.

That day in the bar Alex drank whisky. Bates sipped sarsaparilla. 'Liquor does me no favours,' says he. 'It allows me to do things I wouldn't normally do.'

It wasn't doing much for Alex. Never a heavy drinker he hated the way it clogged his brain. Seeing his discomfort and a Padre for all the missing dog-collar Bates patted his arm. 'You need to let it go, Guvnor.'

'So everyone keeps telling me.' Alex was sour.

'They don't like to see you suffer.'

'I don't like seeing me suffer.'

'Then give it to the Lord. He'll mind it for you.'

'I doubt that,' says Alex even more sour. 'If the magic formula didn't work for you I don't see how it will work for a sinner like me.'

'That was my problem not yours.'

'Yes but you were the guy carrying the flag.'

'I still carry it and shall for evermore. It's you I'm worried about.'

'Don't. My soul is not your problem. It stopped being yours the day you jumped into the ocean.'

Bates wasn't about to be offended. 'Again, that's my problem. Let's get to yours. The Lord loves a sinner. Give him your pain. Tell Him it's too heavy. He'll take it until you're ready to pick it up again.'

Alex said he'd think about it. Then with nothing to lose he gave the wedding ring he bought to Bates. Christmas and lonely in Achnacarry he bought the ring and wore it third finger of his left hand '*Omnia Vincit Amor*' engraved inside. He gave Bates the photograph of Adelia too. 'Take this while you're at it. I don't know why I thought to keep either.'

Frank pocketed both. Last sight was of him staring after Alex, a roly-poly defrocked priest with the all-knowing eyes of a saint.

That night aboard ship bound for Italy Alex thought on Frank and again with nothing to lose offered August 2nd and Suffolk and all that happened in prayer to God. 'Please take it. If I come through this war I promise to go back to Suffolk and pick the pain up again.'

~

That was ten days ago. So far other than finding whisky repellent Alex hasn't noticed a difference. That he is alive is something, a prisoner, yes, along with others but not for long. He's going to do it! He is going to make a break. All he needs is the farmer to make the break with him.

With that in mind while statesmen procrastinate Alex bends his eye and thought to the farmer with this message; '*Tu! Voie primula vicolo!*'

He needs the man to see that Primrose Alley and to think, 'I can cut through that to the market.' If he gets that and say a little distraction, the crowd cheering or Buzz Knowles hamming it up, then Alex can make the break and rolling out the line dive into fifty pounds of steaming shit.

It's a risk. The guards are likely to cut him down the second he moves plus diving into horseshit isn't a thing he'd regularly do, but this isn't regular life, this is a fool's idea of life where a man believes in mind tricks.

'*Tu! Voi Primula Vicolo!*' Like a whip the thought cracked out.

Hey you! You want Primrose Alley!'

'*Tu!*' And again and again, '*Voi Primula Vicolo!*'

Alex doesn't know if the farmer hears a voice in his head telling him where to go yet if sheer desperation carries spiritual weight then the thought is currently ploughing through the guy's brain with the weight of a torpedo.

Until Adelia all thoughts of dreams and spiritual intervention were for writers and artists, 'whackos,' as Dad calls them, 'the dodgers and the bum-shufflers. People who never had a sensible idea in their life '

Mind power! Ghosts! Spirits! Dad has no time for such thinking. 'It's a load of hooey! When you're dead you're dead and that's an end to it.' His argument, if there was life after death why don't people come back to tell.

Alex used the think same. That's not to say there weren't moments when hair back of his head suggested otherwise. But with Adelia dead a door to the Other Side creaked open and every day an aspect of the impossible seeping through until he's starting to believe there's more to life than death.

One such an event occurred moments before Davy Furness pulled the trigger.

Alex knew he was going to do it. It wasn't body-talk, no soldier picking up telltale gestures it was a conversation in his head, Davy asking forgiveness of his mother and her answering 'it's alright, son. The Lord will understand.'

Davy Furness chose that way because he knew an attempt on his part to escape would hamper others. Hands down and arms glued to his sides Alex stood tight and let it happen because to do otherwise would've been wrong.

It takes courage to what Furness did but brooding on another man's choices won't get Alex out of here, however that experience and others like it, namely Adelia breathing down his neck, have opened his eyes to other worlds. Right now he needs to watch and wait. Dung stinking to high heaven, the farmer will do anything to get out the crush maybe even to giving someone a ride.

The chances of pulling this off are slim but as Joe said Alex is a stubborn bastard who believes in seeing things his way. Right now the stubborn bastard needs a kick-start to launch him on his way.

Muscles bunched and nerves tense, he takes a couple of minutes to breathe. Three days on the march with little to eat or drink he's weary, plus his left knee aches where a rifle-butt brought him down. Bottom line he's scared. He knows if he's caught he will be shot, all these people watching, a sniper with an eye for theatre wouldn't be able to resist.

Windows opposite open and dignitaries walk out on the balcony but no Mussolini now, just lesser men in rumpled clothes.

Morose and silent with no belief in this war the crowd begins to break up.

The farmer is on the move! He is heading for the Alley but with so many people on the move he has to pull the wagon rather than push.

Suddenly there it is, a pile of shit not two yards from Alex's nose!

Now or never, he tries to move but his feet are stuck to the ground.

'Help me, Adelia, to get through!'

A racket starts up. A lickspittle on the balcony has dug out a phonograph and now the German National Anthem is blasting about the square.

That's it! That's when the kick-start occurred!

As he had hoped Buzz Knowles and a couple of others had decided they'd had enough of being pushed around. A guy mid column started whistling the Colonel Bogey March, a comic song suggesting Hitler has only one ball and Goebbels none at all. One voice at first and others joining in and to mark the point every man pushes a fist in the air two fingers extended.

The Oberleutnant is yelling. Guards are breaking through the lines toward the centre of the column, threatening men.

The moment is here.

Alex dove into the filthy straw.

There was brief eye-to-eye contact, the farmer's eyebrows shooting skyward and his mouth dropping open.

'*Salve me!*'

Why he chose the Latin prayer Alex doesn't know, but it was there on his lips even as he wriggled deeper under the muck.

'*Salve me!*'

A look, a thousand thoughts and fears, and then the world was stilled, and the sky dark, the farmer throwing a jacket over the straw.

The wagon is moving.

Lieutenant Colonel Alexander Stonewall Hunter, aka the Camera, Ist Battalion US Rangers is still a prisoner, but not for long.

Twenty-three
Cure or Kill
Rustington, West Sussex
March '44

Bobby woke this morning to a note under the door. It was from his co-pilot, Socko Smith; 'Be warned. Booze-up planned tonight Mess Hall re Operation Jericho. I don't know about you but I got better things to do.'

Damn right! He crumpled the note. It had to happen. A top-secret operation, it should have stayed secret but as with all things hush-hush had a shelf-life of zero. It's out, how in February crews from Littlehampton along with other Mosquito MVI squadrons took part in a raid over France, their directive to bomb Amiens Prison, to blow holes in walls, to send them 'tumbling down' giving several hundred prisoners inside a chance to escape.

As one of the pilots Bobby will be expected to attend the late night booze-up but forewarned is forearmed, he'll be anywhere but there.

Operation Jericho is not a thing to be celebrated. A mission of mercy, they said, hundreds of Allied prisoners including members of the French Resistance, due to be executed the following day. 'You are to bring down the walls and give them a chance to escape.'

Bring down the walls! It was a tricky task requiring low-level hedge-hopping by the Mosquitoes and the certain knowledge that however careful they tried to spot the bombs prisoners were going to die.

The raid commenced February 18th Zero plus 13 and though it was bloody, prisoners and Mosquito crews killed, the guard-house was destroyed and two walls breached prisoners seen running into nearby woods.

So far so good, men died but for the good of the whole, a man can live with that. Then last week a whisper reached Bobby's ears. French Resistance prisoners were the real reason for the raid, one or both having information that gained by the enemy would cause an upset to Allied invasion plans.

The message behind the raid was 'cure or kill' get the French guys out to where Resistance people were waiting or flatten the prison and all inside.

The cynicism and casual attitude got to Bobby. Okay, it is only a rumour and as Socko said we have to believe more men escaped than were killed, yet our men died in that raid including Operation leader and his co-pilot. So what's to celebrate? There have to be better reasons for gettin' pissed on warm beer.

Time on his hands, and the Base not far from her husband's farm Bobby plans to call on Lady M. It's a month since they were together. He likes to keep in touch with the old girl, touch being the operative word Mildred never imaginative but always willing.

In wartime a week apart is a lifetime, Mildred now a full-time ambulance driver and Bobby with his ongoing transfers that has been the way of things.

Talk about a Rolling Stone! It's been one station after another until now he's with Avro 'Mossies' at Rustington. It's okay, he wasn't meant to stay in one place for long. Same with relationships! Keep it loose. That's the thing about Mildred and the barmaid in the Horse and Hounds, they don't care to be tied down they want the nylons and the lipsticks rather than the man.

It didn't used to be that way with Mildred. Once she would've given all to be with Bobby but when she saw he didn't want her for keeps, that there was another he wanted more, she switched to booze with benefits, him bringing the booze and her supplying benefits.

It has to be said love gets in the way. A man and woman should be able to meet when they want, do what they want and leave with tails up. Sex should be light-hearted. Forget the heavy weather that comes with passion! B&B is the way forward, booze and benefits... at least that is what he tells himself when once again he is steering the bike away from Suffolk.

It's a month since he saw Mildred and coming up two since he was in Needham. He misses Dee! He's desperate to see her and Sophie. The two of them are all the while on his mind. He dreams about them, hears Dee telling Sophie to drink her milk and 'not to crawl down stairs again or you'll fall and like Humpty Dumpty Mummy won't be able to put you back together again!'

Two months! Dee must be wondering what she's done. Fact is she hasn't done anything. She remains her glittering self, still worrying the honest folk of Needham with her eccentric ways. It's him that's the problem, Flight

Lieutenant Robert E Rourke, DFC, the most fucked-up man on the planet.

A while ago a worm crawled inside his head and started chewing. As usual the worm involves memories of the past. Too much thinking and he's backed into a corner. It happened autumn of '43 over pot-roast and wine. She was willing to be loved and warm and naked in his arms she was everything he'd dreamed. It was good, everything was suddenly possible. Then the worm crept into his brain, a stupid, sour-grapes belittling worm along the lines of, 'I'll give you pot-roast, bitch! You kept me waiting all this time and now you think one lousy fuck is going to make it right! Well think again.'

Fool! Instead of making the most of that evening he decided he was being played for a sucker, that she didn't really want him and that sex was about Sophie. Things are tricky in Needham, witch-finders on the move, the local parson questioning Dee's mental stability - bottom line she is looking to Bobby to save Sophie. She may not have known that was a reason for the come-on. Subconscious fear or straightforward planning it didn't matter, he decided he was a meal-ticket rather than a lover and took offence.

Fool and fool again! Any rational man loving a woman wouldn't care about her reasons for loving him back. A mother wanting her child safe is natural. He should have grabbed hold and never let them go but since when did Baby Rourke do anything rational.

Short-sighted, he decided to teach her a lesson along the lines of 'never mind the past! This is what you've been missing. I am in charge. Play nice, lady, and you can have it again. Freeze me out and we're done.'

A good lesson or so he thought, a sexy lesson him and his wicked fingers and tongue making her crazy, which was fine, but then when she was wet and steamy and expecting him to follow-though he backed off.

His hand clamped over her mouth so's not to wake the baby he really got her going. Then even with his dick screaming mercy he rolled off the bed.

All the while he is dressing she is staring. 'Bobby? Do you not want to think of yourself?' Good question. 'It's okay,' says he. 'I can wait.'

The look on her face left him grinning all week. Further ramming home the point he took his time calling Needham keeping a whole week before phoning.

Fool of a man! Once started he couldn't stop, a week became ten days and then longer until suddenly he's left it too long, it's Christmas and he is alone.

Christmas Eve he was here in the Horse and Hounds, everybody singing and dancing and trying to make the best of it and him staring at a wall.

Next day the telephone lines on overload he couldn't get through. It was the 27th before they spoke. She seemed pleased and no questions asked. Switch-around then it was him worrying why she wasn't bashing his ear?

Off he went on the bike it snowing a blizzard and him hardly able to see through it. It was the same poky apartment but cosy with hand-made decorations on the tree and Dee a Christmas angel with her hair undone.

Sophie seemed suddenly grown. She stared, a thumb in her mouth.

'She doesn't know me,' he says disappointed.

'Of course she knows you. She's shy,' says Dee. 'It's as you said, she has an amazing memory, once seen never forgotten.'

Once seen never forgotten? If ever a diabolical situation is summed up in four words it is that. Bobby felt it that Christmas. Arriving late he stayed over but didn't go near Dee. Instead, he got drunk and slept on the couch. Not due back until the 29th he could've had a ball joining in their limited festive cheer, sang carols round the gas fire and ate a slice of corned beef hash. He tried making a joke of it. 'You didn't try for a pot roast and wine then this time.'

'No,' she says, her face kinda thoughtful. 'I wasn't sure what you were doing and thought it best to stick with what I know.'

Stick with what I know? He had to think about that wondering if there was more to her statement. She said a local butcher was in trouble for selling horse meat and that the tinned beef was a present from the Air-Base.

Then he felt bad because while he was playing silly buggers they were struggling. He had brought a couple of things with him, a bottle of brandy that he managed to drink, a wax toy for Sophie and nylons for Dee. But other than a couple of wizened potatoes they'd nothing much in the cupboard. There were better things he could've brought.

Christmas was not good. He was ready to leave when Nora Jackson and her husband turned up with bottled fruit, that made him feel worse, him with money in the bank and them struggling for food! It all got a bit too much. He'll always love Dee but the whole thing such a burden he was ready to run.

Then she produced the sweater.

'Is this f…for me?' he'd stuttered.

'It's not actually new,' she said anxiously. 'I found an Argyle sweater in the church rummage and washed it and unwound the wool. I hope you like it. It's a lovely shade of brown. I thought it might go with your eyes.'

For once in his life Bobby was struck dumb. So it wasn't new, who cares, she went to the trouble of unpicking and knitting it again.

Overcome, he felt like crying. No one has ever done anything like that for him, no one! It didn't end there. Sophie had made him a present.

'She picked the pattern,' says Dee. 'I thought she might go for a teddy but she wanted a monkey, and so a monkey is what you've got. Sweet, isn't it? It's meant to be a lucky mascot.'

'Does it have a name?' he says, still struggling with tears.

'The pattern is called Coco.'

'Then Coco it is.' He stuck the thing in the top pocket of his RAF blues. Button eyes staring out it looked like a cute little guardian angel. 'I'll keep it with me.'

What a moment, right enough and good enough for a kiss under the mistletoe and every hurt healed but with Nora and her hubby looking on he chose to kiss Sophie instead and lost the moment.

It's Alex. To kiss Dee would be to betray him again. Now, knowing the guy is missing Bobby's not sure he can look at her never mind kiss.

Alex Hunter is listed in casualty figures alongside that of his Godfather, Joe Petowski. There is it, Lt/ Colonel AS Hunter, US Army, MIA, Anzio.

MIA, missing in action believed dead is the official tag. With reports coming in of tens of thousands killed at Anzio he's more likely dead than missing.

Bobby kept the news-clipping in his wallet. Knowing the guy gone and no need to worry about being caught out in a lie you'd think he could rest easy. He can't rest. Adelia Challoner can live the rest of her life not knowing the father of her child but while blue eyes are watching, Sophie's blue eyes, her Dad's eyes, Bobby will always know.

There is something else, the grief that comes with the end of childhood.

Alexander Hunter dead! The Camera smashed and broken! Bobby saw the name in the paper and thought on the laughs they'd shared and the way the guy was always there for him. Knowing the only good thing about yesterday was gone forever he crept into the hangar, climbed into his plane and wept.

It's not just that he's dead! It's remembering Alex staggering round the square calling out for Dee with that look on his face.

Bobby put that look there. It's likely the man died still with that look.

Last night he dreamt of the Old Mill. A shadowy figure in the top turret room Alex was inside. Bobby could see through the window and called out, 'Ash let me in! I've come to say I'm sorry!'

The figure turned. It wasn't Ash. It was Gabe Templar. It was Gabe though not the man remembered, this was someone never seen before, the US Marine, a real tough guy hair razored to his head and coat-hangers for shoulders.

Man, it scared Bobby! He woke with those eyes drilling his soul. Silver eyes that looked right though him, a killer's eyes.

~

Bobby's in a call box. He's been trying to call Mildred but as usual the queue is long and time is short. Finally at twenty-after-seven he gets through. The phone rings for an age then is answered by the butler.

'Can I have a word with Lady M?'

'Lady M?'

'Yeah, Lady Mildred. Is she around?'

'May I ask who is calling?'

'Flight Lieutenant Rourke.'

'One moment.'

There was another wait. When she did come Mildred was not happy.

'Hello?'

'Hi there, beautiful, it's me Bobby, your own private fun-palace.'

'What do you want?'

'What do you mean what do I want? I want to see you.'

'We're about to have dinner.'

'Sorry about that. I would've called sooner but there was a queue.'

'Why call at all when I've told you not to.'

'I thought you might want to see me.'

'This is my home. I don't want people disturbed.'

'By people I guess you mean your husband.'

'I mean anyone.'

'Okay, well, I don't want to disturb anyone. I was hopin' you might pop over for a drink.'

'Pop over for a drink?'

'Yeah, a couple of gins and howdy-do-de. I'm in the neighbourhood. We could call in one of the pubs there. It wouldn't take me a minute to nab over.'

'You've got a damned nerve!' She was livid, spitting down the phone, her accent so sharp she could've cut through overhead power cables electrocuting them both. 'You disappear for days on end with not so much as a hello then you call and think I'll come running!'

'I didn't think anythin', honey, other than you might like to meet.'

'I don't want to meet you. I don't want to think about you. You're a selfish shit, Robert Rourke, and a complete waste of time. I don't know what I ever saw in you. Don't call again.'

Boom! That was it, phone down, over and out.

He had to laugh. Talk about letting a guy down easy.

Plans spoiled, he lit a cigarette. Where to go and what to do? Operation Jericho baloney at the Base tonight he doesn't want to get caught up in that. There is the Horse and Hounds and what's her-name the barmaid.

He could try there.

Whistling, hands in his pockets, he made for the pub. Windows taped and blast curtains drawn you couldn't see much from the outside but then the door opened and noise and light spilled out, people laughing though a haze of cigarette smoke and a piano punching away in the corner.

It was a good atmosphere. They all know him. He's been in several times since transfer. 'Evenin' all!' He doffs his cap. They grin and make room at the bar. What's-her-name was pulling a pint. Oops! Now he is here he's not sure of a welcome. He promised to take her to the flicks Tuesday but forgot.

Smiling, he leans on the bar. 'Hey there gorgeous! How you doin'?'

Face like granite she stares.

'Sorry I didn't make it the other night.'

Still she stares the pint glass under the pump filling.

He leans closer. 'You see I had an appointment with Berlin.'

Silence, the bar-room hushed and everybody listening.

'Yeah, we were told a real nasty guy over there needs blastin' out of his bunker. So me and a couple of pals took a trip over.'

Her face doesn't crack.

'I guess I should've called.'

Beer glass overflowing she empties it over his head. 'I guess you should.'

~

'Hello! You there, Dee?'

It's gone midnight. He's trying to call Suffolk but it's rowdy in the Mess hall. They are drinking way too much. Now some silly bugger has started a Conga. They're singing dirty songs and shuffling up and down in a crocodile and she's on the other end of a phone and can't hear a word he's saying.

'You there, Dee?'

'I can't hear you.'

'Of course you bloody can't! It's these idiots. They've all gone mad.'

'What! What are you saying?'

'I'm sayin' I got the licence and have booked the Horse and Hounds for Friday week. So fetch your best bib and tucker and you're on your way to Virginia.'

'Sorry, Bobby, I'm only getting bits.'

'Oh, forget it, honey! I just called to say I love you and that I always will and that I'm sorry for bein' such an arse.'

Click, the phone's gone dead and he's caught up in the crocodile singing the stupid song along with the rest. Up and down they go, pissed to the eye-balls.

It is a stupid song, a WW1 thing about German soldiers and French whores. A few of them know the words the rest are making it up.

Bobby churns round the hall with them. Guys banging on tables and yelling the noise is insane. He shouldn't be here but Mildred gave him the brush off. Nowhere to go he shuffled round to the pub to what's her name.

'Say, Socko?' He drags the guy out of the crocodile, another who said he wouldn't be here but couldn't get a lift to Winchester to see his girl. 'What is the name of that redhead behind the bar in the H&H?'

'Redhead?' Socko swayed. 'Is there a redhead?'

'You know there is. You were tryin' to make her last time we were there.'

'Oh that one! I don't know her name.'

'As you were!' Bobby thrust him back in line. 'Take my advice don't stand her up on a date. It'll cost you a laundry bill and drinks all round.'

The redhead was another who'd had her fill of Robert E Rourke but who with more class than Lady M emptied a pint of Pipers best over his head. He laughed as did the rest and before the night was out he was her pal again plus a lifelong member of the dart's team.

It was coming up midnight when he got back to the Base. He was plastered then. Even so he had to call to tell Dee the truth.

It came to him earlier to make a clean breast of it, to go to Suffolk and take his chances with the truth. What with Alex gone and her amnesia he's nothing to lose. It doesn't have to be the absolute truth, so help him God. All she needs to know is that Bobby saved her life and that Sophie needs to be safe.

'I mean, what kind of life will the kid get with a mother in the nuthouse? Britain is finished! There's no money. America is the only safe harbour.'

'You talking to yourself, Captain America?' Socko is leaning on him. 'You're surely not still thinking of Audrey in the Horse and Hounds?'

'So you do remember her.'

'Vaguely. She is okay. I like her, a good woman with a great pair of knockers, but don't tell my girl I said so.'

'Lips sealed.'

Socko poked the knitted monkey in Bobby's top pocket. 'What's this?'

'Coco, my lucky mascot.'

'Lucky mascot!?' Socko scoffed. 'More than fifty ops and not so much as a headache, since when did you need one of those.'

'Maybe I don't but I'm gonna keep it. My daughter made it.'

'Your daughter!'

'My little Sophie. She wanted to make me a Christmas gift but a babe and only able to cruise round on her padded little ass her Momma made it for me.'

'You have a kid?'

'Yeah, nine months old.'

'You never said.'

'You never asked.'

'So where is she?'

'Back home in Suffolk with my missis.'

'Hang on a minute.' Socko goggled. 'You've got a wife and a baby?'

'One does usually come after the other.'

'I don't believe it. What's wrong with you? You got a family of your own and a place to go and you're here in this place drinking with us sots?'

'It does seem that way.'

'You must be out of your mind.'

'Yeah,' Bobby frowned. 'I must.'

He snatched his jacket and hit the road. If he takes the bike to the station he can catch the early train to Sudbury. It'll take all of three hours but he can sleep the booze off and wake bright-eyed with the licence in his pocket.

They could be married there and then!

Yeah! He could wake that old fart of a parson and have him do the job! If Dee thinks it's for Sophie she'll do it and she'll know it's for the best because Bobby will tell of 1.75 million. If that don't blow her mind he doesn't know what will.

In all the time they've known one another he's never mentioned Bucky's money, always kept that little gem tight to his chest. If she was going to love him it had to be for him not the money. But then knowing what money can buy, the doors it can open - kindergartens and private schools, the Virginia society ladder that they can climb, him and his well-bred English wife - she may see the light.

He could give them a good life, and a house on the Green with the rest of the nobs. Maybe not Virginia, Ma waiting there with a hatchet, but some place sweet in California where the sun always shines.

Yeah! That's it California, sunshine and lollipops all the way.

Suddenly the door is open to a bright, new future and the resentment felt over years, his Artful Dodger beginnings, how he'd had to fight his way through filth, Ma on her back and him a two-bit pimp dancing attendance on dangerous low-life some of them preferring his young ass to hers, all the bitter pain of so many years began to fragment and fall away.

Being seen for who he is has been a struggle. First there was Ma and Wolfe Street. Then West Point where he was always an outsider. Sure, they laughed at his jokes and slapped his back and thought him a wag, much like they do here but that's as far as it went. You don't take trash home no matter how amusing. The Academy is for Army blue-blood like Dwight D Eisenhower and Alexander Hunter. It was never meant for the bastard off-spring of a tinker.

It's been the same here in England with Bomber Command. Steering metal pigs round the sky was not why he signed up. He wasn't meant to sweat it out inside a metal coffin while braver men played chicken with clouds. Johnny-bright-star Fighter planes were why he was born. But a Yank with no pedigree he came too late and Hurricanes and Spitfires passed to the cream of the crop.

Years of makeshift and mend it's been but not anymore. Here he has a God-given chance to make it good and she doesn't need to know what happened. She only needs to know the truth that is in his eyes; he adores her and would die for her and Sophie. What's more, he brings peaches from the Commissary. Gorgeous peaches, big and juicy. They were on their way to the officer's Mess. Bobby saw them and thought, 'nah, their need is greater than yours.'

Excited, happier than he's ever been he kicked the bike awake. Socko Smith was right! A wife and a baby of his own Bobby is the luckiest guy. Fifty three ops flown and while there were dicey moments he always came back smiling. Now there's the double crackle of important paper in his pocket, a licence to wed and a notice of missing, and it's cheerio and pip-pip, old boy! The future opening before him in a clean, straight road!

Smiling, he put his foot down. It was snowing but he didn't feel the cold. So clear in his head he was happy, so happy he didn't see the bomb-crater or the barricades fencing it in until he was on top of it and no time to manoeuvre.

There was a thud and a long sliding skid, the bike and him parting company. Then there was free-fall through the

air and a brick wall and jagged barbed wire approaching fast
and the thought, 'Lord, you have got to be kidding!

Twenty-four
Shape Shifting
September '44
Evac Hospital,
Solomon Islands.

The Colonel paused at his bed. 'What's your name, son?'

'Gabriel Templar, sir,' Gabriel tried getting up but struggled pain sapping strength from his body.

'As you were, Corporal,' a hand pushed him back on the pillow.

'Aye, aye, sir.'

'Templar, huh?' The Colonel continued staring down. 'Seems to me I've come across you before. You were at Henderson Field. It was you doused that foxhole and brought Colonel Gene Phillips' nephew back.'

'Yes, sir.'

'A pity you weren't with him at Saipan. You might have got him out again. Tough young guy but headstrong. Still,' the Colonel shook his head, 'that is the way it is. We lose our family as well as our friends. I recall you took a hit in the left shoulder in '43. Now you got it in the right. What are you trying to do, Angel Gabriel, make holes to hang your wings on?'

'Seems that way, sir.'

'Well, I liked what I saw in '43 and again in Peleliu. Any other guy would've got the Medal for what you did but the US Marine Corps doesn't give medals to ex-cons no matter how outstanding so you'll have to settle for another stripe.'

'Aye, aye, sir, thank you, sir.'

That was him, the Big Man, Colonel Chesty Puller passing through the hospital as the Hand of God dispensing pain killers and promotions.

Gabriel waited til they moved on and then closing his eyes slept. His back is burning. Left scar open with right he can only lie face down and the pain coupled with morphine brings dreams of childhood and Pa and the belt.

He must get away!

Eyes closed he's gone, running and swooping into space, travelling fast, putting distance between this converted cathedral, and rows of hospital beds and howls of men in pain. Soon he is home in Virginia in the barn.

What a dream! Wood shavings under his bare feet it's like he's actually there! There's the hunk of Lime tree! It still looks good and smelling of fresh resin has a glow about it as if freshly cut down. In this state his carvings look even more alive. There's the fox cub he whittled out of Redwood, Pa claiming sharp teeth snapped when he picked it up. And over by the window is the carving he did of Mizz Baines' pug that died of distemper. The old lady gave him three dollars but wouldn't take it home. She said it was too alive. She'd be wanting to pet it.

Here among the smell of wood he recalls making coffins in the Funeral parlour and snap, the dream takes him there.

Coffins against the wall and biers stacked tidy it's as Mr Simeon left it but a lonely place now the old man is gone. The Parlour was willed to Gabriel but he doesn't want it. After the war he'll sell it and give the money to Ma.

This life is all he knows now, Gunny Emmet said it, 'your soul may belong to Jesus but your ass belongs to the Marine Corps.'

Needing to get away from the stench of death he kicked up into the sky. What a feeling! He's flying over Bayonet Woods, the Rappahannock River a glistening ribbon glimpsed through the trees. Then he's tangling with a skein of geese and has to swerve them squawking and him laughing. Up and up he climbs until the whole of Virginia is laid out beneath, and then the whole of the world, the Earth a gleaming ball of blue hanging in space.

The Colonel made a joke about flapping wings. Now hanging in the sky Gabriel is aware of sutures pulling and of a twitching middle of his shoulders of a bug trapped under his skin.

Impossible feeling! In this dream he's neither a dummy nor a man, he is a Universe. Arms outstretched he spans the Heavens, the Earth beneath and the Sun and Moon and Stars a fingertip away. One kick and nascent baby-feathers in his back will uncurl to become gigantic wings, and he, Gabriel Templar, Child-of-God will fly into the sun and burn.

The urge to join with that ball of flaming fire is strong. Gabriel feels the pull even to his human body lying in the hospital bed. He feels it and knows he'd better resist because once joined with that fiery furnace and skin, hair and eyes shrivelling, his days as mortal man are done and Life in the Light begun.

The need pulled and he is turning, turning toward the Sun.

'No!' A voice whispered. 'Please don't go, Gabriel. Not yet. I need you.'

Snap! The need is broken. He is swooping down to land where-else but the Eyrie. Forget the Sun and the Stars! Heart's dwelling of this life and all lives before and after this is where he longs to be the Eagle's Nest.

What a dream! So strange and yet so real, there's an argument going on, him thinking he's not so much dreaming as remembering before he was born. Whatever it is he wishes he could stay. When he's here in the attic lighting a lamp so that she, love-of-his-life will come, then he can forget angel wings as he can forget the faces of those he helped kill at Guadalcanal.

Good or bad, saint or sinner men died there with eyes rolling and mouths twisted in pain. No single units they died in droves, some shot before getting their feet wet and others as they hit the shore buddies rolling in agony at his feet and the Japs blasted out of fortifications running with their hands in the air, burning to death, oxygen sucked from their lungs.

A K-Bar in one hand and a flamethrower in the other Gabriel was a killer among killers. Until then he didn't know what pain was. He thought Pa's beatings were bad but they were nothing to the killing of a man.

Then later, shot at Peleliu, he thought he had died. A corpsman thought so too, Gabriel heard him yell, 'don't bother. This one's gone!' For a time then there was a feeling of looking down on his crumpled body and wondering why it needed so much blood followed by a notion of hovering, detached from emotion, not a man so much as a fish on the end of line.

He wasn't a lonely fish. Shoals of fishes were caught at Peleliu. No division, American Marines and Japanese foot-soldiers were similarly tethered. Then ping, ping one-by-one the strings would break and the body pass away.

Pass away? Gabriel gets the term now. That's how it is, one minute solid flesh lying on blood soaked ground and then a passing into nothing.

One guy passed right under his nose, a mortar-man his job to feed ammo to the forward line and a joker saying how he'd be back of the queue for St Peter. Face becalmed and hands folded across his chest he was front of the queue.

Waking from that dream Gabriel recalls the serenity of the mortar-man's face and he wants to weep but such is war he doubts he'll ever weep again.

~

A fortnight on and he is up and about. Guys in this hospital are in pain. They want to scream but afraid of being cowards wait til nightfall their faces pushed into the pillow. Gabriel hears them and hugs them tight. 'It's okay,' he says, 'nothin' wrong with tears.' Some get better as he holds them, life from him like a silver river passing into their bones. Others die asking about the music.

Gabriel heard music when gazing at the Sun. Bird, beast and plant and every living thing there was a chirping and a squeaking and a woo-wooing and all at the same time in a melody that filled the heart with longing.

Yesterday he asked the medic about it. 'What is that music you play?'

'Music?'

'Yeah, on the radio.'

'We ain't got a radio.'

'Yeah, you do. I heard it the other night with that guy in the isolation room. It sounded like folk singin'.'

The medic sighed. 'We haven't got a radio and no one here is singing. As for the guy in isolation you weren't anywhere near because isolation means exactly that. No one goes in. The guy was tortured by the Japs. They lopped his hand off. Only Major Stokes tends him and she takes heavies with her.'

'I could've sworn I heard singin'.

'Yeah well, if I were you, buddy, I'd keep my mouth shut about that,' the medic shot gunk into Gabriel's arm. 'You're a Marine. You don't want to be heard saying weird stuff. Put it down to morphine making you antsy.'

Gabriel kept his mouth shut. He heard music, no question, as he knows he sat with the guy who'd lost a hand, but as the medic said he keeps his mouth shut.

If time in the Corps has taught him anything it's to keep his mouth shut. Silence is armour he's learned to wear sliding out of his bunk every morning into a thick brown shell that covers him from head to toe. If he keeps that shell in place then he's seen an okay Marine, brave but a bit stupid.

Mr Simeon suggested it the day Ma finished the first velvet jacket.

Granma's looking-glass back home is tarnished yet even in that you could see how black velvet made Gabriel's hair shine. Ma wasn't happy. She dragged the jacket off him. 'You shine,' says Simeon. 'You need to dull it down or folks will take a poke at you.' He said Gabriel needed to merge with others. 'When you wake in the morning think of stepping in mud then you won't sparkle so much.'

Gabriel didn't get it. What do they mean dull it down? Charlie Whitefeather tried explaining. 'Mr Salmanovitz wanted you to be less of a target. My people merge with nature all the time. We hunt buffalo by becoming buffalo. How else in old days would we eat?'

'I get it!' Gabriel understood that way of thinking. 'It's how I carve animals. I get inside the skin transferrin' their shape into wood.'

Charlie had smiled. 'There's a name for that. It's called shape-shifting. If you want to stay sane in this world, *Shiye*, better learn to do the same.'

If he didn't get what Mr Simeon and Charlie were trying to say he gets it now. Being different gets a man into trouble. In Boot Camp he put an end to being different by denying his little gal. Part of him went missing that day and hasn't returned. Since then he often feels he's looking through another's Gabriel's eyes hearing people talking but unable to make out what's being said.

Morphine has him imagining music and thinking he can fly. This Gabriel, the ordinary guy, doesn't want to hear silent music any more than he wants to fly. To be the same as everyone else is what he wants. Okay, so he's lonely, a hole in his gut the size of a fist, but better that than hankering after dreams.

~

Friday 6th October.

Knowing he's soon to be shipped out Gabriel is lifting weights, working on being ready for recall. Every muscle hurt when he started but it's getting easier. Men here have lost arms and others never to walk again. Gabriel feels like a fraud and with the medical teams overworked, and more wounded being brought in, he doubles as gofer, running errands and helping wash and feed.

Major Stokes, the nurse in charge, says it's against regulations.

Gabriel says yeah but I'm here so I might as well.

Washing bodies it's not so different to washing corpses except these bodies are so badly wracked there's not a place that does not hurt.

'Oh! Oh!' He reaches down to touch and terror starts up in their eyes.

'It's okay,' he says. 'I ain't gonna hurt you.' Most times it does hurt but they manage. If they are real bad he cheats.

There's a spot behind the ear that if pressed real hard knocks an animal out. Charlie Whitefeather called it the 'little death grip'. His sister Isabelle, a horse wrangler, showed him how. 'She uses it when her horses are in pain.'

He said this particular hold sends a horse into a happy state, pain being the last thing the critter feels. 'The term little death refers to sexual orgasm,' says he. '*Le petit mort*, to die of pleasure. You might find it handy one day but don't hold on too long or the critter won't bother coming back.'

Charlie said that spring of '35 and for a time had fun demonstrating on Gabriel, knocking him out when least expected. He said he should learn in case Boss Man rose up. 'Keep pressing and he's dead and not a mark on him. Trust me I know. It's how I dealt with the man who hurt Isabelle.'

Gabriel heard then how Isabelle was raped and how Charlie made the guy pay. It's why he's on Death Row and his sentence in dispute, cause of death never determined his defence arguing against conviction. 'They knew I did it The judge knew and the jury. I didn't deny it. I let them decide.'

Then he'd turned to Gabriel, eyes old as Methuselah. 'Consciousness exists on many levels. That scumbag died from pressure of my fingers then again maybe he died because I wanted him dead. The more we know of the mind the less we're bound by the body. Remember that when meeting your great love. Then you will learn for yourself who is in charge the body or the soul.'

~

Talking, always talking, that's Charlie. You never knew where it was coming from. One thing is sure the hold works. Pressure applied, you can bandage a man from head to toe and he keeps smiling, Gabriel saw that Friday evening when helping Martha Stokes change dressings in the isolation room.

Usually it takes three to treat this guy, one to change dressings the others to hold him down. Captured and tied to a tree, right hand lopped and left almost severed, he's so heavily sedated there's no need for anyone to hold him. But being tortured messed with his head so even when sedated he's howling.

You hear him shouting. 'Don't take me! Leave me here to die!'

A wolf caught in a trap it drives the other patients crazy. 'For Chrissakes!' they yell back. 'Will someone please put a bullet in his guy's head!'

Now dressings need changing and a storm is brewing, thunder and lightning, and two nurses down with gut-rot there's only Gabriel free to help.

They walked into the room. The guy reared up in bed. 'Who's that?''

'This is Sergeant Templar. He's come to help.'

'No fucking way,' says the guy. 'I don't want him near.'

'Why is that?' Major Stokes carried on laying up the trolley.

'I don't trust him.'

'Trust or not he is all you've got. Everyone else is down with beriberi. So you'd better behave and let us get on with our job.'

'Can't you leave it?' The guy stares at Gabriel. 'Do you have to change the wrappings? It's not like I'm gonna grow a right hand again.'

'You won't grow a right hand but if you don't have your wounds dressed you will lose the left. I don't want that. I've worked too hard to keep it.'

Martha Stokes says she left Sydney, Australia, for this godforsaken hole in April '42 when they first started making over the church. 'It was another year before we could make use of it. All I did for weeks on end was stamp on cockroaches. I'm still doing it. It's time I went back to Oz.'

When asked about home she says she's not sure she still has one. She hadn't heard from her kids in months. 'Maybe they think I'm dead and maybe they are right.' Same intense manner and tricky temper she reminds Gabriel of Sue Ryland. Not as beautiful as Sue, a little too heavy round the jaw, but a great nurse and a good woman and mighty generous with her loving.

Glance intent, she's unwrapping the right stump. 'Now you stay steady, Carl Whitner. You know I'll do my best to make it easy but sooner or later it is gonna hurt. So no striking out like you did the last time.'

Eyes like a scared rabbit the guy looks at her.

'Listen to me Carl. Don't hit out because if you do the Sergeant here, who is a master of judo, will put you down. You hurt me last time, d'you hear? It took all my tolerance not to add a broken nose to the rest of your hurts.'

'I hear you, ma'am.'

'Okay then,' she dumps soiled dressings in the bowl. 'That's the right wrist clear. Now I'll start on your hand.' She nodded to Gabriel. 'Carl usually finds this the most painful so it might be an idea if you sat alongside.'

The guy was staring. 'I know you,' he says. 'I've seen you before.'

'Is that right?' Gabriel pulled up a stool.

'Yeah,' the guy was trembling. 'You were there when they did this.'

'Where was that, Carl?'

'They caught me at the off and hung me on the tree. I prayed to Jesus to save me but they got my right hand and was sawing away at the left. Then I saw you with your finger to your lips. You was saying hush, help was coming.'

'Are you sure it was me?'

'Certain.' Carl nodded. 'If it wasn't it was your twin. You came and cut me down and you brought me here even though I begged you to leave me. You should've left me. What use am I to my wife with only one hand?'

The Major interrupted him. 'You're wrong about the Sergeant.'

'I ain't wrong! I saw him sure as I'm seeing you.'

'You're thinking of another soldier.'

'I ain't. And he wasn't a soldier! He was a Marine like this guy.'

'You're wrong there, Carl. It can't have been him.'

Martha was wrong. She should've kept quiet. Until then the guy was arguing with himself. Now he is arguing with her and she is hurting him.

'You calling me a liar?' he says.

'I'm not calling you a liar. I'm saying you've got it wrong. The day you came in the Sergeant was already here under sedation with his right shoulder blown away. You are mistaking him for another.'

Scissors in hand she was cutting through a blood-soaked dressing. Then she was inching it back but taking a layer of skin with it. It must have hurt like hell. The guy struck out with his stump. Then he was fumbling for the scissors with his wounded hand but couldn't make a fist.

'Okay, that's enough.' Gabriel grabbed him. 'It's time you had a rest.'

Finding the spot behind the ear he pressed. It took a while, Carl shouting, telling the rest of the hospital of a sadistic Aussie bitch that got off on hurting crippled men. Then he was gone sliding back on the bed.

'My God, what did you do?'

'I did nothin' but give him and the rest of us a good night's sleep.'

'Have you killed him?' She's leaning over the guy taking his pulse.

'I don't know. You're takin' his pulse. Does he seem to be dead?'

'Not dead but out for the count so you must have done something.'

'I applied a little pressure to ease his pain.'

'Applied a little pressure? Are you out of your mind? When I said judo expert I was joking. I didn't expect it to be true and you to demonstrate.'

'I'm not demonstratin' anythin' other than a quiet way is the best way.'

'What?'

'Like I said, nice and quiet is best.'

'Are you lecturing me?'

'No.'

'Are you sure?' She's checking the guy's blood-pressure. 'Only it sounded to me like you were saying I was noisy.'

'You ain't exactly quiet.'

'Well, I don't know!' She flung the blood-pressure gismo on the bed. 'Why in God's name did I go through all that training in a nice clean hospital in Sydney among civilised people when I could've been here dealing with savages, one patient punching me on the jaw while another gives me a lecture on how to behave. Why take so long Martha? It beggars belief.'

'You should calm down.

'Calm down? You cheeky bugger, who do you think you're talking to? I'm in charge of this bloody zoo. I'm the one to listen to. This is my hospital. You have no authority here.'

'I thought to help you, Martha.'

'You were no help. The guy was scared of you and with cause! You're a patient not an unarmed combat wizard. You do as you're told not as you think. And don't call me Martha! From now on, Sergeant Templar, until you get a stripe occasioning similar rank you will address me as ma'am.'

Later that night, as she does most nights she called him to the office. She brought him in and locked the door. 'I'm sorry for losing my temper. I was scared. I thought you'd killed him.'

'I didn't kill him. I gave him a little peace.'

'I see that now.' She undid the collar of her shirt. 'You seem to have worked some kind of magic. He's sleeping like a babe. Do you want to tell me how you did that or do you want to leave it.'

'I guess I'll leave it.'

Her face weary and her eyes soft she came closer. 'I really am sorry.'

'It don't matter. You got a lot of worry.'

'I do, Gabriel.' She wound her arms about his neck. 'What I need is someone big and strong to make it better. Can you make it better? Can you give me the same smile that is currently hovering on that poor bugger's face?'

'I can sure try.'

~

Gabriel slept that night and dreamt of home. Charlie was outside the barn smoking a cigarette. Thin as a rail and hair straggling he looked ill.

'You don't look so good, Charlie.'

He shrugged. 'It's the fibromyalgia. It's dragging me down.'

'Maybe you should see a doctor.'

'Too late for that. This is a soul condition. No doctor can cure that.'

Overwhelmed with love, Gabriel tried to hug him but Charlie held him off.

'Take is easy, *Shiye*,' he said, smiling, the pockmarks on his face deep and bruised. 'I'm fragile today. A hug from you would finish me off and I need more time on earth. I have things to do.' He lit a cigarette. 'So how are you? I thought I might drop in to see how you're getting on with the Lime Tree.'

What Lime Tree! The barn was empty, the hunk of Lime gone and every carving and all of his tools vanished.

'Where's all my stuff?' said Gabriel.

'I don't know,' said Charlie. 'Looks to me like you've had a spring cleaning.'

'But who took it? It won't be Ma. She knows what they mean to me.'

'Do they mean something to you?'

'Sure they do!'

'Well, someone thought them surplus to requirement.' Charlie puffed on his cigarette. 'Better look inside the house make sure that is as it should be.'

The house was stripped down to the boards, not a table or chair, nor a cup in the cupboard. What's more it was covered in dust as if empty for years.

Puzzled and scared, Gabriel paced up and down. 'I don't get it. I haven't been away that long. How come everythin's changed?'

'Something has changed,' says Charlie. 'Are you sure it isn't you?'

'It ain't me. I'm the same as I always was, ain't I?'

Charlie was gone, just a smoke ring curling. It came to Gabriel then in the dream to run to the Eyrie but thinking that might be altered, the love and faithfulness stripped away he stayed where he was wandering from room-to-room his footsteps echoing. Apart from a mirror on the wall Ma's bedroom was empty and the doll carved in the State Pen that too was gone.

It was here. Ma wrapped it in a towel and stowed it in a trunk the day Gunny Emmet came. 'Don't you worry, son!' she said. 'It'll be here when you come home. I'll make sure no harm will come to it.'

But harm had come and not only to the doll to Ma!

What an awful dream. Gabriel was desperate to wake but couldn't and was forced to stand before Granma's looking glass seeking an answer.

Years ago he stood before this mirror trying on a velvet jacket. Time has moved on and now a Sergeant in the Marine Corps looks back.

Hooyah, what a catch! Hair shaved and shoulders straight he's real smart in Class A blues. Top-notch, you might say. But he doesn't shine as he did in the black velvet jacket. Something has been lost a precious metal gouged out. Now when he looks in the mirror he sees what everyone sees, an ordinary guy who smiles at jokes that aren't funny, who has sex with women he doesn't love, and who looks to life in the Marine Corps and weeps as he kills.

Twenty-five

Life-Lines
December 24th '44
Needham, Suffolk.

Adelia is trapped on the stairs while Edna unloads the latest
batch of village gossip on the mystery of Bobby Rourke.

'... so I said, you want to watch what you're saying,
Mrs Drake, coming up here spreading your nasty rumours.
One of these days you'll say the wrong thing and be up
before the judge. She says it's not gossip, it's God's honest
truth, he's cleared off back to America and you're never
going to hear from him again. That'll be four-pence, lovey,
yes, and a merry Christmas to you too!'

Mrs James sees the last customer off, turns the sign to
closed, the bakery shut over Christmas, takes another
breath and starts off again.

'She wouldn't have it there might be an innocent
explanation. She said what with the Home Guard being
stood down and liberation of Paris Yanks were being sent
home and the women they'd been with worrying what's
going to happen to them and their kiddies though what you
have to do with the liberation of Paris I do not know. She
said it serves you right. You're a bunch of floozies who got

what you deserved. On and on she went until I told her to go and get her bread somewhere else.'

'Alright then thanks, Edna. I'd better go. Sophie needs her supper.' Goose hidden under her coat Adelia hauled the pushchair upstairs. A whole goose and right on time for Christmas she needed to get it plucked and in the oven.

It was a present from the landlord at the Duke of Wellington. She helps out there. Their regular barmaid has fractured her wrist and so Adelia does the lunchtime shift. 'Here you love!' As she was leaving the landlord fetched the goose out. 'Pop it in the oven for an hour or two and it'll see you and your little 'un through Christmas. There's a small bottle of port to go with it.'

Then he'd tapped his nose. 'Me and my Missis appreciate you coming in at short notice. We'd like to have you fulltime. As Annie says, you're a good little worker and unlike our regular, Blanche, you're no flirt. We like having you. So off you go and do what you can to have a happy Christmas.'

The goose under the sink and the port in the cupboard she washed her hands ready for supper. A whole goose! She will share it with the James. They are generous with food and Sophie not a meat-eater it's too much for one.

It's still snowing. Adelia took a blanket from the cupboard. Twice this week Sophie woke saying she was cold. The bakery ovens maintaining heat over night she can't be cold, something else is bothering her busy little head.

A bright child, she's always on the move. There she in the sitting room playing with the toy farmhouse Nora bought. It's a wonderful thing. Sophie loves it and at night lines up the animals with Toby, the cat, to say their prayers.

'We've had it for a year,' said Nora. 'We got it in the January sale and kept it under the bed. By rights we should have waited until Christmas morning but us being away when she opened it we had to bring it.'

Nora Jackson is such a dear. Adelia loves her and Bert. They are lifelines to all that is good and worthy. It's a pity they're away for the holiday. 'I don't know why his mother can't come to us,' said Nora. 'Never mind Bert's not well We still have to traipse all the way to Stepney. But there you are, needs must.'

Needs must is the story of Adelia's life, three days off and then working evening shift at the pub. It has to be done. Pulling pints is not ideal but cash in hand it suits them all plus she can take Sophie who sits out back doing jigsaws with the landlord's aging mother or playing in the garden with the geese.

Ah yes, the goose! Adelia kept it hidden all the way home and must pluck and cook when Sophie's abed. At nineteen months she jabbers rather than talks and yet understands a great deal with a sure idea of what is right and wrong and killing one of the pub's pretty geese could not be more wrong.

'Sophie!' Adelia hiked the potty out from under the pushchair. 'Potty!'

Thank the Lord she really has the hang of this and is happy to cooperate. Hopefully in the New Year she'll be in knickers instead of nappies.

'No rush,' says Nora. 'Don't push. It'll happen when she's ready. Same with her teeth and walking, it'll all come good in the end.'

All come good in the end? Wouldn't that be wonderful!

Suddenly faint, Adelia hung onto the sink. 'Please God not now,' she prayed. 'Let me have one Christmas without making a fool of myself. Please, three days of peace and quiet and goodwill to all men including Bobby Rourke! '

People gossip about the way he disappeared. Those first few weeks when all was silent Adelia thought he had been killed and mourned him. Then when the first note arrived she thought it a poor joke. It was postmarked April 1st and made little sense. *It's me the bad penny. I guess you thought I was dead. No such luck. Me and the bike had an argument with a wall. Tell me you're still my girl because if you're not me and the bike will find another.'*

That was it, no return address. Relieved to know he was alive she waited to hear more. Weeks passed before the next delivery, a card postmarked Sussex and lost in the turmoil of war back-dated to March. Two lines: *'Hi Dee, you shouldn't have given me the monkey. It's done for me.'*

Anxious, she called at the Base to see if they had news but met a stone wall. 'We don't give out information. If the Lieutenant wanted you know his whereabouts he would've told you.' That was when gossip started an open forum everyone adding his or her comment, the latest piece of embroidery suggesting she is pregnant with his baby and behind with the rent.

Rumour upon rumour, Edna said American personnel were being recalled to fight the Pacific War. 'Maybe your chap is one of those.' Adelia doesn't know what to think.

Monday an Airmail Bluey dropped through the letterbox. '*Season's greetings. I'd love to be with you but as you've probably gathered circumstance and the US Air-force have removed me from my heart's desire. I didn't know what to do for a Christmas box so for now I'm sending love in the hope we'll spend the dollars when you're here with me in good old US of A, yours ever Bobby .*'

This time there was a PO Box return address in Virginia. But it isn't right! He is not right! The notes are low-key and not at all the upbeat the man she knew. Though anxious she can't help being hurt by the way he left so abruptly. She'd like to tell him to go to hell but misses his smiling face and his support.

While not exactly worse the blackouts do not improve and if anyone knew and understood her situation it was Bobby.

'How are things?' this from the Andrew Covington Wright who drops by when in Suffolk. 'I understand you're still seeing the psychiatrist. It is good to talk of feelings yet you need to be clear on the physical cause. Come in for tests. There may be pressure on the brain and while I don't want to worry you we shouldn't rule out epilepsy.'

Epilepsy!

'Do I do that?' Horrified she turned to Nora. 'Do I lie on the floor and squirm and foam at the mouth?'

'Of course you don't!' Nora was disgusted. 'Bloody doctors! Why do they have to make such a song and dance about everything?'

'That's what he said, possible epilepsy!'

'You haven't got epilepsy! So, you have trouble concentrating and sometimes get a bit confused. What does he expect? You had a knock on the head. You're entitled to be confused.'

'But that was in '42, Nora. Shouldn't I have got over it by now?'

'Your nerves are bad, lovey. It's this bloody war. It's enough to drive us all crazy. You need to get on with your life, and everyone else, Mr Covington Wright included, needs to mind his own bloody business.'

'He is concerned.'

'Maybe he is and then again maybe he fancies you, the old goat.'

'You don't like him?'

'I don't mind him. It's doctors in general I don't like. Sitting on clouds thinking they're God! You can't have an opinion. They said Bert had nothing wrong with him that it was in his head. Now they say he's got sugar diabetes and should've been treated earlier. Useless sods! I'd sooner see a vet.'

Adelia had laughed. 'I don't think a vet can help me.'

'Maybe not but at least he won't try telling you you're crazy.'

No one has ever said she is crazy. They shuffle words about. The psychiatrist likens her condition to a musical fugue, *'two rhythms playing one against the other,'* which though poetic is of no real help. Nora says it's nerves. Ladies from the Christian Morality League think she's a woman of the streets. Even the ghost she sees now and then has an opinion. He said she'd left a bit of her soul behind in '42 and wouldn't be right until she'd got it back.

Yes, truly, a ghost by the name of Joe.

She first saw him last January. She was in the yard clearing snow. Sophie was asleep in the pushchair. There was a crackle of ice underfoot and there he was a soldier with a pack on his back and helmet in his hand. She knew he was a ghost because he was almost made of smoke, the dustbin by the shed seen through him. Next time she saw him was in the park when he appeared by the pond minus backpack and smoking a cigar. He stooped to pat a dog and the dog clearly aware of him wagging its tail.

He looked up and smiled. 'The name's Joe,' he said. 'Don't be scared. I'm only passin' through.'

A ghost with such a thick growling voice you'd think she would be scared yet strangely she wasn't scared, she liked seeing him, found him comforting.

Once when worried about the fainting fits he appeared at the kitchen door. 'You left a bit of yourself in '42, Missy. You won't get better until it's returned.' It came to her then she'd seen him in dreams and that in one dream he was caught in an explosion. Seeming to hear her thoughts he nodded, 'you were there when it happened but not for me. You were there for the other guy.'

She didn't know what he meant but it didn't matter because let's face it she is crazy. Seeing ghosts *and* talking with them surely proves the point!

It occurred to her he might be Sophie's father. He caught the thought and smiled. 'I don't think so, Missy. I'm too old and too cussed to be father to anyone. Closest I'd get is Godfather, plus my eyes are wrong.'

His eyes are wrong. They are brown as opposed to blue.

She never talks of Joe not even to Nora. She believes that he and the tramp are gifts from God, and to speak of them would be to betray them. Besides, why knock another nail in her insanity coffin. There's enough there as it is.

~

It's quarter to eight. Adelia is outside the bakery waiting for Eddie James. There is a problem with the goose. Hanging down like this, feathers soft and white, she finds she can't touch it let alone cook. It's wrong. A lovely thing like that shouldn't be dead. It should be alive and running about squawking.

She phoned the James. Eddie answered. He was odd on the phone, preoccupied. 'Something wrong?'

'Er... well, we've had bit of bad news.'

'Oh Ted I am sorry! I'll call back later.'

'No, hang on!' There was shuffling on the other end, Edna telling him to shut-up. 'I'm on my way, lovey,' then he said. 'Are you sure about the goose?'

'Certain.'

'What will you eat?'

'We'll be fine. I made cauliflower cheese earlier.'

'Well, if you are sure I won't say no. We've our daughter and her chap coming. A goose will come in handy. Give me a couple of minutes and I'll come by. And don't worry about our bad news. I shouldn't have said anything.'

Now she waits in the snow. So cold, paths treacherous underfoot and temperature well below zero there will be no visiting St Giles tonight. As for the Black Swan, Sam, the landlord at the Duke of Wellington, said it is to be rebuilt.

'No more Mucky Duck! It's to be renamed the Oast House.'

It seems she's not meant to know what happened there. Maybe that's a good thing. As Nora says she needs to get on with life. If she knew what was happening with Bobby Rourke maybe she could.

Sophie's second Christmas and no daddy to share it. She used to ask after him. She'd hold out the blue teddy, 'Dada?' Adelia would shake her head, 'Dada is a busy man.' She never speaks of him now. She knows Dada is long gone, that he lost interest in Mummy the moment she let him into her bed.

Snow scattering Adelia kicked the gate-post. 'So much for America!'

So frustrating! One minute he's declaring undying love and then he's gone. Last Christmas was a washout. He didn't phone and when he did he was insultingly casual his manner suggesting he was too busy.

Thinking he might come for Christmas lunch she was out every morning queuing at various shops, most times coming away empty-handed but then Thursday getting a pork chop. It had to keep until the Saturday but four foot drifts were enough to freeze anything. He didn't come Christmas Day or Boxing Day and so afraid it would go off she gave the chop to Nora, their usual butcher closed down for selling horsemeat.

When he did eventually turn up all they had was corned beef. He was drunk when he arrived and a bottle of brandy under his arm determined to stay so.

He returned to Littlehampton and a repeat pattern, few words and space between. There was one call in March when he babbled of a marriage licence. That was months ago. Now his courtship, if that's what it is, arrives in scribbled notes. He still talks of the States but talk is all it is.

Adelia smiled ruefully. 'Maybe the corned beef put him off.'

'Cooee!' Eddie is coming and Edna too trudging through the snow.

'I didn't expect you, Edna.'

'I wanted to come.'

'Shall we go in?' Adelia opened the gate. 'It's cold out here.'

'No, we won't stop. We only came to pick up the goose.'

There was something else, something terrible. Adelia could see it in their eyes. 'What? What has happened?'

Edna took out her hankie. 'You tell her Ed.'

'Tell me what?'

'It's like this, lovey. There was a V2 strike yesterday. It was on the news.'

'A V2 rocket?'

'Yes, in London, in Stepney on the Vallance Road.'

'Vallance Road? Isn't that where Nora's mother-in-law lives?'

'It is. I'm sorry to say it got them.'

'What do you mean got them?'

'It got them all, Nora and Bert and the whole family!'

'Oh my God!'

Edna nodded. 'We heard the news and knowing they were there called Eddie's brother at Stepney East fire-station. He's a fireman there. He said he'd find out. When you called about the goose he'd just rung. They were killed, every man, woman and child in the apartment building.'

'Poor Nora.'

'We weren't going to tell you. We didn't want to spoil your Christmas but when you rang we had to tell. I'm sorry. I know how much you loved Nora.'

'I did love her and Bert. They were so good to us.'

'They were good to everyone. It's the kind of people they were. Are you going to be alright?' said Eddie 'We can stay if you want.'

'No, you go. You've things to do.' Adelia held out the shopping bag. 'Better take this. You'll need to get busy.'

'Alright then.'

'I'll see you Tuesday.'

Edna hesitated. 'Are you sure you're alright?'

'I'd better go in. Sophie's up there.'

'Right you are. Sorry to bring such rotten news.'

'It can't be helped.'

'Will you tell Sophie?'

'I don't know. I'll have to think about it.'

'Give her our love won't you?'

'I will.'

'We'll come round Boxing Day to see how you are.'

'Yes do.' Adelia waited until they turned the corner and then went into the backyard closing and locking the gate.

Why Nora and Bert? Why them! They were such good people. They never harmed anyone! Now they're gone and the world is worse for it.

Bang! It came then, a sense of body and soul coming adrift, of the frailty of life, and of this awful war and of nothing ever making sense.

Sickness overwhelmed her. Key slippery in her hand she tried staying upright but her legs folded. She fell and could not get up

She lay gazing up at the sky and at moonlight making candelabras of icicles. This is what Bobby meant by unimaginable backdrop. He said this canopy of suns and moons and stars is what a pilot sees when crashing to earth, that God hung the sky at the beginning of time so that from then until forever men and women might die gazing upon the infinite.

A terrible vision!

Panic stricken, she tried to rise but her limbs were leaden. I must get up! Sophie is alone. She will wake and wonder where I am.

Heart pounding and struggling with all her might she pushed against the icy ground fighting to rise until suddenly she was on her feet and running up the fire escape so light and easy she might have been flying.

She went to unlock the door but hadn't the key. Thinking she'd dropped it she looked over the railing. There it was in the snow! And so was she!

What!?

Yes! There she is lying against the bin.

But how is that? If she is down there, what is up here on the fire escape?

Oh my God, I'm dead! A thought tore through her mind. I must have had a seizure and died. 'Oh Sophie! My little girl!'

Terrified, she lunged forward and was propelled into the flat passing through the outer walls as through smoke. Then she was in the bedroom hovering over the cot and Sophie, hand under her rosy cheek is asleep.

'Oh help me!' Adelia cried. 'Someone please help me!' She cried out and help came.

'Take it easy, Missy.' Someone took her hand.

It was Joe. Though she couldn't quite see him she knew his voice. 'Help me, Joe! Tell me what's happening? Have I died?'

'You're not dead. You had a shock that knocked you sideways.'

She clung to his hand. What does he mean sideways? How can she be on the ground, face so pale she merges with snow and yet be here in the bedroom? She hurt her head when she fell! It has to be that, and the strangeness of it all is the result of the fall, at least......

....at least that's what she tells herself when thinking on that day, and she does think about it, piecing together fragments of conversation where she held hands with a ghost and no words were spoken and yet all were heard.

'What's happening, Joe?' she said. 'How can I be in two places at once?'

'I don't know what to tell you,' said Joe. 'I'm no expert. But I reckon that there are times in a person's life when he has such a shock he splits in half, parting company body and soul. I reckon that's what's happening here.'

'I'm frightened.'

'Sure you are. I was scared when I stepped on that mine and found myself lookin' down on my body. I knew I'd hit the big one and should be movin' on, maybe not to heaven,

I weren't that good a guy, but to some place. But you see I was worried about a kid I love and so I hung about him for a while. Then seein' his worries was not for him but for someone else I went lookin' for that someone to see if I could help and that's how I found you.'

Seeing her confused he shook his head. 'But don't worry about that. You can catch up on that another time straight from the horse's mouth, so to speak. Right now you need to reconnect with the you lyin' down in the snow and get on with life knowin' that no matter what happens you and your baby are safe.'

'Safe?' Adelia tried again and again to grab Sophie but found her hands passed through bars on the cot as if they weren't there. 'How can she be safe when I can't touch her? What is safe about that? She's my daughter, my little girl, and she's alone in this world with no one to care!'

'She's not alone. There is always someone watchin'. Yesterday it was me. Today you got new helpers.'

With that he drew her aside so she might have a wider vision of the room.

She saw them.

'Oh!' Her heart rolled. There they were, Nora in her flowered pinny and Bert in the same mustard coloured cardigan. They were standing by the cot gazing down at Sophie their faces wreathed in smiles.

'They're keeping watch!'

'Sure they are. They are her Godparents.'

'No, not her Godparents! I wish they had been. We never got that far.'

Joe smiled. 'You think a bit of paper and splash of holy water makes a Godparent? That is not how it works. Love makes a Godparent, pure and simple, and those two good people loved Sophie.'

Adelia's eyes filled with tears. 'Will they stay with her?'

'Yes until someone with a higher duty comes along. You gotta lot of people lovin' your kiddie, Missy. Some are like Mr and Mrs Jackson, life-lines as you call them, others with a vested interest.'

'Vested interest? Are you referring to her father?'

'Depends what you mean. Most men would give their eye-teeth for a daughter like Sophie. I know of three fellers who'd give their souls! They know who they are and what they feel and you need to know because as with Godparents a man doesn't need a piece of paper to be a father. He needs love.'

'But how will I know?'

'You'll know. It will sing through your bones.'

'And if I choose wrongly?'

'Then you must see it through.'

'Why must I? I've already made one mistake. Surely Sophie would be better if I made my own way?'

'Can you do that?'

'I don't see why not. I have this flat. I have a job and friends. Sophie will be two next year. If I get her into a nursery I could go back to nursing meanwhile...'

'....meanwhile there's a pub and your kiddie playin' with geese.'

'What's wrong with that?' Adelia was angry. 'There's nothing wrong with the Duke of Wellington! It's a respectable job run by respectable people! I like it there. This job allows me freedom with pay.'

'I'm not sayin' otherwise. If you think it's okay for her to be there then fine. Some people might not agree but that's your choice.'

'Yes, my choice and my life! I do the best I can with what I have. I love Sophie and I take care of her. I don't need anyone else!'

'Maybe not but you've lost two of your lifelines. What's to say you won't lose more? This week a V2 rocket took Nora and Bert. Next week it could be another lifeline and not necessarily through death. What d'you do then?'

'I manage! I get on with it the same as everyone else!'

'Sure you do. Being strong is what this war is about.' Joe gestured to the railing and her body below. 'As things are, a bit of you down there freezin' to death and another up here talkin' with a ghost, you have to wonder how strong.'

'I can be strong if only people will let me.'

'Ah, yes, people.' He sighed. 'When I was a kid in Japan I thought I knew people. I didn't know them then and I don't know them now. And neither do you. So look to yourself and your daughter, Missy! In the end there is only you, so get back in that body and be strong because the world is turnin', old life-lines breakin' and people you thought were friends may not stay so.'

With that he gave her a push. Adelia fell over the rail and with a sudden stop was in the backyard covered with snow.

Shivering, hardly able to walk, she fumbled with the key. All was quiet in the flat. The cot was empty. Sophie was in the big bed huddled up with the cat. Cheek wet with tears and animals from the toy farm littered about the bed it would seem she's had a bad dream.

Adelia undressed and crawled into bed. When Sophie opened her eyes she drew her close. She didn't speak. Words were the snowflakes slipping silently down the window and had all been said.

Twenty-six

Rose Cottage
December 31st '44
Behind German lines

'You'll get the Medal for this.'

'Yeah, sure.'

'No, I'm telling you, you will get it. I can see the chit already being drawn up.'

'I should live that long.' Alex carried on stuffing straw into the gap between leggings and his boots. Hiding in the crypt of a bombed out church, his left knee shot to pieces, there's a little more shelter from the wind now he's closed the grating but not enough to stop him freezing to death.

Messing with straw is a waste of time but he's got to get through the night. US Army issue battle dress is lightweight and easy to wear but when you're ankle-deep in the German Eifel snow it's worse than useless the material thin and the soles of his boots conducting cold rather than repelling. It's the same with the treads on US Sherman tanks. Unlike the German Panzer Tigers they are not geared toward the icy terrain and slip and slide all over the place.

More straw and more padding, it seems Alex has spent the better part of the war getting familiar with shitty straw. Not so many months ago he was face down in it.

That guy! The farmer was so scared he ignored Alex's whispered pleas to be taken to Monsignor Brandt and the Church of Mother of Mary. Head down he pushed that cart up and down back alleys and never stopping until he pulled into a backyard. A gate was slammed shut. Orders were to keep quiet. When Alex tried to speak the muzzle of a shotgun was poked through the straw.

'*Zitto! Shut your mouth Yankee boy!*'

The Yankee boy shut up. There was a meeting, two and then three voices arguing. One guy wanted to kill him and bury him in the yard. 'Better that,' he said, 'than caught harbouring a prisoner.' A woman ran out snatching the gun. She told them not to be crazy, the war was lost and the Nazis worse than any Yankees. She said they had to get him out the yard and into the Vatican.

They argued some more. From what Alex could gather St Peters Basilica used to be a way out for Allied escapees, the Holy City declaring neutrality and that as with the word of God any prisoner surrendering within the Vatican grounds would be given sanctuary. So it went, prisoners being smuggled out. But then with the Italian cease-fire of '43 the Germans took over. A Nazi officer, one Colonel Herbert Kappler had a demarcation line painted across the front of the Basilica and issued a notice any Allied soldier crossing the line would be shot and Italian helpers with him.

The farmer and his pals carried on arguing until a layer of straw was peeled back and a slice of melon offered. They fed him and gave water but wouldn't let Alex out the cart. He was to stay put until they'd got him away to the Church of the Holy Sepulchre where *contadini* of the Italian countryside had escape routes.

Those villagers! Talk about guts! If he gets through this alive he'll make pilgrimage to villages in the Salmona Valley thanking them for their help. They didn't have to do it. Not so long ago he was one of those killing their sons. With the Armistice agreement Germany turned against Italy. The fury of the Third Reich unleashed homes were burnt to the ground and people and livestock killed. There was a problem then with information. The British war-machine got it wrong. They had assumed the ceasefire would send the German army in swift retreat behind their lines and with that in mind relayed a message to allied camps all over Italy telling the POWs to stay put and await assistance.

It was a mistake. They forgot they were dealing with a maniac thus thousands of German troops were redirected to Italy. In the confusion POWs in the more Northern camps managed to cross over into Switzerland whereas those in the Southernmost camps were forced to stay under German command.

In February of '43 Alex knew nothing of this. His only concern was breathing through horse shit and getting to neutral ground. Half-suffocating, he was wheeled through the Vatican City under the noses of German guards, his helpers changing again and again until nightfall when he along with the manure was loaded onto a truck and taken via back roads out of Rome.

From then it was a series of anxious faces and of being hidden in cellars and cattle trucks and of being bundled from one village to the next. It was three months before he and other prisoners reached Allied lines and with more than one Italian helper killed along the way.

The risks that were taken! These people had nothing! They scrambled to live. Alex remembers being given a bowl of gruel and of starting to eat but then conscious of eyes following every mouthful realised this was all they had.

'*Mangiare!*' When unable to swallow he stopped eating a woman slapped him. 'You eat Yankee and eat good then you say we did you no harm.'

Every mouthful choking Alex ate.

Back again in Allied territory advanced to Lieutenant Colonel he was allowed a short rest in field hospital and then given new orders. So many killed and captured at Anzio the Rangers were done. Alex was absorbed into the Fifth Army and returned almost immediately to frontline duties.

A hasty move, he should have listened to British SOE advice and accepted a transfer to Army Intelligence. 'We fight the same war, Colonel but with different weapons,' said the Intelligence officer. When asked what weapon they referred to his mental facilities, i.e. the Camera and what that walking, talking Videodrome could do for them behind enemy lines,

When asked what enemy, and where, they said, 'Berlin.'

Good God! Berlin already a new warzone and the old battle not even won!

The Warlords had sensed the dawning of a new day and the end of one war and the beginning of a new. 'We don't trust Papa Joe. When Berlin falls we need to be there for fair pickings or the Russian Bear will overrun us all.'

If Alex had known what was to come, that refusal would see him shipped frontline to the Ardennes and Hitler's Stormtroopers he might have thought again. So little rest! He didn't even get to speak to his folks!

Sick of open warfare it would've been easy to switch but how could he join Intelligence when it meant ducking out on the people that had died to keep him alive. So here he is again back where he started.

'They'll get you in the end, kid. You can wriggle as much as you like but when Sam Jentzen and his OSS guys come calling they get what they want.'

'Chrissakes, Joe, will you shut-up!' Alex slung the empty water-bottle at the wall. 'I'm sick of you in my ear. Go haunt some other poor sucker.'

It's okay. Joe Petowski's not here, God knows, Alex wouldn't wish this cellar on anyone not even one as tough as Joe. This bizarre subterranean one-way chit-chat is of martial arts stay-alive strategy taught at the Academy.

Mind-over-matter and Man Greater than the Sum of his Parts psychology, Joe was into that. Alex remembers him lecturing on the virtues of the Samurai Warrior and Bushido Code in the Academy boxing ring while pinning some poor unfortunate plebe to the deck. 'Physical strength isn't enough,' he was saying. 'There is more to you than a body. If your body is the engine then your soul is the driver. Be as tough as you like. You will still die. Look beyond the body when you are wounded. Seek out friendly thoughts! Fight to live by finding reasons to live.'

In the crypt of the Wounded Heart Alex endeavours to do just that, to stay alive when truly he could care less – which makes the point that any medal after this would be a sham since it's not gained through courage but rather through indifference. It might look like courage, it might even seem so him another Errol Flynn leaping about clearing foxholes with a Browning automatic, but as everyone knows seeming isn't being. The fact is he doesn't give a shit. Such a weight of guilt on his shoulders to lay it down if only for a minute would be peace indeed.

He is not alone in the crypt. Over against the wall are three guys from the British Royal Tank Regiment and alongside a stone coffin two of Hitler's finest.

They are all dead. A rattle of gunfire, it happened so fast. One minute he was with the rest of the Unit creeping through a wooded tract using a tank for cover when out of the mist a column of Panzer Tigers reared up.

Steel behemoths clashing battle ensued. The British tank alongside Alex was soon ablaze. The driver's door jammed he climbed up top and levering it open dragged the Commander out. They then came under fire from Stormtroopers hidden in a cellar. Errol Flynn again he cleared that with grenades but took a round in his left knee and unable to keep up waved the Unit on while he and the Commander took shelter in the crypt.

That was two days ago.

Skin hanging in scorched shreds the Commander was badly burned as was the gunner. He died during the night and the gunner soon after. As for Alex snow or not he'd like to be out in the fresh air but his leg won't carry him.

So he sits tight hoping that someone will remember he is here.

It's cold in the crypt. The *Obersoldat* back of the coffin wears a fur-lined jacket. Alex hopes to relieve him of that and his rubber galoshes. It's a matter of finding the courage to move. Last time he tried the pain was so bad he passed out and found his way to heaven via soft Virginia blue grass and with his head in Adelia's lap.

What a way to go! So damned real, the sun shining in the sky and the smell of blossom and Adelia Challoner smiling down? What more could a man want?

Why, he could even count the golden down on her cheek.

'What are you doing here, honey?' he'd said, a fool questioning delirium. 'I left you on English soil. How come you're in Virginia?'

'I live here.' She'd stroked his hair back from his forehead. 'This is my home. Where else would I be?'

Home? A sweet dream if a little absurd it goes to show how even when things are utterly hopeless the mind needs to dream.

Home. While resting in hospital he wrote his folks letting them know he is alive. Joe's death and their son's long march to freedom through the Italian Alps he kept to himself. Hopefully, they got the letter but things being as they are, it's not certain. A four-star General Dad could push for news. He won't. He despises those using rank for favour. 'Judas H Priest!' he'd thunder. 'If that what it's down to, men pushing their badges across a desk, I'd sooner quit.'

~

Lord, his knee hurts! This interminable cold is a mixed
blessing. On one hand it's freezing his balls off on the other
it will slow necrosis down. The wound is deep but clean
and unlike others in here doesn't stink.

Ham frying was the smell coming off the British tank
guy yesterday.

'I am most awfully sorry,' the Commander was
apologetic. 'Burnt to a crisp the atmosphere in here must
be pretty ripe.'

'It's okay.' Alex had said. 'You may still get through.'

'Oh no.' The guy wasn't to be fooled. 'It's obvious what
is happening and it's alright. It could have been worse. I
kept my nerve, Colonel, that's what matters, though I wish
I might have spoken with my wife. She does worry so.'

Though unable to see how things could be worse Alex
agreed that if he got through he would carry a message to
the wife back in Blighty.

'It doesn't need to be much. My Betty is a brave girl. A
couple of words and she will know I am dealing with it.'

Rose Cottage.

Those are the words. No explanation, just that.

Lips frayed and hands like claws it's a wonder the man
could talk at all. 'Just tell her I'll be waiting in Rose
Cottage with the kettle on. She'll know what you mean.
Thank you. I feel so much easier.'

Blink! A candle snuffed out he died as if with the words
Rose Cottage he was free to die.

'A tough guy that Britisher.'

'Yes, Joe, a tough guy.

'Will you carry the message?'

'Sure, if I can.'

'That's a reason to live then isn't it?'

'I guess so.'

'So let's try livin'. Start with the jacket. The temperature's dropping and though help is on the way it's not much use if you're ass has frostbite.'

'Is help on the way?'

'It will be even if I have to fetch it myself so get going! And get the boots too!'

Teeth gritted, Alex inched across the floor. He grabbed hold on the boot, twisted and pulled. Jesus Christ! The foot came away with the boot, shrapnel cutting through the ankle as neat as any butcher.

It threw Alex across the room his head hitting the floor. When he came to, or thought he did, it was to the Old Mill in Fredericksburg.

Ten minutes timed by the Obersoldat's watch he wasn't out long yet it felt like forever. A filthy place, the windows sealed and hole in the roof there was nothing to see yet there he was gazing at the front door as if the treasure of the world was inside.

It was quiet but for a lone duck quacking. There was a scent in the air. Thick oily attar of roses, it tasted so sweet Alex could've drunk it.

A light sprang up in the top room of the tower, lamplight appearing and disappearing as she, a woman made her way down the stairs.

'Quack! Quack!' Lonely and calling for a mate the duck was going at it and Alex's heart keeping time.

Then Bobby Rourke was in the dream and both gazing at the front door. It was Bobby but not the buddy of old. This was an old man. Shrunken, and with a flier's white silk scarf wound about his face he hung back in the shadows.

'Hi there, Bobby!' Alex spoke to him. 'How are you doing?'

. 'I'm fine, old sport,' he said. 'How are you?'

'Good to see you.' Alex's hand went out.

Bobby turned and the scarf fell away and pain and wretchedness peered out.

Bang! Alex regained consciousness flat out on the stone floor, the Stormtroopers boot plus foot still in his hand. He tossed it aside. No way did he want that! Same with the jacket! He didn't care how cold it was. The thought of taking it terrified him. What else might drop out, the guy's heart!

Alex's head hurts where he fell. He keeps thinking of the Mill. He knows of it. The History of the US Civil War, in particular the Battle of Fredericksburg is required reading in the Hunter household.

The Mill has a reputation and known locally as bad juju. No one goes there, especially at night. It has a dark history, rumours of men shot there in the War of Independence and again in the Civil War. The gossip about those parts is that no one gets into the Mill unless the dead wants them. It's about being welcome. You can take a hammer to the door but you won't get in.

That kind of old wives tales is part and parcel of the South, the common thought if it ain't worth listening then make a mystery of it. Alex remembers pictures in Dad's *Time Books*, black and white shots of the Mill in the 1800s. It was already derelict then, the tower blasted and opened to the sky a cinematic leftover from a Boris Karloff movie.

It surely isn't any Rose Cottage. So why go there even as the result of a blow on the head. It wasn't a dream it was more a trauma induced hallucination. But what called him and why was Bobby there? There must be more to the dream that Alex has forgotten. The Camera retains most things. Even in sleep the film rolls. He does have the odd blind spot. Large or small, important or not so, whack, the Camera has wiped the lens clean.

He's no idea why. Joe says it's a safety device. He reckoned Alex has a cut-off point where his soul says, 'No thanks. I'd sooner live without that.'

No! Alex doesn't buy that. It's too neat. If that were the case, if he were able to reject an image as too painful then why remember Adelia dying?

'You can't get more painful than that.'

~

Churches are always cold. This one is as cold as any grave.

Weary beyond thinking and leg on fire Alex wonders how much longer he can hold out. What if help doesn't come? What if he dies and he and his companions are found a hundred years from now? Of course, there are always dog-tags. Mother dead in Nagasawa and father a Polish sailor Joe has no folks to be told the bad news. David Furness has an aging mother. Alex didn't get to see her but did leave the dog tags with the C/O.

Now there's these guys. Those tags belonging to the tank crew are already in Alex's pocket along with special words for the Commander's wife.

In an absurd whim Alex is tempted to write special words on a scrap of paper and pin it to his jacket. But he and Adelia didn't have any. There wasn't time. There was a church and an empty window and mouse whiskers quivering.

She had his class ring. He bought another ring in Scotland and had it engraved *Omnia Vincit Amor*. Now he wonders how many lovers visiting that church have a similar ring and inscription as remembrance of the day.

Lovers need that kind of memory. Such memories help keep love alive. They are like a tune, the special melody that means so much.

They had the Twilight Lounge and Glen Miller. Music drifting up from below they'd clung together shuffling about that filthy bedroom to the song.

'*I'll be loving you always, with a love that's true, always, when the things you've planned need a helping hand I will understand…*'

Joe says if you want to live you must have reason to live otherwise the body functions as an automaton and the soul remains asleep. 'You have to believe in something, Camera, and if not something then someone.'

Deus ex machina, the god, or in this case the ghost in the machine, here he is again shouting inside Alex's febrile head wanting him to live.

It's cold now, so cold. A little colder, a slight drop in the barometer and Colonel Alexander Hunter, Ist Battalion US Rangers is no more.

She is here! His beloved baby is close by. All he has to do is stretch out a hand and she will bring him through to the other side.

That's what he should do, lie down and sleep.

Who knows, he might get back to the Virginia blue grass.

Eyes tightly closed he lay down and a warm hand took his.

'It's alright, my darling,' she whispered. 'I'm here. You can sleep now.'

So he slept....

..... He regained consciousness to daylight and movement and men talking.

Rescuers were here! They were talking, saying he is lucky, that they were searching for wounded but believing no one here had moved on.

'But for the Polack Sergeant we would've missed you.'

'Polack?'

'Yeah, a big gorilla of guy. He wouldn't take no for an answer.'

A medic laughed. 'I thought he was gonna pull his pistol on me. What a tough guy! He had a voice like a rusty motor.'

'Rusty motor?'

'That's him. You know him, Colonel?'

'I guess I do.' Too weary to tell of the brave man who even in death won't let go of duty Alex was loaded onto a stretcher. Closing his eyes he reached out for Adelia but the dream had melted into German snow. Now all he has is the memory of a girl holding his hand and a duck quacking.

Twenty-seven
Anticipating
April 1945
Johns Hopkins Hospital
Richmond, Virginia

Bobby grabbed the nurse's wrist. 'If you do that again
without shuttin' the door I swear to God I will knock your
teeth back of your face!'

'I did close the door!'

'What, and it opened on its own?' He threw her back.
'Spooky! Maybe some other poor bastard died of
mishandlin'. Better get the room exorcised before he gets
his revenge on you and the rest of the clumsy bitches'

'I'm not clumsy!' the nurse protested. 'It's you! You
make me nervous.'

'Nervous my ass! You're just no good at the job.'

'Thank you, nurse!' The doctor bustled in. 'You can go!
Leave the dressing. I'll finish up here.'

The nurse ran.

'What's the problem this time Captain Rourke?'

'That girl is problem! She has no more sense than that
wall. I've told her before to give a guy privacy. Don't be
flingin' the blinds wide and lettin' in all that light. Does she

listen, no! She comes chargin' in and starts rippin' left and right and leaves the door to the corridor open for everyone to see.'

The doctor closed the door. 'If the nurse did do that then I am sorry. She should have been more thoughtful. But really, was all that shouting necessary? I could hear you arguing the other end of the corridor.'

'And yet you didn't intervene?'

'I was with a patient. I could hardly walk away.'

'I guess not. Why stop some poor benighted guy bein' bounced about the bed and his limitations hangin' out.'

'Limitations? Captain, aren't you a little over sensitive to your condition?'

'Over sensitive?'

'Perhaps a little? What happened to you is tough. It must take some dealing with. But you're a hero, Captain Rourke, a decorated man who served his country with great gallantry. If anyone can manage it's you. I'm sure given time and patience you will resume your life as before.'

'You think so?'

'I do.'

Bobby sat up, removed his dark glasses and shoved his face up close. 'You think I can do that, Doc, resume my life as before?' When the guy automatically stepped back he grinned darkly. 'No, I thought not.'

'I'm sorry,' the doctor apologised. 'Now it is me being thoughtless. Of course the nurse should draw the blinds and at the very least close the door. There's no excusing carelessness. But I assure you such want of feeling is not the norm. We try at all times to do our best by our patients.'

'Do you indeed?'

'Yes, sir, we do, it is our primary concern.'

'Well then, buddy, in that you are failin',' Bobby slipped the glasses back over his nose. 'I've been comin' to places like this for more than a year. Months of bein' pushed and pulled, tubes shoved down my throat and tubes up my ass, and I have to say you medics may be Ace at puttin' a man's body back together again but you're shit at mendin' his soul.'

~

Apologies made and bills paid the Doc didn't stay around to debate. Neither did Bobby. A handful of painkillers down his throat and he's in the Morgan on the Turnpike, foot to the metal all the way until Pamunkey Bridge where raining most of the week the river is swollen and the bridge waterlogged.

'Tally Ho!' Water whaling over the side he sliced on through overtaking an open top Chevy. The guy hung out cussing. 'Yeah, whatever!' Bobby flipped him the finger. 'Get a decent car instead of a rust bucket! Get a Morgan! They're like yours truly, custom-made and great at manoeuverin'!'

He found the two-seater roadster while in hospital waiting to be shipped back Stateside. Motor bike totalled and unsteady on his pins he needed to get around. A combination of scarlet paintwork, brilliant chrome and black upholstery one look at the pic in the Sussex Times and he was sold.

Custom made it wasn't cheap. He didn't care. It is a great car, fabulous as he used to be fabulous. A phone call and it was his. No waiting around. Nowadays Baby Rourke gets what he wants when he wants it. No diddling on the side! Too many precious things get lost along the way.

November '45, a Christmas gift to self, he had it shipped over to Virginia.

Ma was scornful 'It doesn't suit you.'

'Why doesn't it?'

'It's a fancy hotrod that rich kids drive. And it's red!'

'I like red.'

'It's too gaudy! Folks will see you comin' and you don't want that.'

'Why don't I?' He was fool enough to ask.

'Because you look like somethin' kids throw stones at.'

Jesus, she is cruel! Nothing changes! All this time away and in a few short weeks she's telling him to move out because she can't stand to look at him. Now he's living at the Veteran's Hospital. He pays extra for a room of his own. It's not so bad. It's full of guys with arms and legs shot off. Most of them are crazy and whistling to the wind so Bobby is among friends. Anyway, he'll be moving again soon now he has his own place.

He bought the Old Mill in Fredericksburg. Ma hates it. She reckons he's wasted his money and maybe she is right. Pre-civil war, stinking of damp and crumbling tower it's been around so long folks have forgotten it's there. It needs work and plenty bucks to make it habitable also out on the edge of Bayonet Woods with nothing much close by it needs courage to live there.

Even the realtor was doubtful. 'It's a lot to take on, sir. Are you sure you're up to it?'

Sir ain't sure of anything other than he needs to be off the beaten track where's there's no passing traffic and no Ma dropping by, a place where he can sit chewing his finger ends wondering what the fuck happened.

What did happen? How did he get from that to this? One minute he is a movie pin-up, girls falling at his feet, the RAF's finest with 50 plus missions under his belt and talk of a transfer at the end of the war to Dayton, Ohio testing jet planes. Then boom, he's skidding on ice and it's gone, the Lancasters and the Mosquitoes, and the RAF blues that along with the jolly good show camaraderie bullshit kept all pilots and crews from falling apart.

It's all gone leaving him a defunct pilot written off as unfit to command.

January 6th the letter arrived from the Defence Department declaring him unfit for duty. Unfit to command a plane? Him! Robert E Rourke, DFC, the guy that helped shoot down the Amiens Walls of Jericho!

'No way!' Bobby pulled the Morgan into the Mill yard. 'There isn't a man alive that can stop me flyin'! The USAAF and the CAA and every other petty agency on this here planet will not keep this bird from flexin' his wings.'

It's pathetic. People bring out rules about governing airspace when we all know only one power rules the sky and that is the God that with Icarus threw Bobby down, pressing his arrogant, unbelieving face into the dirt.

Forget destiny! Forget icy roads! Conditions were incidental. God caused that accident. This was the God of Moses and of Abraham, the I Am That I Am scary old man with the pointing figure leaning out of Leonardo da Vinci's painting, the God that parted the Red Sea and the same God that but for Noah and his Arc drowned the world in tears.

It's Him! Power Omnipotent working on behalf of Alex Hunter.

Who other than Ash has a bigger axe to grind? Okay, maybe God didn't stick His foot out sending Bobby ass over tit but it was Alex's bike that folded

The accident was payback due to Miss Adelia Challoner currently pining away in Suffolk with Sophie, the twinkle in the hole that once was Bobby's left eye.

Barbed wire took his left eye and his ear. Surgeons did their best but with half his face hanging on the A259 roundabout they couldn't put back what wasn't there. It's left him a bit player for a Horror Movie. Even with dark glasses people don't want to look at him. Old friends rarely stop to chat. Rather than stumble through awkward conversations they turn away.

The other night one old friend did more than chat. Bobby was at the Hawaiian Bar nursing a whisky. Who strolled through the door but Herb Willet's widow? Wow! If Bobby has lost his looks then Miss Sue has gained.

Raven hair hanging down and body like a panther she strolled down the length of the bar to total silence. It was a bad moment. Remembering what they had before the war, giggles among the grave-stones, he'd crouched down in the booth hoping she'd pass but next he knew she's sliding in.

'Hi there, Baby Rourke,' she says in that breathy voice. 'I thought it was you snuck away here on your lonesome.'

Twenty minutes and she was drunker than he. She had to be because another Tequila Slammer and they're out in the back-lot among the trash cans going at it like rabbits.

'Ain't you worried about this Sue?' says he coming up for the air.

'Worried about what?'

'I don't know, maybe you bein' here back of the Hawaiian Bar out of your scull on booze and seducin' the Night of the Livin' Dead.'

'Is that what I'm doin'?' She looks at him with those great dark eyes. 'Funny, I thought I was pickin' up where I left off a lifetime ago. See you around, Bobby.'

Tossing her hair and swinging her hips, she was gone like the Whore of Babylon Ma's always going on about. Too bad Bobby shot his mouth off. If'n he'd kept quiet he'd have seen the tussle in the alley for what it was, two scared kids coming together in the shadow of yesterday.

Now he is parked outside the Mill too scared to go in.

Ma says he's wasted his money. So far he hasn't wasted anything but time. The realtor is bashing his ear twenty-four hours a day but as yet no deed signed. It's not the money! He could buy this place five times over. It is the Mill and the nightmares he remembers!

This was never a childhood hunting ground. A moth to light he preferred down town to the boondocks. Bayonet Woods was Gabe Templar's territory. Yet in dreams Bobby stood in this exact spot staring at hooded windows and afraid to go in. Now he's here and the sun is shining and birds are singing and all he wants to do is to run.

'Good afternoon, Captain Rourke,' the realtor gets out of a car. 'I'm glad you could make it.'

Bobby allows him a grin. 'I bet you are. There ain't too many keen on buyin' this heap I imagine.'

'Probably not in the current market yet things are changing.' He's straight into his spiel. 'With the war in Europe coming to an end and a solution due anytime in the Pacific Theatre properties like this will be seen as investment.'

'You think so?'

'I do. Such houses bestride history and with so many fine old buildings in Europe reduced to ash, I'm hoping America will want to hang onto her heritage, and that this and that other fine house along the way will be seen as memories of a more elegant time. Have you looked at the Eyrie Captain?'

'Not yet.'

'Of the two you might find it less of a strain. Though still in need of work the Eyrie is structurally sound. No tower, you see, and no sails to worry about. It also has very fine gardens.'

'This has a garden. Roses are the one thing I remember about it.'

'Roses?'

'Yeah, a real heady scent.'

The Realtor frowned. He couldn't see any roses. He couldn't see a garden, merely stale ground and rusty machine parts. As for scent, the only thing he smells is a possible sale and goodbye to a White Elephant that's been on the books since the Flood.

'Indeed, there is a deal of land. As you can see it stretches beyond the meadow and into the woods. I'm sure

if you've a mind to grow flowers then this is the place. Do
you grow roses, Captain?'

Bobby adjusted his dark glasses. 'Not yet.'

'No, I imagine you've been too busy winning a war. '
The realtor shuffled his feet. 'I have a key to the Eyrie.
While you're here you might like to take a look. I
understand it to be a copy of an English mansion and that
much of the original building was shipped across the
Atlantic in the early 1800s.'

'Is that a fact?'

'It is. Such history! I say to people by all means build
apartment blocks but let us also try to hold onto our
heritage.'

~

Bobby took both sets of keys but wouldn't stay. 'I have an
appointment the other end of town. If I've time later I'll
take a look.' He does have an appointment with a dress
shop in town but not until later. The realtor got on his
nerves. Going on about the past like that Bobby wanted to
yell, 'look at my face, idiot! Don't talk to me of holdin'
onto history when history is all I got. '

Surgeons have set a time limit on Bobby's ass. They said
they could save his right eye but injury to the optic nerve
meant he will one day be blind. When asked how long they
shrug their shoulders. 'We don't know when only that it
will happen. You're not helped by damage to the bowel
and bladder. Repeated infection will put a strain on your
kidneys. It's a tough call, Captain.'

The spill did real damage. A double whammy he got barbed wire in his eye and with an iron spike in his gut his bladder and lower bowel are compromised which means he's not always able to piss to order.

Further surgery in Virginia brought some relief but he has the occasional accident. The first time it happened he was home in bed. Early morning he crept down to the laundry to get rid of evidence. Ma saw him. 'What are you doin' messin' the bed at your age! Use the privy like everyone else!'

Some mother! She never lifted a finger. It was help he needed not a cussing out. Last month he had another stretch in Johns Hopkins. Things are a little better but he does get caught short like the other night at the ball-game.

Dark glasses and a cap on his head he got as far as the ticket office when it happened, a pain ripping through his gut and piss trickling down his leg.

It's as well he sticks with RAF blues, had his pants been a lighter colour he'd have died of shame.

Maybe dying is the answer! For sure hiding in his room during the day and trolling the dockyard at night is no way to live. If he wasn't so scared of meeting Alex he would shoot himself.

As with most towns bad news travels. Bobby's tragedy was known before he came home. People don't mean to be unkind, they can't help staring. Ruby is Ruby and can't be any other way. The woman in the dress shop understood his pain. He phoned to say his girl was coming from England and he wanted to see if there was anything she might like but couldn't get to the shop til late.

'No problem,' says she. 'I usually close-up around five but if you drop by at six, Captain, I'll be here.'

The Captain is a sympathy title over from England. He could care less about titles pride and glory replaced by a mole scurrying through the dark.

He will go to the shop but around seven when it's quiet. The owner will be there. There's not that much dough about that she can afford to be impatient.

Shop-to-shop women talk. Word has got around that a young English woman and her baby daughter are coming to stay, and that the young woman's fiancé, Captain Robert E Rourke is anticipating their arrival.

Last week he was in Richmond looking at furs. One coat in particular, a full length black Russian sable took his fancy. 'I reckon my girl would look good in this,' he says. 'She's blonde, you know, that white blonde that comes from nature rather than store-bought.'

'My word yes!' The sales-woman was aquiver.

'And she has green eyes as opposed to our babe, Sophie, who has my dark hair but her maternal grand pappy's blue eyes. Say?' Bobby fingered the fur. 'I don't suppose you could get a fur jacket to go with this? Maybe a cute little thing with a hood for a comin' up three-year-old?'

By the time he left she was oohing and aahing at his tale.

People are willing to put themselves out especially if the carrot on the end of the line is sable. He won't buy there. The coat was okay but there's better at Bergdorf's New York where he was told they would be pleased to embroider the name *Adelia Rourke* in the lining.

~

Bobby walked out of Belle Couture and into General Hunter.

'Belay there, young feller!' The General stuck out his arm. 'Can this be you, Lieutenant Rourke, coming out of a fancy lady's boudoir shop with a heap of boxes in your arms?'

'It is, sir.' Bobby did his best to smile.

'Why is that? You're not thinking of swapping tickets? Only it's a little late in the game if you are, you already proved yourself a man.'

Jesus, could that be admiration! That's a first.

'I'm hangin' in, sir,' he replied in kind. 'It's my girl. She's comin' from the old country and them with nothin I thought she might take a look at these.'

'Well, that's decent of you. I'm sure the little lady will be thrilled.'

'I hope so. I was in there long enough.'

'Female doodads?' The General held up his hands in surrender. 'I keep away. My wife and daughter have long since given up asking my opinion on anything, which is as well, them never liking what I like anyway.'

'I'll probably find the same when Dee gets here.'

'No doubt.'

The General rocked up and down on his heels. A question was coming. Bobby saw it lining up in the craggy face. William Hunter must be in his fifties. He doesn't look it. A handsome man, straight and true, he is respected throughout Virginia. His word carries weight. If you are okay with WG Hunter, you're okay with any man. Today it seems Bobby is okay.

'I was sorry to hear of your injuries, Lieutenant (no Captain for this man. He knows what's what). A man with your record deserves a better ending to his career. Are you getting the help you need?'

'No complaints, sir.'

'Good.' The General stared out over the town, the same extraordinary blue eyes but saddened and fading. 'I guess you heard Alex is MIA.'

'I did and I can't tell you how sorry I am.'

'It's hard. His mother and sister worry something awful. We had hoped to hear something now the European push is slackening but so far not a word. '

'I understand the post is pretty tricky in those parts. I'm still gettin' British mail from as far back as '42 (which was true, letters from girls he'd loved and left along the way. Shame! They wouldn't give him a second glance now.)

'So I believe. You two kids were close. I guess you miss my boy.'

'I do. Him and me go way back.'

'So you do. Well, that's war, nothing we can do but bite the bullet. Good to hear your intended is coming. When a man's back is to the wall he needs to know he can depend on his family.'

'Yes, sir.'

The General was making his way through the crowd when he paused. 'It might've been easier if Alex had married. A wife and baby to fuss over his mother would've drawn comfort. But I mustn't jump the gun. Missing isn't the same as dead. While there's life there is hope.'

Bobby waited til the General was out of sight and then ran to the car flinging the boxes in the back. It is God again making Himself known, every word out of the old guy's mouth a stab to the heart.

~

The meeting took the pleasure out of shopping. The boxes sat in the trunk of the car heavy as the weight on his heart. Pretty clothes too, nothing sensational, that'll be Bergdorf's when he takes a look. The blue silk dress was cute, a tulle train like a mermaid's tail and a velvet jacket made to be worn over the top with the collar framing the face, Dee will look sensational in that.

'I take it the young lady is of slender build,' the boutique owner rattled the rails.

'All the women in Britain are slender,' says Bobby. 'They don't need diet books. Dodgin' bombs keeps them busy.'

Folks back here don't see much of the war. They have ration books and shortages and their men are fighting and dying but as to the rest, buildings collapsing and dead babies being dug out, they haven't a clue.

No one talks about the war only about the end of it and a rumoured A-bomb to be dropped on Japan. The war in Europe is done news trickling back how 8th Bomber Command crucified Dresden in Germany, 700 plus Lancaster bombers with massive flight cover dropped thousands of tons of explosives on the city causing a whirlwind fire that could be seen from Mars.

Thinking of the life consumed in that fire, the people and the animals, Bobby wouldn't care if he never saw another Lancaster. He wants to fly but not one of them.

One look and he sees Muggy Danes and co-pilot falling through the sky.

Lately, determined to keep alive to the sky, he's been looking to buy planes with the idea of making mails runs et cet. Not necessarily for him to fly, more for USAAF buddies that can't find work. It's early days yet but he's looking.

It's no good planning too far ahead. He's yet to know how his body is going to work out. He's taken the Beagle out of the hangar two or three times. It wasn't easy. Most of the time he was close to panic, eventually a sense of balance took over, a third Baby Rourke appearing with a light finger on the button. Soon he was flying by gut feeling the Beagle a second skin. It's likely he's always flown that way but never until now appreciated the gift of sight.

~

Time on his hands and not wanting to be alone he drove to Mill and parking up took a flashlight. The moon bright enough to see his way he's thinking of taking a look at the other house. He's heard of the Eyrie through Sue Ryland. She would go there looking for Gabe Templar. Back then the guy haunted the place. If you wanted to find him all you need do was whistle and he'd come crawling out of the Eyrie woodwork.

Sue said it was his home in a life before, and that one day as he had lived there so he would die there.

Gobbledegook! A sexy sorceress believing in omens, she reckons owls are feathered angels carrying the souls of the dead to heaven. If she saw one in the churchyard, and there used to be one nesting in St Jude's spire, she'd leave off fucking and nothing he did would bring her round.

'No,' she'd say. 'It ain't decent while a soul is in transit.'

Hah! Soul in transit! Beautiful to look at and luscious as a juicy plum before it falls off the tree she loved to tease. She'd tease Bobby fooling around with other kids trying to make him jealous. He didn't care anymore than she.

Her main target was Gabe. Along with the rest she'd mock calling him stupid while secretly crazy for him. The day he went to jail she wept. It's why she married Herb Willet, with Gabe gone nothing mattered.

Her and Bobby's rumble in the alley is all about that. The triangle of her, Gabe and Bobby is what she saw. If she was to fuck Bobby, as ugly as he is, she is fucking Gabe.

Sad is a love like that. He sees it sad where before he never would. It takes pain to know pain. Dee is his first and last love, he knew that the moment he saw her. He still feels the same, the need to get her to Virginia as real as ever.

He dropped in the realtors earlier and paid cash for the Mill. The realtor stared. 'All this money! Are you sure you don't want to reconsider?' The die cast Bobby carried on out the door. Dreams and all he owned invested in that goddamn place he wasn't about to reconsider anything.

~

Key in his pocket, he's through the woods and outside the Eyrie. One look and he knew he'd bought the wrong house.

As the realtor said it is an elegant house and in better condition. It does have some problems yet above and beyond all of that it shines!

I know this house, was he first thought. I really do and not because I've seen houses like it in Sussex, the old Tudor black and white mansions with gables over the windows and leaded glass and mullions. I really know it!

A light in his head and he could tell the lay-out, how the staircase splits on the ground floor and scoops out left and right in twin arches. He could tell of the Orangery and of the secret passage back of the panelling that is a copy of the original English house, how it shields a Priest's hole and if you keep going between the walls you come out at the back kitchen and a circular iron staircase that leads up to the attics.

'I do know it! I do!'

He started to run and was brought up short by wondrous perfume.

A thick carpet of blossom clambered over the front facing wall. The flowers hung in pendulous bells and like weighty lanterns in the moonlight gave off a light and a scent richer than any rose.

The need to own this house with its drapery of flowers overwhelmed.

It didn't matter that he's bought and paid for the Mill. No! Why have that when he can have this?

He got to the front door but couldn't get the key to work in the lock. He fiddled but it wouldn't turn. Fuck it! The realtor must've brought the wrong key! The ticket attached says The Eyrie but it doesn't work.

Nothing would keep him out! He squeezed down the side of the house and smashing a window climbed into the Orangery and crunching through broken glass found his way into the main house.

It is a mess and will need work but look at the hand-painted ceiling! And the moulded architrave and the panelled walls! Back in the 1800s this was where people gathered for a summer ball, the musicians playing in the gallery and candlelight from heavy double chandeliers giving light to ladies in their gorgeous gowns.

Excited, heart beating, Bobby made his way up the stairs.

Treads busted through and balustrade rickety it was tricky.

Up and up, his hands thick with dust he kept going to the top floor and the attics where servants would sleep. A door far end of the landing was closed stray moonlight under the door making it seem a lamp glowed within.

Bobby wanted to get in that room. He didn't know why but he needed to get in that room before any other. He tugged on the handle but the door wouldn't open. He put his shoulder to it but stuck over years it would not budge.

Panting, he tried again until, skin prickling he seemed to know he could stand here forever pulling but something on the other side wanted it shut.

Then, God help him Alex Hunter was trying the door with him!

Bobby knew the hand alongside his! He saw the class ring on the finger and felt breath ruffle his hair. It was Ash, his old buddy, no doubt about it.

Shocked, he lurched back and the spell broken. He was alone on the upper landing, Alex's ghost, if that's what it was melting in moonlight.

He stood trying to get his breath back. Then ping! The door opened, swinging open easily and quietly as though on waxed runners.

Beyond an oil-lamp on a table and an overturned chair the room was empty.

He didn't go in. Bobby made his way down the stairs and kept going until he was well away from the house. He didn't look back but kept on pushing through Bayonet Woods the feeling of knowing the Eyrie fading.

The moon was high and the air thick with the scent of the wisteria. He could've tried unlocking the door. He could have taken an axe and chopped his way through but what's the point? Baby Rourke knows when he's not wanted.

Twenty-eight
Packing
The Duke of Wellington Pub
Needham.
May 8th 1945

'Delia!'

'Yes!'

'Any more flags down there?' The landlady called down to the cellar. 'I'm sure I put a box down there.'

'Yes, still some here,' Adelia pulled a tangled heap of red, white and blue bunting from under a dressmaker's mannequin. 'They're a bit tatty!'

'Doesn't matter! Bring them up will you, will you, and another crate of Watneys if you can manage it. They're going mad up here.'

People are going mad. There is singing and dancing in Needham High Street, villagers wild with joy and entitled to be so. It's over. The war that dragged on for four long years is finally over. No more rumours. Mr Churchill has declared it so, Germany has surrendered.

'At long last!' Adelia hauled a crate of beer up the stairs. 'Now maybe we can all get on with our lives.'

'Here! Let me give you a hand with that.' Fred, the publican's son grabbed the crate. 'You're too beautiful to be doing stuff like that.'

'It's okay. I can manage.'

He grinned. 'Never mind manage. Lugging beer about is my job or will be the minute I'm out of this uniform.'

'Don't give up the navy, Fred!' Blanche, the regular barmaid leaned in the back door. 'You look ever so handsome in your blues. But then all men look handsome in uniform.'

Fred waggled his eyebrows. 'But not so handsome out?'

She giggled. 'I wouldn't know. In your case I never got to see.'

'Maybe there's nothing to see.'

'Maybe, but a woman likes to make up my own mind about such things, doesn't she, Delia?'

'What?' Adelia was under the counter stacking bottles.

'I said we never got to see Freddy in the nude. '

'No, I suppose we didn't. Is that it with the Watneys, Annie?'

'That's fine. Fred can always bring more if needed.'

Blanche fluffed her hair. 'I reckon the place will be full of Yanks tonight. They love a good knees-up. Maybe I'll try one of them. See what he looks like in the buff. What do you reckon, Delia, in or out of uniform?'

'I don't know. I never thought to ask.'

'What, you don't already know. Strange, I thought you might.'

'Hey, Blanche,' Fred cut in, 'don't drag Delia into your nonsense. If you're that curious to know you can always sneak a look. I'm in bed by eleven.'

'By eleven?' Blanche patted his head. 'What a good little boy you are.'

'I don't know about good. These days I can sleep anywhere anytime, though looking at that lot out there.' he gestured to the crowd. 'It'll more likely be eleven in the morning before we get to our beds.'

'Eleven in the morning? Ooh! Can I still catch a look?'

'You can catch whatever you like, Blanche. It's a free world.'

'I'll take you up on that but hang on to the bellbottoms! You never know when you might need them.'

'No not me! I've done my bit. I'll not be doing anymore.'

'You don't mean that, do you, Fred?' said Adelia. 'I'm sure if we were in trouble you'd be there same as everyone else.'

'Like hell I would!' Fred was bitter. 'Excuse me, Delia, but all this tub-thumping gets on my wick. It was a sod of a war and for many still is. We paid a price and will keep paying and don't let anyone tell you different. Anyway, come on.' He grabbed the bunting. 'Let's pretend to be happy if nothing else.'

'Can you give me a moment? I need to check on Sophie.'

'Oh yes, do check,' drawled Blanche. 'Stuck out there in the back hour-after-hour, it can't be good for the poor little mite.'

Adelia paused mid-flight. 'What do you mean not good for her?'

'The stink of booze and all the noise! It's not natural for a two-year old. A kid should be out with other kids not cooped up.'

Fred looked at Blanche. 'You mean like yours?'

'Nothing wrong with my kids, Fred Carter! Kitty is fourteen and Bella coming up thirteen so they're old enough to look after themselves. Sophie's a toddler and shouldn't be left. '

'I don't leave her,' said Adelia.

'You left her the other night.'

'When?'

'Saturday and that wedding party when the punters wouldn't go home.'

'I didn't leave her. She was here asleep in Annie's bed.'

'And you think sleeping in a strange bed is alright?'

'I don't see Annie's bed as strange.'

'Maybe not but someone else might.'

'Who?'

Blanche shrugged. 'I don't know, the Town Hall maybe, public welfare or whatever they call it nowadays.'

'You think the Town Hall worries about where my daughter sleeps.'

'Maybe not worries but interested.'

'And why would you think that?'

'I've heard talk.'

'Oh talk!' Adelia smiled. 'There's always talk and not always about me.'

'Meaning?'

'Meaning exactly what I said.'

'If you must know there's always talk of you and the Yanks, that feller Bobby doing a runner and the other one, the big feller, leaving you stuck.'

'Goodness me.' Adelia untied her apron. 'I have been busy and according to you unlucky in my choice of men but I don't see what any of that has to do with Sophie sleeping in Annie's bed.'

'No, nor me.' Annie poked her head round the door. 'Leave the kid alone, Blanche Hobley. She's fine where she is. And what are you doing hanging about here? If you're not working then you're on the wrong side of the bar. So buzz off and leave others to get on with the job. And get that bunting up, Fred! We'll have to let them in soon or they'll be breaking down the door!'

Annie's word being law they went their different ways, Fred to get a ladder, Blanche to rattle someone else's nerves and Adelia to see if Sophie is alright.

And of course she is alright! A contented child, it takes very little to make her happy and a walled off area of garden with ducks and geese and other pets couldn't be better.

A nice man, salt of the earth Sam Carter walks the garden when the lunchtime trade is done petting a rabbit that tomorrow will be in the pot.

'This is Flo,' he'll take Sophie from cage-to-cage. 'And this is Sparky. He's getting on now and a bit cranky. I doubt he'll see another summer.'

Indeed, served up as stew that evening Sparky didn't get to see another day.

Adelia doesn't know how he does it, to pet and then to kill would seem to her like betrayal. But she's glad of the

Carters. Honest people, she can come to work knowing Sophie is safe. People are quick to judge pub life without seeing the full picture. Blanche wants her job back as she wants Fred, the publican's son, just home from the navy and so all comments aimed at another woman are her shaking the tree. It's alright, Adelia's not afraid of the Blanche's of this world nor is she interested in Fred Carter, life is complicated enough without adding to it. At least with Blanche her antagonism is out in the open. It's the undercover stuff, the whisperers and poison-pen scribblers that rankle.

One such a person jumped out the cupboard after a visit to the Gas Works.

One sack of coke per family twice a week is the allowance. Most people stick with a sack others are greedy shovelling directly into an old pram. A man came Thursday with a tin bath on wheels and dug as if burrowing to Australia.

A quarrel broke out that led to fisticuffs, a woman behind Adelia boxing the man's ears. In the melee the pushchair was upended and Sophie with it.

It was nothing, more aggravated humour than violence. Sophie shed a few tears but was shocked rather than hurt. There were repercussions; Adelia pounced on outside the flat by the woman from the Morality League.

Tweed skirt, feet planted wide apart and gold *pince nez* on her nose, she presented herself as 'Dorothea Lowell-Peach, JP.'

She said she was here on Sophie's behalf, the child thought to be in danger.

Adelia asked what danger and from whom. The woman replied, from you, her mother, and then went on to refer to a note-book quoting dates and times of incidents, Thursday's upset at Gas Company including, accusing Adelia of *'failing in her maternal duties.'*

Thinking the woman mad, and already late for work Adelia pushed by whereupon Miss Lowell-Peach went from eccentric to aggressive backing her quarry against the Bakery window, talking of a breakdown of morals and of the current rise of illegitimate children due to the influx of foreign servicemen, and that if decent people didn't put a stop to it these unfortunate children, and the country itself, would be at the mercy of all manner of filthy diseases.

Adelia should've have turned back up the stairs ignoring the nonsense, but a mistake at the best of times chose to defend herself.

It was a foolish idea because in arguing in the street she forgot mob rule. Her aggressor had a high-pitched voice. Reminiscent of a bat squeaking it drew a crowd who were not averse to offering an opinion.

It became very quickly very noisy, and Adelia realising no one was on her side saw that Bobby was right, pitchforks were being waved but at the frustrations and vicissitudes of war and the ups-and-downs of her life collateral damage.

Opinions grew warmer and voices louder until she trembled imagining the debate removed a century and she in a ducking-stool with head shaved.

It was a reference to *'the Mental Health Act of 1930'* that turned curiosity into a distrustful mob, the average Englishman ever averse to mention of mental issues bombarded with uncomfortable facts, how in August '42

'Miss Challoner was confined to hospital under guard, the doctor's recommendation that she be placed in a locked ward in a nearby psychiatric hospital.'

Adelia couldn't believe what she was hearing. Such a betrayal of trust!

The crowd were told that while in hospital the patient escaped her protectors, wandering the streets at night putting her unborn child at risk and that she wouldn't return unless forced to by a member of the local constabulary.

Not only that, when released from medical care she was offered a home above the Bakery and visited by members of the Morality League, whose only desire was to help, but who along with nursing staff at St Faiths were accused of persecution, Miss Challoner seeing herself a victim of ill-will, more sinned against than sinning, 'as do all such loose women when brought to book.'

Adelia knew her then. This is she, the poison-pen, or her alter-ego.

But what a shock! This spitting venom and evangelistic fury was not what she'd imagined at the end of the pen. The attack seemed almost personal!

The nonsense continued for a good thirty minutes. And it was nonsense! Seen afterward from the safety of the flat it was a ridiculous affair, people goggling and a woman wagging her finger. Ridiculous, yes, but so much known of the Challoner's doings, her starting and leaving to times at the Duke of Wellington, whether she brought Sophie and whether they stayed overnight at the pub, or as in latter months were accompanied home by the publican's son 'to the flat above this Bakery that we understand is supported by an American serviceman, yet another male caught in her web.'

There was reference to black-outs and dates and times of visits to her doctor and psychiatrist. There were notes on her trips to St Giles and 'to that notorious blot on the landscape the Good Lord thought fit to remove in the summer of '42, the Black Swan, for assignation with a wild-looking individual, unshaven and filthy, who oughtn't to be anywhere near a child.'

There was a whisper then of 'shame!' Only one woman hissing but it was enough to get Adelia indoors and the mob to disperse.

It was so upsetting. Adelia couldn't stop shaking and lost a day at work with such a migraine she couldn't see. The following day she tried explaining to the boss but Annie Carter didn't want to know, a well-run pub her criteria.

Neither did the affray help the Challoner's relationship with Edna James who apparently unwilling to take sides hid at the back of the shop throughout and who later followed Adelia up to the flat defending her position.

'All that shouting, I thought I'd best keep out the way. I mean, you didn't need me coming to your aid you were doing alright on your own.

Adelia listened but offered no comment knowing as did Edna that a true friend would have stepped between her and the mob.

'People can get every tricky and we couldn't afford to take sides,' Edna continued. 'They are our livelihood. We depend on them, don't we, Ted?'

Embarrassed, Ted looked away. A quiet sort of man he hated upset.

Adelia understood that but what a revelation! It brought home advice from a ghost; '*Look to yourself and your daughter, Missy. In the end there is only yo*u.'

The confrontation brought a new sense of unease and Edna James viewed with a wary eye. Adelia knew she ought to challenge the leaking of patient information. She ought to go to Andrew Covington and cause a stink demanding to know how a stranger can be in possession of private and confidential information. But to what end! This is the work of Matron at St Faiths and as a battle isn't worth fighting. Better save her energy and add another personal treasure to the box when packing for America.

Packing for America is Sophie's idea. One evening Adelia found her putting toys into a cardboard box, the blue teddy and the sheep from the toy farm, precious toys she would not be without.

When asked what she was doing she said she was getting them ready for the boat. When asked what boat, she fetched out the cloth alphabet book and pointed to the letter B. 'B is for boat,' she said.

'Yes, it is. Well done,' said Adelia.

Sophie turned back to the beginning of the book and a picture of a shiny red apple.' A is for America.'

This is Bobby. He gave Sophie the book. 'It was a free gift with the buggy,' he said, 'and so they ought to give somethin' the dough that cost.'

The buggy went into the canal, the book stayed. Bobby would sit with her on the floor pointing to various pictures and offering a running commentary.

'A is for America where I wish the hell I was. B is for the Burlington Buggy your Ma didn't want. C is for clown, otherwise known as Bobby Rourke, and D is for Damned if he can do anythin' to please her.'

In the end Adelia hid it. After Bobby was transferred Nora dug it out and would sit patiently going through the letters. Most children forget their early teaching, not Sophie, her ability to retain information has her mother walking on eggshells. This is one child you cannot fool. White or red don't tell fibs or promise a treat you don't intend to give, she will remember.

'He must've had a good memory,' this from Edna recently.

'Who must have?' Adelia was sweeping the stairs.

'Sophie's father. Earlier she was helping at the til putting coppers into bags. I told her how many per bag. She did it and not a ha'penny over or under.'

Adelia used to wonder about the man, was he kind and was he clever. Did he have a wonderful smile? Did he love her and if not why the ring?

Then realising wondering didn't help she closed her mind erecting a steel door between her and the past. As a result while she hardly thinks of him during the day she dreams of a blue-eyed man every night.

Most dreams are of being kissed and held in his arms. She wakes happy. Others are in the midst of battle where she watches men die.

After being heckled on the doorstep she dreamt that night she was digging a body out of a snowdrift and this in May the sun clear in the sky!

The psychiatrist at St Faiths reckoned dreams are a reflection of our innermost desires where we indulge in night theatre acting out our joys and sorrows. Of loving dreams, yes, she can see that, everyone wants to be loved. But digging a body out of snow? If that is a reflection of an innermost desire then Miss Lowell-Peach was right to call her mentally defective.

Mentally defective, horrible words!

It was her parting shot. 'I understand you were hurt in a bomb blast in '42 and that it has left you mentally defective,' she bawled up the stairs. 'That may be the clinical opinion for your case but it's not one I support. From what I've seen and heard of you, Miss Challoner, you are another example of the malady affecting the whole of Great Britain, namely a lack of moral fibre.'

~

Scary woman, jaws snapping and prominent eyes peering through a gold wire pince nez, you wouldn't want to be up before her at the Bench. She'd have you in irons and on the way to a Penal Colony before you could say Captain Cook.

It's not funny. People gaping and a finger wagging under her nose! Though she tries making light of such events tonight after another desperate headache she will add an item to Sophie's box.

'Bring whatever you want,' writes Bobby. 'As much or as little. You don't have to bring anything. I can get everything you need here in Virginia.'

She hasn't said they'll go. In fact this whole idea of packing feels more a game of truth and dare than reality.

Dare she go if she doesn't love him? Dare she bring Sophie to a strange country and a man known to be unpredictable? Ought she be truthful and say she this is for Sophie? But then he knows that.

'I know this is more about Sophie than it is about you and me,' he wrote,' but given time it can become about you and me.'

Every day she gets a letter, sometimes two or three. Yesterday there was a brief person-to-person call to the Bakery, not a lot was said, Edna James longer on the line than Adelia.

It's all so hit-and-miss. She'd be more inclined to go if she heard from his mother. It's all she needs, just a line saying how much Mrs Rourke was looking forward to meeting them. The idea of a loving Nana waiting for Sophie with open arms would be more than enough to make the bridge, as would a picture of the house he raves about, ' I bought a house and you're gonna love it. It's old and elegant and has masses of land where a kiddie can play.'

The house is under refurbishment, he says, the carpenters in.

She misses his smile and long, lean frame decorating the doorway. She longs to feel his arms about her but still doubts nag, his letters and entreaties to come to America are a Giant Hand pushing and Adelia with her heels dug in and never really knowing why.

It's likely she's looking a gift-horse in the mouth but there it is, a pointer on a set of weighing scales perpetually fluttering between Stay and Go.

The battle over a sack of coke and Miss Lowell-Peach's wagging finger came close to pushing the pointer to Go.

Then today the message came over the wireless and joy-of-joys the Prime Minister, Winston Churchill, putting rumours to bed; '*My dear friends, this is your hour, a victory for the great British Nation, Germany has surrendered.*'

Once again the scales tip toward Stay. The sun is shining over the sea and battered and beloved Suffolk rises up out of long, dark night. America shrunk to a dot on the map then Adelia is in love with England again.

Twenty-nine
Under Review
US Marine Base,
Quantico, Virginia,
June 1945

'Fill her up, will you?' Gabriel wound down the window

'Yes, sir.'

'And maybe clean the windshield?'

'Sure thing! It is kinda dusty out today.' The old guy on the pump leaned into the windshield. 'I guess they did it then, Sergeant.'

'Say what?'

'Them German's surrendered?'

'Seems that way.'

'Do you reckon that'll be Japan done next?'

'Maybe.'

'I hear they plan to drop a big old bomb on Hirohito's head. You know, one of nuculer bombs. Jumpin' Jehoshaphat!' The guy rolled his eyes. 'Imagine the mess that'll make and the people and houses smashed to pulp. I don't think they'll do it. There are rumours but...! Do you think they'll do that, Sergeant?'

'I wouldn't like to say.'

The old guy talking enough for both Gabriel gazed over the Creek. It's a beautiful day, fresh and clean, a good day for taking out the trash. With only a couple of days left and chores waiting back home he needs to get moving. First stop getting the Funeral Parlour ready to go on sale. The realtor says no rush. 'Not much call for the horse and buggy nowadays. It's limousines and fancy electronic gismos, but I guess the old way still appeals to empty pockets.'

Gabriel left it with him, as the man said no rush. From the Parlour it's the Mission for cookies for Ma and then back to oil the privy door so it locks easier.

There's nothing wrong with the door. It's Ma trying to hold him still.

Yesterday he was told his service within an active war-zone entitles him to at least one home tour at Quantico. While he didn't turn it down he wasn't in a rush to say yes. Ma wants them to spend time together but the thought of another day among ugly memories is enough never mind six months!

'So where are you coming from, Sergeant, if I might ask?' The gas-jockey swapped the pump for wash-leather. 'You guys in and out from all four corners the Base is busting at the seams.'

'Iwo Jima was my latest tour.'

'Yeah, I know that place. That's where our boys raised Old Glory top of a mountain. I saw a picture. It was in all the papers. Anyways,' he grinned. 'Us with a nuculer bomb them slant-eyed bastards won't be hanging any of their own flags.' He flicked the wash-leather. 'You on R&R now, Sergeant?'

'Waitin' orders.'

'I thought so. Nuculer bomb or not Marines are always ready for something.'

Gabriel paid the pump and left.

The bomb is topic of conversation everywhere. He doesn't care to talk about it. As the old guy said the Corps first boots on the ground it don't matter who's fighting who, there's always one war following another.

Sun bright in his eyes he flipped the visor and got onto the highway. Back-pay mounting, he bought the truck so Ma has use of it. He's given some time to the house, realigning shingles and so forth, and figures next furlough he'll build on a shower room. If he'd put his back to it he might've done more this time but everything confining he couldn't stay in one place for long.

The town never felt so small. It was always an open place with avenues and fine-looking houses not a choking mass of people and buildings huddled together. Here among familiar faces he finds it hard to breathe. Even in Bayonet Woods, a place he used to love trees and bushes crowd in.

Gabriel can't stand being crowded. He needs space and silence. He used to like the sun, could stare at the heart without troubling his eyes. Now any light is too bright. Same with noise, 'hush up world!' he thinks, 'you're too loud.'

Even with Ma he finds chat and physical contact awkward. She stares trying to work him out. 'Still the quiet one,' she says. 'I thought bein' with others might bring you out but no. You were closed-off as a boy and now you're closed off as a man.'

Poor Ma! She's looking old, still upright with plenty hair but lines in her face now where there was none.

'I know.' Guessing his thought she nods. 'Waitin' on a call sayin' your son is killed ages a woman.' She sighs. 'Aunt Belle's boys gone I was thinkin' if you are set on stayin' in the Marines I'll go to Baltimore, two widows together.'

He says she must do what's best for her. She can have the money when the Parlour sells but he has had no real thought of giving up the Corps.

'You should get out,' she says. 'Twice wounded you're pushin' your luck. And it doesn't have to be the Parlour. I don't care about the money. That job at Shenandoah Park is still open to you, the Sergeant said so.'

Gabriel says he'll think about it, he will think but not too long. Town loon and jail-bird he always was a curiosity. Now folks don't only stare they come right up asking questions, how was it in the Pen? How is it in the Marines? Did you kill many Japs? Will you be there when they drop the bomb?

And they want to touch! They pat his arm commenting on his stripes like they want to make sure the stripes, and he, are real.

'Yes, a fine looking man you turned out to be!' the Baptist Minister yesterday outside the Courthouse. 'I always knew you'd go far.' He turns to his wife almost pleading. 'Didn't I say that? Even in the midst of his troubles didn't I say that boy will go far?' The Minister's wife nods her eyes sad.

It ain't true. It's a bubble, the Minister puffing as he puffs his life. It doesn't stop there. People Gabriel's never laid eyes on smile saying how smart he is in uniform, a regular dandy, and how they too always believed he would go far.

That he doesn't laugh in their faces is a miracle. The town owes him nothing. A loner, inward looking, he was never part of town life. He's still alone only now instead of looking in he looks out observing life from afar.

Ma says he's lost his kindness, the same on the outside but inside all glued up. 'You weren't the brightest but you was always the kindest even to your Pa. I don't see that kindness now.'

'The war, Ma,' he says. 'It changes people.'

'You are changed but it ain't jest the war. It's you. You've lost your way.'

Gabriel shrugs. State Pen and two holes in his back what does she expect? A boy left home in '34. That boy ain't never coming back, not even for Ma.

'The war will soon be over.' She keeps at it.

'Well or not I'm still a Marine.'

'Maybe, but that don't mean you need sleep at the Base.'

'I'm waitin' on orders.'

'I don't care! You're home and should stay home.'

Gabriel's sleeping habits are nothing to do with orders. Quantico doesn't want spare parts kicking about. Under siege, they want those Marines here making room for those in-coming. It's the house. How can he sleep under that roof and Pa everywhere he looks? He can't do it! So, for the first time in his life he lied to Ma saying he was at the Base when he was at the Eyrie.

She ain't fooled. She knows where he is. Like Daisy, the old dog waddling along on his heels she knows it is his sanctuary.

Five nights, the dog alongside, he's bunked down in the one place he can feel free, though if he was waiting on a welcome home party he is wasting his time. So far he's had nothing, not even a mouse come out to say howdy-do.

Everything is upside down. He gets a welcome home from the 'burg but from this, his heart-home, he gets closed doors.

That first night the Eyrie wouldn't let him in. All former routes were closed off, front door jammed, side door choked with weeds and the alley to the back kitchens blocked by fallen masonry.

There was only the Orangery.

He smashed a window.

Oh! The sound of breaking glass! It might have been his heart.

It was cold inside, not a trace of wisteria in the air, only the must and dust of dead leaves.

Upstairs the attic forbad him. An hour he stood beseeching entry. The lamp was lit inside and then again it might have been moonlight under the door but it sure smelled of oil.

An hour! The message came through loud and clear. Go Home Sergeant Gabriel Templar, you don't belong here.

It hurt. He ran down to stand in the hall yelling up the curving staircase, 'why are you doin' this, old Eyrie? What did I ever do to you?'

No answer, not even an echo, and there's always an echo, a snowflake falling on a window-pane or a fly caught in a web the house always knew.

Shut out like that made him angry. Ungrateful! Years of faithful service he's given, years of shoring up rafters and blocking draughts, of mending leaks and tearing up weeds, not to mention keeping faith with yesteryear, him a go-between lighting the oil-lamp guiding lost souls home.

Seems none of that now matters. He has offended and must pay.

'Okay then, if that's how you want it,' he said that first night, moonlight flashing on his jacket buttons. 'I'll mend your window and clear the broken glass and everythin' else beside. I owe the Past that much. But I won't come again. You and your miserable secrets can go to Hell!'

~

Today is Mission day where ladies gather to sell their wares. Fruit and veg and home-grown produce, they sit with their baskets in the yard sharing gossip.

Ma in need of Mizz Matilda March's ginger-cookies he made his way through.

Ten minutes and he's loaded down, folks giving of their wares, apples from one basket and a posy from another. He thanked them and moved on to where Miss Abigail and Miss Emilee perch selling home-made cakes.

They already had a customer, Bobby Rourke's mother.

He should've turned away but the press behind blocked him.

In the past Ruby Rourke hadn't a good word for Gabriel or for that matter anyone. A cruel-mouthed woman she could cut a man down to size in two easy bites. Now she's here - his nemesis, as Charlie Whitefeather would say - eating sugar-doughnuts and the cherries on her hat bobbing in time with her jaws.

Sugar on her lips and poison in her heart, she turned. 'Well, will you look what the cat dragged in!'

He tipped his cap. 'Mizz Rourke.'

A stringy woman with a mean fist she barred the way. 'Don't you tip your cap at me Gabe Templar! I ain't fooled by your good looks. I remember you as you was, the Sheriff marchin' you away in chains. But dog to vomit you're back, your Pa cold bones in his grave and you, his murderer a struttin' peacock!'

'I'm jest passin' through, Mizz Rourke. Ain't no need for this.'

'There's every need as my eyes do bear witness to the folks hangin' on your shirttails!' She waved her arm. 'What's wrong with people of this town they want to glad-hand you? Are they so quick to furget murder and that you havin' tasted more killin' no man or woman is safe in this place?'

'Oh hush up, Ruby Cropper, and leave the boy alone,' said Miss Matilda. 'What is wrong with you, woman? You are never happy unless you're skinning some poor cat.'

'What do you mean leave him alone? I don't want to touch him. I wouldn't want to soil my hands.'

'No, you'd sooner soil your tongue, vicious critter that you are'.'

'That's right, Matilda March, pick up where you left off wipin' his ass!' Ruby sneered. 'You two was huggin' and kissin' him when he was in his cradle. You couldn't manage a child of your own so you borrowed some other.'

At that Miss Emilee, the quieter of the sisters snatched Gabriel's hand. 'Yes and look at the wonderful choice we made! We know who he is. Don't need you spinning your malicious tales. We've always known and I tell you this, my brother Lawrence would've been proud to know Sergeant Templar as we are proud. Go your ways and leave decent folk in peace. And give me that!' She snatched the sugar-bun. 'If you're not willing to pay don't handle our stuff.'

Gabriel smiled. How could he not? It wasn't that he found the situation amusing, these little pets defending his honour and them no bigger than his thumb. It was Ruby. In this ever changing world she is one remaining constant.

She saw him smile. 'He's laughin' at you, Emmie March! He's sees you and your sister suckin' up and he sees a pair of foolish old women. And so you are wastin' Christian charity on such as him 'cos despite the uniform and the shinin' hair he's nothin' but dross. The Lord knows dross when he sees it.'

Then she waves the bible she always carries around. 'It says so here in the Good Book, Proverbs 17:3. The crucible for silver and the furnace for gold but The Lord God tests the true heart. I tell you now, Emmie March, I see his heart and it is empty!'

Miss Emilee packed her basket. 'Go away, Ruby. You're making the gingerbread droop. Me and my sister follow our own way. We don't need instruction. And it's Miss Emilee March to you! Always was, always will be.'

Upset and trembling, the ladies began packing the cakes away.

'I'm mystified.' Ruby wasn't done. 'What kind of a world do we live in where a man like him comes home to flags wavin' and folks sayin' what a great feller he is, and my poor boy, a real hero, medal pinned to his chest by the King of England, comes home wounded and for shame no one comes near nor by. '

'We've seen your boy,' said Miss Matilda. 'We visited when he first came home. We offered help as did others. Then he moved out and no one knew where he went, not even you, Ruby, I imagine. So don't accuse us of wasted charity. Good Christian Charity is never wasted especially as he, poor fellow, was fending for himself you never there.'

'I had my duties to attend to. The Lord needed me in His church.'

'Phoee!' Miss Emilee took Gabriel's arm and Miss Matty the other. 'You're the one should be ashamed. Your duty is to your son. Charity begins with those we love and those we don't, which is why in good charity we're off home leaving you to stew in your own juice.'

~

Gabriel is in the barn looking at the Lime tree wondering why he hung onto it. What was he doing, thinking on Charlie Whitefeather and his love of marble sculpture? That man was forever comparing the dolls with Italian sculptors. He used to say, 'one day, my son, you will stand before

Michelangelo's David and other such a work of genius and will not be ashamed of your own.'

What a thing to say! He believed it and had Gabriel believing. It's a fact Charlie is persuasive. He could dream for the moon and have everyone else dreaming with him. But not this! Those Italians had magic in their hands. They could paint and read and write while Gabe with his thick fingers and wishes for brains can barely sign his name.

If this is what dreams have come down to a hunk of Lime and wooden toys, then he'd best drag them out root and twig and set fire to them.

So thinking he dragged a can of petrol from the pick-up.

Ma came into the barn. 'What you doin'?'

'Gettin' rid of the trash.'

'You think this is trash?'

'It ain't far short.'

'Oh son, how can you think that? You put too much work into them to throw them over. Besides, they're worth money if not to you then to me.' She picked up the fox. 'I could've sold this five times over. The feller as runs the antique store on the Avenue told me to name my price!'

'Next time he comes tell him he can have it.'

'Is that so?'

'It is. Go ahead. It's nothin' to me.'

Ma stared. 'And what about the other thing?'

'What other thing?'

'The doll in my room? Should I sell that?'

'Sure. I told you it's nothin' to me.'

She shook her head. 'You sure have changed.'

'How have I?'

'For a start you're lyin' as you never did before. You're lyin' about sleepin' at the Base as you're lyin' about this, sayin' it means nothin' when we both know it's means heaven and earth and always has.'

She marched away. A minute later, red faced and boiling, she's back with a bundle in her arms. 'I hung onto this as I hung onto the blanket you was wrapped in as a babe. Most things in life aren't meant to keep. Come-day, go-day, you can toss 'em away. Others are blood in your veins and meant to be cherished. But if you're thinkin' your work is trash then maybe you're seein' yourself as trash.'

'Now hold on!' Gabriel had had his fill of being told what to do. He didn't come through Guadalcanal to be yelled at by his mother or anyone else. 'Back off and leave me space! I gotta get on with my life which means makin' choices. Some of them choices won't sit easy with you but that's how it's got to be.'

He unscrewed the petrol cap. 'And the first choice I'm makin' is to clear my head of old business and that doll is old business.'

'And am I old business that you need lie to me?'

'I'm sorry about lyin' but I can't be in this house. You say I should hold on to precious things. What happened here took seven years of my life. I don't know that I'd call those years precious but whether or not they are gone and I won't get them back. I don't want to hurt you. I know I'm not the kid that left in '34. Time etched its mark on me as it did the Lime tree. I need to find out who I am because if I don't know pretty quick I'll go crazy. D'you understand?'

'I understand more than you think. I understand your comin' home ain't been easy as I understand you need to start over. I just don't want you doin' anythin' you'll regret and you will regret settin' fire to that Lime tree as you will surely regret sellin' that doll, 'cos it ain't a doll, is it, son?'

Gently, she peeled the blanket away, the face emerging, pure and lovely as the day it was carved. 'This was never a doll. This is someone you have loved since before you were born. Sellin' this would be to sell your soul.'

'Don't say that!' Gabriel held up his hand. 'I left that way of thinking on Pariss Island! I saw believin' in dreams was more dangerous than carryin' a rifle. Keep the doll and all that goes with it! I can't have that life again.'

'I ain't keepin' it!!' She thrust the doll into his arms. 'It's your burden not mine! You want to make choices start with this doll and that can of petrol, for misuse of one will surely kill the other. And don't be so certain you are right! Swap the stripes and polished boots for a little humility. The good book says pride goeth before destruction and haughtiness before a fall.'

Tears in her eyes, she kissed him. 'You've had falls enough, Gabe. You don't need any more. Now go wash up for dinner before spendin' another night with the spooks in your hidey-hole. And take the dog for company! You may be done with the past but I doubt the past is done with you.'

~

He was hanging his shirt on a hanger when another piece of the past wandered in lamplight shining on her silky hair.

'Hi, there, Gabe.'

'Hi Sue.' He wasn't surprised to see her. As with Daisy dogging his feet she's been two paces behind this whole week. Why she didn't make herself known he couldn't say. But that's Sue, always in charge of her own doings.

She knelt, ruffling Daisy's fur. 'You're lookin' good, Gabe.'

'You're lookin' good yourself.' She did look good. She was always a good-looking girl. Not pretty, her colouring too strong for that and wild. Now her eyes dark as damsons and mouth a bitten plum she is beautiful but with a dangerous beauty sharp and like to cut you.

'You seen Bobby Rourke yet?'

'Nu-huh.' She rarely called him Baby, she said it was a loathsome name given to a pet bulldog you aim to kick now and then.

'Do you plan on seein' him?'

'No.'

She shrugged. 'I guess not. You owe him nothin'.'

'I hear he's not doin' so good.'

'He ain't.'

'Do you reckon I should go see him?'

'Wouldn't go amiss.'

She carried on stroking the dog. With no reason not to Gabriel carried on hanging his clothes. Last week he put requisition in for a new khaki rigout. Right now he is managing on two pairs of everything, one to wash and one to wear. Ma's good with his stuff. He could trust her with his shirts but particular about his things launders his own.

In war a man can't worry about the state of his underpants any more than he can piss in any one place. He does what he does when he does it. Yet when there's time and hot running water and clean cotton about his ass what fool would turn away.

Ma says he's picky. She watched him the other day polishing his boots.

'I thought you Marines wear boots.'

'These are boots.'

'They look too good to be boots.'

'They are good boots. They was given to me in New Zealand.'

'What do you mean given?'

'A present.'

'Who gave you them, a lady-friend?'

'They belonged to a Marine who never got to wear them.'

Ma was shocked. 'You wearin' a dead man's boots!'

'He wasn't dead when he bought these. As I say, he never got to wear them. They was passed to me by his commanding officer.'

Ma scowled. 'Why would you want to step into a dead man's shoes? Why not wear what's given?'

Gabriel said how most Marines start out standard issue but along the way they want better, and that there are tailors everywhere who for money, and even with shells careening overhead, will get you what you want. It's the same with shoes, or jewellery or side-arms or drugs. If you want it it's there including flesh, male or female any colour and any age.

Wanting tailor-made uniforms is not about rank or money. It's about personal pride. Every Marine knows of a guy on the Base who can make dress blues sparkle, just as Gabriel knows that along with two pairs of immaculate boots Gunny JJ Emmett willed him his Commendation Medal and Mizz Jeanie's best love, but there being only so much he can tell Ma he keeps that to himself.

'You like bein' a Marine?' Sue was watching.

'It's okay.' Gabriel hung his pants seam-to-seam, a handkerchief over the bar to stop creasing, another between collar and hook to stop rubbing. Stripped to his skivvies he slid the whole caboodle in a dress bag and with JJ Emmet in mind hung the bag from a rafter. '*Hang your stuff high, asshole, and keep watch! There are rats loose in every hut and not all with four legs. If you're stuff goes missin' look to the next bunk rather than a hole in the wall.*'

Gunny Emmett was a master of information, what he didn't know about Corps craft could not be known; Gabriel misses him now more than ever.

'You shouldn't have come home, Gabe,' says Sue. 'You should've stayed on an island with one of them Hula girls.'

'You think so.'

'I think you comin' back was a mistake.'

'Maybe.'

Fingers stroking she crept up behind him. 'You got holes in your back.'

'I took a couple of hits.'

'Did it hurt?'

'Yes.'

'Poor Gabe.' Sliding her hands about his waist she laid her head on his back. She'd been crying her tears wet.

'What's wrong?'

'Nothin'. I'm jest blue.'

'I'm sorry about Herb. He was a good guy.'

'He was a mutt but house trained so he did for a while.'

'What do you want, Sue?'

'What I've always wanted you to love me.'

'I can't do that.'

'Why can't you?' Ain't I pretty enough?'

'You are pretty but I still can't love you.'

'Is there someone else? Somebody you met when you was away?'

It came to him then that there was someone and that there was always someone and that as Ma said if he threw that someone on the fire or sold her it would be selling his soul.

'There is someone.'

'And do you love her?'

'I do.'

'Does she know you love her?'

'No.'

'Will you tell her?'

'No.'

Slipping her blouse she hung on her breath hot on his neck and her skin smooth against his skin. 'Then you got nothin' to lose by lovin' me.'

'I told you I can't love you. I can never love you.'

'No but you can pretend, if not for you then for me.'

~

Four in the morning he woke with a start. Sue was gone and the dog with her. He'd been dreaming he was across the way in the Old Mill. A dumb dream with no particular sense he was on a step-ladder hanging kiddie's fairy- lights from the ceiling and threading them in and out of rafters.

There was a noise in the background, a motor humming, insistent, the buzz of an overgrown fly.

Bzz! Bzz! Bzz! On and on getting louder until it was hurting the ears. Then out of nowhere Bobby Rourke rushes in. 'For Chrissakes will you turn that thing off?' he yells. 'My head's killin' me!' Boom, his head did explode, blood and brains staining Gabriel's dress-shirt.

Some dream! He lay thinking about it. Standing on a step-ladder hanging fairy-lights, what is that about? And why Bobby? Other than his mother talking of him earlier and Sue wanting a visit why dream of him?

There doesn't need to be a connection. Dreams do that, take the craziest images and string them together. When he was last injured and on morphine he dreamt he had wings and was able to fly through the air.

He had those dreams all the time then, him flying and music from the gods.

Now he rarely dreams. This one, an exploding head was like a clip from a Tom and Jerry cartoon, the cat getting bashed over the head with a mallet. It made no sense and yet left Gabriel feeling responsible for the cat.

This place and this town! Thank God he's only one more day. The sooner he's out and on the other side of the world the sooner he can rest. An open warzone has to be better than the pain sitting on his heart.

Sex last night with Sue was wrong. It shouldn't have happened. It was the past being dragged out all over again, him and her battling it out here in the Orangery with starlight for back-lighting and green eyes watching. .

Yes, last night he had been aware of eyes watching, green eyes with long lashes as familiar to him as those seen in a mirror every morning shaving.

Eyes that had come alive under his knife, fashioned, you might say, by Gabriel as the Creator fashions eyes that can see.

What those eyes saw last night doesn't bear thinking about! Him and Sue rolling about the floor and all the huffing and puffing and disturbing of dust! My stars! They wouldn't have watched for long. Disgusted, they'd have shrunk away as he shrinks from the memory. He should've said, 'no, Sue. You and me are worth more.' But enjoying what she did, them locked in velvet battle, he kept quiet self-respect rolling down her throat through sucking lips.

Yesterday he walked away from the Mission with a woman hollering contempt in his ear. 'Don't you worry about Ruby Cropper,' Miss Matilda had patted his arm. 'She's only happy when she's tearing some poor soul to pieces.'

He wasn't worried. It was Ruby and her always bad-mouthing someone he took it on the chin. She called him a sham! She said he was dross not gold. Now with remembrance of his lies to Ma and casual use of Sue her words got through and Sergeant GH Templar, US Marine Corps, began to dissolve.

Stitch-by-stitch the stripes on his sleeve came undone. He saw them unravel as he saw the buttons on his jacket that shone yesterday are tarnished, and the soles on his boots bequeathed by a good man, were coming away.

Everything, all borrowed glory was stripped away until there was only him naked in a house of glass and like a suit of old clothes, comfortable but shabby, the former man rolled back and it was autumn of '34, a Killing Judge banging his gavel and an unfeeling brute with chains on his hands and feet.

This time he didn't need Ma's mirror. Under review he is revealed a sham. No wonder the Eyrie wanted him out. Forget Peleliu and Guadalcanal and stripes earned by killing. Forget sexy ladies who missing their men accept what he is only too willing to give. And for God's sake forget cutting wires and saving lives! It don't matter who was saved and who died. This is him as Ruby Rourke said, Gabe Templar, town loon and murdering ex-con minus a hard on.

Thirty
Crucified

Bobby saw him coming through the trees and grabbed his jacket and ran.

Two minutes and he's in the Morgan heading out the back way. They can't meet. No! He couldn't bear it.

Hearing Gabe was home Bobby's been on the move this last week, dodging back and forth trying to be everywhere he isn't. It was okay before the war. They could have run into one another every day and it wouldn't matter. He was the Man then, Baby Rourke, a cool guy with movie-star looks whacking a ball about a tennis court and buzzing the clouds over Chesapeake Bay.

Gabe Templar was the blonde kid with holes in his shoes that lived in a shack with a drudge for mother and a bum for a father. Now look at him striding through Bayonet Woods like he owns them. Buttons flashing and duffle bag on his shoulder, Esprit de Corps he defines the Marine Corps.

'Semper Fi my ass!' Bobby stared into the rear-view mirror watching the Mill retreat. 'Who does he think he is General Eisenhower?'

Now thinking Gabe might wait Bobby must drag about town until dark and he won't be able to see to collect wood. Even in July it's cold in the Mill and with only memories to keep him warm Bobby sleeps in the tower on an old couch. It's still cold but at least up there he sees the world before the world sees him.

He was scratching about for kindling when he saw Gabe coming. That's okay; he'll get logs delivered and hire a guy to plant the rose cuttings he has stashed in the garage. Bobby Rourke doesn't dig. That's for slaves like Gabe Templar.

Sergeant Gabe Templar? Fuck off! He's still a slave. I mean, how much can he be making? If it's anything like RAF pay it's not worth drawing. But then he isn't in it for the dough. He's in it for the glory.

Bobby was outside the Mission yesterday. Shades over his eyes and baseball cap he hid among the crush. A familiar face and name round here you'd think someone would recognize him. Nah! They were too busy watching the parade.

Smooth buzz cut and firm jaw Gabe was a swell in good khaki! None of your standard issue he'd laid out bucks for tailor-made and it showed, women smiling and schoolgirls on the way to College fluttering their lashes.

No wonder Ma roused up. She wasn't blinded by the braid. She let rip saying folks were seeing gold where there was dross.

The minute she started Bobby quit the scene. She was right to lay into Gabe but spitting and snarling she was more bear-pit than human.

This is her denying the past. Having appointed herself God's mouthpiece, and folks too scared to argue, she circumvents memories of Wolfe Street and in blinding people to her sins points out theirs. In the evening she sits chewing liquorice and learning bible quotes. She has a saying for every occasion, and because money and the getting of it is her main preoccupation she's majoring on thieving: John 10: 10. '*the thief cometh not, but to steal and kill and destroy.*'

Ruby sees everyone a potential thief her son included. First day back he caught her checking his bank-balance. She said if they were to live together, and him likely to die, she needed to be co-signatory at the bank. When he said nix she spat out a new saying, '*he that covereth his sins shall never prosper.*'

Bobby laughed but the words went deep. He doesn't prosper and with his secret sin never will. He shouldn't have bought the Mill. So decrepit, he doesn't know where to start. Builders say flatten it and begin again. If he was his old self he might take a swing at it but he can't lift his head never mind an axe. Madness took over. Why buy a house to live next door to a man you hate.

Rumour says that, though his Ma don't want it Gabe's about to sign for a four year stint abroad. Let's hope rumour is right. But why should Bobby run? And where can he run to? A mutilated spider seeking the dark he hides in an old theatre watching old movies. From there he has two ports of call, picking up tail at the dockyard or getting drunk at the Hawaiian Bar.

'It ain't fair.' He is so lonely. He didn't know loneliness until he bought this place. Builders are right. Maybe if he offers enough one of them will get a stick of dynamite and blow the Mill sky high and Bobby with it.

~

Shaky, he hit a couple of bars tossing beers down his neck. Still shaky, and with an empty gut he makes for a cafe where they do a decent steak. He got a table and was chewing on his steak when the General tapped on the window.

A different General today, smiling. 'Sorry to break in on your lunch but seeing you here I had to tell you the news.'

Suddenly the piece of steak in Bobby's mouth is dry sand. He couldn't swallow. The look on the General's face said it all. 'You've heard from Alex.'

'Yes, by golly we have, and though he's been knocked about a bit in Italy and then in the Ardennes he is sound of heart and mind.'

'That is good news.'

'Isn't it just! As I said before, you two kids being pals I thought you'd sleep better knowing him alive.'

'I will. And is he on his way home?'

'Well, there's a thing, he is on his way but to DC rather than here.' Face wreathed in smiles, proud dad, the General bent low. 'He's got an appointment with the White House, a certain ceremony being called.'

'Ceremony?' For the life of him Bobby couldn't make sense of the word. He kept thinking wedding bells and folks getting married.

The General bent closer. 'The Medal, you know.'

'Medal?'

'Uh-huh. *The* Medal. The Big one.'

'Oh, I get it. Wow! That is somethin'. Are you and Mrs H goin' with him?'

'Flying visit.' The General's face darkened a trace. 'He's got a couple of days in Washington and then heading right back to Europe.'

'As quick as that?'

'As quick as that. Naturally, he should be home but between you and me and the Kremlin the young fool's got caught up with OSS guys. It's a Special Ops behind the lines set-up though what can be more special than spending time with his folks I do not know.'

'You must have missed him.'

'Yes and the way things are looking we'll carry on missing him. The word being Berlin and deep cover it could be years before we see him again.'

'And yet he is alive!'

'You're right! He is alive!' The General slapped Bobby's back, dislodging the lump of steak. 'And what in the world can be better than that.'

With that he was striding out the door, back straight, head high and shoulders swinging, a father with a living son.

~

Bobby left the steak for his regular haunt in the old Regal Cinema. A matinee performance, but for the usual flashers and the drunken sots the place was empty. What a dump! Cigarette-ash and other unmentionables littering the floor it's filthy but it's also warm and dark and no one can see you cry.

Stunned, he stared at the screen. Ads were running, a fat guy in a checked shirt, though what he was selling Bobby couldn't tell. Alex Hunter alive? It is a shock yet truth to tell a weight off his mind. Alex didn't have to die thinking he killed Adelia. He will always hold himself responsible, he's that kind of guy, but now he stands a chance of meeting someone new.

Here's another thing, Special Ops or not sooner or later he will come home. Which means Bobby needn't worry about being discovered for a liar by either Alex or Dee because she won't be here. She'll still be in England and beauty that she is will find someone and be happy. It's only Bobby that will die alone.

It's over. He dug the whisky bottle from his pocket and took a long pull.

What an anti-climax! All the fuss and conniving has been for nothing. And the letters, reams of them!

Every night he used to fall into bed thinking tomorrow I'll I tell her to forget coming to the Promised Land because there is no Promised Land, there's a broken down guy living in a broken down house with a broken down life.

That's him at night. In the morning he wakes wishing that she was here taking care of him. Because she would, you know! Angel that she is she'd forgive the lies and flapping her wings rise up to draw him to her breast so that he might rest enfolded in her feathers.

So he sits and writes another letter telling of a great life in this great house and how she will love being here, that Sophie will be in loving hands, Ma longing to meet her, and that Fredericksburg is a great place to live with great schools and great doctors and great hospitals and great cemeteries!

Then he races to the nearest post-box pushing the letters through one-by-one, '*signed with a loving kiss.*'

Now letter writing is done and he has nothing.

It's not been bad news for everyone. The woman at Belle Couture believes Dee a lucky lady and Bobby a living saint, the bedroom closet so full he has trouble closing the door.

Shopping for her and Sophie used to be the highlight of his week until he started thinking folks were staring and stayed closer to home. Some do stare but most are busy with their own lives. It's him, sensitive to every turn, like the day he walked into Bloomingdales and the door-man thinking him blind took his arm. 'Let me help you, sir.' Bobby let him help him out the door into a cab.

Then he began home-shopping and Belle Couture's cash register ringing.

This last couple of months he's been sending to England. Nothing expensive, trifling bits of fun, fancy items you wouldn't find in war-torn Britain like a silk boudoir cap covered with blue bird feathers for Dee and a diamante Mickey Mouse glove puppet for Sophie.

As he said fun items! Dee will see it as money wasted which is why he drew the line at a sable jacket for Sophie. Momma might stand one herself but not for her kiddie. 'I'll buy the coat,' he said to woman, 'if you will embroider the name Adelia Rourke in the lining and knit me a toy monkey.'

'A toy monkey?'

'Yes, by name of Coco. Can you do it?'

'Certainly I can.'

'That's good. And one more thing?'

She smiles. 'And what's that, sir?'

'Give it a patch over the left eye.'

The woman burst into tears! 'I'm sorry,' she says, 'I shouldn't cry but you are such a brave man. Your wife is a lucky lady.'

That was it; his RAF badge pinned to the monkey the coat was to go special courier in time for Christmas. Now he may as well give it to Ma.

Flat as a busted balloon he sat in the dark remembering how he set fire to the original Coco. Yes he did, set fire to it. Pathetic! So he went into barbed wire? That was him pissed out of his brains not a toy offering a hex.

Stupid ass that he is he set fire to it one night at the Veteran's Hospital and stood in salute watching it burn.

Three years wasted! Bobby should be glad it's over but he's not. He almost had her here. One last trick via the baker's wife and he would've pulled it off.

Edna James has been a constant source of information, not exactly a paid informant but not averse to help with the rent. He'd phone asking how things were. She didn't like him calling but he didn't care. Last time Dee was working at the pub. Her daughter expecting Edna was chatty for a change. 'We'd like to be nearer,' she says, 'but we've a hefty mortgage and now is not a good time to sell. Shame! I'm sick of it here. I wish we could pack up and go.'

The phone call gave Bobby a jolly wizard idea but echoing other jolly wizard ideas he kept quiet. Now it doesn't matter because any idea is wasted. God has made up His Mind. Dee is not meant to come. Bobby must live and die alone.

~

Sick of his own company he went to the Hawaiian Bar in hopes of seeing Sue and coaxing a quickie out of her. No sign of Sue he ordered a tray of Tequila Slammers, his mission to drink himself into oblivion

The bartender hovered. 'Don't you think you've had enough?'

'Nah!' Bobby waved him on. 'Enough is never enough, my good fellow. Bring on the champagne and the dancers! There's always room for more.'

'I'm not carting you back,' said the bartender. 'Once was enough.'

'No sweat. I can make it on my own. Don't need your help.'

Then a kid in Navy Cadet pea-jacket walked up. 'It's okay,' he says. 'I'll take care of the Captain.'

The bartender shrugged and walked off.

Bobby peered up. 'Do I know you?'

'No but I've seen you around.'

'Hah!' He laughed. 'Everybody's seen me around. I'm like the Lincoln Memorial, a national treasure and not to be missed.' He waves the kid in. 'Pull up a booth, my amiable sailor friend and we'll splice the main-brace together.'

The kid sits. 'I don't drink.'

'Wha..?'

'I don't touch the stuff. Root beer's as far as I go.'

'Then what the fuck are you doin' here?'

'It's as good a place as any.'

'Whoah! Now hold on!' Bobby held up his hand. 'If you're another lonely soul come to drown your sorrows then keep walkin'! I've enough sorrows to fill an ocean without listenin' to yours.'

'That's okay.' The kid lit a cigarette. 'I don't tell my sorrows to anyone.'

'Damn right!' Bobby emptied his glass. ''Cos nobody wants to hear, not even your own mother!'

They sat in silence, the kid smoking and Bobby ruminating on the sable coat. He's decided Dee should have the coat. Why not? It was his fault she missed out on Alex Hunter so why not have a sable coat!

On the way here he dropped by the shop. The light was still on the woman out back with a vacuum cleaner. He knocked on the glass. At the thought of another thousand dollar sale she was quick to open the door. He asked if the coat was ready. She fetched it out the name Adelia Rourke embroidered in gold thread and beside it Coco, a woollen monkey.

It was cute, not a carbon copy of the original but cute with a pair of bright red flying goggles stitched round the eyes. He asked why goggles.

'Don't you like them?' she said.

'They're fine. I just wondered.'

'I chose red silk because you gave your sight to your country, Captain, and it should be remembered! I can make it a patch it if you like.'

'Leave it is,' he says. 'You chose right. I bled and I am still bleedin'.'

The woman's sensitivity got to him. Close to tears he asked for a gift card.

'How about this florist's card,' she said. 'It's rather plain but then a sable coat arriving in the post any good wishes speak for themselves.'

He took the card and still thinking blood red goggles dashed off a note shoving the card deep within a pocket and the knitted monkey after it.

The saleswoman boxed and wrapped the coat. When it was done, co-conspirator and partners-in-crime, he slipped her a couple of big bucks.

'Get it posted and keep what's left.'

'Don't you want to see it go?'

'No. I've done my bit,' says he grimly. 'Now it's down to her.'

Now he sits in the bar watching the clock believing that one way or another, the coat, and what's in the pocket, will decide the future.

Why did it have to be this way? It could have been so much better. They could be here now and him about to go home with a bunch of roses and a loving kiss. A tear slipped down his cheek.

The Navy Cadet patted his arm. 'It's okay.'

Bobby turned. 'What!?'

'I said it's okay. You'll get through this.'

'Get through? You tryin' to be funny?'

'No! As I said, I've seen you before and I know you're struggling. I just wanted to say hang on. You're still the Bobby Rourke you always were.'

Bobby ground his teeth. This is hospital hearts-and-flowers shit again, the build 'em high and make 'em strong.

He didn't like it then and doesn't like it now. 'Piss off!' he spat. 'And take your phony baloney with you!'

'Sorry.' The kid was on his feet. 'I didn't mean to upset you.'

'Well you have upset me! Tellin' me I'm still the guy I was! What are you eighteen and your ass still wet? How can you comprehend my feelin's? I'm nothin' like the man I was. That Bobby Rourke was a winner. This Bobby is ugly and half-blind. He's a thing rather than a person, as his mother quaintly puts it somethin' kids throw stones at. Go home, Navy-boy, you're not helpin'!'

'And neither are you!' Bobby lurched to his feet giving the finger to those staring. 'So turn round all of you and mind your own fuckin' business!'

The kid was trying to get out the booth. Contrite, Bobby pushed him back onto the seat. 'Sit down and stay put! You don't need to go!'

'I'm sorry. I had no right to speak.'

'You're okay. It's me. I'm crucified, hung, drawn and quartered! Or as my doctor would have it I need to see the wider vision.'

Heart pounding, he slumped back. Hell, he thought! I'd better get a grip or they'll be carrying me out in a straight jacket.

The kid was shaking. Shame! He was trying to help but the fact is there is no help. There is Hobson's Choice, a miracle or a bullet.

Tequila Slammers all gone Bobby dug into his reserves. Hefting a bottle of JD from his pocket he drank until his throat burned.

The kid was babbling, saying he knew how it felt to be on the outside. The Academy was his father's idea. He hated the Navy and couldn't wait to get out. Bobby let him talk. Another unhappy soul pleading with God what difference did it make? Then the kid did something, a word or gesture, something, and Bobby knew why he was an outsider.

His heart gave a tug. You poor little shit!

The kid was waving his hands describing life at the Academy.

'Hush up!' Bobby dug his ribs. 'You're lettin' it show.'

'What?'

'I said be quiet. You're lettin' your secret show and there are guys watchin' who trust me, sweetheart, are not what you're lookin' for.'

The kid stared a thousand emotions passing over his young face.

'Take a hit.' Bobby offered the bottle. 'It's late and you've had a bad day. And you ought not to come to this bar. It's not a good place.'

'I was lonely.'

'I know.'

'It's difficult.'

'Always is.'

'I need someone of my own.'

'Don't we all.'

'I look but I don't find.'

'You gotta keep lookin' because someone is out there.' Bobby took a snap-shot from his wallet. 'This is my someone.'

The kid looked. 'She is beautiful.'

'She is and she has a little kid just as beautiful.'

'Your kid?'

'No, though I'd be more than happy to claim her.'

'So what's the problem?'

'I haven't seen her in a while.'

The kid didn't cut corners. 'You mean she hasn't seen your face.'

'No.'

'I'm sorry.'

'Me too.'

They sank into a mutual melancholy him chugging the bottle and the kid with the photograph. Head aching, and guts blown up where he hadn't eaten all day, Bobby was feeling real nauseous. He needed to go home and sleep but to what, a couch in the attic with the rest of the rats.

'So?' Trying to find diversion he turned to the kid. 'What do you look for in your somebody? What's your preference, young or old, long or short or tall?'

The kid wasn't listening.

'Did you hear what I said? What's your preference?'

'Him.'

'What?'

'Him! The blonde guy at the door.' The kid was gazing down the Bar. 'He would be my someone.'

Bobby didn't need to look to know who he was talking about. The kid's voice said it, the Marines had landed.

~

Gabriel had to take a minute before going in. It wasn't only the damage to Bobby's face, a gouging hole for a left eye and another for his left ear, it was the man. Clothes hanging on his bones and not shaved in days he looked terrible. He was always a sharp dresser. You knew him by the quiff in his hair and expensive shoes, and in latter-days the Royal Air-force uniform. Now he wears the uniform but the pants and the jacket are wrinkled like they're slept-in. This isn't Bobby Rourke. This is a graveyard.

No wonder Sue is fretting. She mourns Bobby as she mourns her own life. He needs help, though why Gabriel is here he doesn't know as he didn't know this morning Ma reckons Bobby bought the Old Mill. If he has he's bought trouble. There's history there as there is with the Eyrie. It's said Atlantic traders were dropping supplies into the mid 1800s but that Civil War rivalry hit both families, father-against-son and brother-against-brother as is the case in many parts of the South.

This morning Bobby saw him coming and bolted. Gabriel didn't hang about. Though built at the same time the houses don't feel the same. Walk into the Eyrie and you walk into warmth— at least, that's how it was. Walk into the Mill and you freeze. Sails tattered and innards gouged out, it's not a place to linger misery hanging in the air as smoke from a funeral pyre. Now Gabriel peers through cigarette smoke and sees the man and the building the same.

Yesterday it was Sue looking for help. Today it was the bartender.

Gabriel was at the gas-station when he came running. 'Hey, Sergeant!' he yells. 'Come get your buddy will you before he does something stupid.'

Gabriel had frowned. 'What buddy's that?'

'The flier that got shot-up. What's-his-name, Rourke? He's drunk and looking for trouble. I took him to his mother's last week but I'm damned if I'm doing it again. He threw up all over the wagon! I'm not chancing that twice.'

'And I can?'

'He is your buddy.'

It was news to Gabriel. No buddy and never will be but he's here and might as well get him home. 'Hi Bobby.'

Bobby grins. 'Well, if it isn't my old sparrin' partner! How you doin' champ?'

'I'm okay.'

'You look okay.' Bobby waved at a Navy Cadet sitting the other side. 'Pull up a pew, Sergeant, and meet a new drinkin' pal of mine.'

The kid was on his feet. 'It's okay. I need to be going.'

'Shame,' says Bobby. 'We were only breakin' the ice. But if you have to go then you have to go. Cheerio, old chap, pip-pip, as we say in the RAF! Do drop by next time you're passin'. You'll find me here.'

The kid was gone. 'Poor little lamb!' Bobby stared after him. 'Another lost soul tryin' to negotiate the hell that is Life. I don't hold out much hope for him.'

'You need a lift home?'

'Home?' He leaned his chin on his hand. 'That's a nice soundin' word! I love the sound of that word. It has a ring to it. But the word is no good on its own. You need a home to go with it or it means nothin'. You got a pile of bricks and ghosts in the lobby but you ain't got a home.'

'Only if you do wanna lift I can drop you some place.'

'Yeah, you can drop me some place.' Bobby was on his feet any humour dropped away. 'How about Chesapeake Bay.'

Gabriel hauled him out to the truck. It was like pushing a barrow, a stinking barrow at that yesterday's sweat mingling with today's.

'You could use a shower.'

'I know but the Mill don't oblige. I have to pump any water I need. Same as with the electricity. There ain't none. It's lamplight all the way.' He grabbed hold of Gabriel's arm. 'But that's okay, ain't it, sugar. We-all look so much better by candlelight, even me.'

They were at the truck when he decided to go back. 'Hold on a minute!' He starts grabbing at his pockets. 'Where is it?'

'Where's what?' Gabriel was losing patience.

'My photograph! The kid was lookin' at it, sayin' how beautiful she is though she wasn't his bag, you were.'

'What!'

'The photograph! I've dropped it.'

'Get in.' Gabriel hoisted him into the truck. 'I'll go back.'

'No, I'll go!' Bobby's trying to climb out and he was weeping, tears running down his cheeks. 'I can't lose that. It might be all I ever have.'

Gabriel locked him in. He got to the Bar as the bartender is coming out.

'Take this!' The guy thrusts out a photograph. 'But for Chrissakes don't lose it! Poor bastard sits half the night staring at that.'

'Okay!' Gabriel turns back but in haste drops the photograph. He picks it up and is looking at the doll. Only it's not the doll. She was never a doll. She was and is a grown woman, a beautiful woman, the only woman, his Little Gal, his Other Self.

Thirty-one
Soul's Passion
August 1945.
Little Shelford,
Cambridge, England.

'No! I agree with Dad. It's not a thing to have on show. It has to be shown when required and beyond that fetched out of mothballs once a year to show the grandchildren.'

This was Alex back in May getting between his mother's pride in her hero son and the General's reservations regarding the displaying the Medal.

Mom said Alex should wear it all the time; 'then the world will see how my boy suffered for his country.'

The General said it should be worn only when circumstances dictate.

Mom chipped in. 'What's the point of winning a medal if no one knows.'

Alex tried to say it's not about winning. 'You can't win in war. No one can.'

From then on, as is customary with any difference of opinion, his parents fell into a drag out grind.

It doesn't take much to get them going. Theirs is not an easy marriage, the General a rigid man demanding of right manners and high standards, and Mom Ellen, a disappointed woman who trained as a classical dancer but who never got to fulfil her dreams and so is always feeling in some way cheated.

They argued on the way to the White House and on the way back. As far as Alex was concerned regulations dictate the wearing of any medal ribbon left side of his jacket along with other military decorations, beyond that the actual hunk of metal goes in the kitchen drawer along with balls of string.

The Medal of Honour being the most prestigious of military decorations awarded to US service personnel who 'distinguished themselves in acts of valour,' it's likely Mom thinks Alex reluctance to accept is him behaving like a spoilt kid. He does have misgivings. When looking back on his contribution to the defence of his country he finds nothing to shout about.

Maybe if he were to see it again, a slo-mo replay of every action he might find something worthy but his memories of each day of his own particular war are of a lump of flesh responding to outer stimuli not unlike a rat in a maze.

There was a moment during the ceremony, the ribbon about his neck, when General Eisenhower nodded. In that moment Alex thought perhaps he did do something worthy, for sure if he needs reminding of Anzio and the Ardennes the smell of horseshit and the ache in his left knee will do it.

Ike's approving nod aside the moment was only a moment and soon overtaken by the faces of those lost in battle.

'I'm sorry about Joe,' Dad was shocked by the news. 'He was a good man. The world is the worse for him going.'

Joe's loving tutorage ever close to his heart Alex agreed but of that other loss, that great personal loss, burning, burning he said nothing.

'Yes, a good man,' Dad continued, 'but you can't think on that. I realise you got Granpappy Frobisher's memory to navigate and by that it's harder for you, son, but you got to get beyond the loss and look to the greater good. If you dwell on the negative you won't survive.'

This from hardened soldier who as far as Alex knows never lets a day go by without making penance for those he fought and killed in WW1. A big guy with a tough shell you don't get to hear William Hunter say sorry as you don't get fond words instead a heart attack in the spring of '29 - and according to Mom another in '43 when Alex was posted missing - his body speaks for him.

Choked up inside is a family trait more obvious in Hunter men than the women put up and shut up being Academy Law, even so if Alex hears the phrase 'the greater good' again he will have to kill the person that says it.

The good of the whole is a lie. He is not alone in thinking so. Friday he was present at a briefing regarding his ticket to Berlin where among others he will operate an undercover cell, the purpose of which to 'find out what Uncle Joe Stalin has in mind.'

An Englishman by name of Tom Farrell, a walking skeleton recently escaped a German POW camp said they were too late. If they wanted to know what Stalin had in mind they should visit Katyn Forest in Silesia where they would find the graves of thousands of Polish officers murdered by Russian Secret Police. 'That's what he has in mind,' said Major Farrell. 'For Stalin and the ideology he represents there is no greater good than the systematic removal of anyone standing in his way, and you are mistaken if you think titting about with secret codes and invisible ink will change that.'

Alex hadn't heard of the Katyn massacre but as time goes on and the Allies move further into Germany more atrocities are revealed, not least a Nazi pogrom regarding the gassing of hundreds, maybe thousands of Jews. Now there are rumours of the US about to drop an atom-bomb on Japan.

There can be nothing good or great about that.

~

Sunday evening Alex sits in the front parlour of 55, Oakbridge Drive, a pretty house in a leafy Cambridge suburb, taking tea with Mrs Elizabeth Beveridge, widow of Captain Peter Beveridge of the Royal Tank Regiment. A gentle woman in a blue cashmere twinset, Mrs Beveridge is soft-spoken and with a Scottish burr. Alex has to lean forward to catch what she says.

'I believe you were wounded in the same conflict, Colonel Hunter.'

'I took hurt to my knee.'

'Is it mending?'

'It's coming along, thank you, ma'am.'

'Good, I'm glad.' She set down her cup and folded her hands, a gesture Alex took to be her ready to hear what he had to say. 'And my Peter?'

'It was a tough situation. There was little opportunity to talk other than thinking of you the Captain asked me to bring a message.'

'So he was thinking of me?'

'Indeed he was. You were the one person on his mind. He knew you would worry about him and wanted to put your mind at rest.'

'Did he indeed? And how did he propose to do that?'

'Sorry, ma'am?'

'Put my mind at rest.' She retrieved her cup of tea, the spoon rattling in the saucer. 'I wonder he thought anything he said could put my mind at rest.'

'Those were my words, Mrs Beveridge, not his.'

'Of course. Excuse me.' Down went the cup. 'Please continue.'

'His actual comment was, 'she's a brave girl, my Betty. A couple of words and she will know I'm dealing with it.''

She smiled. 'He always called me Betty, never Elizabeth. My mother hated it. She said I sounded like a back-kitchen maid. Mother was not over-fond of Peter. She didn't think him good enough for me as my mother-in-law didn't think me good enough for him. Silly isn't it, how our parents make these judgements. As if any of us know who or what is good for us.'

Alex waited.

She sighed. 'What words?'

'Rose Cottage.'

'Oh!' She closed her eyes

He looked away. Mrs Beveridge is angry. She blames her husband for getting killed, and, poor woman, feels guilty for it.

'Why do men do it,' she said, reading his mind. 'Why can't you be peaceful and stay alive. Why must you fight?'

Alex stayed quiet. There was nothing he could say.

She opened her eyes. 'You must have wondered at the message.'

'No ma'am. It was not for me to wonder.'

'Well there is a simple explanation, innocent really. Peter and I spent our honeymoon at Loch Garry in Scotland and while there we fell in love with a wee cottage. A picture-book place, magical, roses round the door and bottle-glass windows, it was perfect, and in a moment of romantic madness we made a vow that whoever died first would wait there for the other.'

'A good vow.'

'You think so?'

'I do.'

'We were young and hopelessly in love. It seemed right at the time.' She shook her head. 'I had forgotten about it. So many years ago, the children and all since then, schools and teeth and tonsils, things get put aside.'

Eyes brimming, she looked up. 'But my dear Peter didn't put it aside. He kept it in his heart for such a moment and as he is there waiting in Rose Cottage so one day shall I be.'

He left soon after. She showed him to the door. They shook hands. 'Thank you for coming, Colonel Hunter. If I seem ungrateful it is only because I miss him so. Your message helped and as time goes by will help even more.'

~

The car was waiting. 'Where to Guvnor?'

'Back to the hotel, if you please.'

'Right you are.'

Alex took off his cap. Wearied by the interview he closed his eyes. This is the second such meeting. While stateside he visited David Furness's mother in Long Island but other than to say her son died a brave man there was little he could say. As it was Mrs Furness was another Mrs Beveridge, taking it on the chin. She said with the war in Europe at an end and soon to be so in the Pacific, she hoped 'Colonel Hunter would never have to do anything like this again.'

Neither had great faith in her hope.

The driver coughed. 'Is it back to the hotel or a deviation, Guvnor?'

'Deviation?'

'As I mentioned this morning we're not far from the county of Suffolk. I wondered if you might like to visit.'

'Negative! I do not want to visit!' Alex snapped. 'Just get me to the hotel.'

'Yes Guvnor.'

'And quit calling me Guvnor! Stick with the regulation sir. It simplifies matters.'

'Yes sir. Sorry sir.'

There are certain situations in life that stuck in a groove prove to be a repeat pattern. Alex's current driver is such a pattern, and while Sergeant Franklyn Bates is a good man, brave, a designated minder and not afraid to do his job, the association has drawbacks in that it is a little over familiar.

Ex-padre to the Battalion Frank Bates knows what Suffolk means to Alex and how despite his protestations his Guvnor yearns to go there.

For all that he dropped the dog-collar and wears a sidearm and other items of self-defence Bates is still the father-confessor and of late so much an Aunt Sally Alex wonders if Frank moved in where Joe moved out.

'It might help you to visit, Guvnor,' he said earlier. 'It won't resolve the pain. Nothing will do that but you might get closer to the reality of it.'

'And what is the reality of it?' Smarting, Alex went in with both feet. 'Is it a granite marker with her name on it or the magic-wand of laying the past to rest that once waved renders the girl and her death a non-event.'

'I wasn't thinking of any one thing,' said Bates. 'Only that it might help to tread the path again.'

'Do you mean your favoured Way of the Cross? Surely you can't mean that, the one that you tried to circumvent?'

'No sir, I meant where you two met.'

'Same thing, padre. It's a path I've never left.'

Alex stared out the window. He regrets saying that to Bates. Such petulance is unworthy. This is not his fault. This is Alex's own loose-lip subconscious chewing at the past. He brought up the subject not Frank. Knowing they were coming this way he just happened to mention that the Beveridge house was close to where Bobby Rourke was stationed when he met his accident.

Latest news on Bobby is that he's in a bad way. No one seems to know how he got his injuries, whether it was a plane or what. Other than he was hurt and shipped home to spend weeks in hospital there is no real information.

Rumours abound and none of them good. It's said he sleeps rough in a derelict building in Bayonet Woods and that he gets no help from his mother and beyond dashing about in a sports car is rarely seen.

The General said he's not the man he was.

That got to Alex. 'As I recall you didn't care for the man he was.'

'No one cared for him!' said the General. 'He was ruined from birth by that woman, Ruby Cropper. What's more he passed the ruin on. Your sister was able to see him for the womaniser he was. If she'd been as blind to his faults as your surely are then that woman would have been her mother-in-law.'

Alex tried defending him. 'Bobby is not his mother!'

'Maybe not but he's sure inherited her ways. That tinker Buckminster left him more than well provided so he can't keep blaming the past!' said the General. 'He got the DFC for Pete's sake and served his country with distinction! He should be proud and hold his head high not roll in the gutter.'

'You've seen him rolling in the gutter?'

'No, but stinking of booze at ten in the morning he might as well.'

This is the General, black or white and never a shade of grey.

Then Mom waded in saying fate had a hand in the tragedy. 'It's as they say, what goes around comes around. You know how he was before the war, Alex, so don't try to defend him. As your father said he was a dreadful flirt. And it wasn't just flirting. He was careless with those girls, got them into all sorts of scrapes. Now he's finding there's more to life than good looks.'

Sarah, who once had a thing for Bobby dashed in. 'You ought to consider your words, Ma. All this judging! How would you feel if this was Alex scarred and drinking to ease his pain? Would you see that as payback for past sins?'

'Now then daughter,' Dad was at the ready. 'There's no call to talk to your mother that way.'

'There is every call! People should be more forgiving. Badmouthing and giving a dog an endless bad name! The war's not over yet and here's Alex with a busted knee and a head full of nails. We don't know what was and we don't know what is still to come. Things can still happen. Bad things! And talking like this tempts fate.'

Then Mom was in tears, and Sarah was in tears, and Dad spluttering, and all Alex wanted was to be on the next plane out. It was more peaceful on the front-line than at home. Besides, the argument isn't all about Bobby. It is about Alex heading straight back to Europe.

Sarah said it: 'How can you be away all this time and then fly in and fly out? Two days and you're off again! Couldn't you have stayed a little longer? You don't seem to consider Mom and Dad's feelings. All this time away and not knowing whether you were alive or dead, it's been a great worry.'

He said he was under orders and couldn't pick or choose, which is true, though had they heard themselves bickering they might understand why he chose not to argue with orders and why he will choose not to argue again.

A good reason for not staying longer is the third-degree he'll get when he does finally touchdown. Sarah senses there's more to his wounds than battle-scars 'What's wrong with you?' She saw him off at the airfield. 'Why so heavy? The end of the war in sight and us mostly unscathed you should be thankful. What happened? Is there more to your brooding gaze than a wounded knee?'

No ma'am! He kept quiet. Not a word of what happened in '42. A knife to an oyster shell Sarah's curiosity is sharp. He must hold off as long as he can because once the issue is known she'll be calling her girlfriends, arranging dates and organizing dinner-parties, her motto of life through her own none too secure marriage, 'if at first you don't succeed then for Pete's sake try something new and do it now!'

He can't tell her about Adelia. Sarah wouldn't get the speed of that day in Suffolk or the magic. She'd apply commonsense to roaring passion; 'Don't be absurd! You can't fall in love in a day! Forget it and move on.'

There is only one person he can talk to of that time and that is Bobby Rourke but aware of his situation Alex can hardly dredge up old news.

Is it old news? Is it hell! There's nothing old about his feelings and never will be as he learned again with the wedding ring.

It was Frank Bates. Assigned bulldog to Alex in Berlin he asked for a meeting.

'I want to know if you're okay with me taking care of you.'

'What do you mean okay?'

'In '43 my job was to guard your soul. Now I am to guard your body. I need to know if you are comfortable with that.'

'Why would I not be?'

'Because you know who I was and what I did! I was a troubled man in North Africa. I lost my way and I let you down. I want you to know I'm not that man anymore. I know who I am and I know my job and that is to guard your life and I will guard you with my life. You have my word.'

'Thank you, Frank.'

'No sir, it's me thanking you. You saved me from a great sin and gave me a second chance. I am grateful. One other thing, Guvnor?' He'd fetched an envelope from his pocket. 'What do you want done with the ring?'

It's a valid question. What does he want done with the ring?

February of this year when handed back it went into Alex's pocket. Since then every day the ring and the photograph are moved from pocket to pocket depending on the jacket. It was in his dress uniform in the White House when he got the Medal and again in khaki in Berlin. It's here now pressing hard against his chest! When he moves the photograph crackles, a reminder of love and grief as poignant as the scars in his hands.

The scars bled in Italy, so cold there. A priest in one village saw them and took fright making the sign of the cross. 'It is the soul's Passion that bleeds, Colonel,' he said. 'Your hands bleed as my Dear Lord bled.'

Soul's passion.

Alex took the ring from his pocket. It lay in the palm of his hand as a heavy weight. There was a moment when he was tempted to tell Elizabeth Beveridge of Adelia and St Giles and of their wedding vows under a non-existent window. He seemed to think she would understand. But

Mrs Beveridge's grief was her own, private and precious, and was not to be muddied.

'Frank?' He rapped on the glass partition. 'Did you manage to get a break while I was with Widow Beveridge?'

'Yes sir.' Frank nodded. 'I took tea in a cafe in the village.'

'Good. Look, I'm sorry about earlier. I was wrong to speak to you like that. You supported me in my sorrow. The least I can do is support you.'

'Maybe we can support each other, sir?'

'Better that than at odds. Anyway, I've thought about what you said and decided I should visit Needham if only for an hour. It might help lay the ghost.'

'I don't know about ghost, sir.' Bates eyes in the rear-view mirror were lanterns. 'From what you told me your lady was more an angel.'

'Yes, you're right, my lady was an angel. And though I feel her around me ghost is entirely the wrong word. How far away are we?'

'Not that far. I looked at the map and thought if you wanted to take a look we could go via the A14 to Newmarket and then to a place called Bury St Edmunds which as you say is close to where your friend was stationed.'

'Okay then. Let's do that.'

'Begging your pardon, Guvnor, but are sure?'

Alex spread his hands. 'I'm not sure of anything. But if I don't try to get by this, I never shall.'

~

It was a bonfire that did it. He didn't get by anything! To even think of going there was a mistake. It is autumn and the harvest brought in farmers were setting fire to stubble, smoke blowing across the fields, thick and acrid and too much like another bonfire.

The car moved through the smoke. Alex tried fighting off memories but to no avail. A switch was pulled inside his head and a reel of film began to turn.

Click! They are in the Bistro and she was talking to Luigi who owned the place; '*Alex is a coffee enthusiast. He sees it as a cure-all, don't you, love.*'

Click! They are in the ruined church and a mouse sits on the altar. She is asking God to bring Alex safely home: '*not necessarily to me, though I would be so glad to see you! I thought He might bring you home to your family and the world in general.*'

Click! He is looking down at her. '*I love you.*'

Click! Her eyes are wide. '*What?*'

Click! '*I love you.*'

Click! She is shaking her head. '*You mustn't say things like that.*'

Click! '*I do love you. From the moment I saw you I loved you. I am pretty sure I was born loving you.*'

Click! '*That's a big thing to say and cruel if you're playing games.*'

Click! '*I'm not playing games.*'

'*Really?*'

'*Really.*'

'Really *and Truly*!'

'No! Stop the car!'

Alex is shouting. The car swerves onto a verge and he's out and vomiting, English tea and biscuits puddling the ground.

Head down, he is sick and sick again until he is empty.

'I got you, Guvnor.' Frank opened the car door.

Alex crawled in and head spinning slumped back.

It is a year to the day she died.

Goddamn memory! It will be the death of him.

'Here, hang about!' The car was about to pull away when a labourer from the field taps the window, a glint of gold in his hand. 'You dropped this.'

He pushes the ring through the gap.

'Sorry?' Alex stares at the ring.

The labourer grinned. 'It fell out your pocket.' Then with shades of Cockney fire-fighters and gallows humour and other unfortunate words he laughed. 'Better not lose it, Captain, or you'll have some explaining to do to the Missus.'

The ring back in his pocket Alex stares out of the window. Leaving the A14 they pass more labourers at work. Here in Britain the war is over, signposts are being erected people and things returning to the rightful place.

The right-hand post points to Needham Market and other possibilities.

The left-hand post points to Ipswich and the continuation of a private war.

The car pulls left and keeps going.

Thirty-two
The Coat

The coat arrived the Saturday before Christmas. A corner of the packaging was torn and though the coat was in a box and the box wrapped in heavy-duty cellophane a portion of fur was visible.

The post-office van dropped the parcel at the Bakery as they were closing for the holiday. Adelia heard the van arrive but in a hurry to be ready for work carried on decorating the tree. There was a moment when the shop below was suspiciously quiet and then a yell. 'Delia! Come down here!' Edna was at the bottom of the stairs. 'You've a parcel from the USA.'

'Hang on a minute!' Adelia was on a step-ladder about to pin the angel to the top branch. The tinsel wings were dented. She was trying to straighten them.

'Never mind a minute! Come on down! You've got a mink coat!'

'Oh Lord!' Adelia climbed down. 'What has he sent this time?'

It could not have been worse. Every year on this day Ted James bakes ginger biscuits and bagging them in festive paper three biscuits a bag for the village children.

Something of a tradition people queue in the bakery to receive them.

Ted cussing and Edna red in the face as people push and jostle it's always a bit of a scramble. One woman is bound to complain of broken biscuits as another will say her allotted three seem smaller than the rest.

Tradition, noise and laughter and today an added amusement a brief pantomime show and this time with Adelia and the coat a star turn.

The parcel was on the counter.

'Quick!' Edna was breathing down Adelia's neck. 'Open it up!'

'My hands are dusty from the tree. I'd sooner take it upstairs.'

'Never mind dust! It's Christmas! Open it here then we can all have a look.'

With Edna pulling at the wrapping Adelia could only comply

The box opened and tissue-paper peeled back people crowded close.

'It's not mink,' said one.

'Looks more like squirrel,' said another.

'It's not squirrel. It's fox.'

'It's neither. It's sable!' Edna pointed to the label. 'See! Genuine Black Russian Sable imported from Minsk.''

'Where's Minsk?'

'A place in Russia.' Edna stroked the collar. 'Feels so soft.'

A woman sniffed. 'I bet that cost a packet.'

Sharp and meant to wound remarks flicked back and forth.

'I bet it did. Hundreds of pounds I would say.'

'More like thousands.'

'Nice trinket to find in your Christmas stocking.'

'I wonder which Santa climbed down the chimney to bring this? It can't have been the regular. He's skint like the rest of us. '

A man winked. 'Whoever he is I bet he didn't climb down so much as run knowing what was at the other end was tastier than any mince pie!'

Amid laughter Adelia took the coat and made for the stairs. Mid way up, the fur slippery she dropped it and had to gather it up again.

'That's it, love, scoop it all up!' a woman sneered. 'You worked hard for that so don't leave any of it behind.'

Three days the coat lay sprawled on the sofa firelight making molten silver of the fur. Adelia gave it a wide berth and Sophie, as though dealing with a wild animal, would pat it warily. 'Pretty pussy-cat!'

Utter luxury, the coat is every woman's dream. Ankle length and with hood that falls back into a collar it is simply gorgeous and yet quite useless as are most things Bobby sends. Silk boudoir caps, perfumed scarves and scratchy diamante toys? What's the good of them? The diamante razor sharp Sophie couldn't play with the puppet as Adelia couldn't wear the coat. To what event, queuing in the butcher's for a quarter pound of mince or picking potatoes direct from the field? Ridiculous!

Snowing throughout the night it's cold today. It. People are out clearing paths. Not to labour the point, you can't wear sable clearing snow neither can you wear it to the pub. If Adelia were at Barts she might get away with it for the opera or the ballet but never to the Gas Works shovelling coke.

It 's likely she won't wear it at all in Needham. Everybody knows the workings of the village including what comes through the post. Bobby said she was to watch out for pitchforks and not stir the mud, but damn it all his gifts have stirred up resentment. Everyone is struggling to make a happy Christmas. While a pound box of sugared almonds is an acceptable gift, especially when offered to the family next door as too much for Sophie's teeth, but a feathered cap and diamante Mickey Mouse are too rich for the National blood.

Adelia knows she ought to be grateful but a fish on the end of a line she can't help wriggling. It is the man, all or nothing is how he lives. She should be used to it. So what if super-glamorous the coat doesn't go with navy dresses and lace-ups, too bad, as with a silver butterfly belt she's not that woman anymore.

Bobby says he was left money by a wealthy relative. '*I got so much I could buy the Empire State Building and have change,*' was what he said in the latest letter. '*So don't worry about me sending stuff. I'm on my lonesome here in Virginia. What better way to pass the time than spending dough on the two people I love.*'

Oh, poor Bobby! He sounds so lonely and almost apologetic about the money, like a kiddie finding sixpence spends it quickly before someone wants it back. Tonight when she gets home she'll write a long, chatty letter. She could phone but Edna doesn't like them using the phone. They've already sent a parcel, Adelia knitting another pullover and this time with new wool. Sophie wanted to

send another Coco but recalling the message that the
monkey had done for him they sent a drawing of the cat
instead.

~

Christmas Eve and the pub is packed. Annie and Blanche
serve in the Lounge bar, Sam and Fred in the tap-room, and
Adelia in the Snug.

Annie hired a chap to play the piano and has had the
tables pushed back so people can dance. Sam Carter's not
happy. 'I don't know why we need to have folk jigging
about. What's wrong with singing carols? All that noise,
some of the regulars are finding it too rowdy.'

'It's the Yanks we want coming in.' Annie dismissed
him. 'They spend more in a night than regulars in a year
and if they are going home we need to make hay while the
sun shines. As for jigging about, the more they jig the more
they drink and unless you've forgotten, Sam Carter, selling
beer is what we're about. Never mind rowdy! There's
always the Snug and Miss Delia for anyone who thinks
having a good time is beneath them. They can sit in there
and sip sherry and moan to their heart's content.'

Miss Delia! Things here at the Duke of Wellington are
not as friendly as they used to be. There's a chill in the air
that has nothing to do with the weather.

It's Fred's continued interest. His mother doesn't like
it. It's why bandaged wrist or not Blanche is back behind
the Lounge bar and it's why Adelia's days working at the
pub are numbered. The only reason she's not already out
on her ear is the Christmas Rush.

Annie made her feelings clear. She has told Fred to 'settle for a decent girl and stop making sheep's eyes at that Delia when any bloke with sense can see she's set her sights on something better than a pot-man's son.'

That was said last night on the way out and Adelia meant to hear.

Fred apologised. 'I'm sorry about Mum. She's fixed in her ideas. She thinks if I get bored I'll reenlist in the Navy and so she keeps throwing girls at me. She can't see that if anything will keep me in Needham it's you.'

'Your life is your own, Fred. You mustn't make me the reason you stay.'

'You are the reason I stay. Right now you're the reason I do anything. You're the woman for me and that's all there is to it.'

'I'm sorry.' Adelia told him then as she had told him before. 'You are a good man. Any girl loved by you is lucky.'

'But not you!'

'No.'

'Why not?' He'd frowned. 'What's wrong with me that you can't see me in a romantic way? Am I that lacking in what you want?'

'There's nothing wrong with you. As I said, a girl that has your love is lucky.'

'I don't get it.' He'd shoved his fists in his pockets turning the conversation as he does at such moments to Sophie's welfare and her mother's shortcomings.

'It's not like I come empty-handed. I'm no slouch. I've served my country and with the pub I have a job that's mine for life which is more than can be said for most. I've money saved, not a lot but enough to keep you and your kid. You could live here. There's plenty room. I'd be a good father to Sophie. I know she's not my daughter but I'm willing to take her on as is Mother.'

'Your mother has other ideas. It's why Blanche is back.'

'Blanche is here for the Christmas trade. If not for that she wouldn't be here at all for the simple reason Mum can't stand her. She thinks she's a tart.

'Which goes to show how keen your mother is to be rid of me!'

'She's not keen!'

'Oh, come on, Fred! She hates the idea of you caring for me.'

'Only because she's not sure of you! She knows the way I feel and that having set my mind on you I won't give in. If she thought you'd settle down and be content she'd go along with it. But she's scared. She sees you as flighty.'

'Flighty?'

'You know what I mean, uncertain, a butterfly likely to fly away any minute.'

Sunday evening after a busy shift Adelia was too tired to take offence and it wasn't the first time he's said it. Every time he walks them home he offers marriage and then when turned down tells her why she is wrong to reject him. Today it's because she's an uncertain butterfly.

'I don't know about uncertain. I have always been certain with you, Fred. From the first, when you talked of your feelings I told you I wasn't looking for romance and in the weeks since I've never said otherwise.'

'That's true.' He'd nodded grimly. 'You've always been clear on that. I've never had the door slammed in my face so many times and by the same person.'

'And yet you keep asking as I keep saying no and not just to marriage, to you acting as chaperone every evening!'

'I walk you home because I want you to be safe.'

'Kind of you to think that way but I can take care of myself. I don't need a guard and I don't need you to fetch and carry in the pub. I can manage. It's my job to manage. It's the constant fuss that annoys your mother.'

'You think I'm fussing.'

'Yes and I'd rather you didn't.'

'If I fuss it's because I love you. You're beautiful. You're all I think about. I know you're way above my league and that there are men with more to offer. But flighty or not I can't imagine another woman in my life.'

'Then I am sorry again.' This was said at the door to the flat. 'I think it's probably best if I don't come in tomorrow. I'll phone Annie and tell her.'

'No, don't do that!' He snatched her hand. 'Take no notice of me. Come in tomorrow and do your job. You need the money and Mum needs you working especially now we're so busy.'

'But what about you?'

'Forget about me. I still live with the idea that if I persevere I might win you and if silence has to be the way then fair enough.'

'But why won't you listen! I don't want a romantic attachment with anyone. Won't you let it go and allow us to be friends?'

'Don't talk to me of friends!' Collar up, he'd turned away to the night. 'I don't want to be your friend and I don't want to be like the others leaving you in the lurch and then trying to buy you back with fancy stuff. I am what I am. What you see is what you get with Fred Carter. You either want me or you don't.'

~

That was last night. Now it is Christmas Eve and the pub so crowded people can't breathe let alone dance. Knocked over twice the Christmas tree is removed to the backyard as are redundant stirrup pumps and sandbags.

The noise! It is Bedlam! The piano banging, people singing and shouting and calling out, not to mention the queue of drunken men from the Air Base keen to tell their troubles on this their last Christmas in England.

They are going home! Having done their bit and fought like heroes and dropped their bombs American servicemen are leaving in droves, planes thundering out across the skies and tanks trundling down the road.

'This is some rodeo! Can anyone hear themselves speak?' Bobby's former commander dropped by earlier. 'You don't have it much longer. This time next week most us will be home picking up on our nine-to-five lives again.'

'Will that be a hard task do you think, Squadron Leader?'

'I don't think it will be easy. Some may struggle. There's a certain degree of freedom in war that can't be found in peace time.'

'Needham will be sorry to see you go,' said Adelia.

'Hah!' He grinned. 'I reckon more than one will be glad to wave us goodbye. We are a noisy bunch and haven't always served our hosts as politely and as gallantly as we should. It is time we moved on.'

'You must be looking forward to going home.'

His smile was wry. 'If you'd said that a year ago my answer would have been straightforward but life is strange. It leads you down unknown alleys and suddenly what was right last year is wrong this.'

Having seen the Squadron Leader lately in the company of Effie Gardener, the pretty widow florist from the High Street, Adelia's smile was sympathetic. 'Life can be bewildering at times.'

'You can say that again!' He sighed. 'I guess all we can ever do is keep going.'

'As I have often been told.'

'You have reservations about moving on?'

Adelia nodded. 'I do.'

'Me too.' He emptied his glass. 'I shall miss this place. If I had my time over again there are things I would do differently and I doubt I'm alone in that way of thinking. It's not what we did while we were here in England, Mizz Challoner. It's what we didn't do to help leave a trail of glory.'

~

The Squadron Leader's soulful pondering over a whisky set a pattern for the night. From then on every other man had something to say about his time in England. Quarter to eleven and another pilot leans against the bar saying how much he'd enjoyed his stint in Suffolk.

'You are all so very complimentary,' said Adelia.

The fellow grinned. 'That's because we're leaving.'

She laughed. 'I suppose so.'

'It's also because we're alive! We've come through a war and lived to tell the tale. A lot of guys weren't so lucky. Here we are on Christmas Eve drinking booze and talking with beautiful women while other guys lie face down the mud. It's a lot to take in, especially with the debit and credit business. Some fellows will go home sporting Silver Stars. People will call them heroes. I did the same as everyone else yet I go back as I arrived ornament free.'

Adelia ventured a word. 'I'm sure you earned your stripes, Lieutenant.'

The pilot shrugged. 'I fought my war. I drove a pig of B29 through the skies. I got shot at every which way and I watched my buddies die. I did my best for King and Country. I can do no more.' He kissed Adelia's hand. 'You, my lady, are the saving grace of all. If I take nothing back from this kerfuffle other than the memory of your lovely face it is medal enough for me.'

The airman was drunk. He was gentle and sweet. He was not a problem. Left alone he would've returned to the States with no thought of England beyond a headache and an empty pocket. But Fred Carter had been drinking since lunchtime and contrary to a promise to bide his time decided the pilot was a pest and followed him to the Gent's threatening to bust his nose.

A scuffle developed, US airmen coming to their buddy's defence and local men, who resented men from the Base wading in on Fred's side.

A pitch-battle raged up and down the yard. Windows were broken. Beer bottles smashed. The police were called, a Black Maria and a Military Police jeep screeching into the yard. A towel over the pumps the pub was closed down. People were sent home and the midnight extension withdrawn.

Annie flew into a rage. 'This is your fault Delia Challoner!' she yelled. 'You and your Yanks! Look at this place! I've a pub full of beer and no one to drink it!' She told Adelia to collect Sophie and leave and not bother coming back.

'Why are you yelling at Delia?' Fred appeared with a bloodied nose. 'It's not her fault. It was me. I got myself in a stew.'

'Yes and it was always going to happen. I warned you about her. I told you it would all come to grief!'

'But I'm the one to blame!!' Fred protested. 'She didn't do anything.'

'I don't care who's to blame! I want her out of my pub! It was always going to come to this, you making calf's eyes and her mucking you about for some other bloke. You should've nipped it in the bud like I said.'

'But Mum!'

'Please, Fred!' Adelia couldn't get out fast enough. 'Don't say a word on my behalf. If this is what your mother thinks of me then I'm glad to go!'

'Yes go!' shouted Annie. 'And don't bother coming back!'

Hands shaking Adelia fastened Sophie's bonnet. It was bitterly cold outside and fetched from a warm bed and frightened by all the shouting the child was sobbing. 'It's alright,' she said. 'Don't cry. We'll soon be home.'

'Better take this before you go!' Annie threw an envelope on the counter, the paper splitting and coins scattering. 'Though why I should pay you for emptying the pub of hard-earned trade I do not know. By rights I should be deducting your money. Thanks to you I've barrels on tap and a kitchen full of ham-sandwiches that no one's going to eat'

Adelia crouched picking up coins.

'I'm sorry.' Fred crouched beside her. 'I don't know what got into me. I saw that bloke slobbering over you and couldn't stand it.'

'Don't talk to me.' She pocketed her wages. There were more coins scattered about, a half-crown under the piano and a shilling or two by the chair but be damned if she'll scramble for them.

'I'll walk with you,' said Fred.

'You will not!'

'I'm sorry.'

'Don't apologise to her!' Annie flew at Fred. 'What have you to be sorry about? You did what any self-respecting bloke would've done seeing a bloke pawing his girl. You told him to lay off.'

'The pilot wasn't pawing me,' said Adelia. 'As for being Fred's girl I was never that. I have told him repeatedly I didn't want his attention. It's not my fault he wouldn't listen.'

'Get you!' Blanche pitched in. 'You think you're so special. With your reputation you ought to be grateful a decent man bothered to try. The others didn't hang around. They got what they wanted and buggered off!'

'Belt up, Blanche!' Fred shouted. 'I don't need you butting in.'

'There was nothing decent about what happened here,' said Adelia. 'The man was talking, that's all.'

'Yes, that's right, Delia,' said Blanche. 'You and your big eyes and your la-di-dah voice, you're good at listening to men. It's how you get your twinkly bits and your fur coat. You should set up a lonely hearts club, hands across the sea sort of lark. You'd be a millionaire in a year.'

'Oh, be quiet, you silly woman!' Adelia pushed by into the yard.

Fred followed still apologising. 'I am sorry, really I am.'

Adelia kept walking. 'I don't want to talk to you.'

Then Annie Carter who'd also had too much to drink ran into the street shouting. 'Get back here Fred Carter and stop making a fool of yourself!'

'For Christ's sake, Mum, go inside!'

'I'm not going anywhere until you stop saying you're sorry. She's a tramp and not worth an apology.'

'Mum! You are making things worse!'

'I don't care. She's nothing but trouble. Everybody says so. I should never have taken her on. I should've listened to Edna James. She said I'd rue the day.'

Adelia turned. 'What's that about Edna?'

'Yes, at the bakery. She's always complaining of you bringing men to the flat. She says one day the police will raid the place and she'll be before the law for keeping a brothel. I said I wouldn't put up with it. If it was my place I'd have slung you out long ago. I dare say she would too if it wasn't for Sophie.'

'What's Sophie got to do with it?'

'She's everything to do with it. She's the reason you're not behind bars. People say you're mad and can't help it. I say you're a slut and the best thing that could happen is that poor little kid taken into care and you in jail. So sling your hook and don't let me see your face either side of bar.'

Furious, Adelia pushed the buggy down the road Fred following behind saying he never wanted this to happen, that he loved her and wanted to marry her and had tried to keep quiet but couldn't take all the others.

'Others?' Adelia demanded. 'What others?'

'The chaps that fancy you.'

'Oh please stop! I don't look to be fancied, as you call it, but if I am it's the man's problem not mine and it shouldn't be yours.'

'How can it not be mine? That bloke tonight leaning on the bar peering down the front of your dress. Christ, his eyes were on stalks.'

'So what now? Are you telling me I shouldn't have worn this dress?'

'No, I'm not.'

'I should damn well hope not because if you thought my neckline low you might have a word with Blanche and everything else hanging out.'

'I don't care about Blanche or what she wears. She'd have looked a tart in her Christening robe. It's you I care about and those leering at you.'

'Well, you can stop caring now because thanks to you I shan't be working at the pub anymore so you won't have to see anyone leer.'

'No!' He shook his head. 'You'll be working there. It will all blow over and you'll have your job back. Mum will come round!'

Adelia stared. 'Maybe she will but I won't. I'm not putting me and Sophie though that again?'

'She didn't mean it. She'd been at the gin. She does it when she's stressed.'

'Of course she meant it! She wouldn't have said it if she didn't! It doesn't matter! I couldn't possibly come back. So, it's best we keep our distance.'

'So that's it, is it? You just going to walk away?'

'God's sake Fred! Have you any idea how I felt there, you making a fuss about nothing and men bashing one another. It is Christmas Eve! Peace of earth and all that! We've only just finished one war and here you are starting another.'

Fred didn't like that. 'And I suppose you had nothing to do with it?'

'I didn't have anything to do with it! I was doing my job listening to a drunk and trying not to yawn and thinking of Sophie and wishing we were home in bed and glad that tomorrow was Christmas Day and no pub which meant I wouldn't have to listen to another drunk.'

'That's not very nice.'

'Possibly not but that's what I was feeling.'

'I thought you liked working there.'

'I didn't mind. It was a job and I needed the money.'

'And was that all it was? Nothing more than a job and everything we did to keep you happy, the goodwill, Mum letting you keep your kid there and me walking you home, that didn't matter?'

'Of course it mattered. I was glad your mother was kind to Sophie. It made life easier but if I'd known it was against her better judgement and that she believed me a tart I'd have worked anywhere rather than be in receipt of that kind of goodwill.' Seeing Sophie upset Adelia bit anger back. 'But I've said enough. The best thing now is we go our separate ways and no hard feelings.'

Adelia set off down the path and he followed.

'No hard feelings?' He was angry. 'You must be joking! Of course there are hard feelings! Any man would be pissed off after that. All the hand holding and kissing fingers, it made me sick to watch it.'

'Then you should've looked away! You had no right to be watching as you have no right to be following me around! My life is my life. It has nothing whatever to do with you!'

'Hey!' He grabbed hold of the pushchair swinging it round. 'Don't you bloody talk to me like that! I'm not one of your free and easy Yanks who you can pick up and put down at the drop of a hat. I don't wear a fancy uniform or flash my wallet buying fur coats and Christ knows what! I'm just an ordinary bloke who had the nerve to care for you but who got sick of being left dangling.'

Furious, spittle on his lips he leaned close. 'I don't think my mother was so far off calling you a tart. I reckon she was spot on because deep down that's what you are, a tart who promises one thing but who inside is cold as ice.'

Adelia slapped him, the slap echoing down the street.

'Why you!' He grabbed her wrist and was pulling her forward when suddenly he was pitched backwards, sliding through the snow to cannon into the wall.

Adelia didn't know what happened and didn't stop to find out. Head down she ran the last few yards only turning to look as she put the key in the lock.

Fred was up on his feet staring back down the path as though watching someone walk away. She looked but couldn't see anything beyond swirling snow that in the lamplight might have been wings.

Thirty-three
Trail of Glory

Adelia woke the following day with an aching head and echoes of glass breaking. Through the open door she could see the sable coat. It had slid off the sofa onto the floor. She ought to hang it up. It's worth that if nothing else.

Sad today and feeling terribly lonely she lay thinking about the Squadron Leader's 'trail of glory' and how she will miss the Americans and the energy they brought. Such faces, so alive and so intent on being so! They brought new blood to Needham. England will never be the same.

Last night the Squadron Leader addressed her as Miss Challoner. Either he forgot to append her former married title or Bobby's prolonged absence has exploded the myth. Having seen the name *Adelia Rourke* inside the sable she's guessing Bobby prefers to perpetuate the fairy story but then having laid out hundreds of dollars he probably feels entitled and plans to further his claim by branding it on her backside the moment she sets foot on Virginian soil.

'He's letting the world know ownership,' she brooded. 'A bit like the 'Kilroy was here' graffiti seen on lavatory walls.' But then what's in a name. Few people actually use her true Christian name, always a variety.

She drew the curtains and stared out of the window. It's snowing. A radio next door plays 'Jingle Bells.' Events of the night are bitty the major memory being a piano playing and Annie with her mouth open and malice in her eyes.

It's back to names again and this time she is a tart. 'I wonder if that's a step up or down. I mean, in marks out of ten do I get less marks for being a stuck up cow than I do for a tart. I'll ask Edna. She'll know.'

Tart is a small word yet cruel when said of a woman by another woman. Adelia had thought she and Annie got on. They used to laugh about Sam and the mini-zoo in the back garden, nothing nasty, two women sharing a working day. Now Adelia is the joke and Sophie seen as a poor little kid.

The poor little kid is in the sitting-room sucking a lump of barley-sugar and singing her version of a song to what looks to be another knitted monkey.

'*Here we are again, 'appy s'affer be, all good pals and jolly chumpany.*'

Silly, but hearing her sing made Adelia cry. It was the way she sang and rocked the toy monkey, innocent and carefree and ready for a new day.

Adelia took to the bathroom to sit on the loo hiding her tear-stained face. Nothing seems to work out. If she believed in fate she might think they're not meant to be in Needham, that greater forces are leaving hefty clues along the way and pig-headed or blind she is missing every one.

She ran a bath, climbed in and lay looking at cracks in the ceiling and going over Fred Carter's last shot. He followed them home last night pleading forgiveness but with his apologies rejected another Fred surfaced, a bitter man able to say things a man should never say to a woman no matter the cause.

Then Sophie shuffled out of her pjs and into the bath. She hugged Adelia. 'Don't cry mummy. ' Mother and daughter against the world they clung together all hurts left outside the door.

~

Later that morning they took flowers to the cemetery. It's ten years since her parents died and a year since Nora and Bill. Adelia misses Nora so much. She remembers the James bringing the news. Such a shock!

It was an odd day, displaced. She slipped in the snow and fell against the dust-bin and in a dazed state thought she was with Joe, the soldier ghost, who talked of grandparents, that love made them not an official bit of paper.

She hasn't seen Joe in a while or for that matter the tramp, that other will-of-the-wisp with whom she used to share a sandwich.

It's weeks since she's been to St Giles. Working at the pub nights and busy during the day there hasn't been time. There was a notice yesterday in the market-place, ten o clock tonight a Candle-lit Mass marking the end of the war to be held in the ruins. Though late they will go so that Sophie can send love to the Nana and Granddad she never got to meet and a kiss to the Grandparents who for a short time so enriched her life.

They'll take flowers. Norah loved poppies. Last autumn she and Adelia went picking potatoes. It was hard work but they didn't mind because the sun shone and the tractor unearthed pink-eyed King Edwards to take home to roast.

Land-girls worked alongside singing as they worked their voices ringing out over the fields. Lunchtime they picnicked on bread and cheese and milk from the churn. Then it was back to work everyone taking turns to sit in the shade with Sophie. It was a day filled with the love of ordinary things, of flowers in the hedgerow, red poppies for Nora and blue cornflowers for Adelia, a wonderful day noted by a Land-girl tipping her face to the sky, 'heavenly.'

Today Adelia brings a poinsettia. Scarlet leaves bright against the snow it shines out over the graveyard. It will be dead tomorrow as those underground. The frost will kill it. It doesn't matter. Norah will have seen the flag of love fluttering and know it was for her.

~

Sophie is playing with the knitted monkey.

'What's the monkey's name?' Adelia asked.

'Coco.'

'And where did you find Coco?'

'Pussy-cat had it in her pocket.'

It was a sweet little toy and beautifully knitted, so much neater than the original. 'I see Coco has red flying goggles!'

Sophie nodded. 'Like my Daddy.'

All this time you'd think she'd forget Bobby but she forgets nothing. Mr Covington Wright says she has an eidetic memory, the ability to vividly recall both audio and visual memories. He said, 'it will be useful in her education.'

Andrew Covington Wright came to see them. He said he was retiring from peripatetic work and will be based in London but that she was to think of him as always there for her and Sophie. Adelia kissed him. She said she was grateful for his kindness. His response was symptomatic of the man. 'I wish I could've helped more. Your case has been of some concern to me these last years and will remain so.' He gave her his card. 'If you need help I am here.'

This total recall comes of Sophie's father. If it helps with education then fine. It's a darn sight more useful than sable. Then again total recall won't buy food whereas you can always sell a sable coat.

The idea of selling the coat was prompted by this morning's mail.

Coins jingling, an envelope was pushed through the letter-box. Two shilling pieces and a half-crown it was the rest of her wages. There was a note.

'I'm posting this so no one can say you were cheated of what was owed. We've always tried to treat you fair and square. Our Fred heartbroken it's a pity you didn't return the favour. Annie Carter. PS. You left a blanket in the spare room. If you want it you'd better collect it by the end of the week or I'll burn it.'

The door is really closed. Not that Adelia could've gone back, not to Fred's injured glances. She woke in the night and remembering his anger looked to see if he was outside in the street gazing up at the window as he had done before. He wasn't there, hopefully that's the last she'll see of him.

Unnerving, the flat at the top of the stairs is beginning to feel like a tiny island eroded by the sea. Every day a bit more nibbled away, it only needs a heavy tide and they are high and dry.

~

Five o clock Edna knocked on the door. 'Can I come in?'

'Of course! Happy Christmas, Edna!' There was a strange hiatus then, both women offering a kiss on the cheek but the kiss never really landing.

'No Ted?' Adelia surveyed the landing.

'No. He woke with a sore throat this morning and thought best not to pass it on. He sends his best.'

'Poor Ted! I understand there's a lot of it about. Do give him our love.'

'I will.' Edna hovered. Then seeing Sophie with the monkey swooped down. 'What's that, a monkey! And with an RAF badge. Did it come with the coat?'

'It was in one of the pockets.'

'Isn't that nice. He was a thoughtful bloke that Bobby if a bit common. So, are you pleased with the coat? Does it look good?'

'I don't know. I haven't tried it on yet.'

'You haven't tried it? My word, Delia! You are a cool one! I wouldn't have been able to resist.'

'I will try it sooner or later. Can I offer you a sherry, Edna? We have some left over from last Christmas.'

'No thanks. I just dropped by to bring Sophie a gingerbread man Ted made.'

'That is kind of him. We'll keep it for later.'

'And one other thing.'

Adelia was suddenly afraid. Edna is the bearer of bad news. Last time it was of Nora and Bill and the V2 rocket. What is it this time a surging tide?

Edna offered a box. 'I came to give you this.'

'What it is?'

'Open it and you'll see.'

It was a powder compact.

'We've had it engraved on the inside. Click it and it opens! See what it says, 'to an angel with amnesia try not to forget us ''

'Oh, how thoughtful.'

'We thought you might like it.' Edna coughed. 'It's a going away present.'

'You are going away?'

'Yes, well not straight away, but yes, eventually. It's Ted. He's not getting any younger and I've more than had enough. It's why I am here. I thought best to tell you what we've decided.'

As though a switch had been pulled and a curtain raised last night's revelation popped into Adelia's head, how Edna advised against employing her.

She set the compact on the table. 'And what have you decided. Is it about me working at the Duke of Wellington? A belated reference perhaps, saying what an honest person I am. How I always keep up with the rent and am tidy and quiet and worth having as a lodger?'

Edna stared. 'er...no.'

'That's as well because as you've no doubt heard I don't work there anymore. I was sacked last night.'

'Sacked?'

'Yes, sacked! Given the boot! Chucked out and my wages thrown at me.'

'What do you mean?'

'I mean I was told to leave. That I was a trouble-making tart who should never have worked there and that Annie had been warned against me.'

Edna shrugged. 'I hadn't heard that.'

'Really? I am surprised.' Fingernails cutting into her palms Adelia stared. 'It wasn't exactly a quiet sacking. It was a noisy event, glass breaking and noses being punched. I would have thought half of Suffolk heard about it and as always ever there when passing on the news I felt sure you would've heard.'

'I didn't. Ted being ill we didn't go out much.'

'Of course! Poor Ted, such a gentleman. I'm sorry he is not well. Now what was it you came to say? There is a service this evening at St Giles, a Candlelight Mass for those killed during the war Sophie and I plan to be there.'

'At St Giles? I didn't know about that.'

'You didn't? Good heavens, Edna, this is not like you! You're usually so on top of village affairs. What's happened to get between you and news?'

Cheeks flushed, knowing she was found out Edna bit back. 'I've had a lot on my plate! What with Christmas and our Beryl being pregnant and wanting us nearer, and trade as it is, people never satisfied and always grumbling about something, and you can't get the help nowadays, and...and...!'

'And Ted not well?'

'Yes! And with Ted not very well we've come to a decision. We're going to sell the shop and move closer to the new baby!'

'Of course you are!'

Adelia let go of anger. What is the point of it? It's not Edna's fault she got the sack anymore than she is to blame for the upheaval that continually threatens their life. This is Adelia Challoner's life one problem after another and the poor little kid, Sophie, suffering because of it.

'Of course you are,' she said it again aware that the Black Hole that is her memory is already at work taking the sharper thorns and spitting them out to places unknown, and that while she knows what is being said here and now at quarter past five on December 24th 1945 the chances of retaining the exact matter of the day and the conversation are nil.

'It's alright, Edna. I understand.'

'You do?'

'Yes. I would want to be near my daughter if she was pregnant.'

Surprised to be let off the hook so easily Edna made for the door. 'It's not the best news for you, I know that, but you see I must do it.'

'I do see. You must do what's best for your family.'

'Yes! Family must come first and our Beryl is not the best manager.'

'Have you put the bakery up for sale? I heard you were thinking of selling but that you didn't think there was much money about.'

'That was the case but.... but we've had a bit of good luck. We had a win on the pools. Not much, but it will bridge the gap.'

'Bridge the gap?'

'Pay off the mortgage and make life that bit easier all round.'

It struck Adelia then that Edna was fibbing and a silly fib at that. 'What a coincidence. Didn't Nora have a similar win some time back? I should have spent more time with you, Edna. Your luck might've rubbed off.' The sable on the floor again she swooped lobbing it back. 'When do you want us out?'

'Oh, there's no rush! You've plenty time to find a place. Our Beryl's not due until May and the shop needs decorating before it goes on sale. I just thought to give you fair warning.

'Thank you, I appreciate your concern and on Christmas Day too!'

Edna left. Clearly irate at being mauled by her tart of a lodger she paused on the stairs to shout 'that bloody Yank rung their home number saying he'd booked a call person-to-person on the bakery line for six o clock.'

'He called about a government programme, women being offered free trips to America to see their men-folk. GI Bride programme, he called it. Says it's in all the newspapers. I made a note of the address you're to contact and left it by the phone. Take the call but don't keep him talking.'

Edna stomped away. 'Bloody cheek calling us at home! Ted wasn't at all amused. People should get a phone of their own if they want to talk long distance. We're not the GPO!'

~

When the phone rang Adelia was dressing. 'Stay put, Sophie! I'm going down to answer the phone.'

Sophie got down off the chair. 'It's Daddy so I come!'

'Not today, love. It's Christmas. Others will want to call their families.'

Adelia ran down. The operator put them through. 'Hello?'

There was a click and there he was. 'Hi, honey, how you doing?'

Such warmth in his voice, it wrapped round her like a bandage.

'Hello, Bobby. It's good to hear your voice.'

'Yes, and you, sweetheart. It's been an age.'

'Thank you for the coat.'

'Oh you got it! I'm glad. Is it okay?'

'It's wonderful. I've never seen a coat like it.'

'I'll bet.' He laughed. 'What did you do sell it to the pawnbroker under the bridge where you got the buggy?'

Good God! Adelia blushed. He might have been reading her thoughts. 'Of course not! You bought it for me I wouldn't do that.'

'You can do what you like with it. It's your coat. If you wanted to swap it for cash go ahead. Once it's left me it's all yours.'

For a minute she couldn't speak.

'Hello? You still there?'

'I'm still here. I was thinking what a generous man you are.'

'You think so?'

'I do.'

'Well, honey, let me tell in terms of givin' if I thought it would help I'd lay down my life for you never might a fur coat. That's how much you mean to me.'

'Oh, Bobby, I do miss you.'

'And I miss you. You have no idea how much.'

'Did you get the pullover?'

'What d'you think I'm wearin'.'

'It was new wool this time.'

'I don't care, honey. New or old there's a piece of you in it and that's present enough for me.'

Adelia began to cry. She didn't mean to. She felt so alone and he was kind and so sad, she could hear it in his voice. 'Are you alright, Bobby?'

'I've been better. Did you get my message about the GI programme?'

'Hold on a minute.' Adelia wanted to wipe her eyes but Edna a fanatic for tidiness there was nothing on the counter, not even a paper bag. There was a note-pad with address and phone numbers regarding the US Military GI Bride Programme.

Phone under her chin, Adelia tore off that sheet and was fumbling for a pen when she saw the poison pen letter. It was there in her hand, the same red ink and angry scrawl.

Those poison pen letters! The writer was angry when she wrote them. You could see how the pen had dug into the words almost tearing the paper. It's the same here with this note, same heavy hand, plus the letters are the same, they swirl and loop in the poisonous D in Delia as they swirl and loop here in the Department of Defence, every D blown out at the top and narrow at the bottom, pouter-pigeon, you might say and not unlike Edna James.

Everything matches, every letter the same as those in the notes upstairs in the bottom drawer of the dresser. An angry woman wrote this, the same anger heard on the stairs; *'Bloody cheek using our phone. People should get a phone of their own if they want to call long-distance. What are we the GPO?'*

'Oh Edna!' Adelia felt sick. 'How could you?'

Edna wrote the notes! It made sense, how the notes were on the mat early morning and how details of Adelia's day was known, what she did and when.

Edna of all people! Adelia had thought it was the woman from the Morality League but as Bobby said pitchforks were waved and this time by a friend.

'Dee?' Bobby is on the line. 'Say, Dee? Are you there?'

'Yes. I'm here.'

'Are you okay? It went so quiet I thought we'd been cut off.'

'No, I'm still here.' Adelia wiped her nose on her sleeve and then stuffed the note in her pocket. 'Bobby, can I ask you a question?'

'Sure! You can ask me what you like. If I can answer I will. If I can't and it keeps you on the line a bit longer I'll pretend I can. So fire away.'

'What do you want for Christmas?'

'Beg pardon?'

'Simple question. What do you wish most for Christmas?'

There was a moment then he said, 'what I've always wanted, you and Sophie to come to the States to be with me.'

'Then happy Christmas, Bobby. You have your wish.'

'What?'

'You have your wish. We'll do this GI Bride thing and come to America.'

Then it was Adelia's turn to think they'd been cut-off. He was silent for so long she laughed. 'Oh my God! Don't tell me this has always been a joke. That it was never anything but a game?'

'No way!' His voice crashed back through the line. 'This is no joke. It never was a joke nor ever will be! This is the God's honest truth. It's what I want and have always wanted. Come! Never mind the GI Bride watchamacallit! Get on the first plane out or a berth on the Queen Mary! Anyway you like! Just come.'

'I will come.'

'You will?'

'Yes.'

'Promise?'

'I promise.'

'Swear on Sophie's life.'

'I swear.'

'That'll do it. Now you have to come.'

'Yes.' Adelia turned. Sophie was at the door listening. 'Now we have to come.'

~

Adelia is getting ready for church. She was ready before the telephone call but as the Squadron Leader said things happen and what was right last year is wrong this. Before the telephone call an everyday coat was right for the vigil but St Giles being Patron Saint of the Outcast, and Adelia surely that, she believes a change of clothes befitting.

With the exception of the red raincoat everything in the wardrobe was bought with the idea of mingling with the crowd. Be damned with the crowd! The Mass at St Giles under the magnificent East Window is not for creeping about. It is for making an entrance! For striding down the nave looking fabulous in a sable coat and boots with heels and the black lace mantilla Bobby sent that looks so well against her hair.

Yes, damn them! What is it they say, if you've got it flaunt it and the coat is certainly It.

'Pretty mummy,' Sophie is dressed and sits in her tiger bonnet watching.

Adelia took out a lipstick, and real lipstick at that, no beetroot tonight, Chanel's *Red for Danger* Bobby sent through the post: '*you so pale skinned it might be a bit red for you but better red than dead and lipsticks are considered good for morale and the one thing NOT rationed here in the US.*'

It is red, very red and that Other Adelia, the one who is called tart by so-called friends, wouldn't be seen dead in it!

'But that's okay!' This Adela likes it and smiles in the mirror. 'A woman should wear the colour that suits her soul, don't you think?'

Earlier she came away from the telephone call hating the world and everyone in it. Angry, a pain deep within her soul, she wanted to march down the road and rake Edna out asking why she would sink so low.

'What made you do it? Was it because I chose Nora for Godparents and not you? Or is it closer to home and your daughter too long conceiving because that was your regular moan, a drab of a daughter and feckless son-in-law who wouldn't know an honest day's work if it jumped up and bit him but always losing money on the horses and putting you, his mother-on-law, into a constant state of worry and not at all good for Ted's Health.'

'Mummy.'

' Is that it? Was it jealousy of me and Sophie behind it? But then how could you envy my crazy head and fear of becoming more crazy? Did you want to change places with that nightmare!'

'Mummy!'

'I should call her out so everyone knows! She'll there tonight at the vigil. She wouldn't miss that, not with everyone else there.' Hand shaking, the lipstick making a clown of her mouth, Adelia reddened her lips again. 'And she can have her stupid compact back. I don't want it!'

'Mummy!'

'And I shall say my name is Adelia, not Delia. ADELIA, don't you know! If you can't say it right don't bother saying it at all!'

'Mummy!' Sophie is tugging her arm.

'What!'

'Don't Mummy!'

'Don't what?'

'Please don't shake so!'

'Oh Sophie!' Adelia snatched up. 'I'm sorry, darling, did I scare you?'

'Yes you did!'

'Well, I'm alright now, sweetheart. I am shaking because I've had a bit of a shock but it's over now.'

They wept together, Sophie stroking her mother's tear-stained cheek. 'Pretty, mummy.' Adelia sobs and kisses her again and again, 'and my pretty Sophie.'

~

Late arriving they found the church thronged with people and the service almost over and so took a place at the back by the West Gate.

So many people! Most of the village are here, the High Street shopkeepers and local tradesmen. There's the Minister from St James and his wife talking with the librarian. Edna and the ailing Ted, poor fellow wrapped in scarves, stand by the wall along with Sam and Annie Carter and over there standing apart is Blanche Hobley links arms with Fred.

Ted sees them and waves but Edna tugs his arm and he turns away. Sam Carter, always a genial fellow, smiles. Adelia returns his smile. She has no quarrel with Sam or anyone else if it distresses Sophie. It's alright, everything is alright. There'll be no more scenes and certainly no bringing Edna to book. Now it's a question of looking forward and biding time until they are gone.

They missed the dedication service but in time for communion.

A queue is already forming, people moving toward an altar table where the priest and his servers prepare the Host.

'I get out, mummy!' says Sophie.

The harness released and the chair pushed to one side they join the queue and hand-in-hand shuffle toward the altar.

Everyone has brought a candle. There are a few long tapers left yet most now are flickering nubbins of wax. Sophie wanted to bring the purple hippopotamus candle that Bobby gave her Christmas '43 but couldn't bear to set fire to it and so carries a nightlight in her gloved hands.

It is cold out yet the sky is clear and the stars out in abundance.

A choir sing carols, the words of 'Oh Holy Night' drifting over the crowd.

'*Oh Holy Night the stars are brightly shining it is the night of Our Dear Saviour's Birth. Long lay the world in sin and Error pining Til He appeared and the Soul felt its worth.*'

There's not a breath of air, the bare bones of the church stand out against a dark sky and the East Window a trail of glory amid a sea of twinkling light.

Adelia knows the window is gone, that it was destroyed in 1940 when a bomb blew it and the congregation to glory yet in this dreaming state she sees it alive and glowing as she sees the people and hears them singing. Maybe it is a lie and as everyone says she is quite crazy yet there's kindness tonight in being crazy and such comfort she wishes others could see what she sees.

Sophie smiled. 'So pretty, mummy.'

Adelia grasped her hand. 'Do you see it, Sophie?'

'Yes.'

'What do you see?'

'An angel and a pretty lady in a blue dress.'

'Yes.' A tear slipped down Adelia's cheek. 'An Angel and a pretty Lady in a blue dress.'

It is their turn at the altar. They kneel together.

A breeze passed through the crowd, a hundred candles flickering.

Sophie's night-light flickered and seems to go out.

'Oh no, mummy!' she gasped.

A hand reached out cupping the flame so that it sprang out again in a golden crocus of light.

Adelia knew who knelt beside them on red velvet cushions her sable coat swirling about his knees. It could only be one person, the one who in sharing a cheese and tomato sandwich shared her isolation. But then the Communion Cup was offered and she looked and saw that she was wrong.

If only for a moment a man did kneel beside her accepting the pain of the Lord Jesus Christ it wasn't the tramp, not he of the silver eyes and golden hair, at least not wholly. It was a man with eyes as blue as the living sky, and seeing him there, if only for the moment, anger slid away lost in his eyes.

Thirty-four
Business Deal
February 1946
The Old Mill, Fredericksburg.

'Shit! Shit! Shit!'

Bobby rolled under the blanket stuffing the flying scarf in his ears.

It's five in the morning and he's here again, Sergeant Gabriel Templar hammering and sawing like a crazy man.

Bobby hates the sight of the fucker. He doesn't want him here! He'd sooner drop off the edge of the world than need him but he does need him and needs him fast because every minute of every day brings them closer.

They are coming! They are truly coming! It's all arranged; they've got the tickets booked on the Edmund B and arrive the first week in May.

Okay, they are not coming in an upper deck cabin on the Queen Mary or flying first-class as was suggested. He got round that as too sudden and began dropping hints how Dee should get used to the idea and that paper-work regarding the GI Programme was needed and that it's cold in the early months and better for Sophie if they came toward the summer, and that he's working with ex-fliers setting up a flying school.

Waffle, waffle, and a thousand excuses, he couldn't go in too hard because she might wonder if he wanted them to come. So shocked was he when she did agree Christmas Day he almost blew it, silence offering a million words.

She laughed. 'Was I not supposed to say yes? Was it only ever a game?'

Then the scared Bobby, the one who'd deceived them all wanted to yell, 'of course it was a game, you silly bitch! I played with the idea of you coming but never in a million years believed you would!'

For good or ill Bobby kept his trap shut in the hope that once here she would stay. Then he panicked. What were they coming to bare boards? He needed to get the Mill sorted, to buy furniture and make the place half-way decent.

Now there's hammering and banging and it's his fault, Gabe Templar out there chipping ice off the water-barrel. But for him Bobby would've found a way out but that man kept the nightmare alive asking what was he doing bringing a girl like that to a dump like this, and then not content with the answer started busting his gut trying to make it less of a dump.

This kicked off last June. Gabe Templar was home on leave. They met in the Hawaiian Bar, yours truly so drunk he could barely breathe never mind walk. He got a lift back here to the Mill at which point, as a gesture of goodwill, you might say, he got the galloping trots and shit his pants.

'Oh my God!' He groaned thinking about it. The shame of it! Standing bare-assed in the yard sobbing his heart out and the man he hated most in the world hosing him down! If he was to live to a hundred he'd never get over it.

Gabe Templar made it worse by not cussing him out and after cleaning him up all but carried him to his couch in the tower. When Bobby woke next morning the guy was gone but came back later with coffee and a steak sandwich.

That's when he asked, 'who is this girl and what is she to you?'

Bobby couldn't tell the truth, how he'd stolen Dee from his best friend and lied to keep her and was still lying, that she'd no idea of his accident, that as far as she knew he was the guy she met in '42, the Dashing Captain America, and that he strung her along in the hope she and her kid would come to America.

Unable to say any of that he pared it down to the bare bones, his fiancé and their little girl are coming to Fredericksburg, that he and Dee Challoner plan to marry but being ill he hadn't been able to get the house right.

Templar was ill himself that day. Pale as death, he had some sort of ague and shook so the couch he leant on shifted halfway across the room. It shocked Bobby. He's never known him ill. Even in '34 when he got fifteen years did he didn't look like that a painted puppet with the guts pulled out.

Bobby asked if he was okay but the guy was gone, 'I gotta sort a couple of things.' The couple of things turned out to be him laying off a four-year stint in the Philippines with the Corps in favour of Quantico and home-rotation, not that he said any of that to Bobby, news of that came as it always does via Ruby.

She came to the Mill one morning daggers drawn. 'What's this I hear about you havin' a foreign finance.'

'I think you mean fiancé,' says Bobby.

'Never mind what I mean! Is it true you got a girl back in Britain and are bringin' her and her kid here to live?'

'What if it is?'

'It ain't gonna happen.' She's goes on a rant. 'You're not bringin' any foreign girl here to shame me, Baby Rourke, and you certainly ain't bringin' her kid to let the world know what you've been doin' these last years.'

He told her to mind her own business. It was his life to live as he chose. He could bring whoever he liked. It was nothing to do with her. 'I could bring the Queen of England and her two princesses home and you couldn't stop me.'

She grins then real nasty. 'But you're not bringin' a princess. You're bringin' a two-bit trollop who's had a kid and wants you to pay for it.'

That's the trouble with Ma. She knows when he is lying. She's always known and once again was on the money. 'Yeah, that's right,' she's still grinning. 'This is some other man's leavin's. You're the fool got caught with the bill.'

She said she wasn't going to be grand-mammy to any foreign bastard and had a quote from the bible ready to make her point: Deuteronomy 23-2:' *A bastard shan't enter the church of the Lord even until the tenth generation.*'

That was when Gabe turned up with a wagon-load of wood and rolling up his sleeves starts unloading.

'What's he doin' here?' says Ma snapping her jaws.

Bobby shrugs. 'He's lookin' to make a few extra bucks.'

'I heard he'd passed on fightin' for settlin' with his Ma,' she says. 'I wasn't surprised. The Marines get him out of jail free and he pays them back by droppin' out the first chance he gets. Yellow-belly coward, I call it.'

Bobby said he was helping put the Mill back to rights.

'I hope you got him cheap,' she says. 'He ain't no master craftsman. He'll do more harm than good. And I wouldn't leave anythin' valuable lyin' about either when he's around. You're likely to find it missin'.'

If he heard any of that Gabe never said. He was busy unloading wood and setting up a work table in the yard. Then without a by-your-leave he's kicked the cottage door open and is in ripping loose tack off the wall.

'What d you think you're doin'?' says Bobby.

Gabe turns and with such hate in his eyes Bobby was flung back against a wall. 'What do you think I'm doin',' he says. 'I'm savin' your ass.'

It was hot that day. He started hammering and hasn't stopped. Morning, noon and night any break from Quantico he's here. Bobby keeps quiet. Words are dangerous, a little sympathy and a lot of Jim Beam and before you know it the truth is out and whilst he doesn't know what drives the man he sees the outcome, a phoenix rising from the mess that was the cottage.

Gabe won't touch the Mill. 'That's your problem,' he says. 'I haven't got time. Hire a couple of guys you go flyin' with and fix the roof if nothing else.'

Bobby did that. He went to the abandoned airfield where ex-USAAF pilots hang out and spread the word that if they wanted to earn dough they could help with the Mill. A restless bunch with nothing to do and nowhere to go they are unreliable and like Bobby prefer drink to work, even they got the roof fixed and the generator working.

~

March '46

The cottage is all but finished, Gabe presently fixing shutters on the windows. Bobby took a photograph of it yesterday to send to England. He sends a pic nearly every day detailing changes. He writes on the back, '*the latest on your boudoir, ma'am,*' that kind of thing. She wrote the other day saying how well he'd done and that she couldn't wait to see the house. He's not inclined to send pics of the Mill. The dark humour hanging over the place would put anyone off. He never mentions Gabe. If she thinks Bobby does the work that's okay. As long as everything is tip-top when she arrives no one need know otherwise.

Every night when Gabe's gone he nips inside to see how he's doing. The place is looking good. Walls re-plastered, floors sanded, no rough edges to hurt a little kid everything is smooth as silk, if you didn't know the circumstance you'd think this a labour of love and Gabe the man waiting for his bride.

You have to wonder why he does it. I mean, why does he? What's in it for him? It can't be the dough! The whole thing of him being here freaks Bobby out. He has nightmares about it. The other night he walked in his sleep and woke in the cottage bedroom with muck under his fingernails where he had been scratching the newly plastered wall.

Next day Gabe asked about the marks. Bobby said it was probably mice. It was the dumb dream. In it he was paying Gabe for the work done and he was paying him plenty but not with bank notes with bricks!

Yeah bricks! He was taking bricks out the wall and piling them up in his arms and what's more Gabe was refusing. 'I don't want them,' he is saying. 'I never wanted them. They don't belong to me.'

It the whisky! That's what it is! Bobby has got to stop going to the old hut on the airstrip. Mixing with them layabouts does not help. He had a whole bunch of them down the other night drinking and making noise. In the end he threw them out, one guy thinking it clever to play with a tray of rose-cuttings.

No respect for people's belongings! Bobby doesn't care what they do but they are not messing with his roses. They are his life-line! While he's working with them he's not thinking how alone he is. You want Bobby these days you'll find him in the greenhouse by the willows or top of the tower layering the cuttings in best compost.

Fragile things they are not to be messed with. The Gloire de Versailles and white Damask took a hammering. It took ages to get the poor little buggers comfortable again. It's cold up in the tower. He sat up most of last night with a heater trying to warm the compost. They are recovering but it was close. At one time they were so close to dying he thought of asking Gabe to lay a little spook in them like he used to do with people's sick pets.

I mean, what's the difference between a dog and rose? If he can make a dog feel better he can do the same with a tray of rose cuttings?

Weird guy! Everybody used to talk about his way with animals. Bobby knows of horse people who regularly sent for Gabe when they were off their food. You don't hear it so much now. It's Gabe Templar the hero now. Not the spook.

See! He's down there now stripped to the waist white-washing walls! Why is he here all the time? Doesn't he have any other life? And what's happening with Sexy Sue? She comes and stands on the edge of Bayonet Woods but never speaking to Bobby or Gabe, only watching, her eyes big and dark as though seeing a door closing in her life.

It is a mystery. Bobby gets scared. He feels his life is out of control and that a Great Big Wheel is rolling toward him and it's turning round and round and one day it's gonna crash through those trees and mow him down.

There's no sense to anything anymore. And what about money! All that wood and paint Gabe's bought but not a mention of payment. Bobby wasn't going to let him work for nothing. No sir! And every day would stuff a bunch of notes in the top-drawer of the dresser Gabe was after rubbing down.

Weeks went by and him not taking and Bobby giving it got to be quite a bundle. Then May turns up and starts hanging drapes in the bedrooms. Something must have been said because by evening the money was gone.

It's her collecting it. A thrifty woman and having to scrape when Hodge was alive May keeps an eye on cash. But why wouldn't Gabe take what was owed when craft's man or not he's doing a first class job. And why is May Templar helping. Her pitching in and him working all hours, there has to be a reason. Is it more spooky stuff? Is Bobby the latest sickly critter he's chosen to help?

Working and getting paid to do it is one thing but doing a favour for a cripple is another. Just thinking about it Bobby wants to pull a pistol and run down shouting, 'tell me what's going on because if this is you doing me a favour you can stop right now. The only favour you could ever do me is to start walkin' and never come back!'

Though every minute is harder to stomach he holds back because deep down he suspects it's not about him. This is about the girl in the photograph.

Gabe knows Adelia Challoner. Recognition was there in his eyes. There is a link though what Bobby doesn't know. Maybe he was struck by her face.

She does have that affect. Everyone stares, they can't help themselves.

Last night he was upstairs on his hands and knees measuring the back bedroom. Bobby stood at the door. 'What you measurin' for?'

'A bed for the kiddie.'

'Should you be doin' that?'

'Why?' Gabe looks up. 'Have you thought of gettin' one then?'

'I have been thinkin' along those lines,' says Bobby.

He leans back on his heels. 'And what have you decided?'

'I don't know. I guess I could nab into Richmond and get somethin' sorted.'

Still he leans, one hand on his knee and those lazar eyes cutting through flesh and bone. He knows Bobby's not going anywhere, especially Richmond, a creature of the night he finds it nigh impossible to go out during the day.

As for thinking of beds and where they might sleep he hasn't thought of anything, not of them sleeping, or eating, or doing anything real because to him they are still in the realm of dreams.

Bobby retreats. 'I'll leave the cot with you then, old sport. You seem to know what you're doin.'

'Your choice,' he says.

'Sure, and anythin' else you feel like doin'!' Bobby backs off. 'I'm busy with the main house so best you carry on here. This is where they'll be livin' until me and Dee get to know one another again. It's been a while, if you get my drift.'

Gabe carried on measuring.

Bobby hovered. 'Was you thinkin' of makin' a bed for her?'

'I had thought of doin' it.'

'Good, then go ahead. Make them a matchin' pair, mother and daughter. Same with linen and rugs! Get everythin' you need. Don't worry about cost. And while you're at it maybe you could make my little Sophie a doll. I know you're good at stuff like that.'

He rattled on about nothing, saying how grateful he was for the work Gabe was doing and that he couldn't have managed without him and that when Dee is here maybe he and his Ma could come for dinner.

Talking, talking and all the while Gabe is measuring, head to one side and shoulders square and tense as though waiting for a question.

Then a question comes. 'You ever been to England, Gabe?'

'No.'

'Spent most of your war in the Pacific, Guadalcanal and the like?'

'Yes.'

'And never anywhere near a place called Needham in Suffolk.'

'No.'

Gabe packed up and drove away. Bobby climbed to his lonely perch. He could have asked if he knew Dee but that would've been stupid. If he's never been to England how can he know her? It's just Bobby being paranoid.

Yesterday Bobby called England but not to speak to Dee, he avoids talking with her. Though hopeful of things working out in the US she's scared. He hears it in her voice. It makes him feel bad. Last time he called she said she'd had a visit from the Red Cross and was told she and Sophie would be staying in an army camp the week before leaving and they would be seen by doctors.

'For yet another medical check, would you believe,' she said. 'I tell you, Bobby, if this wasn't so very important I would've told the US authorities what they can do with their GI programme.'

He said not to fret, that he'd had visits from the Red Cross. Fact is he did have one but via the phone and it was more or less a check list.

It was Dee's jailor he called yesterday, Mrs Edna James.

That woman hates him! He hears it. She'd like to tell him to go to hell but them conjoined twins in the Devil's Deed she must suffer him a while.

War does things to people. It brings out the best and the worst, his offer at Christmas to loan her and her old man money brought a burst of indignation. 'What sort of a person do you think I am?' she spat down the phone. 'I can cope with you helping to pay the rent. It's a good flat. You said she needed help and so we agreed thinking it helped everyone. But offering us a loan so she has to move is underhand. I'll not be part of it.'

It was a tricky moment. Edna James is no fool. She knew he wanted to force Adelia's hand and though she didn't fancy being a pawn in the game she still wanted rid of the shop. So, having checked the going price for the bakery and offering enough for the donkey to appreciate the size of the carrot, he said she'd misunderstood; he was offering to *buy* the bakery not loan them money, that there was nothing underhand about it, that buying the bakery would relieve Dee of all her monetary worries so that if in the end she chose to remain in England she could and keep the flat while running the bakery.

Edna almost slid through the phone into his arms. She said they wanted to sell but owed a bit on the mortgage and wouldn't be able to buy anything decent in Brighton where their daughter lived. She said Ted had a weak heart and was wearing himself out and that she couldn't wait to retire.

'Problem solved,' says he. 'I'm sure there'll be enough left from the sale for you to find a place near your daughter and there's no rush. You can take your time. Dee doesn't need to know I fund the sale any more than she needed to know I help with the rent. I'll come clean when the time is right. 'Then he thought off the maid, Nora, and applied the *coup de grace*. 'Of course if she wonders how you can suddenly afford to move after saying you can't you can always have a little joke with yourself and say you won the pools.'

'I couldn't say anything like that,' says Edna. 'While I understand about keeping quiet there's no need to fabricate. It's a business deal fair and square.'

'Exactly,' says he, 'a business deal, fair and square.'

~

April '46.

Bobbie is writing a letter. He's been thinking on a comment he made to Gabe Templar about Dee and Sophie staying in the cottage when they first arrive and him sticking to the house. The more he thought about it the more it made sense. It covers all grounds and could be the making of the deal. So he wrote to her suggesting that very thing, '*it will be your own private space. You can live there and not feel pressured into anything. I'll be more than pleased to make you a weekly allowance so you can buy whatever you need. I don't want you worrying about anything especially the intimate stuff. It's some time since we were together, Dee. We need to get to know one another again.*'

It is a real winner because once in the cottage nice and snug and with an ice-box full of food and logs for the fire and all the comforts of home she might think her and Sophie lucky and not be inclined to rock the boat.

Having heard from Mrs J that Dee gave up her job on account of customers getting over-friendly he figures they are struggling for cash and any money left over from her Aunt's place used up. He could send a few bucks but he won't.

Sounds harsh but she needs to struggle. It'll make her think twice before running back home. She may not run. A steel backbone and a kind heart, God willing she'll take one look at him and fight for him not against.

Seeing the letter a last hope he wrote with tears pouring down his cheeks and for a sweetener added a photograph taken in '42 at Biggin Hill, him standing beside a B17. Uniform, flying jacket and all, he looks good in that.

It's how she'll remember him. It's how he remembers himself, one of the few, Flight Lieutenant Robert E Rourke DFC, RAF Eighth Bomber Command.

Letter finished and Gabe gone he did his usual tour of the cottage.

Things are changing all around. He hired a firm of decorators to gussie up the Mill house. They pretty much cleared the ground floor and are now starting on the bedrooms. He'll pay them off soon. There's plenty more needs doing but he can't stand having them around. They were always staring.

The Mill house is old and dangerous. He rattles about inside like a broken toy. He is lonely and afraid and not just for himself. Every night he's on his knees pissed out of his scull begging the Lord to keep them away. If they come here they come to danger because no matter what happens it can never be right.

In the morning he wakes even more scared and cries out to God to bring them. 'Don't let me die like this alone and miserable!'

Back and forth his head is spinning. Sometimes he thinks it would be better and braver to walk away from the Mill and never come back, find a sea to walk into or that old pond, which incidentally has a duck swimming on it now it's been cleaned, one duck as lonesome as he honking half the night.

The thing is he doesn't know how he's going to be able to pick them up. Just can't see how he can meet them looking like this. Someone else will have to go. He did think of paying Ma but she'd sooner leave them stranded.

Of course, there is Gabe Templar. Maybe he would go.

Last night he was upstairs in cottage doing the plumbing. Bobby tiptoed up and stood on the landing trying to pluck up courage to ask. Gabe knew he was there and stopped tinkering, the silence so deep and heavy Bobby could have rolled it.

An hour Bobby stood there and then tiptoed down again.

He won't ask. He can't! Asking is for beggars and Baby Rourke was never a beggar. But what will happen? All those guys on the quay waiting on their girls! Everybody excited, bands playing and flags waving! He saw it on the cinema newsreel when the first boatload arrived. Talk about razzmatazz! Speeches and National Anthem playing, no way can he go through that.

Now, stone cold sober he sits looking out over the pond breathing in linseed oil and polish and listening to a lonely duck calling. He can't stop thinking of Dee, the shock on her face when she sees him! And what about little Sophie! She's likely to run and hide. Dee will want to be kind but will struggle realising the man she crossed an ocean to marry is not a man. He's a bogeyman.

Bobby figures he needs to talk to God because this is God punishing him. Her coming here is payback for a thief and was always going to happen.

He knelt down and prayed. 'I can't do it, Lord. Gabe Templar's the only one I can ask but I'm fearful of him meetin' her. He'll see how beautiful she is and try stealin' her away. I know I stole her from my best friend but don't let him have her. He's okay. He's good-lookin'. I'm the one that looks like shit. So it wouldn't be fair to let him have her. Send him to pick them up but remember you're supposed to love people and forgive their sins! So forgive mine and let me find some fuckin' peace at last.'

Thirty-five
In Thrall

Ma's old dog decided to let go of life. Gabriel was out on the stoop. It is too hot to sleep in the roof and too busy with old news. The night air and Ma's rocking chair is a better option. Daisy lay at his feet. Another who couldn't get comfortable she whimpered until struggling to her feet.

'What is it, old girl?' he asked. Eyes filled with pain she laid back her head and howled. Gabriel knew what she wanted. She wanted to go to the Eyrie.

'Hold on,' he shoved his feet into his boots. 'I'll take you.'

He didn't wake Ma. Twelve years and more of company she loves the dog. It's true that since he's been home nights and at weekends the place is as it was when he was a kid overflowing with critters. All the same Ma can do without watching an old friend die.

Such a quiet night not a breath of air and the moon full he thought on Charlie Whitefeather and how he'd give anything to see him coming through the trees, pock-marked face wobbling fat and all. Then like the old days they could sit and think on life, Charlie philosophising and him the dumb mute.

There's no word among the Corps of Navajo Code Breakers. Working for the military it's likely they are so highly classified as to be non-existent. 'They'll bury it!' this from Gunny Emmett the day he died. 'If Top Brass thinks it a waste of time and resources even if the code were to prove useful the world won't get to hear. It'll always be some dumb asshole's idea and therefore doomed to silence.'

Gabriel wishes Jim Emmet was still alive and that he had his friendship rather than his best boots. A sensible guy, he could advise about taking the truck to New York to collect the girl who has pursued Gabriel's dreams since he was a kid, a girl once thought to be a romantic dream but now known to be a flesh and blood reality on her way to Virginia to marry Bobby Rourke.

Such inner turmoil, the Lord God would have a job advising on that never mind Gunny, much easier for Gabriel to cry for the moon.

Frederiksberg to New York by road is reckoned to take around seven hours. The truck being slow he figures he'll leave around three am.

Bobby Rourke asked him to collect them from the Reception Centre and Gabriel will do it but let it be known he wishes he'd never heard of the woman. Not even here yet already she has screwed his future.

This time last year he was on the brink of becoming the man he'd always wanted to be, a respected man, Sergeant GH Templar, a regular Marine signed into a four-year rotation abroad with the Corps of his own free will not dragged from a prison cell. That was last year. Now he's stationed at Quantico on home-rotation. He's still a

Sergeant and who knows maybe even respected but there's nothing free about his will. He is…what is it Ma says, in thrall.

Ma was angry when she said it. She wanted to know why he was every spare minute working at the Mill. He said he was helping Bobby out of a jam.

'So he got a girl into trouble,' she said. 'What's new? He's always spoilin' someone's daughter. It doesn't explain what you're doin' but then you know what you're doin' and it's nothin' to do with Ruby Cropper's boy. It's that girl. You got some idea in your head about her.'

Gabe said he hadn't any idea. The feller was ill and asking for help. And hadn't Ma seen that place? 'It's filthy with rain comin' in. You wouldn't want your worst enemy to sleep there never mind a woman and her child.'

She wasn't fooled. 'That's right, Gabriel Howarth Templar. Keep tellin' yourself you're doin it out the goodness of your heart and I'll keep sayin' what I am seein'.'

'And what are you seein'? says he.

'You in thrall to a dream.'

A couple of years back Gabriel was trying to figure the word pariah. It meant outcast. Now he has two new words to figure.

As it happens the meaning came in the shifting shape of Sue Ryland. She showed what it meant. He was in the Mill cottage ripping up damp floorboards. A shadow slid through the door and with it the smell of crushed strawberries and a memory of golden freckles on another woman's breast.

'He got you at it then,' she says.

'What's that, Sue?'

'Servicin' his gal.'

He didn't like the phrase. 'What do you mean servicin'?'

'Lookin' after her interest.'

'I ain't lookin' after anybody's interest. I'm tryin' to lift damp floorboards.'

'Uh-huh,' she nods. 'I guess you are.' She leans against the doorjamb. 'Seen the photograph of his gal?'

'I've seen it.'

'Beautiful, ain't she.'

'I suppose.'

'Bobby's cracked about her. To hear him talk she is a fairy queen. All she has to do is wave her wand and men fall under her spell. I said is that what happened to you, Bobby. Do you know his reply?'

Gabriel shrugged. 'Somethin' dumb I imagine.'

'No, not dumb, the God's honest truth I reckon. He said she didn't have to wave a wand. He fell the minute he saw her and never got up.' Sue sauntered over the way she does. 'Do you want to know what I said?'

'Not particularly.'

'Don't matter 'cos I'm gonna tell you anyhow. I said that's how I feel about Gabe Templar.' She slides her arms about his waist. 'I'm enthralled by you.'

He pushes her away. 'What's that you're sayin' enthralled?'

Maybe she knew the impact of her words for she smiled. 'It's what I'm always sayin'. I'm under your spell and always will be.'

In thrall means bewitched. He'd like to say it's a lie that nobody bewitched him but how can he when he's rushing back from Quantico every evening to get to the cottage. Neither would he be here in the barn until late working on a beds for her and the baby if it was a lie, nor counting the days, crossing them off on a calendar every cross lessening the distance between them.

If being dragged by your heart to do and say things you shouldn't is in thrall then he is in thrall to something. Maybe if Bobby hadn't asked him to collect her there would have been a way back. If they hadn't to meet face-to-face and he to see the living doll then he could've sorted the cottage and walked away if not unscathed then at peace knowing he did the best he could. But Bobby asked and once the words were out his mouth there could be no unsaying.

Thursday evening he came asking. Ma was visiting the Mizzes March. Gabriel sat in the darkness watching the door as he'd watched all week. Rain or shine Bobby came every night to stand outside shivering. Any other guy your heart would ache but this is Baby Rourke and not to be trusted.

Gabriel had his answer ready. No way was he going to collect her. Bobby could hire one of his pilot buddies. But then when the door opened the feller looked so ill he hadn't the heart. So, this morning soon as the sky gets light he is off to New York to bring back Adelia Challoner. He knows her name. He checked the Edmund B passenger list. There it is, Miss Adelia Challoner and daughter, Sophie, on route to Virginia via the US Military GI Bride Programme.

Marrying Baby Rourke! Gabriel doesn't get it. What's wrong with British guys? Are they blind they can let such beauty slip through their fingers?

Ma wasn't so sure. 'Never mind men bein' blind what about her? Can't she see what's she's gettin' into?'

Gabriel said Bobby would have been on his best behaviour with her.

'Maybe, but a leopard doesn't change his spots as she'll find out. And her with a little girl and him with a filthy mouth!! The woman must be mad.'

Though he agreed he didn't like Ma running her down. 'We don't know what's gone on. Bombs droppin' every day British people have had it tough.'

She wasn't impressed. 'What are you sayin'? That she's comin' here to get away from trouble because I tell you give it a month and she'll be beggin' to go home again. Poor girl, she couldn't be in more trouble if she tried.'

Her feeling sorry for someone she's never met is nothing new. Open hearted, May Templar is always looking to help. Gabriel worked on that sympathy asking her to run up drapes and bed linen for the cottage bedrooms.

'At least that way her and her kiddie will have a place to sleep.'

She was chary at first, didn't want to get involved, but changed her mind and not only made drapes made clothes for the doll he's carving and other bits for the dolls-house.

'Why are you doin' this?' she says. 'Up all night fiddlin' with bits of wood! First the beds and now this and a doll? Don't you think you're oversteppin' the mark? I mean, her not knowin' you she might wonder why you bother.'

Other than to say Bobby asked he says nothing. How can he explain what he doesn't understand? Making a doll is no big deal. He's done plenty in the Pen. It's true he's finding the doll's house tricky but that's because it's a copy of the Eyrie and him and the house not getting on these days.

Fact is he needs to keep busy or he'll go crazy. All this waiting! Beyond a bomb exploding he has no idea what he's waiting for.

It started last summer when he drove Bobby home, the truck stinking where the feller had shit his pants. Gabriel hosed him down and got him up to a makeshift bed. Then head reeling, he ran to the Eyrie for help.

Once again the house tried keeping him out every pathway blocked, until he laid back his head and roared. 'Better let me in Old Eyrie because if you don't I swear I will burn you to the ground and piss on your ashes!'

Recognising it no empty threat the shadows let him in but grudging a footfall at a time.

The Eyrie was in a fine old temper. Wind whining through the rafters there was one heck of a noise. You couldn't miss what the wind was saying, there was a demand, he was to return certain items once considered on loan from the house but now regarded as stolen.

They were talking of the bit of wallpaper and the doll made in the Pen.

The wallpaper he understood but not the doll. 'Why must I bring that?' he wanted to know. 'I made it. I didn't steal nothin'!'

Didn't matter, beyond that demand the house was mute.

All other demands he made upon himself and the first was at Quantico switching the proposed the four-stint abroad to home rotation. His Gunny was not pleased. 'I thought you were looking forward to the challenge, Sergeant.'

'Yes, sir,' says Gabriel. 'I thought so too.'

Ma pondered the change of heart. Though glad he is to be stationed close-by and able to come home nights she is anxious. 'Why did you switch? I thought you couldn't stand being home? Is this about Bobby's girl?'

What could he say? Everything he does these days is about Bobby's girl, each day a pattern. He works while Bobby watches.

Lord, the state of that guy! Even now with hot water on tap he is a mess. The damage to his face rules his life. He wallows in self-pity trailing after Gabriel saying how unlucky he is, that he served his country, got a DFC and should be able to fly not 'grounded by cowardly fuckers who only ever flew a desk.'

Other than tend roses he complains of being ill-used and then switching to his 'Dee', how beautiful she is and how kind and a nurse at a local hospital she'd given up her home and friends to come care for him.

It drives Gabriel crazy. He wants to knock him to the ground and grind his face under the heel of his boot so he'll never speak again because the feller is lying through his teeth and not only what he says in what he doesn't say!

There is something counterfeit about whole deal. Gabriel arrived the other night to smoke pouring from the cottage chimney. He went to investigate and found Bobby feeding the stove with photos ripped from an album.

So absorbed, he didn't hear Gabriel coming and startled hid stuff behind his back. 'It's nothin',' he said, his hands shaking. 'It's stuff Ma sent over. High-school photos and suchlike, I couldn't see the point of keepin' it.'

Watching him wriggle and knowing him a liar fear grabbed Gabriel. Sensing danger he is scared for the girl and her baby. It's the Mill. A Killing Ground if ever there was it reeks of blood, the heavy green blinds on the windows closed against the memory of what was and what may yet be to come.

Gabriel spent yesterday checking the plumbing and making sure the generator works and that they had fuel for the stove and food in the ice box. They had food but it was foolish stuff that a child couldn't swallow.

Ma was disgusted. 'Why has he bought this? Comin' all that way they'll be dog tired and will want eggs and soft stuff not lobsters!'

She said not to worry. She'd drop by in the day with milk for the baby and bread. Though anxious, she has taken those two lost souls to her bosom. The notion of a kiddie being nearby has set her wishing her son would settle.

Poor Ma! As much as he'd like to give comfort he doubts her wish for grandchildren will be granted. Now close to midnight he's removing another of her joys, he is taking Daisy, the English Staffordshire Terrier home to die.

Odd how the dog took to this place! From the start she preferred the Eyrie even to Ma's and would take off two or three times a day checking in. Gabriel used to feel the same and in his heart still does; it was home and as Daisy seeks to die there so he always felt it would be his last resting place.

Though it don't agree he follows orders bringing the doll.

Gabriel never thought he was fickle but recently in a fit of pique wanted to put the doll and the Lime Tree and everything to do with past in the fire. Now the thought of leaving it in the Eyrie worries him. That doll means so much. It is time spent in the Pen. It is Charlie and all that he meant. It was his little gal. Now it is a living doll, a stranger coming across the ocean to rattle his world.

It is Adelia Challoner!

When he left prison rather than it fall into wrong hands he was prepared to destroy it. What now? Is it meant for a kid that will live here, because if so he's not sure he likes the idea of a snot-nosed brat mauling it especially in a house that abandoned the maker.

Once upon a time the Eyrie was his sanctuary. Now it doesn't want him. It is his fault. The house abandoned him the day he abandoned his Other Self. In running from his little gal he ran from himself. Having sex here with Sue Ryland hasn't helped. The shadows are against the misuse of power. He used Sue that night and now feels the Eyrie's displeasure.

It was bitter sex, heartless and empty. It was fuelled by anger. Starting with Pa and prison and on to Guadalcanal this last fourteen years have been fuelled by anger. He tried fighting it and did think he was getting on top but it's back again any progress stripped away by a photograph.

He should sign out of the Corp as not worthy to lead men. He's not Sergeant Templar anymore, he's the blonde kid that can't read or write his old self clinging to his soul like muck to weeds.

Yesterday before leaving for Quantico he pressed his Class A blues thinking to wear them to the Harbour. Later that day he sat in the barber's recalling a dream of being at the Harbour in Marine Class A blues and then in the same dream of wearing West Point swallow-tail greys and carrying a sword.

Furious, he drove back from the barbers swapping his blues for khaki. 'To hell with it,' he'd raged. 'I am a Marine not a fool ruled by dreams!'

As a Marine he is strong. He can go anywhere and do anything. Now look at him worrying about what to wear and whether to pack shaving tackle and is his buzz-cut too close and Miss Adelia Challoner seeing him a plucked turkey!

For Christ's sake, he is going backwards and everything he wanted snatched away. On his way out yesterday his C/O dismissed him. 'I was considering you officer candidate material, Sergeant Templar. Now I'm not so sure.'

Bang! Another chance gone! Why lose out! He should mind his own business and let Bobby Rourke sort it. Who is Gabriel to appoint himself Guardian to Miss Adelia Challoner when she may well turn out to be nothing of his?

Now he outside the Eyrie hoping the house will let him in, if not for him then for the dog who always loved being here.

His shoulders ache from carrying Daisy. Heavy she has ripped open the wounds on his back. But then they never heal. They bleed especially at night. He's tried everything but nothing works. Last night Ma tended his back.

Gabriel said he remembered as a kid he didn't have to worry about Pa beating him. An angel would come heal him by morning.

Ma yelled at him. She said not to talk foolish! 'Everyone bleeds when they're hurt. It's nothin' to do with angels. It's just that you're lucky. You're like Aunt Belle. You have good healin' skin.'

She didn't want to remember that time. Blaming herself for him going to jail and other sad memories she chooses to forget bugs wings.

It's a good way if you can do it. Memory can be fickle. There are plenty people he would like to forget and a few he'd like to keep. Mr Simeon nor Mrs Jean Emmett and Gunny would be top of the list to keep. Then there's Martha Stokes and the medics and Sue Ryland who underneath is pure gold.

Charlie singing is a memory worth keeping. Gabriel recalls one night in particular when he slashed the doll and woke to singing and the doll made whole again. A miracle you might say.

~

Here's another miracle the front door to the house is wide open.

'Well lookee here, Daisy,' he whispered. 'It seems you are expected.'

He set her down in the Orangery. Glassed-in ceiling and wooden panelling on the far wall it's always warm in here. Now there's a scent of early wisteria.

Gabriel's not fooled by the warmth and the scent and the soft susurration of the bats asleep in the rafters. This isn't for him. This greeting is love of Daisy.

The dog in his arms he sits on the floor. Time is getting on. He needs to get back to shower and change but he won't leave Daisy until she's ready. She's been a good dog. Sixteen or thereabouts they didn't think she'd last this long.

Bless her, she is weary, her heart fluttering under his hand. Gabriel thinks of Gunny Emmet and how he helped him pass over. Maybe he should try doing that in reverse. Ma does love this dog. She will miss her. Would it be so wrong to give Ma and Daisy a little longer together?

At the thought his hands grew warm. Soon they were blazing as if jam full of a backlog of energy.

Daisy stirred and panting struggled to get away. She looked at Gabriel but not with hope in her eyes with terror. This is not Jean Emmet a tough woman in her forties eager to fight to be well again. This is a creature who has reached the end of her natural life. She has arthritis in her bones. She is old and tired. She aches. She wants to die! It's why she's here.

'Sorry, Daisy,' he whispered. 'Forgive me! I don't know what I thinkin'.'

The heat in his hands receding he hugged her close. She wagged her tail and licked his hand as if to say, 'it's alright, Gabriel Templar. You meant well.' Then she turned her head into his chest, closed her eyes and died.

'Oh God help me!'

Gabriel wept. Tears falling on her fur he cried. Her body so softly giving in his arms it hurt to hold her. Such dignity and grace! Such understanding of the natural order of things! Compared to her instinctive trust in what should and should not be he sees his endeavours as pathetic.

He will bury her here under the willows. She would like that.

How he sobbed. Such ancient pain, very kick and shove from the battered three year old child to the man, from Pa's fists and from the scornful laughter of kids at school, every felt and forgotten tear poured out, and above and beyond a dreadful suspicion that blind with anger he had wasted time squandering the Light within.

As he sat head bowed all was so silent, the Eyrie seeming to be waiting.

Then wham! One minute the dog was cold and then the warmth that had been in Gabriel's hands was rekindled through the dog.

He was on fire! Heat zigzagging up through his body into his shoulders.

Zippppp! A red-hot needle pulled thread through the hole in his left shoulder.

Zippppp and again the same searing pain through the right.

The wounds were closed up.

It hurt! Lord, did it hurt!

Crying out, he lurched to his feet and trying not to drop the dog reached out to the wall for balance. His hand hit a wooden post.

There was a click and a sliding movement and a hole appeared in the wall.

It was the Priest's Hole!

Gabriel had forgotten it was there. A dusty space between a false wall and a brick probably means nothing to twentieth century man but to a practising catholic in Tudor England it means a terrible secret, a blessing and a place to hide for the priest who risked his life bringing the holy sacrament.

It's almost twenty years since Gabriel saw this. He oughtn't to remember it because the narrow passage leads out to the back kitchen and a circular iron staircase and up to a cupboard in the attic.

'Of course!'

Where else is the doll meant to be but with the wallpaper in the attic.

'Sorry Eyrie!' He whispered. 'I should've known you'd have a place ready.'

He wrapped Daisy in her blanket and laid her on the window-seat. ' Rest and be still. I'll come back for you.'

The Priest's Hole is the way in. Gabriel must go this way. If he were to try the main staircase the attic would be blocked and the Eyrie lost to him forever.

It's narrow between the walls barely the width of a child never mind a man. He was seven last time he squeezed through here. He remembers as if it was yesterday because he was angry then. They were playing Hide 'n Seek, him and his little gal, and he was angry because no matter how he searched he could never find her.

That day he was in the Orangery then and a voice whispered in his ear, 'lean on the dog's face, Nathan, and get in,' though that someone had his name wrong young Gabe did as he was told. He leant on the panel with a dog's face carved into the wood and click, same as now it opened to the Priest's Hole.

It's dark in there. He inched his way through a century of dirt and decay. He was finding it hard to breathe and just for a moment was a little kid again and scared of the dark and what might be in the dark hiding.

'Oh Lord!'

Then ahead down the passage a light bloomed. Someone was carrying a lamp!

Carrying a tiny flag of light the lamp bobbed up and down. Gabriel peered into the gloom and thought he saw her. Yes that's her! Look how the lamplight catches her hair. It's her, his little gal.

Heart full he can barely speak. 'I'm sorry,' he whispered, his words echoing. 'I never meant for you to go. I guess I just wanted to lead a normal life.'

She didn't answer. But then why should she when for years he's blamed her for all his troubles. Blaming her is why the Eyrie locked him out and will keep on locking him out until he faces the truth, if you want to be ordinary and fit in with the crowd you will be ordinary and the Light within reduced to a spark.

Flip! She's gone. He is through the passage and climbing the circular stairs. There's a door ahead and lamplight beyond the door. He pulls on the latch and is in the attic but there is only moonlight shining through the window.

Gabriel knows he can't stay. He has to go back to Ma's and wash the cobwebs out of his hair. But first there is the doll and the wallpaper.

From inside the attic you wouldn't know there is a cupboard and stairs leading down. All you see is an oak-panelled wall. There is a boxlike shelf on the stairs side of the door. That must be where he's to put the doll.

With nothing to wrap the doll he removes his shirt and folding the doll inside places it on the shelf. He'd like to say something but can't find the words. And what is there to say other than life goes on and he must bury Daisy and get started for New York and whatever is waiting there.

One thing is sure as always when leaving this house he leaves a piece of himself behind, today it is childhood and Pa and bugs wings, and Charlie Whitefeather and Tsohanai, the Sun Bearer. He can't carry them anymore, a least not for now. They will be here and live but not as his memories. They belong to the house and the doll and the wallpaper

Finding the place on the wall he squats down and peeling back the layers resets the piece inside, returning winter to the other seasons.

Compared to the other layers the paper is faded, the message almost worn away, just the odd word visible...' *goodnight and goodbye...Rosamund.'*

One day, he thinks, I'll come back for the doll and for this paper and the house itself. It will be my house. It will belong to me as the memories belong.

Gabriel once told Simeon Smith that he felt he didn't belong in this world. That somehow he'd got mixed up in a birth and life he never wanted.

Simeon quoted poetry by a guy called Wordsworth who says that to be born is to forget heaven. It's the price we pay for living.

Right now Gabriel can't see the point. A man scorned by others, an outcast and in thrall of a dream? Why would any man leave heaven for that?

The only heaven he's ever known were moments of childhood and his little gal and she belongs, if she belongs at all to another life and another Gabriel.

The lamp is flickering. It'll soon be out. It's time he was gone. Daisy needs to be warm under the willows and he on the way to New York.

He knelt smoothing the wallpaper down. He got to his feet. Then the moon slid behind a cloud and Zippppp! As with the wounds in his shoulders so the panelled door on a retracting hinge closed shut.

Gabriel didn't bother to search for the way back in. He could look for now and forever and wouldn't find it. It was meant to stay shut, it, and the dog's face panel and the entry to secrets is for another time.

And anyway, the door to the attic is open. The Eyrie may not have forgotten his sin yet for now it seems he is forgiven.

Keys to the truck jingling in his pocket and the scent of morning in the air Gabriel made his way down stairs, Mr Simeon and an English poet whispering in his ear. '*Our birth is but a sleep and a forgetting: The Soul that rises with us, our life's Star, Hath had elsewhere its setting, And coming from afar: Not in entire forgetfulness, And not in utter nakedness, But trailing clouds of glory do we come, from God, who is our Home.*'

Printed in Poland
by Amazon Fulfillment
Poland Sp. z o.o., Wrocław